THE SHADOW FIXER

DIVISION ZERO BOOK 6

MATTHEW S COX

DIVISION ZERO PRESS

Cover art by: Alexandria Thompson

ISBN (ebook): 978-1-950738-24-3

ISBN (paperback): 978-1-950738-25-0

CONTENTS

THE MADDENING

Hopeful someone at dispatch confused the report, Kirsten clutched the patrol car's control sticks tight—she had no idea if she could handle a psionic child murdering people.

It *had* to be an error. Command wouldn't have sent *her* to contain a psionic freaking out. Division 0 had plenty of Tactical personnel for situations involving living problems. Unless the kid going crazy had a serious rating in Mind Blast, there'd be no reason to send her. A handful of others had higher ratings, like Commander Ashford. The man didn't routinely pull field duty, but for something like a powerful mind blaster on a rampage, he definitely would.

She'd already dismissed the idea anyway, as Mind Blast couldn't technically kill anyone, and the dispatch made it clear people had been killed.

They might send her out to deal with a Suggestive. She had a middling rating, no slouch but hardly Division 0's best at it. They *might* send her to deal with someone using Suggestion to kill, but not as a primary. This came through under a 21-49 code, a paranormal manifestation resulting in death—but the accompanying information from multiple witnesses described a little girl murdering people.

Someone messed up. She closed her eyes and tried making a wish. *Please don't force me to shoot a kid.*

"Spend enough time working as a cop in West City, the day's going to come when you have a little kid pointing a gun at you." Dorian spoke in a tone of voice like he hated the words coming out of his mouth.

"I know…" She sighed, not wanting to say it already happened to her.

Dorian flicked a bit of lint from his uniform sleeve, the same bit of lint he always plucked.

Such a situation happened to him once, long ago when he'd been alive. He *had* shot a young boy, but in the leg. He got lucky. When forced to choose between a child's life or his, he gambled on a non-lethal shot and survived. Kirsten bit her lip, thinking about Shani. Bad enough having a seven-year-old point a gun at her, but the daughter of Dorian's former partner? Kirsten, too, got lucky. Shani's a good kid who fell victim to a psionic suggestion—not a street punk who gave up and didn't care if she lived or died.

At least I'm not Div 1.

The average Division 1 patrol officer had guns pointed at them 47.8 times a week—often by teens—and took between six and fourteen bullets each week. Even if most firearms couldn't penetrate their armor, a bullet still left a mark, possibly a broken rib.

No Division 1 officer runs into abyssals…

Compared to the awful things abyssals or true demons could do to a person, being shot while in police armor ranked as pleasurable. She didn't want to jinx herself by thinking about them. Several months of sanity would end sooner or later. Her life had gone back to the boredom of sitting at her desk in the Police Administrative Center most days. She hadn't made the same mistake again. Kirsten stopped complaining about boredom.

But the Universe heard her thinking it.

She banked the patrol craft around a silvery high-rise office building in Sector 1157, within 380 meters of the pin on the NavMap. A small army of Division 1 patrol craft, both on the ground as well as the roof parking area, made the computer navigation assistant pointless. Someone in orbit could probably see it from all the flashing lights.

"Damn. This is going to be nuts," whispered Kirsten. "Seventeen patrol units? What are we walking into?"

"A mess." Dorian smiled at her. "Probably a big one since most of them haven't gone into the building."

"Sounds like our kind of mess." She breathed a mirthless chuckle, then slowed the car to a hover. "Dispatch, this is 1815-014. In position at destination. Should I take the front door or the roof?"

A holographic face appeared above the middle of the console, a boy no older than fourteen in Division 0 blacks. "Lieutenant, there isn't much information coming in from the patrol units on site. The initial distress call came from apartment seventeen on the sixty-fourth floor."

"Roof it is," muttered Kirsten.

She pulled the patrol craft up into a climb, weaving through a layer of advert bots 300 feet off the ground. A few broke from the pack to chase her as she skimmed the windows in a vertical climb to the parking deck at the top of the building. As soon as the car passed the edge, she leveled off. The entire roof, except for one cube-shaped structure at the center, consisted of landing spaces for hovercars. A silver set of double doors on the south face of the cube belonged to an elevator for residents to enter the building. The west face had a small stairway door.

A formation of Division 1 officers stood behind their cars, pointing weapons at the elevator as if expecting the entire Diablos gang to come charging out at any moment.

A dull, droning whirr vibrated in the cabin as the ground wheels extended. Kirsten aimed for an open spot behind the patrol officers, setting her patrol craft down at almost the exact second the wheels locked into place. She pushed the door upward, got out, and found herself standing amid a group of advert bots displaying ads for legal representation, specifically those with experience defending against traffic citations. It took them a few seconds to realize the car they followed up the side of a building belonged to the National Police Force.

Somewhat sheepishly, the bots collapsed their holographic displays and glided away, dropping off the edge of the roof.

Kirsten sighed, shook her head at them, and hurried over to the blue-armored cops prepared to annihilate anything inside the elevator if the doors opened.

Dorian materialized beside her. "If someone farts too loud, they're going to shred that poor elevator. I'd suggest you tell them to calm down, but when in human history has telling someone to calm down ever worked?"

"When a telempath says it," muttered Kirsten.

"Ahh. True. Good point."

She hurried over to the middle of the police line, approaching an armored man with sergeant stripes. "How bad is it?"

He jumped at the sound of her voice, almost firing into the elevator, but managed to catch himself—likely due to having heard a patrol craft land behind them. "It's real freaky in there."

"Have you sent anyone inside?" asked Kirsten.

"Two." The sergeant lowered his weapon, faced her, and froze in shock.

Given the urgency of the situation, she peeked at his surface thoughts to skip past the twenty questions routine. His brain ground to a halt at the sight of what he thought to be a fourteen or fifteen-year-old girl wearing Division 0 lieutenant insignia. Psionics scared him, but the fear conflicted with his solidary toward a fellow cop and his need to protect a 'young kid.'

"We don't have time for sniffing each other's butts, sergeant," said Kirsten. "I can handle the weird stuff. Just tell me what the situation is."

He cleared his throat. "We received multiple reports of assaults inside the building, so half a dozen units responded. Howe and Greene were the first officers inside. They made contact with... something. Howe threw himself off the roof in a panic. We found Greene in the lobby, catatonic. Looked like she had a heart attack, but the stimsuit shocked her back."

Dorian whistled.

Telempaths aren't usually strong enough to cause people to die from fear. Sending someone running off a building is easily possible, but a heart attack? "Did their cams catch sight of any suspects?"

Sergeant Peters shook his head. "Nope. Just some weird distortions. A few of the calls described a small girl attacking people, between ten and twelve."

He held up his left forearm guard. A holographic terminal appeared floating above the armor, showing video from a helmet cam. Text at the bottom indicated it came from Officer Greene. She walked behind another officer, likely Howe, down a hallway past two dead— or unconscious—people. Blood trails sprayed on the walls appeared to be the result of arterial spurting. Kirsten cringed. Officer Greene followed her partner around a corner in the apartment building hall, stopping short at the sight of a bright glow most of the way down the next hallway, near an open door. Even in video, the brightness somewhat hurt Kirsten's eyes.

"Shit," whispered Howe. "It's a little girl."

The form didn't resemble anything even close to a person shape, being a smear of light hovering at doorknob level.

"Hey, sweetie," said Greene. "Put the knife down, okay? Let's talk."

A flicker came from the light mass. Howe shrieked in terror, whirled, and shoved his partner to the floor to get past her. Greene dragged herself back as the light raced toward her. It hovered up in front of her... and the video died.

"You can see why we haven't gone inside." Sergeant Peters lowered his arm. "Greene hasn't been able to speak yet. Howe..."

Kirsten bowed her head. "No need to say it."

"Any idea what this is?" asked Peters.

"Looks like a ghost. They don't usually appear *that* bright on camera, though."

"This one's probably quite old." Dorian eyed the elevator. "Going to be... interesting."

Sergeant Peters swiped at his holo-panel, opening a different screen. "Div 2 tapped into the hall cameras. There are at least six bodies on the sixty-fourth floor. Two on the sixty-fifth. Whatever's in there isn't straying too far up or down."

"All right. Try not to riddle me with bullets when I come back out." Kirsten slipped between two Division 1 patrol craft and hurried toward the elevator, her heart already in her throat at the idea of a murderous child ghost.

Howe and Greene saw a child, not a light blob. Everything about the situation worried her, but at least she didn't have to deal with a living psionic child going on a rampage. Normal people seeing a ghost clearly enough to believe it a physical person didn't happen often, hinting at a powerful entity. A spirit powerful enough to appear brighter on camera than any she'd ever seen before would be a pain in the ass. Worse for being a kid. She'd have to fight guilt as well as the ghost.

A beep came from the call panel in response to her police override code. A moment later, the sliding doors opened. Kirsten stepped in and turned to face out. Someone's perfume hung in the air. The carpet appeared cleaner than most places she'd been to. Small handprints smeared on the silvery wall, too little to be the child going crazy. Dorian stepped in to stand beside her and stuck his finger into the console. The sixty-fourth floor appeared as the selection for no apparent reason.

She bowed her head as the doors closed, thinking about the first time she saw Evan. The boy had been astrally projecting out of his body, so she'd initially mistaken him for a child ghost. Another case of her sensitive side getting the better of her thinking side. She should've recognized an astral form apart from a ghost due to the amber coloration of the energy body, lack of clothing, and also the lack of detailed anatomy. Astral forms had an almost cartoonish quality to their nudity, as if the person projecting wore a sheer bodysuit. The faint silver cord coming out of his forehead should also have been a clear giveaway.

But she'd become so caught up in the tragedy of a dead child, she stopped thinking.

In ninety-nine percent of cases, ghosts linger in the mortal world for a specific reason like revenge, a need to finish something, or—like Theodore and *The Kind*—shits and giggles. Kirsten considered it exceptionally good luck that throughout her entire life she'd only run into one legitimate ghost child, a boy who dwelled with his ghostly parents down in the Beneath. Peyton and his parents died during the Corporate War, hundreds of years ago before West City existed. He'd been thrilled to have Kirsten for a friend when she'd lived down there, hiding from Mother.

As far as she knew, the three spirits didn't have any unfinished business or need for revenge; they'd simply not realized they'd died. Peyton's dad was the first person to ever tell her about the 'demonic' presence out in the Badlands, a monster calling out to everyone who lost their lives during the war. They refused to become part of the creature.

Except for Peyton, Kirsten had the fortune not to run into any other actual ghostly children. She clung to the hope kid spirits didn't linger around and almost always transcended right away. What little data Division 0 had on ghosts suggested most apparent child apparitions came from malevolent spirits adopting the guise of innocence to trick the living into being sympathetic. At the time she met Peyton, she'd been a child herself, so never considered things like demons or evil ghosts might impersonate kids.

People like me are the reason they pretend to be children. Such a sucker.

Bands of light scrolled up the walls of the elevator, indicating the passage of floors.

"You okay?" Dorian nudged her, his touch a mere brush of cold on her arm.

"Yeah. The usual."

He plucked the same piece of lint from his uniform. "Precisely why I'm asking if you're okay."

"Can't be a real kid." She shook her head. "Children aren't evil."

The doors opened on the sixty-fourth, allowing in the odor of ballistic propellant and a hint of fragrant feces. Unnatural dread hung in the air, making her feel like a little kid afraid of the dark, wanting to run away from here. She knew this sort of paranormal radiance well; most hauntings of angry spirits had a similar quality to the environment. However, she'd rarely encountered it this potent, strong enough it took effort to resist. Kirsten winced, stepping out into a small lobby.

A late-thirties woman in a dark skirt suit huddled behind a huge fake plant. She bled from multiple slashes over her arms, chest, and face, though the wounds appeared shallow. Two passages led away from the elevator room, one left, one right. On the left, a man's legs protruded into view from behind one corner of a T-junction at the far end of the short hall. Considering the amount of blood on the floor around him and the *feel* of the body, she assumed him dead.

"There have been some truly evil children in history." Dorian walked out of the elevator.

"How?" Kirsten approached the woman. "Ma'am?"

The woman looked up, making the same surprised face most spirits did upon realizing she could see them, despite not giving off energy like a ghost. To confirm if she'd discovered a live person or spirit, Kirsten grasped the woman's shoulder—solid.

"You're okay. The elevator is safe. C'mon, I'll help you."

Mute, the woman kept staring at her.

Kirsten took a stimpak from her belt case and pressed it into the woman's left arm near the biggest cut. As soon as the hiss from the autoinjector stopped, she looked at the woman's recent memory. Scattered images danced around her brain, showing a nightmarish version of the building's hallways. Insectoid limbs extended from stretched, twisted walls covered in black gunk. The pale figure of a young girl in a white nightie stalked after her, brandishing a large kitchen knife.

The woman struggled to run past dozens of inhuman arms jutting up from the floor, grasping at her legs, tripping her. A man came out of nowhere and grabbed the evil child, trying to protect this woman. She didn't look to see what happened to him, rushing into the lobby and hiding behind the plant, too terrified to understand the concept of elevators.

Kirsten broke the mental link, her hands shaking. The woman obviously hallucinated the hallways being so alien, but the fear fed back across the telepathic connection. Worse, the sinister little dark-haired girl seemed so gleefully evil. The child couldn't have been older than nine.

She coaxed the woman to stand, guiding her to the elevator, then leaned in to hit the button for the roof, ducking out before the doors closed.

"Peters," said Kirsten into her comm, "sending a civilian up to you. Make sure your team doesn't freak and blow the crap out of her."

"Copy, lieutenant."

Dorian looked at the ceiling. "Hope they resist. Whole building's saturated in radiant fear."

"Yeah…" Kirsten went left, down the short corridor connecting the elevator lobby to the loop of apartment doors.

Like many residential century towers of this type, the sixty-fourth floor contained the 'nice' apartments, meaning they had more than one room, unlike the lower floors packed with super-economy single-room pods. She thought it ironic the poorer tenants closer to the ground had a better chance of surviving a catastrophe like a major fire.

Kirsten paused at the corner to check on the man lying face down in a pool of blood. She didn't need to touch him to realize he'd been killed, as his ghost stood a few paces away. A wound under the chin appeared to line up with the notion of a child stabbing a large knife upward into the brain from below.

"Damn," muttered Kirsten. She looked up from the body at a hallway containing four additional bodies: three adults and a boy not yet old enough to shave. Horrified, she sprinted past the ghost to the boy.

The smell of shit intensified.

Kirsten dropped to one knee and put a hand to the boy's neck. Warm. Rapid pulse.

"He's alive. Probably fainted instantly in terror." Dorian pointed down the hall. "Listen."

A faint little girl voice warbled in a sinister, yet familiar melody, singing a children's song in a minor key, the words too distorted or mumbled to make out. The dirge emanated from the second-to-last apartment near the end of the corridor.

"Excuse me…" The ghostly man walked over to them. "I couldn't help but notice the two of you looked right at me. Everyone else is ignoring me. Why?"

"I'm sorry." Kirsten struggled to gather the twelve- or thirteen-year-old boy up in her arms. "You are dead."

The man braced his hands on his hips. "Kinda figured that seeing as how my body's on the floor right over there. This kid's parents ran off and left him there. Is he okay?"

"Scared shitless." Kirsten hurried back to the elevator, carrying him.

"Literally." Dorian wagged his eyebrows.

She sighed. "Must you?"

The ghost followed them. "It's Melanie's daughter. She's gone crazy. I saw her chasing Alexandra down the hallway, tried to help, but the damn brat stabbed me in the head. She must be on serious drugs. Kids shouldn't be so damn strong."

"How long ago did Melanie lose her daughter?" Kirsten elbowed the elevator call. "Peters? Copy."

"I'm here," replied Sergeant Peters via the comm.

The ghost gave her a weird look. "She didn't. The kid's not dead. Just crazy."

Kirsten glanced at the spirit, mildly perplexed at him thinking the girl alive. What sort of ghost would continually manifest itself? *She can't be a technokinetic who can delete herself from video… they don't make light apparitions or flood an area with dread like this.* "Sending up another one. Unconscious minor."

"Roger."

The elevator opened. Kirsten gently put the boy down, hit the roof button, and backed out.

"You're saying this kid's alive?" asked Dorian.

"Yeah." The new ghost scratched at the back of his head. "I mean, I don't really know them well. Just live on the—well, *lived* on the same floor. Just my luck. Try to do something nice for someone and get killed."

"Happens to the best of us." Dorian patted the guy on the back. "Give us a moment to resolve this situation. If you need any help, we'll be back after it's over."

The guy laughed. "I'm a bit beyond help, but thanks."

"Help in the sense of sending messages to friends or family," said Dorian.

Kirsten hurried down the hall, drawing her E-90 despite hating doing so. If a knife-wielding psionic child came running at her, she'd try Suggestion first. But she knew this girl couldn't be alive. The light blur on video had to come from a powerful spirit. Technokinetics able to influence cameras simply didn't appear at all. Few ghosts had the power to manifest so solidly they appeared to the living as ordinary people—and hold the manifestation while knife-murdering random strangers.

"Oh, shit," whispered Kirsten.

"You'll have to give me more than that. I can't read minds anymore."

She paused six doors from the open apartment, E-90 aimed. "Think this is a possession? Live kid, abyssal?"

"Darn. We've had a good few months without a demon." Dorian fake snapped his fingers. "Makes sense though. Might as well get this over with."

A door on the right lazily swung inward as she neared, revealing a forty-something man pinned to the wall by three kitchen knives, one through his left eye.

"No kid is strong enough to put a knife through a skull." Kirsten swallowed.

"Telekinetic?"

She shifted her jaw side-to-side. Sometimes, adolescence brought with it spikes of uncontrolled psionic power. It happened most often with Telekinesis, and typically at a subconscious level out of the child's control. About half the 'object throwing' poltergeist calls she investigated turned out to be a tween in the house with runaway power they didn't even realize they had.

None of those kids had the precision and power to ram knives into a body, stapling it to the wall. Wild telekinetic storms raged with all the finesse and predictability of a hurricane, not surgically staple a guy to a wall. Nothing about this situation made any sense.

"One way to find out," whispered Kirsten.

"Hmm?" Dorian raised an eyebrow.

"What exactly we're dealing with here. One way to find out."

"Ahh, yes."

She squeezed her grip on the rubberized grip of the E-90 and advanced the rest of the way down the hall to the open door. Shoulder to the wall, she paused, listening. The sinister nursery rhyme came from deep within the apartment. Someone else rasped for breath.

Kirsten swung into the doorway, E-90 up.

The living room lay in a state of mild shambles, no worse than two guys getting into a fistfight over a Gee-ball match. A woman lay curled on the floor near the sofa, cradling a stomach wound. Kirsten rushed over, keeping her weapon aimed at the interior hallway. Dorian walked past the couch, also aiming a ghostly version of an E-86 toward the singing.

"Help..." wheezed the woman. "Lily is..."

"That's Melanie." The ghostly man appeared in the doorway. "Wow... her own daughter stabbed her."

Kirsten crouched next to Melanie, sneaking a few glances down at her in between watching the corridor for the approach of a crazy child. The girl appeared to be in her bedroom, singing to herself.

"Lily is..." Melanie swallowed blood. "Possessed."

"Hold on." Kirsten pulled two stimpaks, bit the yellow safety caps off the tips, and jammed them simultaneously into the woman's leg.

Melanie drew in a sharp breath. "Cold..."

"Means they're working," whispered Kirsten.

"Why did... why did God let this happen?" Melanie looked up at her.

Dorian facepalmed.

Kirsten clenched her jaw. 'Because he isn't real' wanted to jump off her tongue, but it felt cruel to say to a delirious woman bleeding out after being stabbed by her child. 'Because he likes watching people suffer' didn't sound terribly nice either. She knew her instant negative reaction to the g-word came from Mother torturing her for four years, using him as an excuse for her cruelty. No need to take it out on this woman. "Dunno."

Melanie passed out.

Damn. She's lost a lot of blood. Kirsten used another stimpak on her. *Six left... hope this spirit doesn't kick my ass too bad.*

The singing stopped.

Kirsten raised her arms, peering over the E-90's glowing blue ring-dot sight at the empty corridor. She eased herself up to stand, slipped around the couch, and crept toward the girl's bedroom. Silence hung thick in the apartment, the thump of Kirsten's heartbeat noticeable in her ears. Whatever happened in the next few minutes would undoubtedly give her nightmares and probably an interstellar freighter's worth of guilt.

At the bedroom doorway, she paused, took a quick breath, and peeked around.

A girl in a blood-soaked white nightgown knelt on the floor, staring at her bloody hands. She appeared to be around ten years old with light brown skin, like most of the city's population. Long, fluffy dark hair obscured her face. A giant carving knife lay on the rug by her right knee. Except for the bloody footprints and droplets around her, the bedroom looked immaculate, like a demo apartment no one lived in. As sweet as Evan was, even he didn't keep his bedroom *this* perfect.

Paranormal energy drenched the area, strong to the point Kirsten's entire body tensed as if she'd been doused in ice water.

"Help me," whispered Lily. The girl lifted her head, half her blood-spattered face visible through a gap in her hair. "It made me do awful things. I'm scared."

Oh, no... Kirsten's heart sank. She slid the E-90 back into its holster as she entered the room. "It's all right, hon. I'm here to help."

Lily reached both hands up like a five-year-old wanting to be held. She sniffled, shaking in fear.

Kirsten took another step closer, eyeing her surroundings warily. Far too much energy remained in here for the spirit to have gone far. At least, she hoped so. If *residual* energy had so much power, the ghost itself would make the Wharf Stalker seem as weak as a goblin from the Monwyn universe.

"Is it still here?" whispered Lily between sniffles.

She definitely thought so, but didn't want to terrify the child any worse. "Maybe."

"It hurts," whined Lily.

"What hurts?" Kirsten crept closer to her, still looking around for the ambush. Something about the room didn't feel right. Too perfect, like a grieving parent keeping a shrine to a lost daughter. Too much energy in the air, and it didn't seem stronger to either side, no sense of direction... everywhere.

"My whole body. Like I fell down the stairs." Lily bowed her head, keeping her arms raised as if asking to be picked up.

The rug in front of Kirsten's boot filled her with dread, as though it held land mines. Stepping forward even one more inch felt as if it could kill her. She tensed, expecting the dark spirit to come flying at her any second. The instant she lowered her guard to focus on the frightened child, it would strike.

Dorian moved into the room, circling to the right.

Kirsten took another two steps closer, overcome by guilt at making the poor girl wait for comfort.

Lily glanced sideways at Dorian.

She can see him? Kirsten hesitated. Like a droplet of black ink hitting water, doubt fell into her overwhelming concern for this child. She shifted her gaze from the room to the little girl kneeling in front of her. At last, what her Astral Sense had been trying to tell her made it past her sensitive heart. The spectral energy didn't emanate from the room—it came from the child.

Lily rose up a little on her knees, stretching to hug Kirsten, whimpering.

A creepy chill teased down her back. *This isn't right.* She held still, gazing at the girl, and tried to peek into her head. Though she sensed Lily's presence—clearly not a doll—the storm of mental energy lacked substance to telepathy, as though she tried to grasp a cloud in her hand.

She's a ghost.

The instant Kirsten's posture changed from comforting to guarded, Lily sprang upward, slashing at Kirsten's throat, a knife seemingly teleporting into her hand. Kirsten caught the child's wrist, repeating a maneuver she'd rehearsed endlessly in training. She smoothly disarmed the girl and tried to chicken-wing the arm behind Lily's back.

Growling, Lily rammed her elbow into Kirsten's stomach. Superhuman strength behind a tiny, pointy arm knocked Kirsten stumbling, momentarily stunned in pain. Dorian pounced on the girl, grabbing her from behind. For an instant, he appeared surprised to get a solid grip on her. Kirsten doubled over, cradling her stomach. Lily slipped down out of his grip, dropping to her knees, then spun, biting Dorian on the leg above the knee while raking her small clawed fingers down the back of his leg.

He yowled in pain.

Kirsten summoned the Astral Lash, unfurling a slender cord of scintillating white-blue energy from her right hand. Lily detached herself from Dorian, whirling to face Kirsten, growling past black-stained teeth.

"Lily, what's happened to you? Why are you attacking people?" whispered Kirsten. "Let me help you."

Dorian, clutching his leg, fell over backward. "Don't trust it."

Snarling, Lily spun into a kick, punting Dorian's head like a Frictionless orb. He disappeared through the bedroom wall, leaving a thin layer of clear ectoplasm glooping down to the floor. When she faced Kirsten again, she attempted to look innocent. A droplet of black ichor dribbling over her chin kept her firmly grounded in creepy.

"I'm okay now." Lily raised her arms and approached as if wanting a hug. "It's scary sometimes."

Kirsten never imagined she'd be capable of lashing a child spirit—but this one's eyes held malevolence, not innocence. Lily had already tried to trick her into getting close once. She had no doubt there would've been a knife in her heart had she lowered her guard all the way and attempted to pick the girl up.

"Why are you doing this?" Kirsten took a step back.

"Don't be scared." Lily grinned, releasing more black sludge from her mouth. "I'm only a little girl."

"Bullshit!" yelled Dorian from the next room.

Her sensitive heart wept, but everything else—psionic senses, her gut, her rational mind, disagreed. If she thought too much about it, she'd end up dead. When the child took another step closer, Kirsten rounded the spectral whip in a half-committed strike. Too focused on staring into her eyes, Lily didn't see it coming until the energy cord sliced across her chest.

The child arched her back, up on her toes, screaming in a polyphonic voice part little girl part grown woman on the deeper end of monstrous. Hearing a kid shriek in agony as though someone tortured her with a stunrod stabbed Kirsten in the feels—however, the second voice reminded her way too much of the abyssal, Mariko Moriyama, for guilt to overwhelm her.

Demons pretend to be children to fool soft-hearted people. Kirsten clenched her fist around the lash, refusing to believe a genuine child could end up in the Abyss… then escape.

She coiled the energy cord back for another strike.

Lily ran—curiously using the door instead of going through the wall.

Kirsten chased her out into the hall. Dorian dove in an attempt to catch Lily, but the child hurdled over him. Kirsten leapt him as well, pursuing the girl across the living room and into the corridor. Despite the spirit being old and likely powerful, its child-sized form had short legs. Kirsten overtook her in seconds, close enough to snap the lash into the entity's back.

Lily wailed in agony, dropping to her knees and sliding to a stop on all fours. Kirsten skidded to a halt, raising her arm. Cat-like, the girl pivoted to face her, trying to look pathetic. The pleading stare stabbed Kirsten in the heart, making her feel like Mother for abusing a little girl. She almost caved in to guilt and lowered her arm, but caught sight of three corpses in the hallway behind the child.

"I don't think you're really a little girl." Kirsten mentally called out into the aether in hopes a Harbinger might be listening. If they seemed interested in Lily, it would prove beyond a doubt this 'child' had zero innocence.

Snarling, Lily dropped the scared act and glowered.

A wave of mental force slammed into Kirsten's senses. The hallway turned black-and-white. Demonic, insectoid limbs grew up from the floor and walls, shadowy swaths of bio-organic horror replaced the ordered flatness of human construction. Two gigantic human arms thrust up from the carpet in front of Lily, stretching the floor open into a hole big enough for a grotesquely oversized woman to drag herself up from parts below. The monstrous form of Mother climbed upright, filling the hallway to the ceiling, her shoulders touching each wall. She towered over Kirsten, making her feel as though she'd shrunk down to being six years old again. The woman's body bore dozens of open holes from which flesh-eating bugs spilled out, tumbling down her legs to the floor. Two stubby horns jutted from her temples. Missing skin sliced from her forehead made the shape of an upside-down cross.

Sudden, intense fear gripped Kirsten—but only for a few seconds.

The searing energy of the lash burning at the edge of her vision reassured her. No longer would she be powerless to defend herself. Mother was dead. This *thing* in front of her came from the darkest recesses of her mind.

Not real. She's forcing me to be scared.

Kirsten roared a war cry and swiped the lash at Mother.

The energy whip passed without resistance through the horrible woman, dispelling her back into the nothingness from whence she'd come. Aware of the illusion, her brain rejected it. The alien-demonic corridor of spikes and organic matter flickered back to normality.

Lily gawked at her, the fear in her eyes genuine.

Dorian leapt out of the wall in a flying tackle, crashing into the girl and stopping short as if he'd leapt into a tree. "Oof…"

"Don't!" yelled Lily. She grabbed Dorian, pulling him around in front of herself.

He grunted, trying and failing to overpower her. "This kid is too damn strong."

"She's not a real child!" yelled Kirsten.

Lily backed away, hiding behind him. "You're not gonna burn your pet spirit with a stupid light noodle!"

"Don't count on it," wheezed Dorian—right before he vanished.

The child gasped in surprise at losing her shield. Before she could even attempt a pitiful, pleading stare, Kirsten swung the lash, bright and thick, empowered by the emotional spike of seeing her monstrous mother. Screaming, Lily tried to leap out of the way, but the lash caught her in the side, giving off a pulse of light and resonant *boom* on impact. The hit threw the false child off her feet, sending her flying. The child landed about twenty feet away down the corridor, tumbling over herself a few times before sliding to a stop and deflating into a melted puddle. Dark goop, formerly hair, mixed into a pool of white muck from the disintegrating nightgown. Squiggles of light brown where hands, face, and feet used to be blended into an ooze expanding over the carpet.

"I'm going to be seeing 'melting child' in my nightmares for the next few months." She sighed. "Thanks for that."

The temperature dropped twenty degrees.

Two clouds of black smoke emerged from the walls behind Kirsten, one on either side, coalescing into the vaguely humanoid shapes of Harbingers—a billow of darkness with a head and two arms. Their sparkling silvery eyes fixed on her, giving off a sense of 'why did you call us?'

She swallowed saliva. They radiated dread, though it didn't feel directed at her. After being around them fairly often, she'd somewhat become accustomed to their presence, but still worried about doing something stupid in front of them. To be fair, she felt the same way when standing before the Division 0 Command Council, but there, she blamed her subconscious fear of authority figures. Mother had a short temper.

Kirsten gave off a sense of gratitude for answering her request. Both Harbingers bowed their vaporous black heads in acknowledgement. She gestured at the puddle as if to ask them if the ghostly 'child' spirit bore enough of a dark stain to be worthy of their interest. Again, the Harbingers nodded in unison, but made no move to do anything.

Crap. She's not done. Kirsten faced the puddle again. *Playing possum.*

As soon as she started walking closer, raising the lash, the puddle burst upward, gathering into a hideous amalgamation of praying mantis and human female. Though it had mostly human arms, back-curved spikes sprouted from wrist to elbow. Its wide-faced head bore two bulging compound eyes, aglow in dark crimson light.

Free of any guilt at striking an innocent child, Kirsten charged.

Screeching, the fiend opened its mandibles, spewing fiery liquid in a stream. Kirsten fell into a slide, going under the inferno spray and walloping the beast in the chest. The energy whip sliced into the entity, leaving a glowing crack in its chitinous shell. Kirsten scrambled past the hairy insect legs and got back to her feet. The creature toppled forward, crashing to the floor. It shrank from insectoid to fully human, taking on the appearance of a tall, slender woman in her later thirties, cut in half at the torso.

The creature struggled to pull herself together—literally.

Both Harbingers rushed forward, each one seizing half the spirit before dragging it down into the floor. A series of bangs, screams, and zapping noises grew progressively quieter. Division 0 would no doubt soon receive more calls about electronics randomly exploding, dying, or temporarily shutting off.

Kirsten exhaled, relieved. "Dorian?"

He didn't answer. Of course, he didn't like Harbingers, so might have kept his distance. How he abruptly disappeared out of Lily's grip looked like the way ghosts could always instantly return to their mortal remains. Dorian's actual remains sat in an urn at a mausoleum sixty or so miles away from the PAC. He might be able to use the same trick to get back to the patrol craft, but he should have returned already if he'd only gone to the roof.

"Sergeant Peters?" asked Kirsten.

"Copy, Lieutenant Wren. Proceed."

"The entity is gone. Area is secure. Division 1 can come inside now."

"Understood. On our way. Yeah, uhh, now that you mention it, the whole feeling in the air is different."

Kirsten released the lash, the energy cord dissipating as soon as she ceased concentrating on it. She trudged down the hall to Melanie's apartment. The woman still lay on the floor by the couch. Three stimpaks had been enough to seal her wounds but wouldn't have fixed internal damage from the deep stabbing injuries. Kirsten scanned her PID, attaching her record to the call for medical aid.

"Dispatch, if we don't already have medtechs on site already, send a van."

"They're on the roof, lieutenant," replied the voice of a young teen, likely an Admin cadet.

Shimmering light in the corner of the room caught her eye. Kirsten glanced over at a small table holding several holo-bars displaying photographs. Most contained only an intense light smear, like on Officer Greene's helmet video. Some showed a smiling Melanie Avila standing next to the glowing swath, her arm around it as if holding her daughter.

Each holo-bar cycled among numerous photos, not one containing an image of an actual girl, only the glowing patch.

"Not real," whispered Kirsten.

"What's that?" Dorian walked up behind her.

She spun, staring at him. "You're okay!"

"Why wouldn't I be?"

"Took you too long to get back here. Worried me."

He put on an expression of fake innocence. "Gave Bob and Ray a wide berth."

"Bob and Ray?" She blinked. "Oh… Harbingers."

Dorian wagged his eyebrows.

"Relax. They're not interested in you anymore." Kirsten pointed at the holo-bars. "Look at the photos. I think Lily—whatever she is— tricked this woman into believing she had a daughter. Must have been here for a long time."

"What the heck for?" Dorian looked around at the apartment. "Though it does explain how the kid's room was so neat."

"Poor woman." Kirsten hurried over to check on her again. "She's not going to believe her 'daughter' never existed."

"Depends on how deep it got into her head."

Satisfied the woman remained alive, Kirsten accessed her armband terminal and pulled up the citizen record for Melanie Avilla. Sure enough, she had no legal dependents. No record of her ever having a child at all.

"Some psychiatrist is going to finance their next car from this woman." Dorian shook his head. "Would be cheaper to get one of those fake kid dolls and make it look like the ghost so she can keep on pretending."

Kirsten shivered, unsure what bothered her more between the idea of false children and an abyssal impersonating one. The world had so many orphans, buying artificial kids seemed wrong. But then again, some people shouldn't be trusted to take care of actual children. Nothing in Melanie's file raised any alarms.

"I guess," whispered Kirsten. "No idea if this woman even wanted a kid, or the abyssal took over her mind."

Medtechs rushed into the room along with Division 1 patrol officers. Kirsten stepped back to let them treat Melanie.

Dorian moved to stand beside her, watching the medics work. "I suspect she wanted a child quite badly. Creatures like this need some weakness to pick at. It most likely got into her head and made her obsessive. Wonder what set it off on the killing spree?"

"If I had to guess, Melanie started to doubt. Or someone who knew her told her she didn't really have a child. Something. Who knows? Maybe the spirit simply got bored with her. It's not like anything they do is required to make logical sense."

Dorian chuckled. "Are you talking about abyssals, ghosts, or children?"

"All of the above, but if Lily had anything human about her, she was a grown woman. Got a glimpse of her right before the Harbingers pounced. Bet she enjoyed tormenting people." Kirsten sighed at the holo-bars. "Why do some people enjoy hurting others?"

"No idea." Dorian shrugged. "Fortunately, the majority of those who enjoy torture end up managing boy bands or working for health insurance companies. Clawing one's way back into the world from the Abyss is a bit more work than the average psycho is willing to undertake."

Kirsten accessed her armband terminal to create the Inquest record and subsequent reports she'd have to fill out. "Speaking of torture…"

"You okay?" Dorian leaned close. "Seem a little somber. Wasn't a real kid."

"Yeah, I know." Kirsten pictured Lily staring up at her from the bedroom floor. "I almost fell for it. She almost got me."

Dorian smiled. "She didn't. You're not as easy to fool as you think."

"Maybe." Kirsten frowned at the terminal screen. *I'll fill in the basics and do the rest later. Too upset to deal with reports now.*

2

FUTURE STUFF

A working Comforgel bed still made Kirsten feel like she'd snuck into someone else's apartment.

The bed didn't need to work too hard in April, the weather being relatively mild. The first time it went into cooling mode and turned pale blue, she almost panicked until she remembered they had more colors than 'Hades orange,' a surprising demonstration of how much the one in her first apartment bothered her. Obviously, the Division 0 dorms had working Comforgel pads. Her childhood bedroom even had a working one, though after age six, she spent more nights asleep on a closet floor.

She lay there, more or less awake, gazing at the ceiling. Her bedroom's windows—basically the entire wall to her left—tinted out the early morning sun, rendering the world outside in brownish tones. Constant thrumming, the ion thrusters of endless hovercars passing by ten stories up, occasionally drowned out the myriad of advertising jingles.

Who the heck are those bots trying to sell to close enough to hear on the forty-first floor?

By no means extravagant, this place still easily doubled the size of her old home. For some stupid, prideful reason, she'd insisted on getting her own living quarters as soon as she turned eighteen. It would've been far cheaper to remain at the dorms, an option for her since she'd grown up there.

Division 0 didn't have barracks like Division 6, so normal Tactical or Investigative Operations people *couldn't* opt to live at the PAC. Even the dorms would've given Kirsten the boot at twenty-one. Still, it would've been four more years not having to pay rent or buy food. Division 6 troops required barracks since they rotated in and out from active military duty. The line between police and military was thin to begin with, but Division 6 didn't have one.

Any member of the National Police Force, except for Division 6, could resign at will. The worst punishment they'd face for things like refusing an order would be getting fired. Unlike the 'proper' military, where even giving the finger to the wrong officer could land a person in jail for a while.

I don't usually wake up before the alarm. What am I worrying about this time?

Except for having to confront an abyssal, yesterday hadn't been *too* bad. The mental aftereffect bothered her more than the actual confrontation. She couldn't stop thinking about Melanie Avilla's heartbroken expression when told her daughter never existed. As part of her investigation, Kirsten delved as deeply as she could into the woman's memories to determine the extent to which she'd been a victim of paranormal attack. Her suspicions proved true. The woman had a deep-seated craving to be a mother, but never found a man she trusted enough. She lacked the money for adoption or going to a place like FamilyPerfect where they'd make a child using her DNA and some random synthesized DNA based on her preferences.

Lily—or whatever her true name was—approached her in the parking area where she worked five months ago. Within minutes of looking at the girl, Melanie believed she had a daughter and became obsessively devoted to her. Apparently, other people saw the kid, believing her as ordinary as any other child. Until yesterday's meltdown, the abyssal appeared content to simply be doted on, though didn't attend any manner of school.

As far as Kirsten, Captain Eze, or anyone in 'the lab' could guess, the abyssal's motive had likely been feeding off psychic energy while gradually driving Melanie insane. The woman's memories contained zero clues as to what potentially set 'Lily' off on a murderous rampage. She only remembered the fake child calmly walking up to her, saying, "I'm done here" in an adult woman's voice, and stabbing her in the stomach.

Unfortunately, Kirsten lacked the telepathic power necessary to fix the damage. Melanie continued believing her beloved daughter had been possessed. She seemed incapable of rationalizing the girl had never been real. Fearing the woman would try to kill herself if told 'Lily' was gone, Kirsten lied to buy time, claiming the girl had run off and the police were attempting to locate her.

Commander Ashford had likely cleaned up her head by now.

It surprised Kirsten she didn't cling to Evan all night... only for a few hours.

At least the woman's not going to spend the rest of her life pining for a daughter who never existed. Kirsten sat up, hit the button on the alarm to keep it from going off, then got out of bed nine minutes early. Not enough time to try grabbing a little more sleep. She stretched, then headed for the attached bathroom. Her old apartment only had one bathroom. Considering how tiny the place was, it might as well have been attached to the bedroom since only five steps separated the end of her bed from the bathroom door.

Kirsten slipped out of her night shirt, tossed it on the sink, then stepped into the autoshower tube. Sensing her presence, the holographic control screen appeared, displaying various settings and virtual control knobs. She stuck her finger through the preset-one button for a normal morning. The screen played a chime as a text box opened, displaying a notification a firmware update was available.

Whatever...

She poked the 'download' button.

The prompt vanished and the shower whirred to life.

Kirsten stood still, eyes closed, basking in the spray of warm, soapy water from a descending ring of spray jets. This tube—unlike the cheap one in her old apartment—could sense longer hair and spent a little more time applying the scalp-scrubbing water pulse. She ran her hands through her hair after the spray ring went down below her waist. When it reached the floor, she raised her feet one after the other to let the spray wash her soles. Soon, the machine started a rinse pass, then the high-powered hot air cyclone dried her off. The whole process took a little over eight minutes. While the whine of electric fans faded to silence, Kirsten stepped out of the tube, grabbed a clean pair of undies from the machine on the wall, and pulled them on.

Her bedroom windows automatically de-tinted in response to her being awake, allowing in more natural sunlight. Their large size made her feel like a mannequin in a store window, but at least she lived on a floor away from the hovercar lanes. People on the fiftieth, plus or minus one story, had to deal with cars passing right by their bedrooms. They probably set their windows as dark as possible all the time.

She hurried into her uniform top and leggings, leaving boots, belt, and arm guard for later.

Evan streaked across the hall from his bedroom to the other bathroom as she emerged from her bedroom. "Morning!"

"Morning," chimed Kirsten back.

The autoshower in the hall bathroom whirred to life.

Since she woke up early, Kirsten 'semmed toast and whipped up jalapeño eggs with cheese, cheating by making one giant omelet and slicing it in half. Evan rushed into the kitchen within seconds of her setting the plates on the table. He hung his backpack on the chair, sat, and sniffed.

"This smells like ouch."

"No spicier than last time." Kirsten winked at him.

He grinned, then proceeded to attack the food like he'd never eaten before.

Though the doctors called him healthy, Kirsten still worried he remained too skinny. The medics said his Accelerated Healing ability amped up his metabolism, but he no longer lived with an unstable asshole who beat the hell out of him almost daily, so his body didn't need to continuously repair itself. It shouldn't be burning so much energy.

Suppose I shouldn't panic if the medtechs are okay with his weight. At least he doesn't look starved anymore, just skinny.

"Mom, when you were in school, did the other kids keep asking you to talk to ghosts?"

Kirsten shook her head. "Not really. Kids didn't really talk to me much."

"Aww. That's sad. How come?"

"Some did." She looked up from her plate, smiling at him. "Everyone knew I had a really awful mother who mistreated me. My first couple months at the dorm, I was afraid of just about everything. Had no idea how to deal with other children. I'd spent two years living with ghosts under the city. A handful of kids, mostly empaths, treated me like an injured kitten they needed to take care of."

Evan laughed.

She smirked, but also chuckled. "A few years later, it went around that Mind Blast came up on my screening. Once they heard, people mostly avoided me... except for Nicole. Still haven't figured out if she genuinely likes me or if she merely lacks any sense of self-preservation."

"Ugh." Evan rolled his eyes. "People are stupid. Having a power doesn't make someone dangerous. Having a dangerous power *and* being a butthead makes someone dangerous. An' you're not a butthead."

"Hah. Thanks."

"Seriously, you're not." He stabbed a bit of omelet on his fork, grinning. "I'm not just saying it to make you feel better."

"Easy then." Kirsten traced her hand in the air as if writing. "I'll tell Captain Eze to put 'not a butthead' on my next psych evaluation."

Evan almost choked on eggs trying to laugh. Tears streamed from his eyes. "Hot pepper... nose..."

"Ack." She raced around the table to check on him.

Still coughing, he gave a thumbs-up.

"Drink some water… and sorry for making you laugh while you're eating."

"It's okay," rasped Evan, before grabbing the glass and drinking. "And Nicole really likes you."

"Oh, I know. Making a joke." Kirsten returned to her seat. "So, the kids are asking you to talk to ghosts all the time?"

"Not really. It kinda creeps them out. They keep bugging me to guess future stuff, but it doesn't work."

Whew. She breathed relief out her nose. Perhaps she'd been around Dorian and his cynicism too long. If Evan developed the sort of precognitive ability capable of giving him glimpses into the future for trivial things, military intelligence would kidnap him in the middle of the night. His having precognition at all *still* made her worry someone would grab him, but as long as he only saw the future when someone he cared a great deal about faced serious danger made him relatively useless to the military or other unscrupulous people who might try to profit off him.

"Precognition is one of the most difficult powers to control." Kirsten nibbled on toast. "It's super rare, and most people who have it can't control it. They experience prophetic dreams or waking visions out of the blue."

Evan nodded in an exaggerated, comical manner. "I know. Been trying to tell them, but they keep asking me to guess what a random number generator will say, or what someone's gonna be wearing when they walk into the classroom."

"It bothers you?"

"It doesn't bug me they ask. It bugs me I can't do it." He ate another bite of eggs.

He doesn't like disappointing people. "If someone asked me to use Pyrokinesis, I'd never be able to do it."

"Yeah. But you don't even *have* pyro. Totally different. I've got precognition… sorta. Am I doing it wrong?"

"No. In all the time we've been aware of and keeping track of psionics, there have only been three people capable of accurately seeing the future when it didn't involve them personally, or someone emotionally close to them."

"Wow." He blinked. "Only three?"

"Yeah."

Evan made a series of determined faces.

"What are you thinking about?"

He relaxed. "Maybe precog is like *really* hard to do, so it needs the emotions to make it work at all. Like you know how stuff gets stronger when we're scared, or mad? Precog's gotta be like tryin' ta pick up a patrol craft with Telekinesis. Can't do it unless someone you really like's gonna die."

"That's a good way to look at it." She winked, then ate the last of her omelet. A large piece of jalapeño ambushed her, making her feel like a dragon spewing flames from her nose.

Evan laughed the whole time she gasped for air.

"Shani plus one at the door," said the genderless voice of the apartment AI.

Weird. Plus one? It knows Nila. She swatted herself on the chest twice before rasping, "Open the door for them, please."

A faint hiss came from the hall.

"Welcome," said the AI.

The rapid footfalls of two children running preceded Shani and a slightly older girl zooming into the kitchen. Shani hurried right over to Evan and began chattering away, but the other kid stopped short at the edge of the kitchen, staring at Kirsten. Her long, wavy dark-brown hair and big hazel eyes seemed so damn familiar. She'd *definitely* seen this girl before. Four seconds after appearing at the end of the hallway, the mystery girl started crying.

Having never made a kid cry before by simply existing, Kirsten raised an eyebrow.

Where have I seen her—oh, shit! Willow Stephens.

Months ago, Kirsten found the nine-year-old chained to a metal beam while a group of zealous idiots tried to burn her to death for being psionic. Only due to her Pyrokinesis ability had she survived long enough for Kirsten to get there in time to help. She'd almost become too tired to hold back the burning.

Willow bolted forward, racing around the table, and hugged Kirsten.

Evan and Shani stopped talking to blink at her.

"Willow?" asked Evan. "What's wrong?"

Kirsten put an arm around her. "Hey, kiddo. Shh, it's okay. You don't have to cry."

"Thank you for saving me." Willow sniffled, struggling to rein in her emotions. "Sorry. I knew you'd be here, and I still cried. Ev said you were his mom. Seein' you made me think about the bad people."

"Is everything okay?" Kirsten bit her lip.

"Mostly. I sometimes have nightmares and burn my room." Willow wiped her eyes. "Daddy's haunting the school. I think he checks on me at night."

Evan carried his empty plate to the dishwasher. "Yeah. He said he's gonna be around 'til you're grown up. Maybe even stay longer if you want him to."

"Mommy's helping her learn fire stuff." Shani beamed. "Will slept over last night."

"Did you two have fun?" Kirsten ruffled Willow's hair.

"Yeah." Shani nodded.

"Speaking of… where is your mother?"

"'Mergency call. She sent us over here," said Shani. "Can you take us to school?"

Kirsten got up and carried her dishes to the machine. "Of course. Give me a sec to grab the rest of my things and we'll get going."

———

THE KIDS FOLLOWED HER DOWN THE HALL TO THE ELEVATOR AND UP TO the parking area. Living in a building with actual hovercar accommodations made life far less stressful. The walk from elevator to patrol craft took a bit longer, but she didn't have to worry about getting in trouble for illegal parking. Her former landlord didn't seem the type to want cops around, but a passing Division 1 unit might swoop down to issue a citation for a car wedged between HVAC units. Most would ignore an official vehicle, but some might relish the chance to make life difficult for a psionic.

Evan hopped in up front, the girls in the back. Dorian didn't manifest, remaining wherever he went while 'sleeping' in the vehicle. It had become more of a home to him than his burial urn, seeing as how he'd been killed in it. Thinking about former Division 0 personnel who'd been assigned to this car unknowingly butting heads with him and complaining about a 'cursed' PC got her laughing as she lifted off. Most of the crew in motor pool thought her some kind of 'car whisperer' because they didn't believe in ghosts. This patrol craft's problems didn't originate from mechanical or electrical issues, merely a personality clash between the previous drivers and Dorian.

The kids spent the ride to the PAC talking about Pyrokinesis. Much to Kirsten's discomfort, Willow generated a little flame in her hand. Being able to summon fire out of thin air was pretty rare, a sign the girl had serious potential. Most pyrokinetics started off struggling to ignite combustible materials; this girl sustaining an open flame in her hand on pure psionic energy alone put her on par with adults who had been practicing for years.

For a moment, Kirsten wondered if the child might be 'awakened,' like Kate… but the woman's fire turned blue due to being hotter than normal. The flame in Willow's hand remained orange.

She's still a kid, and she's this far along. Wow, I hope she stays happy and well adjusted.

Rumor had it people with Pyrokinesis tended to be short-tempered. Granted, rumor also claimed everyone with Mind Blast should be a creepy, gloomy, morbid sort of person. Kirsten stuck her tongue out in spite at whoever decided on the stereotype she totally didn't fit.

Eleven minutes after liftoff, Kirsten brought the patrol craft down for a landing on the road outside the PAC and drove into the underground parking area. Most satellite precincts had roof parking, but the central Police Administrative Center roof held too many sensitive electronics, including an interplanetary communication array for Mars uplink and a small landing pad used by military aircraft.

She drove to her designated space and shut down the patrol craft. Dorian appeared in the empty passenger seat once Evan got out. He and the kids walked with her across the garage into the PAC. At the entrance to the school wing, she hugged the kids one after the next and sent them off to class. Watching all three of them happy and laughing kept her standing there until they rounded a corner out of sight.

"You've got this mom thing down pretty good." Dorian patted her arm.

"I have no idea what I'm doing. Every decision feels like desperation and panic wrapped up in a whole lot of 'please be the right thing,' followed by like twenty seconds of 'oh shit,' then 'oh, whew, they're alive.'"

Dorian laughed. "Yeah, that's pretty much normal."

"Thanks for the moral support." She started back down the hall, heading for the elevator.

He fell in step beside her. "If anyone ever came up with the perfect way to be a parent applicable to every possible situation, they'd already have published it and become a quadrillionaire—or whatever they call it when someone has so many damn credits they could buy the universe."

"True."

A triple beep—the alarm tone—came from her armband. "Lieutenant Wren, copy?"

She stopped walking, raising her arm. The holo-panel scrolled open automatically, revealing the face of a dispatch doll, a relatively generic-looking mid-twenties woman. "Go ahead."

"21-47 in progress at Bixton's restaurant. Multiple reports of an active paranormal manifestation," said the doll.

I haven't even made it to my desk yet. "Understood. On the way."

"Race you to the car," said Dorian.

She shook her head and started running.

3

GOING ON A RIP

Eighteen minutes after leaving the garage, Kirsten dove her patrol craft out of the sky.

Bixton's restaurant sat in the approximate middle of a block where the ground floors of residential high-rises all contained commercial properties. Restaurants, clothing stores, cybernetic boutiques, electronics shops, jewelry places, and so on stretched for miles in both directions. Thick pedestrian traffic scurried back and forth under a swarm of advert bots.

The nearest open street-side parking space to the restaurant sat a block and a half away, but only a few ground cars moved along the road. So... she swooped down, landing half on the sidewalk, blocking one lane. Intense snap-flashes from the emergency bar lights painted the surroundings blue in strobe, drawing the attention of any pedestrians not absorbed in augmented reality. Most stared at an all-black police hovercar, unsure what to make of it beyond wanting to get well away from the area before bullets started flying.

Kirsten leapt out and ran to the restaurant.

About twenty-eight people seated at tables, two waitresses, and a waiter all looked over as she shoved the door out of her way. She gazed around the room, everything appearing quite ordinary. No disruption, no one screaming, no mess, merely a bunch of people wondering why a cop barged in.

Dorian appeared on her right. "This is the coordinate Dispatch sent us."

"Yeah… Dispatch?"

"Go ahead, lieutenant," replied a generic female voice.

"I'm at the site of the 24-47, but there's nothing going on here. Can you confirm my location is correct?"

"You are at the correct nav point, lieutenant."

She glanced at Dorian. "Thanks, Dispatch. I'll have a look around, but it seems like someone's playing a prank on us."

"Logged," said the doll.

"I'll check the back." Dorian crossed the dining area to a hallway at the far end.

Kirsten glanced around at the people, most of whom continued staring at her. "Did anyone here call in a report of unexplained, possibly paranormal or psionic activity?"

"Yeah," said a woman sitting alone. "Someone grabbed me, but no one was there."

"Same here." A man closer to where Kirsten stood pointed at his arm. "Felt like a kid tugging on my shirt for attention."

"My drink flew off the table." A teenage girl pointed at the floor.

Both waitresses talked at the same time about seeing various objects move on their own.

A woman with shoulder-length metallic silver hair rushed out from a flapping door at the back of the seating area, heading toward her. Upon noticing the woman had glowing violet irises, Kirsten scanned her surface thoughts, concerned she might be trying to use a psionic ability, but saw only the intention to plea for help.

"You're from Division 0, right?" asked the woman as soon as she got close enough to talk.

"Yes."

She offered a hand. "Alina Sandoval. I'm the manager. There's a whole bunch of crazy shit going on in here."

"Looks pretty quiet at the moment."

Alina gestured at the door. "That's because the four customers who suffered the worst attacks already ran out."

"What happened?" Kirsten raised her left arm, opening the holo-panel to create an Inquest record.

"Plates and stuff flying off tables. One lady had her dress torn halfway off. Another man fell when the chair shot out from under him, and the other woman... umm." Alina looked around, then lowered her voice to a whisper. "Lost her underpants in the bathroom."

"Lost?"

Alina whispered, "She said something ripped them off her."

Dorian phased through the wall, his body wispy and glowing for a second before regaining its normal lifelike appearance. "Nothing in sight."

Theodore? Kirsten tapped her foot. Sure, despite his age, he still liked to scare people and did have a fondness for getting more than a little handsy with women. However, she doubted he'd been here. Not only did the place lack the residual energy a ghost as old as him would leave behind, no one complained of an 'ice finger' in a sensitive place.

She squirmed at the memory.

Also, Theodore didn't do 'annoying' things, like throwing food around, yanking chairs out from under people, and so forth. When he got playful, he scared the crap out of people. Or made political statements, like ripping the skirt off the politician who wanted to shut down Sanctuary Park in the middle of her speech and making her chase it around the park.

"Hey!" shouted a man in the back hall. "Get off!"

Alina twisted to look. "Here we go again. Whatever's doing this loves the bathrooms."

"On it," said Kirsten.

She jogged across the dining room to the hallway. A door close on the left bore a sign reading 'kitchen – employees only'. Thirty feet away, two bathrooms stood opposite each other on the left and right. Another door at the end presumably led to the alley behind the building.

"What the fuck?" yelled a man in the left bathroom, grunting as if struggling.

A frustrated feminine growl followed.

Kirsten approached the door. "Are you okay in there?"

"Something's yanking on my damn shirt. Ripped it."

Sensing a buildup of paranormal energy, she took a step back. A woman phased through the closed door, phantasmal vapor surrounding her otherwise naked body for a few seconds until she reintegrated to a visually solid form. She looked hyper manic, as if she'd consumed thirty pots of high-grade espresso. Her lavender hair fluffed out into a ball, awash in crackling sparks. Water dripped down her body, forming a spectral puddle around her feet.

Between her nakedness and the water, Kirsten assumed she'd died in the autoshower.

The ghost disregarded Kirsten, heading toward the dining area.

Dorian clamped a hand over his mouth, seemingly fighting the urge to laugh.

"Umm, hey?" Kirsten trailed after her.

The spirit walked up behind a seated woman and tried to grab her dress, yanking on it with enough force to tear the material from collar to beltline. Screaming, the victim fought back, pulling on the dress in a tug of war until the spirit dragged her out of her chair to the floor.

"Stop that!" yelled Kirsten, pushing at the ghost with her astral psionics, somewhat like how Telekinetics could move objects using their mind.

Emitting a startled yelp, the naked ghost slipped in her puddle and landed on her butt.

"What the hell?" shouted the torn-dress woman.

The ghost scrambled upright, looking around. She lunged at a man approaching to offer a coat to the woman sitting on the floor. Kirsten 'caught' the spirit, using her psionic ability to push the ghost away from him.

"Knock it off," yelled Kirsten. "What are you doing?"

"Uhh..." The man blinked. "Giving her something to cover—"

"Not you, the ghost." Kirsten pulled at the spirit, trying to hold her back from stealing the coat.

Giving up on her first target, the ghost whirled, grabbing the skirt of the first woman's friend. Dorian ran up and seized the ghostly woman's arm, stopping her from tearing the fabric.

"Eep! It's got my skirt!" The other woman grasped the garment in the same spot the ghost did.

"Let go." Kirsten stared at the chaotic spirit. "Hey. Over here. Look at me. I can see you."

The ghost squirmed away from Dorian, ran through Kirsten, and grabbed the shirt of the man who gave his coat to the torn-dress woman.

Grr. Kirsten channeled her power into her body, making herself solid to spirits. She whirled and grabbed the ghost by both wrists, peeling her grip away from the guy's shirt.

He squealed, backpedaling, most of the color draining out of his cheeks. "W-what the hell is going on here?"

"Ghost playing pranks." Kirsten spun the female spirit around to face her, still holding her wrists. "Talk to me."

"Holy shit! You're touching me." The wet spirit squirmed in a half-hearted attempt to pull away. "Wow, yeah. You're solid."

Dorian looked the woman over. "Autoshower malfunction?"

"No. A stupid bot crashed into the tub and electrocuted me. I'm stuck like this, and now it won't stop," yelled the ghost.

"Wow, a tub?" Kirsten blinked. "People still have those?"

"Nicer apartments and actual houses do," said Dorian.

"I can't stay naked all the time." The ghost tried to pull away from Kirsten again, hard enough to seem like a genuine effort to get away. "I'm not a damn Neko."

Kirsten struggled to hold on. Making herself solid shifted things from psionic strength to physical strength, giving the taller woman a mild advantage. "You're not stuck. I can help you learn how to change your appearance. And what did you mean it won't stop? What won't stop?"

"Argh!" shouted the ghost. She surged forward, her wet arms

slipping through Kirsten's grasp until she gripped the collar of her uniform top.

Dorian grabbed the spirit's arms, preventing her from ripping the stretchy fabric. Frustrated, the ghost screamed in anger. He wrenched her away from Kirsten, swept her leg, and pinned the spirit to the floor as if taking down a living suspect.

"Make it stop!" shrieked the spirit.

"Make *what* stop?" Kirsten flailed.

The ghost dove down into the floor.

Dorian went after her.

Kirsten rubbed her forehead.

Alina approached, her expression hopeful. "What just happened?"

"Most of the floors above this place are apartments. Pretty sure the ghost of a woman who died upstairs is trying to find something to wear. Looks like she died in the bath, so she thinks she's stuck permanently naked. A spirit's latent self-image is mutable. She doesn't realize she can change it if she wants to."

"Right…" Alina chuckled. "I'll pretend I understood you. Did you get rid of her?"

"Sort of. She ran away. My partner—also a ghost—is chasing her."

"Is it gonna stop?"

Kirsten shrugged. "Hard to say. She'll probably continue pestering people until she figures out how to make herself look different. If we're lucky, Dorian will convince her to leave people alone since she can't actually wear any clothing she steals."

"Wow." Alina exhaled. "So, that's it? Just letting her go?"

"Yeah. Sorry. We don't have a way to drag ghosts off to jail."

Alina blinked, then cracked up laughing. "Okay, yeah. Guess it's pretty dumb to think you'd be able to do anything more than chase one out of here, huh?"

"Not dumb." Kirsten put on her best Division 0 public relations smile. "Most citizens don't understand the nature of the paranormal. It's perfectly understandable to be confused and frightened. The spirit here can't seriously injure anyone and isn't trying to be malicious.

Death is hard to process, especially for the person who died. She's embarrassed and freaking out, not a serious threat to anyone."

"Right..." Alina whistled. "Should I call it in again if she comes back?"

"Yep. She's pretty disoriented and upset. If not for her having the ability to exert force on physical objects, I'd say she died pretty recently."

Dorian glided up out of the floor. "Lost her. She took the shortcut back to her remains. Didn't say much. Just kept yelling 'make it stop' repeatedly."

Hopefully, she doesn't come back here. Kirsten exhaled. "Drat."

"Hmm?" asked Alina.

"She ran off. I'll be out of your way in a minute, just need to collect a few statements." Kirsten opened her armband terminal. "This won't take long."

4

SUSPICIOUS THERMAL ANOMALY

K irsten emerged from Bixton's to a minor traffic snarl around her patrol craft.

Since she'd blocked one lane, drivers risked oncoming traffic to get around the patrol craft. A woman wearing a skirt suit probably more expensive than the tiny ground car she drove argued with a Division 1 cop two storefronts away to the right over it 'not being a big deal' to use the sidewalk to avoid an obstruction. Two advert bots floated by them, one showing lawyer ads to the woman, the other displaying headache medicine to the cop.

Hundreds of pedestrians flowed past the argument, lost to the obliviousness of augmented reality or simply ignoring them. A queue of at least nine cars stacked up behind the patrol craft, waiting for a chance to use the oncoming lane.

Head bowed, Kirsten hurried to the driver's side and got in. The drivers of the ground cars stuck in line most likely gave her dirty looks, but she didn't make eye contact with any of them. Whatever courage her guilty body language might have given someone to make a comment about her blocking the road failed to overcome the cloud of fear surrounding the all-black car and all-black uniform. Most citizens mistook black for Division 9. While true, they used black patrol craft, theirs didn't have bar lights or markings—and they had no official uniform. Much like people's fear of Division 0, their opinion of Nine was overblown. Contrary to rumor, one of their operatives couldn't randomly kill people free of legal problems. Granted, if they could present the least bit of justification, it didn't take much.

Only a ghost ripping clothes. Safe behind the armored windows where no one outside could see her, Kirsten watched the sidewalk driver continue arguing with the cop. Sensing where she looked, the patrol craft's electronics directed the audio pickup onto the conversation, making it as clear as if she stood right next to them. The woman argued since the police blocked off the road, it gave people permission to go around, even if they had to use the sidewalk to do it.

She gripped the sticks and pulled the patrol craft upward. The driver behind her accelerated hard, nearly sideswiping a merging car going in the same direction who'd attempted to go around in the oncoming lane.

"You seem far more upset than normal for a haunt like that." Dorian leaned his head back and closed his eyes. "Is Lily still bothering you?"

"Nah. Just thinking about idiot drivers. The woman over there could've hurt or killed a pedestrian. For what? A prank ghost? This spirit wouldn't have hurt anyone."

Dorian chuckled. "Only their dignity. What idiots do isn't your fault. You aren't less of a cop because you sometimes deal with issues like this."

"I know, but is it worth blocking a street over?"

"Div 1 routinely blocks traffic to get their morning coffee."

She sighed. "I'm not Div 1. And I wouldn't inconvenience hundreds of people to save myself a bit of a walk for breakfast. Why don't their captains yell at them? Or for ignoring traffic rules when they're not responding to an incident?"

"Being able to park like a jackass is a small perk of the job to keep them from burning out and quitting."

"It's not right."

Dorian smiled, eyes still closed. "It's not in the books, but you can bet their captains have bigger issues to yell about. Don't turn into one of those lieutenants who runs around 'issuing demerits' for every tiny thing."

"Not what I'm saying." She pulled up into the hover traffic lane at 500 feet and set the auto-drive for the PAC. "That woman in the microcar could've run someone over because a ghost yanked on people's clothes. Not even close to a legit emergency."

"We could cite the spirit for public nuisance."

She huffed. Dorian laughing made her angrier, but not at him. True, she had no way to know what kind of situation they'd been sent into and she much preferred to encounter a dress-tearing spirit than a 'Lily' where multiple people died.

I shouldn't be this upset over an idiot cutting onto the sidewalk. Kirsten looked down at her stomach. *Crap. It must be hormone time.*

"1815-014, please acknowledge," said a young voice.

"Go ahead, Dispatch." Kirsten shifted her gaze from her angry ovaries to the middle of the console.

The head and shoulders of a thirteen-ish boy appeared.

I always get the baby cadets. Do they think my calls are cute or something? Light stuff for the new class to play dispatcher?

"Lieutenant?" asked the boy. "We have a report of suspicious thermal activity at the Lyris Corporation building in Sector 882."

This sounds fairly tame. "Cold spots?"

The teen blinked in surprise. "Wow, you can read minds over comm?"

Kirsten grinned. "Nah. The only reason you'd be contacting me about thermal anomalies is cold spots. Most people think they indicate the presence of ghosts."

"It usually does." Dorian opened his eyes. "Hmm. Lyris. Sounds familiar, but nothing stands out. Guess they're only mildly shady."

"Acknowledged," said Kirsten. "Send the Nav pin. On the way."

"Roger, lieutenant." The boy smiled, reached off camera, and disappeared.

Seconds later, a waypoint marker appeared on the Navcon terminal.

Since they already headed south toward the PAC, the car didn't make any course corrections yet. To reach the Lyris Corporation building, she had to fly farther south. She pulled up the company's GlobeNet presence, skimming the basic information. The company manufactured dolls, they formerly made synthetics (it had become illegal to produce fully sentient synths), various types of bots, and consumer-grade cyberware. The company also had a subsidiary involved in chemical production, mostly medical tank gel and hydroponic growth media.

"Hmm. Someone had a bad reaction to a Lyris-made cybernetic implant and went back to haunt them?"

"More likely a spirit would blame the cyberdoc who implanted it." Dorian poked a finger into another small screen, opening the incident report.

The complaint originated from Seth Rivera, listed as a 'security manager' for Lyris. It contained little useful information beyond their systems picking up inexplicable cold spots bearing a striking resemblance to a human form.

"No mention of the ghost actually *doing* anything. Could be a walk-by." Kirsten shrugged. "Love the easy ones."

"Agreed."

KIRSTEN TOOK MANUAL CONTROL OF THE PATROL CRAFT A LITTLE UNDER a mile from the Lyris building.

The company occupied the entirety of a 112-story high-rise shaped like a shiny dark metal version of the Washington Monument. She thought of it since Evan had been talking about it over breakfast recently as it came up in history class. When they built the plates over East City, the government used the idea of moving the entire monument up to the new surface as a big public relations-slash-patriotism fundraiser.

She followed glowing yellow drive assistant lines on the screen to a parking garage entry door at the fiftieth-story level. Dozens of advert bots swarmed around, flashing all manner of glowing, colorful displays. A few delivery bots—recognizable due to their faster, straight-line flight paths—whizzed by, going into the building.

An information box popped up on the windshield screen. For an instant, it displayed a 'no Lyris ID detected, please proceed to visitor parking' message, but changed to a message welcoming the police with directions to emergency parking area near the door—or 'follow the yellow line to visitor parking if this isn't an emergency'.

I'm technically on a call, but no one's in danger.

The yellow line guided her to a ramp up one level, then over to a cluster of parking spaces reasonably close to a group of elevator doors on a square section of wall at the center of the fifty-first floor. 'Emergency' parking would have spared her a sixty-foot walk. She hopped out and started toward the elevators.

A thirtyish man in a dark blue jumpsuit emerged from one pair of sliding doors and raised a hand in greeting. She recognized Seth Rivera from the ID photo linked to the inbound contact to Division 0 requesting assistance. His jumpsuit shoulders bore Lyris Corporation logos, as did the buckle of his utility belt. His belt held a medium-sized handgun in a holster, likely a Class 3 or 4, as well as a stunrod and some utility compartments.

Some Division 1 officers had such a strong dislike for private police they couldn't help but turn every interaction argumentative. Kirsten didn't mind them much, except for a mild distrust of the concept. People who 'enforced the law' at the behest of a corporation could easily end up doing the bidding of their company against the interest of the public. It smelled too much like the ACC for her liking. In the Allied Corporate Council, which had taken over most of Europe, profit ruled. Their entire police system operated mostly to safeguard company interests while making money on the side. Citizens who didn't pay monthly policing fees were left to deal with crime on their own. Worse, she'd heard some stories about innocent people ending up in prison for defending themselves against a criminal who *had* paid their policing fees.

The UCF was far from perfect. Some even called it a military police state. However, it felt like the government mostly tried to do the right thing, even if often seemed misguided.

"Officer?" asked Seth as she approached.

"Lieutenant Wren, Division 0." She offered a hand. "You called about a cold spot?"

Seth shook hands. "Oh, sorry, lieutenant. I'm kinda surprised they gave me the okay to involve you guys at all here."

"Why?"

"Well, you know... start talking about cold spots and everyone thinks ghosts. Who takes 'ghosts' seriously?" Seth chuckled.

Kirsten fake laughed. "Yeah... I get that a lot."

"I think the executives are concerned it might have been a psionic spy." Seth entered the elevator and held the door for her. "I couldn't find anything in our systems indicating a person entered the building and made it into the conference room, so before I go nuts doing diagnostics on a thousand sensors, figured I'd jump straight to the most illogical explanation and eliminate it first."

"You don't think a ghost was here?" Kirsten raised an eyebrow.

"I'm not sure one way or the other." Seth poked the button for the ninety-eighth floor. "As far as I'm concerned, ghosts are probably real. I've seen stuff on the security cameras in this place for years, and no one can explain any of it."

Bands of white light slid down the walls of the elevator cab, offering a visual indication of going upward past each story.

"This building is haunted?" Kirsten reached out with her Astral Sense, hunting for any trace of a paranormal presence, but only picked up Dorian, who stood right next to her. "I'm not sensing any spirits nearby, but the place is pretty big."

"Everywhere in West City is haunted," said Dorian. "We built a city on the ruins of an old world, leaving everything down there as it was. Even corpses in some places."

Kirsten fidgeted. As far as she knew, the universe didn't care at all about 'proper burials,' but many ghosts did—especially from 300 years ago, before society considered religious belief to be a mental illness. If a dead person truly thought they needed a specific ritual performed during their burial, they could stick around as a ghost like someone who'd been murdered and demanded revenge. Most of the spirits she'd encountered in the Beneath died centuries ago and haunted their old homes or death sites because their remains had been left wherever they dropped. The government of the time didn't think it worth the money to 'clean up' areas they intended to bury under city plates and forget existed. In a way, they'd made the entire Beneath into a tomb.

Seth smiled. "If you're not in a hurry to be anywhere, I've got a whole bunch of saved video clips. Chairs moving, doors moving, cleaning bots behaving in weird ways. Even have some audio of people talking in empty hallways."

"Anything violent happen here? Scratches, attacks?" asked Kirsten.

"Nah. All the activity our cameras picked up occurs in empty rooms or hallways. The ghosts here are pretty shy. The weird stuff always stops when security goes there to check on it. Seemed weird for one to stand around in a room with sixteen people."

Kirsten glanced over—and up—at him. "What happened?"

"You're probably going to be mad for us calling you over such a non-event." Seth offered an innocent smile. "We picked up a human shaped cold spot in the room during an executive meeting. It didn't do anything more than stand there the whole time, dissipating once the meeting ended. Management is on edge about it due to the confidential nature of the meeting."

"Mind showing me the video?"

"Sure. We don't record sound in those rooms since they're used for highly confidential discussions, but no problem showing you the thermal."

"Makes sense they're worried about a person eavesdropping if the meetings are sensitive." Dorian gazed around. "Not feeling any other spirits in the area. You think a ghost might've been actually spying?"

"Umm. Probably not. I mean, why? They don't need money. If a spirit did invade the conference room, they were probably lost or simply curious."

"Huh?" Seth glanced at her.

"Talking to my partner." She nodded toward Dorian. "He's a spirit."

"Whoa. There's a ghost in here with us now?"

Dorian waved a hand past Seth's eyes, getting no reaction. "He's as psionic as a doorknob."

"Yeah."

"Wait. I've seen actual doorknobs more psionic than this guy."

Kirsten stifled a chuckle.

The elevator doors opened.

"Cool. Gotta be helpful having a ghost along to help find other ghosts." Seth waved for her to follow and fast-walked out into a sleek silver-and-grey corridor.

Fist-sized orb bots glided back and forth above head level, set to some mysterious task. A mirror-finished disc-bot roamed about cleaning the highly polished floor. Surprisingly, most of the workers in sight wore relatively casual attire, not the usual expensive, fashion-conscious stuff usual for big corporation towers.

"Dorian's a lifesaver. Literally." Kirsten grinned up at him.

"Cool," said Seth. "So, umm, does everyone end up as a ghost? How long do they hang around?"

"Everyone has the potential to be a ghost. Circumstances of death and what's on a person's mind at the time of death make the difference. If you *want* to hang out as a ghost, you're going to. People who get hung up on some unresolved thing can also get stuck here when they want to move on. Could be justice for their murder or something as weird as not getting a promised slice of pie."

"Wow. Pie? Seriously?" Seth chuckled.

"Honest. This one poor guy sat around the hospital waiting for the pie he'd been looking forward to all week." Kirsten gave a sad sigh.

Seth led her through several hallways and sliding glass doors marked 'authorized personnel only' to a small security station acting as a mini lobby in front of the executive conference rooms.

Holographic signs at the entrance to the conference area announced a ban on all personal electronics beyond this point.

A woman in a security jumpsuit seated at the counter smiled at them. "Hey, Seth." She looked at Kirsten, her smile weakening.

Kirsten braced for the usual nasty comment about psionics.

"Oh, please tell me they're not thinking of outsourcing security."

Seth laughed. "Nah, Jamie. Lieutenant Wren is NPF, not a security contractor on a tour."

Jamie's expression mirrored Kirsten's relief.

"Wow." Jamie looked her over. "Since when do the cops wear black? Are you like special forces or something?"

"At my size?" Kirsten laughed. "I'm with Division 0."

"Oh, wow." Jamie gave Seth a creepy look. "Who's getting brain scanned?"

Kirsten blinked. "Brain scanned?"

"They don't really do brain scans." Seth went around behind the desk, gesturing for Kirsten to follow. "I don't think the VPs would even ask and I'm sure Division 0 wouldn't go sniffing around people's brains because the bosses thought someone might be committing espionage."

"Yeah, that's a big no." Kirsten held a hand up. "We don't raid people's thoughts except in the most extreme circumstances, and someone in a suit not trusting their employees isn't extreme."

"Wow, so you guys *can* read minds?" Jamie blushed, looking away from her.

She either thinks I'm pretty... or she's embarrassed for thinking we're dangerous. Kirsten sighed mentally but didn't peek into the woman's mind.

Seth tapped at one of the screens, bringing up a blue-toned video showing the interior of a large conference room. "What counts as extreme?"

"Not *all* psionics can, but telepathy is the most common ability. Extreme is cases where someone is going to die if we *don't* look at what a suspect is thinking."

Dorian laughed. "The paperwork is totally not worth it to use for small stuff."

"Here we go." Seth pointed at the holo-panel, then moved a slider to fast forward a few minutes in before letting it play.

Sixteen bright orange-yellow heat forms filed in and arranged themselves in seats around the table. A minute and eighteen seconds after the last person sat, a dark blue shape exuded from the wall. It started off as a formless cloud, but gradually took on a more human outline. The head, torso, and arms of a fairly large man stood out in obvious clarity, while the legs remained more of an indistinct foggy mass.

"Yeah. Definitely a spirit." Kirsten pointed at the legs. "A live person in a thermal suit wouldn't be a cloud below the waist."

"Could it be a psionic hiding from the cameras?" asked Seth.

Kirsten scrunched her face, thinking. "I can't say with a hundred percent certainty it isn't. However, we've never documented anything like this as the result of a Technokinetic using their abilities to hide from electronic systems. They wouldn't appear at all."

"Whoa." Jamie stared at her "You guys can delete yourself out of videos?"

She exhaled. "There is no need to panic. Approximately eight percent of the population has psionic abilities, though it could be as high as ten considering those who don't come forward. Among people with psionic abilities, Technokinesis is fairly uncommon. Less than twenty percent of psionic individuals display some degree of influence over electronics. The ability to remotely affect recording devices not to register them is... pretty hard to do. I'm not a techno, so I can't really explain it in too much detail, but it sounds like a pain in the ass from what I've read."

"So, twenty percent of eight-to-ten percent of people *might* be able to pull a vampire and not show up on cameras." Seth shifted his jaw side to side. "Yeah, doesn't sound like it would be a real problem."

"Also, that ability does nothing to stop live people from seeing them. They'd only be invisible to cameras. No one in the room is reacting to him." Kirsten again pointed at the foggy mass. "I've seen plenty of ghosts on thermal. This one is either fairly recent or lazy."

"How so?" asked Jamie.

"Do you have a thermal view on us right now?"

Both Seth and Jamie nodded.

"Put it on a screen." Kirsten smiled.

Dorian sigh-chuckled. "You know, some telepaths can make themselves functionally invisible to people."

"Yeah, but they also have legs. And wouldn't appear cold on camera."

Jamie tapped a few buttons and another holo-panel opened.

The two Lyris Corporation security officers stared at the screen for a few seconds before noticing a faint blue silhouette where Dorian stood beside Kirsten.

"Your partner." Seth looked back and forth from the screen and Dorian a few times. "Awesome."

"His legs are solid because he's been around for a while and has a strong sense of self-image. It takes effort to hold shape."

"Squeak," said Dorian.

She glanced at him.

"Guinea pig."

"Huh? What's that?"

"Pardon?" asked Seth.

"Talking to my partner."

Dorian whistled. "Wow. Guinea pigs were medium-sized rodents stereotypically used as test subjects for experiments."

"Are they rodents or pigs?"

"Rodents."

Kirsten furrowed her brow. "Kinda dumb they call them pigs."

He sighed.

She turned back to Seth. "Can you show me this room?"

"Yeah. It's empty now." He swiped a hand at the thermal video, shutting the holo-panel off, then headed through the 'no personal electronics beyond this point' sliding glass doors into a long corridor between two walls of floor-to-ceiling frosted glass. Small silver placards bearing room numbers stuck out from the walls by the entrance to each conference room, a near seamless door-sized glass panel.

"What do you guys do about cybernetic implants?" asked Kirsten. "I get you don't want people recording sensitive meetings on their NetMinis, but lots of people have headware."

"Yeah. Easy. In order to gain access to these meetings, they have to accept monitoring. We don't ban company-issued NetMinis since those are monitored."

Dorian rolled his eyes. "I'm sure every executive is compliant with the monitoring requirement."

She smiled.

Seth stopped by ECR-3. The glass slab door swung inward, revealing an executive conference room with seating for twenty-five. Silver-and-white chairs around the table looked like they belonged in a high-performance sports hovercar. A small metal dot stuck up from the surface of the white-glass table in front of each seat, holo-emitters most likely.

The room held a faint paranormal energy, but no spirits.

Kirsten walked around the table three times, mentally searching for lingering traces. The spot where the cold figure stood for over an hour gave off a moderate paranormal imprint. However, the dent Dorian punched in Nila's wall more than doubled it. Even Nila sensed the energy in it, and she lacked any Astral Sense ability.

A spirit definitely stood here, but he had to be totally calm. Maybe even bored.

"Mind if I check the rest of these rooms?" asked Kirsten.

Seth raised his arm to the side in a 'be my guest' gesture.

She went room to room in the conference area, finding no spirits or detectable amounts of spectral energy residue. Fifteen or so minutes later, Seth met her in the hallway where she stopped to type in some notes for the incident report.

"Any luck?" he asked.

"I'm certain a ghost visited the conference room during the meeting, but the energy he left behind is weak. My guess is he's a random spirit who happened to wander by during the meeting and decided to hang out. Could be, he's related to someone in the meeting and came to say goodbye, but maybe not. If he'd come to say farewell, he would've left a stronger imprint. Whoever this ghost is, he had little emotional investment in being there."

Seth pursed his lips. "So… real ghost. Huh. First time one showed up with people around."

"That he knows of." Dorian feigned innocence. "The man simply stood there."

"True," said Kirsten.

"Pardon?" Seth looked around as if searching for Dorian. "Talking to him again?"

"Yeah. You've observed ghostly phenomenon in empty rooms on the security cameras, but if a spirit didn't affect solid objects, no one would know they existed. Well, except for thermal."

"Uhh…" Seth whistled. "Yeah. We've only got thermal on sensitive areas."

Kirsten smiled. "Not trying to scare you. Just saying… a ghost existing in a room with people isn't necessarily unusual for this building. Maybe they only swat stuff around in empty rooms."

"Oh. So… should we be concerned?"

"Doubtful." Kirsten swiped a finger across the holo-panel above her forearm guard, closing it. "If the spirit wanted to cause trouble, he'd have left a much stronger imprint on the room."

"Cool." Seth fake-wiped sweat from his forehead. "At least I don't have to check every security system on the floor to explain how someone got in here. Thanks. Sorry if it wasn't anything exciting."

"Fine. Totally fine." She followed him out of the secure conference room area. "Love the quiet ones. Way better than the alternative."

"Umm." Seth smiled pleadingly. "Can you please give me something official stating a ghost was here so I can convince my manager *not* to make me audit every system in the building?

Kirsten grinned. "Of course. Unnecessary work sucks."

"Like reports," muttered Dorian.

Ugh. Worst part of the job. Thirteen pages of needless crap for every damn Inquest. "Seriously."

THE ELEVATOR CLOSED BEHIND KIRSTEN AND DORIAN, WHISKING SETH off into the building.

She gazed around the parking deck, searching for paranormal energy. A faint sense of spiritual presence came from the left. It didn't feel like the same spirit as the conference room, so she disregarded it. West City had tons of ghosts, the vast majority benign.

"Two in one day." Dorian started walking toward the patrol craft. "Highly unusual, though I suppose we should be grateful both happened to be tame."

"No doubt. My second day as an active agent, I had six haunt calls."

"Six? Wow…"

Kirsten sighed. "Yeah. Didn't know it at the time, but the Wharf Stalker's presence stirred them up. He made other ghosts stronger and agitated just from being nearby. Like, totally passive sweet spirits would get all chaotic and dangerous merely for being close to him."

The whirring of an ion thruster drew her attention to the right. A footlocker-sized delivery bot zoomed across the parking deck toward the elevators. Such a sight ordinarily wouldn't have demanded more than a second or two of acknowledgement, but this one appeared to be going too fast for indoors.

She shook her head, muttering, "Idiots."

A man walked out from between two parked cars, directly in the bot's path.

"Look—!" shouted Kirsten.

Whud!

The delivery bot struck the man in the head, spraying blood on the column and swatting him to the floor. It fishtailed, swaying side to side from the force of the hit, but stabilized before crashing into a column or parked car.

"…Out." Kirsten blinked. "Shit!"

Undeterred, the bloody delivery bot kept right on flying for the doors.

"Dispatch, need a MedVan at my location *stat*." Kirsten ran to the guy lying on the floor.

"Unbelievable," muttered Dorian.

The front left region of the man's skull appeared cracked, his jaw and nose broken. She hastily injected him with four stimpaks in hopes of stopping the bleeding. No ghost sat up out of his body yet, a good sign.

Light washed over her. Kirsten cringed, expecting to peer up at a spirit. Reluctantly, she looked up—at a twelve-inch orb bot. Multiple holo-panels surrounded it like the petals of a flower, all showing advertisements for medical supplies, rapid-care MedVan protection plans, and a few lawyers.

"Seriously?" Kirsten frowned. "Comm, dispatch, need a medical unit to my location ASAP."

The orb bot drooped as if ashamed of itself, then popped back up, adding another panel hawking helmets. She smirked at it.

"Copy, lieutenant," said an adult woman's voice from her armband.

A *pssh* came from the elevators.

"Whoa, the bot's covered in blood," said a woman.

Kirsten looked.

A blonde girl and two boys, all about eighteen or nineteen, stood by the delivery bot making squeamish faces. Likely, someone sent the interns down to pick up lunch or catering for a meeting. One of the guys began unloading giant sub sandwiches from the flying box-bot.

"Speedy-Nom..." Dorian whistled. "They got 'speedy' down. Wonder if the food's any good?"

Rips in the victim's face foamed pink as the nanobot-laced fluid reached the injury site, mending the skin. His jaw quivered, realigning itself—a little. Stimpaks could only do so much, after all. None of Kirsten's psionic abilities were of any to help, so she gave him another injection and knelt there holding his hand.

Once empty, the delivery bot closed its front hatch and pivoted around, flying for the parking deck exit.

"Bot," yelled Kirsten. "Stop! Get back here. You hit a guy."

It kept flying away.

"Police!" shouted Kirsten.

The delivery bot didn't even slow down.

Kirsten pulled her E-90, sighted, and fired, missing by a few feet, drilling a hole in a column. She tried again, hitting the wall. Her third shot clipped the ass end of the bot, slicing into its rear left ion thruster, causing a spinout crash. The wayward bot slammed into the plastisteel floor upside down and slid into the wall amid a hail of orange sparks.

"Flight system error," said a male voice from the bot.

Her two missed shots left tiny holes in the building's wall; hopefully, the laser used most of its power getting out of the building and didn't damage any passing hovercars.

"Dispatch, I also need a Civ 1 patrol unit here to clean up a dangerous delivery bot." She scowled at the smoldering wreckage. "Stupid, reckless damn companies. They probably disabled the safety systems to shave a few seconds off delivery time."

The advert bot switched its ads from medical supplies and helmets to anger management services.

Kirsten pinched the bridge of her nose.

Dorian cracked up.

5

WORKED OUT

E ager to keep her promised appointment, Kirsten set the Lyris Corporation incident report aside for later.

She hurried through the PAC to the secure dormitory, where Division 0 housed criminally inclined psionic youths. The whole concept of it bothered her for more reasons than the simple tragedy of children who needed to be kept behind locked doors. Radicals often accused the UCF of being a 'fascist military police state.' Compared to the countries it used to be, the United States and Canada, perhaps it *did* sorta count as one. For the most part, Kirsten tried not to dwell on the negatives. Her country was *way* better to live in than the ACC. Of course, the ACC had a 'kill on sight' policy regarding psionics, so it made preferring one over the other a simple decision. As scummy as corporations could get in the UCF sometimes, they could do whatever they wanted overseas. When the corporations *were* the government, the people had no protection.

However, the reality of the secure dormitory painted a black cloud over her idealism.

The unofficial mission of Division 0 involved keeping a positive face on psionics for the world to see. Consequently, anyone who had psionic powers, as well as a strong inclination to use them criminally, ended up being held in detention for undefined terms. It didn't matter what legal sentencing guidelines said, the government would hold a psionic in custody as long as it took to ensure they wouldn't do anything to turn the public against psionics as a whole.

Fortunately, most kids who ended up in the secure dorms came in for relatively tame offenses like simple assault or gang warfare. Once given a chance at a life where they didn't *have* to literally fight for survival, most adjusted. Psionic orphans picked up for minor crimes like shoplifting usually went straight to the normal dorms, not treated like suspects at all unless they had bad attitudes. The few truly disturbed individuals had a lifetime of incarceration to look forward to. Or, worst-case scenario, a mind wipe from Commander Ashford.

Kirsten had been visiting Rafael Esparza, the ten-year-old she'd brought in a few months ago, on a regular basis. The boy had Suggestion—a power set which made the brass nervous—and he'd used it on a pair of Division 1 officers, forcing them to point their weapons at each other. Rafael hadn't acted out of malice or even as a sick prank. His older brother was murdered not long after their parents died, leaving him a street orphan, and he felt the police ignored the crime.

Since she'd—more or less—solved the case, the boy had no further problem with police. Kirsten couldn't say for sure she'd found the exact person responsible for Juan Miguel's death, though she and Officer Solomon—mostly Solomon—wiped out the entire pack of Diablos connected to it. Part of her believed the 'black bishop' had been the one who personally murdered Rafael's older brother, and he died a rather gruesome pyrokinetic death.

So, Kirsten felt secure in telling the boy his brother's killers had been brought to justice.

Except for the 'compliance band,' an electronic bracelet equivalent to wearing a remote-control stunrod, Rafael didn't seem to mind the secure dorms. One of the chaperones tried to scare him into obedience on his first day by telling him how the compliance band would shock him so bad he'd wet himself. Months later, the boy still practically trembled in fear it might go off accidentally. Due to his smallness, they'd put it on his left ankle instead of his wrist. He'd gotten into the habit of limping around, afraid to disturb it for fear of activating it.

Kirsten filed a complaint, but it only resulted in the chaperone receiving a warning.

She approached the outer security checkpoint. The armored door opened once the system read her ID. Inside, two tactical officers and a handful of chaperones sat at their desks in a large white-walled room. Lockers and storage cubbies took up most of the wall on the right. Straight ahead, another armored door led to the secure dorm facilities. They didn't detain enough children to warrant adding a second full school, so the juvenile inmates received custom tutoring via datapads and AIs. At least they had thrice-weekly visits with a psychiatrist and counselor.

No one questioned the secure dorms' mission to help rather than punish the detainees. Even the idiot who terrified Rafael about the compliance bracelet only did it in hopes they'd never have to use it on him.

Protect psionics from ourselves. She sighed out her nose and approached the main desk.

Senior Specialist Cole Hernandez looked up at her, offering a courtesy salute. "Afternoon, lieutenant. Here to see Esparza?"

"Yes. How's he doing?"

"Wow. I've never seen an arresting officer visit a detainee even once after the inquest closed," said one of the female chaperones behind her. "You got a big heart."

For the thousandth time, Kirsten argued with herself about seeking to foster him. She had Suggestion, so she could both mentor and keep his power under control if necessary. But, as an active I-Ops officer, she couldn't be around him all the time. She already had Evan, and—as Dorian kept telling her—she couldn't collect every stray she found. Evan might adore having a brother. She knew him well enough at this point to dismiss any worries he'd suffer jealousy. Mostly, she doubted her ability to keep up with *two* kids. She'd be twenty-three in September, still five months away, and shouldn't have kids at all yet, much less a nine-year-old. Facing wraiths and demons frightened her less than the responsibility of being a mom. Failure out in the field would only get *her* killed. Failure at 'mom' would ruin a child's life.

She pictured Evan smiling and clung to the hope she stumbled through it all right so far.

"So they tell me," whispered Kirsten.

"Esparza's doing well." Hernandez brought up the boy's record on his terminal. "He's totally compliant. Racked up a bunch of privilege points. The psych team is concerned he might be borderline depressed, though."

Kirsten frowned. "How would *you* handle your entire family being killed, then ending up stuck in a locked room alone most of the time? He *still* thinks the compliance stunner is going to randomly make him piss himself."

Specialist Hernandez held his hands up in a 'what can ya do' way. "Can't do much about the bracelet, but he's perked out of tier one security. His door isn't locked until lights out. He can go to the common areas whenever he wants. Oh, good news."

Kirsten raised both eyebrows. "Hmm?"

"Based on the report from the telepaths, the psych team, and the two patrol officers he attacked he's probably going to be transferred over to the standard dorms soon. Psych thinks he'll respond better over there."

"I barely qualify as a high school graduate and even *I* could tell you treating a kid like him as a child and not a detainee is going to be better for his mental health."

The chaperones all chuckled.

Hernandez leaned back in his chair, smiling. "Yeah, well. Not every kid we get in here has his attitude."

"He's not a delinquent. Rafael acted out of grief and desperation." The meaning of what he said finally hit her. "Wait, you said he's getting out soon? When?"

"Maybe end of the week, maybe end of next," said Hernandez. "Waiting on a judge to review the statements from the two officers he used his powers on. If the judge agrees, they'll suspend the sentence for now. It'll come back to bite him in the ass if he does anything else. If not, it'll disappear when he turns eighteen."

Thrilled, Kirsten had to fight the urge to bounce on her toes. "Can I tell him?"

"Yeah. We'd been keeping it quiet so you could be the one to let him know." Hernandez gestured at the storage cubbies. "Go on in whenever you're ready."

"Thank you." She crossed the room, stashed her E-90 and stunrod in a locker, then headed through the armored door.

A short hallway led to another armored door. She walked past the suite of offices used by the counselors, telepaths, and psych team to an internal security checkpoint. A synthetic named Pila with Marsborn white skin staffed the desk. She waved at Kirsten, buzzing her through another secure door into the hallway containing Rafael's bedroom, one of thirty doors on either side. The far end of the corridor connected to the common areas, where the detainee kids who'd racked up enough privilege points could play games, watch holovids, or spend time in a room larger than their personal quarters.

Kirsten squeezed her hands into fists at being surrounded by locked rooms. They reminded her too much of Mother's closet. At least the girl who'd spent hours scream-begging for someone to let her out last week no longer yelled.

She found Rafael sitting on the bunk in his room, one leg up, one leg—the one with the compliance bracelet—stretched out as if keeping it as far away from as possible would help. The open door eased her nerves, as did the numerous 'warm' touches around the room. His good behavior had allowed him to accumulate several toys, two datapads, and cartoon-print sheets on the bed instead of the bland white ones. If not for his blindingly pink detainee jumpsuit, he could've been a normal boy in a normal—if somewhat sparse—small bedroom.

"Hey there." Kirsten knocked on the doorjamb.

Rafael looked up from the datapad in his lap. His hair appeared noticeably longer, touching his shoulders. He seemed healthy but had the frightened demeanor of a child whose parent would beat them mercilessly for the slightest infraction. Kirsten knew the feeling well. Granted, the boy feared a jolt from the metal band locked around his ankle, not a physical beating. Kirsten had to suffer being tapped with a stunrod during training. They didn't hurt anywhere near as bad as Rafael feared it would, but she couldn't bring herself to suggest zapping him to prove it wouldn't be so bad.

"Hi." Rafael tossed the datapad aside, jumped off the bed, and ran into a hug.

Kirsten held him for a moment, hating herself for putting him here and not being able to carry him out with her. Eventually, he relaxed his desperate clinging, tried to act casual, and sat on the edge of the bed.

She sat beside him. "Are you doing okay?"

"I guess. It's nice having clean food an' my own toothbrush." He rambled about not having a toothbrush after he and his brother got kicked out of their apartment.

Rafael didn't have to say anything about being lonely. His big brown eyes spoke volumes. She couldn't blame all of it on secure detention. He'd lost both parents and his older brother in the span of a few months. She put an arm around his shoulders and let him talk about whatever he wanted. He seemed okay with doing school stuff but missed having friends. Surprisingly, he used Suggestion a few days ago and *didn't* get in trouble for it as he'd only told a bigger boy to 'leave me alone.'

"What did he do?" asked Kirsten.

"Picking on me for being short. Said I'm the size of a seven-year-old, not ten. Kept telling me to fight him." Rafael rolled his eyes. "Zack's like taller than you are. He just wanted to hit me, so I told him to leave me alone. Thought I was gonna get fried, but they didn't even yell at me."

"You used Suggestion properly." She squeezed him. "Defused the situation without causing harm to anyone."

"Yeah." Rafael shivered. "If I'm good enough, will they take this thing off me?"

Kirsten ruffled his hair. "Totally."

"Seriously?" He gasped, staring at her in shock. "They will? I hate it *so* much."

She nodded.

Rafael clung to her arm. Tears streamed down his face. "I'm sorry for using my psi thing on those police officers. I swear I'll never use it bad again."

"They know you're sorry." She rubbed a hand up and down his back. "It's okay. Don't cry."

He continued sniffling, though appeared to be trying to collect himself. The way he clung to her felt like a plea, begging her to get him out of here.

How did we let things get so bad Div 1 gets to P-10 a damn murder investigation because the victim had gang connections? Whoever even came up with priority ten? Fancy way to say 'don't care.' She let a long, sad sigh leak out of her nose. *Worked out, I guess. Div 1 couldn't possibly have handled Diablos.*

Once he quieted, she nudged him. "Can you keep a secret?"

"Yeah. Umm." He peered up at her. "Is it a good secret or a bad secret?"

"A good one." She winked.

He nodded.

"They're going to move you to the normal dorm. Maybe by the end of the week, even. Depends on the paperwork. Might be next week, but it's definitely happening soon."

Rafael stared at her, open-mouthed for a few seconds before breaking down in sobs and mumbling 'thank you' over and over. It took him a while to calm down again, but as soon as he did, he ended up grinning. "Really?"

"Yes, really."

He bounced.

"Try not to flip out too much. You still need to put up with this place for a few days more, okay?"

Rafael nodded. Already, the hope of not being stuck in 'jail' for years completely changed his presence. He'd gone from a sad little waif to a ball of energy. "What's it like?"

"Your new room's going to be about the same, but you can have as much fun stuff in it as you want. And they don't lock the doors at night. You'll have classes with other kids."

"Awesome!" He flopped back on the Comforgel pad, beaming, arms out over his head.

"I know it won't be a problem for you, but..."

He stopped smiling. "But?"

"What's probably going to happen is the judge will take the thing you got in trouble for and put it in a box. Everyone's going to pretend like you didn't break the law. The but is, if you do anything really bad, they're going to take the trouble out of the box."

"Eek." He went wide-eyed. "No. I'm not gonna even stay up late. I swear."

She laughed. "Kid stuff is not bad enough to get you in big trouble. I mean, like if you break the law again."

"Oh." He exhaled hard. "Whew."

She pointed at his ankle. "And you're going to leave that thing here."

"Best part," whispered Rafael.

"You realize he lied to you, right? Trying to scare you?"

"Kinda. I guess. Still scary."

Kirsten fidgeted at the sheet beside her, grateful she'd been so shell-shocked when Division 0 took her in at twelve. Suggestion *and* Mind Blast—even though she hadn't known of either ability at the time—she'd probably been one freakout away from secure detention purely out of paranoia at what she *might* be capable of doing. Thankfully, the dorm staff didn't regard hiding under the bed as threatening behavior. She spent a while grinning while Rafael rambled about how happy he was to be essentially forgiven and allowed to be a normal kid soon instead of a prisoner. Her mind circled around the idea of Suggestion. If she'd known about the ability as a child, she could have told Mother to leave her alone the same way Rafael kept the bully away.

Or not... Mother would've thought me using the voice of the Devil. She'd probably have thrown herself off the roof or come after me with a knife.

Knowing her mother capable of killing her—the reason she'd run away from home at ten had been a warning from Ritchie, a powerful old ghost, about her mother killing her that night. Granted, by accident during a beating, but still. Kirsten had no doubt Mother would've been capable of murdering her on purpose if she'd used Suggestion on her.

Out, out bad thoughts. Kirsten scrunched her eyes closed. "Want to go play something?" She gestured at the door. "They've got games in the rec area, right?"

"Okay." He got up.

She followed him down the hall to the game room. Older kids, mostly teenagers, monopolized the Yume Koujou systems, so he headed for the physical games. Spending an hour or two playing gravity pong with him helped ease the guilt she carried for putting him in here. Not like she had any real choice in the matter. Kirsten would've preferred bringing him right to the dorms. Had he used Suggestion on anyone other than cops, she likely could have.

Oh well. At least they finally accepted he's only a scared kid... not a criminal.

6

THE BIG ONE-OH

The next two days felt like someone stuck the world on repeat.

Wednesday had a staggering *five* 21-47 calls, though they'd all been within a roughly seventy-mile area. Of those, three had been wailers: ghosts manifesting and simply moaning or crying—freaked people out, but harmless. One manifested in the middle of the road, causing a nine-car wreck and one fatality. Number five waited until after dinner, dragging her away from home to chase a poltergeist around an apartment building in Sector 2838.

Injuries had been minor, but the damn thing had to have caused several hundred thousand credits in damage across dozens of apartments.

Thursday started off bad, Kirsten's legs sore from all the running, and only got worse with four more haunting calls. Those spirits, at least, had the courtesy to go crazy during office hours. All four had been largely harmless pranksters, zooming around and pushing/grabbing people. Two raced off the instant they realized she could see them, but the other two, both former construction workers who died on the job decades ago, said they had uncontrollable levels of energy and hadn't been so happy ever before—including while alive. She asked them to go easy on people.

Friday morning, the alarm jolted Kirsten awake, but she neither moved nor grumbled.

Her body felt like lead poured into a person-shaped mold. Two days in a row of nonstop running around made her want to spend the next twenty-four hours in search of bed transcendence—how to become one with a Comforgel pad. Even blinking hurt.

However, she already had the day off, being Sunday.

Provided no crazy emergencies happened.

Captain Eze had her back. Wailers, pranksters, and other harmless ghosts could wait a day. She'd been planning today for six months. Sunday, April fourteenth, 2419, Evan's birthday. His technical birthday, anyway. No one knew what his actual birth date was. Even if his biological mother would be inclined to share the information, she'd rotted her brain with drugs to the point she likely couldn't remember it either. Nor would she care. Evan had been an unexpected side effect of sex, like a speed bump in the road she ran over and kept on going barely aware of having hit it. It really had been an astounding bit of luck he'd lived to nine.

Kirsten hated to think if she hadn't found him one year ago today, he'd have been dead by now.

Even her running into him had been a million to one odds. He'd lived in a grey zone, which meant little police presence and even less interest among the locals to call the cops about anything. If anyone else in the apartment building suspected Mick beat the hell out of a little boy, they didn't care. If Evan hadn't been psionic, he'd most likely have died forgotten in a shitty, bare bedroom. Without Accelerated Healing, he wouldn't have made it to nine years old. Only because he'd astrally projected out of his body to escape the pain of being hit, and then decided to explore a nearby cyberware store, had she ever become aware of his existence.

The owner's dog reacted to the astral being floating around playing with the various implants on shelves. He called the police who transferred it over to Division 0 as 'unexplained paranormal crap,' which ended up landing on Kirsten's proverbial desk.

So many moving parts. If any one thing hadn't happened... Tears gathered in the corners of her eyes. She couldn't explain how she'd become *so* attached to a boy she hadn't given birth to, nor did she care to dwell on it. Doctor Loring, Kirsten's shrink, told her they likely saved each other. Having Evan in her life pulled Kirsten out of a depression she hadn't realized she'd fallen into. How many twenty-two-year-olds believed they'd die unloved and alone some day?

No one knew his actual birthday, so when the judge asked about the missing information during the adoption hearing, Evan piped up to ask if his legal birthday could be the day Kirsten found him. She still choked up thinking about it.

Her bedroom door opened.

Evan, bare-chested in pajama pants, walked in carrying a plate. "Morning, Mom!"

"Morning," she wheezed past the lump in her throat, then sat up. "What are you doing?"

He set the plate on the bed next to her. "Bringin' you breakfast."

"Thank you." She hugged him, kissed him atop the head, then looked at the offering: a jalapeño and egg sandwich. It looked and smelled just like the ones from Cabrera's, the tiny eatery Nicole introduced her to. "Wow, did you 'sem this?"

"No." Evan shook his head. "It's from the place you like."

She gawked. "Who took you there to get it?"

Evan flapped his arms. "No one. It came here."

"Cabrera's doesn't deliver."

"Speedy-Nom."

Ugh. Hopefully, the delivery bot didn't kill anyone on the way. "Oh…"

Evan ground his toes into the rug. "I wanted to do something nice for you today, an' Dorian said moms like breakfast in bed."

"Thank you, Evan. Very thoughtful of you." She picked up the sandwich.

He grinned. "Gotta shower and get dressed, so you can have the peace quiet stuff mom's like but can't find."

Kirsten laughed. He zoomed out, leaving her to eat. A trip in a delivery bot made the sandwich somewhat less hot than it ought to be, but it still tasted perfect. Evan obviously hadn't forgotten the significance of the day, though seemed to treat it as the anniversary of her saving him more than a birthday.

He probably doesn't know kids get presents on their birthday. Kirsten sighed egg-jalapeño fumes out her nose. *She* hadn't realized birthdays meant presents until thirteen, when the dorm staff got her a few plush animals and gifts. Mother certainly wouldn't buy nice things for an agent of the Devil. It had been a miracle she let her keep the dolls Dad brought back from his business trips.

This is his first real birthday. She chewed another bite of breakfast, wondering if there might be something wrong with him since he hadn't started bouncing around with excitement. *Other kids would've definitely told him about birthdays by now. He should be expecting some presents.*

After eating, she jumped in the autoshower, got dressed in civilian clothes—a periwinkle blue mini dress over black leggings.

On Friday, Kirsten went into the classroom to help hand out cupcakes for a mini birthday party. Abernathy the ghost popped in as well, even if only Evan and Kirsten could see him. He still had some citizenship points to burn off, but the administration let him skip out on chores for his birthday.

For today, Kirsten made 'birthday reservations' at a Funzone, which included a big semi-private table in the corner, food, cake, and a few perks. She'd snuck away on Saturday for a few hours while Evan went to Nila's apartment to set things up at the Funzone. Two employees helped her put up decorations around the table as well as arrange the stash of gifts.

She and Evan had a nice, lazy morning at home. A little past noon, they flew to the PAC, specifically the dorms to meet up with his school friends, Walter, Shawn, Maela, and Willow. Nila and Nicole met them there, both in uniform due to being on rotation for the weekend. They had the okay from Captain Eze to attend the party on the understanding they might need to rush off for an emergency.

Everyone piled into three patrol craft and flew to the Funzone.

A family crossing the rooftop parking deck paused to stare at a pair of police vehicles swooping in. When it became clear no emergency went on, they kept walking. Kirsten hopped out and snuck around to the trunk, quietly retrieving 'present number one.' Evan didn't notice her concealing the small, squishy package as the group walked across the parking area to the elevator entrance. The Funzone took up the seventh and eighth floors of a high-rise entirely devoted to commercial space.

Samuel Chang met them at the entrance, in costume as Sir Halek from the Monwyn universe.

Evan cheered at him, then stopped to glance down at his normal clothes before giving Kirsten an 'am I supposed to be dressed up' look.

She handed him the package.

"What's this?" He took it, turning the soft bundle over in his hands.

"A little gift for your birthday." She grinned.

"Cool. Thank you." He hugged her, then opened it to reveal a kid-sized dark blue Monwyn wizard's robe. His expression of complete awe would have been worth a thousand times what she paid for the costume. "Oh wow! Awesome!"

He pulled it on over his clothes, then high-fived Sam.

The group made their way down to the Funzone, dealt with the check-in process—which involved everyone getting a temporary electronic bracelet as a mark of having paid the admission fee—then headed to the reserved table.

"What's all that stuff?" Evan pointed at the wrapped gifts.

"Birthday presents, dork." Walter elbowed him.

"Oh…" Evan twisted to look at Kirsten. *It's so much!*

She patted him on the head. *It's from everyone.*

"Cool!" Evan grinned.

"Do you want to open stuff first or go play games?" asked Kirsten.

Evan made a clueless face. "Uhh. We can play games first. Don't wanna make everyone wait for me."

The kids cheered and zoomed off to the various games,

amusements, and mini-rides set up around the massive room—almost an entire story of the high-rise.

Kirsten, Sam, Nicole, Dorian, and Nila sat at the table, talking about random stuff for a while. Nicole yammered endlessly about a new holovid series she'd started watching detailing the exploits of a privateer starship captain. The show took some liberties with the fantasy starship combat, as few real spacecraft transporting cargo out to colony worlds had weapons. Ships cost *way* too much to blow up. Any real-world conflict happened via boarding parties, usually swinging axes or swords at each other to avoid a stray bullet or laser punching a hole in the hull.

Dorian didn't say much other than offering a few well-timed quips that made Kirsten burst out laughing.

Eventually, the kids returned to the table for dinner when summoned by flashing lights on their pass bracelets. Pizza went over well. Birthday cake even more so. A Funzone employee named Allie brought the cake to the table, then lit ten candles shaped like wizard staves.

"Think of a wish, then blow out the candles," said Kirsten.

Shawn, Walter, Maela, and Willow chanted, "Wish… wish… wish…"

Evan looked at Kirsten and smiled.

Maela covered her mouth, making a face like she just saw a stray kitten.

Evan blew all ten candles out in one breath—but they popped back to life. He blinked.

Nila raised an eyebrow at Willow.

Again, Evan blew out the candles, and they reignited.

Kirsten blinked once in confusion, then realized the look Nila gave Willow. They both had Pyrokinesis. Nila must have sensed her using it. Evan tried to blow out the candles again. For the third time, they flared back to life. Willow continued staring at the candles, though appeared to be having trouble not smiling.

Aww! said Maela's voice in Kirsten's mind. *He used his wish so you wouldn't get hurt doing cop stuff.*

Kirsten's heart swelled. *Shh. You're not supposed to tell anyone what the wish is or it doesn't work.*

Really? Maela blinked. *Are you teasing me or is this real?*

Fun superstition. No idea if wishes really work. Kirsten smiled, more than a little amused at the slightly older—almost thirteen—girl believing in wishes.

Maela laughed.

Shani tickle-attacked Willow. "Stop messing with him. We can't eat cake if he's blowing out candles all night!"

Evan's non-reaction gave away he knew she'd been doing it the whole time. He blew the candles out, and they stayed out. Allie, the Funzone employee, cut the cake for them and distributed pieces to everyone.

While his friends had cake, Evan opened his presents. Kirsten didn't want to go *too* overboard with the Monwyn stuff, even though they had a theme birthday party. She got him a toy spaceship as well as a couple Monwyn action figures and a wand that projected holographic versions of spells. Nila's gift came in the largest box: a red dragon bot capable of flying, breathing hologram fire, and emitting a startlingly loud, screechy roar.

Evan probably said 'wow' about a thousand times.

You did say you were going to get him the most obnoxious toy you could find. Kirsten narrowed her eyes playfully at Nila.

Hah! Nila snickered. *Mostly kidding. There are lots of toys more annoying than this one's scream.*

It looks expensive.

Nila waved dismissively. *Way cheaper than a personal defense bot. You know they have a version of these dragons with Class 1 lasers in the eyes?*

Are you serious? Kirsten gawked.

Yeah, but they're not toys—at least not toys for children. I can see a guy like Sam keeping a few around for home defense.

Kirsten whistled innocently *I dunno. The boy's kinda got me into the whole fantasy thing. Used to think it kinda silly, but it's grown on me.*

Sam, of course, got him a new Monwyn video game for the Yume Koujou system.

Evan practically fainted from happiness. Kirsten leaned on Sam, holding his hand while watching her son bask in the joy of having a birthday while surrounded by family and friends. A few minutes after all the kids finished with their cake, Evan glanced toward—more past —Kirsten, jaw open. He shook his head slightly, then shifted his gaze to make eye contact.

Uhh, Mom. That's way too much.

"What is?" She followed his gaze to another robotic dragon. It looked much like the one powered down on the table, other than being the size of a tiny car. The thing probably cost *more* than a Chīsai compact. "Whoa. Uhh… wow."

A teen girl in a Funzone T-shirt and matching lime green hair, peeked around from behind it. "I heard there's a birthday boy at this table who might like to ride a dragon."

Realizing none of her friends had spent a ridiculous amount of money on a giant toy they had no room to keep, Kirsten melted against Sam.

"Yay!" Evan jumped up, cheering.

He scrambled out of his seat and bounced over to the Funzone employee. The big dragon bot lowered itself so he could climb into the saddle on its back. She tapped a little device in her ear, and her voice boomed out over the whole Funzone, announcing Evan's tenth birthday. Except for kids in VR games, everyone looked over at him waving his arms and shouting lines from the Monwyn movies.

Shawn shrank in on himself, blushing. Maela hunched down as well, obviously not a fan of being in the spotlight. Walter stood on his chair, also cheering. Kirsten found it weird—but awesome—the kid who started off trying to bully him ended up a friend.

Evan cruised off on the flying dragon. The bot spat holographic flames randomly while the boy 'fought' holographic winged goblins in a full 3D immersive experience around the entire room. It didn't look anywhere near as realistic as the senshelmet games but based on the delighted cheers coming from her son, he loved it.

Seeing him so happy got her all choked up. Fortunately, she didn't need to speak.

A high-pitched scream came from the plastic ball pit, not an unusual sound in a Funzone. Kirsten didn't pay it much mind until the same small child shrieked again, adding a, "Daddy, help!" At that, she stood for a better look. Several people rushed over to the ball pit.

One man shouted, "Bree?"

The child's voice wailed again.

Evan steered the dragon bot toward the ball pit.

"Bree?" yelled the man. "Where are you?"

"Here!" screamed a voice likely belonging to a four- or five-year-old.

The adults around the ball pit scurried to the left.

Evan's friends all stood on their chairs to see over other tables.

"Should we help?" asked Nila. "Can't tell what's happening."

Mom! Evan's voice entered her thoughts. *There's a ghost in the ball pit holding a little girl down at the bottom. He's dragging this kid back and forth like he's mopping the floor with her.*

Bree's father jumped into the ball pit.

"Dammit. Bad ghost. Nikki, need you." Kirsten jumped out of Sam's lap and ran down the aisle, slaloming around kids, workers, and parents.

Evan, his eyes glowing bright white, stood in the stirrups on the flying dragon, shouting, "Stop! Leave her alone!"

Nicole followed. "What do you need me to do?"

"Grab the kid out of the ball pit. She's all the way on the bottom," yelled Kirsten.

"Okay."

Kirsten ran into the area surrounding the ball pit. The father had gone neck deep, feeling around blind for the missing girl—who had stopped screaming. Nicole and Kirsten simultaneously located an unconscious toddler at the bottom of the swimming-pool-sized pit via Telepathy, their thoughts bumping into each other inside the child's mind. Nicole began shoving the plastic spheres out of the way, burrowing a tunnel. Fortunately, despite its vast size, the 'pool' was only three feet deep.

People in the area reacted with gasps of awe at the sight of a large 'tunnel' forming by itself in the plastic balls.

A man stood out of the multicolored spheres—without disturbing them. He lunged and grabbed a small boy running along the side, dragging him into the pit. The same adults staring in awe at the open space expanding in the balls seemingly for no reason screamed in alarm when Kirsten summoned the lash and dove like an idiot straight into the pit while swiping the fifteen-foot energy whip straight down on top of the spot where the ghost went under. Her sense of a spirit presence and a screaming small boy gave her a good idea of where to aim.

The lash passed through the plastic orbs as easily as air, striking a gelatinous substance close to the bottom of the pool an instant before Kirsten went face-first into the multicolored balls.

"Kid's clear," yelled Nicole.

"Bree!" shouted a man nearby.

Kirsten got her legs under her, struggling to stand. An unconscious toddler in a purple dress glided by on the left, into Nicole's arms.

A hail of plastic balls burst upward as the ghost wrenched the little boy into view, still howling in pain from the lash strike. The spirit had devolved into a vaguely human figure lacking any features. His limbs darkened to black near the extremities.

Crap. He's turning into a wraith...

Kirsten raised the lash again, hesitating when the spirit chucked the screaming boy straight up.

"I got him!" yelled Shani.

The four-year-old boy appeared to stick to the ceiling, twenty feet overhead. Bewildered, the spirit gazed upward as if he couldn't understand why the boy wouldn't fall. Kirsten sliced the glowing whip across his torso, blasting him out of his humanoid shape into a cloud of phantasmal light everyone reacted to. Spirit energy imploded to a point, vanishing with a dull *thud*. Kirsten cringed at the unexpected sense of obliteration, stunned at the surprising weakness of the spirit. She stared blankly at the spot until scream-crying from the left distracted her. She twisted to look.

Nicole knelt by the little girl, who'd regained consciousness apparently after CPR. The child's father scooped her into a hug. Kirsten looked back and forth between the floating boy and Nicole, bewildered how her friend could telekinetically levitate someone without looking at them—until she noticed little Shani standing with the rest of Evan's friends by the ball pit entrance, staring fixedly up at him.

The bad ghost is gone, said Kirsten telepathically. *You can let the boy down now.*

Nodding, Shani lowered the boy into the arms of a woman reaching toward him and screaming.

Evan, still perched on the dragon bot above the ball pit, thrust both hands in the air and cheered.

"What the hell's going on?" asked an older, slightly chubby guy in a green Funzone polo shirt.

Kirsten dispelled the lash. Everyone around the ball pit except for Bree's father stared at her, their expressions unreadable. Possibly awe, possibly fear. "Give me a sec to get out of this pit and I'll explain."

She fought her way through the nearly waist-deep plastic orbs to the edge. Nila and a random guy took her hands, lifting her out of the pool. Shani amused herself by telekinetically flicking the stray balls back into the pit.

"Hand-shaped bruise on her chest," said Nicole. "He squeezed the air out of her."

Kirsten growled, then looked at the guy she assumed to be the Funzone manager. "This is probably not going to be easy for you to believe, but a ghost attacked these two kids. It's gone now. Destroyed."

The manager gestured at her right hand. "The glowing cord?"

"Yeah."

"Some kinda psionic thing?" asked the manager.

Kirsten nodded. "Yep."

"You seriously let psionics in here?" shouted a woman at the narrow end of the ball pit.

"That *psionic* just saved two kids' lives, you idiot," barked another woman.

Almost everyone in sight—including several small children—gave the woman the finger. People near her loomed in a mass until she scurried off to the exit.

"Call the police," shouted another man somewhere in the back.

"We are already here." Captain Eze, in uniform, slipped out of the crowd.

Two teen boys near Nila and Nicole—who also both wore their uniforms—pointed at them while making 'duh' faces.

"Captain?" Kirsten blinked at him.

He smiled. "Couldn't miss Evan's birthday. Am I late to the party?"

"A little." Kirsten exhaled. "Angry spirit attacked some kids in the ball pit."

Bree's father showered Nicole with thanks.

Kirsten and Captain Eze spent a few minutes explaining what happened to the manager—and everyone close enough to overhear. It surprised her no one truly flipped out; however witnessing the light flash of the destroyed spirit made for convincing evidence.

Evan resumed flying around for a while longer before his birthday ride officially ended.

Twenty minutes after the spirit exploded, the Funzone had largely gone back to normal—though no one went near the ball pit.

KIRSTEN LAY ON HER SOFA, STARING AT THE CEILING, CUDDLING UP to Sam.

Wrangling five kids at a Funzone exhausted her as much as a fight with an abyssal, even if it had been a lot of fun. Fighting abyssals was the opposite of fun. More than her group, all the other kids in the place wore her out as they appeared incapable of talking —they screamed everything. Shani came out of her shell and got loud, too, as did Walter. Then again, the boy had two volume settings: loud and sonic assault. Fortunately, Maela, Evan, and Shawn were sedate for kids, Maela being the quietest. Like many of the dorm kids, she had issues to work out. Evan making friends with a twelve-year-old relative outcast gave her a big case of the 'awws.'

Still, as much fun as they had, she couldn't wait for bedtime.

In further celebration of Evan's birthday—and Saturday—the kids all got to sleep over. She had to stay awake until at least their bedtime. Somehow, Sam didn't look tired. He could probably keep an eye on the kids while she crashed early. Alas, getting up off the couch to go to bed required energy.

"What are you thinking about?" asked Sam.

"The ghost."

"Ahh. Should have guessed."

She snuggled against his side. "He's the second spirit I've run into in only a few days who did stuff way past what they should be able to."

"I have no idea what you mean."

"Heh. Okay, so a ghost starts off really weak after they die. Can't even make candles flicker, right?"

"Mm-hmm."

"The longer they exist as a ghost, the stronger they get. Theodore, for example, can pick people up and throw them around."

Sam whistled. "Damn… scary."

"A ghost has to get *really* old, like a couple hundred years, to reach that point. The one at the Funzone today… he had the strength to drag two toddlers around and throw one boy way into the air."

"So, he was pretty old?" Sam kissed her.

"Didn't feel like it. I only hit him twice and obliterated him. And sure, I was angry at him for attacking children, but hardly furious enough to amplify my power much. Certainly not to the point of destroying a spirit powerful enough to physically touch people in two hits."

Sam pondered. "Think something else kicked his ass before you got to him?"

"Possible, but not really. The older a spirit is, the bigger they go off if they're obliterated."

He chuckled. "Why do you keep using such a fancy word for death?"

"Because they're *already* dead. Obliteration is complete destruction. Nothing left of them." She exhaled. "Spirits can also transcend or end up in the Abyss."

"Ahh."

"So, yeah. If this guy had been old enough to throw children around, obliterating him would have at least fried every NetMini in the room and probably all the lights plus the bot Evan was riding. This spirit fizzled out with a mild flash. He couldn't have been more than three to eight months old as a ghost—but had already gone proto-wraith."

Sam tickled her side. "You keep using these made up words."

"Hah." She squirmed. "Like not all the way wraith. I think he was becoming one. So, an evil prick. Never saw a wraith-in-progress before."

"Good thing you got rid of him before he hatched."

She buried her face in his chest and laughed.

"Mom?" asked Evan.

Kirsten looked up as the boy walked around the end of the couch, already having changed into his pajamas. "Hey. Bedtime already?"

"Yeah." He walked up to her for the goodnight hug.

She wrapped her arms around him, clinging, getting all emotional again from remembering what Maela told her about his wish. "Happy birthday, kiddo."

"Thank you for being my mom. Today was way better than a bio birthday." Evan leaned back to make eye contact. "This is the day you gave me a real life."

Kirsten's heart burst into metaphorical little bits. She held him like a teddy bear, expecting him to start squirming soon, embarrassed at such a childish display of affection in front of his friends… but he didn't.

"You look tired, Mom. You should have bedtime now, too."

"Yeah. You're right." Kirsten exhaled and released the hug. "I'm gonna go to bed."

"Night!" Evan hugged Sam, then ran off to his room.

Sam stood, overacting a glance back and forth between her and the front door.

"Where do you think you're going?" Kirsten grabbed his hand. "I need someone warmer than a rune rabbit plush tonight."

7

RANSOMWARE

K irsten found herself sliding face-first down a hospital corridor in the middle of an earthquake.

Old wheelchairs bounced past her. Sections of wall collapsed in billowing blasts of white dust. The floor calved like a splitting glacier beneath her, throwing her into a yawning void... for all of two seconds before she woke up to Evan sitting on top of her, shaking her by the shoulders.

"Mom! You're gonna be late."

She babbled, trying to speak before her brain produced any specific words.

Evan rolled off to the side. "Alarm turned itself off already."

It took Kirsten's brain a few seconds to process the meaning of the small human making sounds and moving around. Birthday party Sunday, followed by a tremendously shitty week—and weekend—of back-to-back 21-47 'emergency' calls. They all turned out to be irritating, about half potentially harmful to the living, but nothing more serious than a guy being shoved down a flight of stairs. Not like an Abyssal ran around biting people's heads off. She hadn't gotten home last night—Sunday again—until well after two in the morning, thanks to a prankster ghost in a commerce center tricking her into an elevator shaft and sealing it—forcing her to climb through a maze of ventilation shafts to get out.

The small person ran across the room on his way out, but caught himself at the doorjamb, watching her. The last thing he said sounded kind of important. Something about the alarm. She glanced at the little silver bar on the table next to the bed: 6:18. Blink. She realized she sat up in bed.

Evan hung in her doorway giving her a 'why are you not getting up' look.

That's weird. The alarm should've gone off at six.

"Mom?"

She looked at him. "Morning, hon."

"It's Monday. Are you off 'cause of havin' to do so much work stuff all weekend?"

"No." She glanced at the clock. 6:19 a.m. "Crap!"

Evan smiled cheesily and darted out of sight.

"Crap!" Kirsten leapt out of bed while attempting to pull her oversized sleeping T-shirt off.

Momentarily blinded, she stumbled over something painful into a spin, trying not to fall on her ass. Her effort to stay on her feet worked, at the price of mashing her toes into the corner of her wardrobe cabinet.

"Ow! Shit!" she yelled, hopping backward.

The whirr of the hall bathroom's autoshower started.

After contemptuously yanking the shirt off, she gingerly examined her toes. Fortunately, none appeared to have broken, though it sure felt like she'd pulverized two of them. Grumbling, she limped into the attached bathroom, still warm and smelling like Sam. He had to be in the office by six, so would've left well before her alarm went off.

Kirsten dragged herself into the autoshower and hit the 'fast' option, which compressed the normal eight-to-ten-minute cycle down to four, making up for haste with higher water pressure and less thorough spraying.

The tube hatch secured itself with an audible *click*. Warm, sudsy water sprayed on her, the soap so strong she tasted it despite a closed mouth. She helped the machine out, manually scrubbing the critical points—face, pits, crotch, and crack as the military guys often said. Spending more than ten minutes around a Division 6 trooper would invariably result in them starting to tell a wild story about living out of a canteen for a week while stranded in the Martian desert, single-handedly fighting off a Cydonian crab with only a knife.

A strange warbling beep came from the control panel in time with the hot air tornado of the dry cycle winding down.

Kirsten pulled her hair apart like a theater curtain.

A computer animation of a flaming bird somewhere between hot pink and electric lavender on an all-black field took up the entire screen, no trace of the usual operating interface behind it. Confused, she tapped the screen.

The bird zoomed up to the top left corner. The word 'Plasmahawk' appeared across the middle of the display, drawn in the same colored fire. Beneath it appeared a text box:

Greetings, citizen in search of a squeaky-clean feeling. This autoshower unit is currently locked down by Credit Sudzer v 3.1. Sorry for the inconvenience, but a GlobeNet king must collect his taxes. To remove my little virus and open the hatch, swipe a NetMini to pay C5000.

Kirsten poked the screen.

Nothing happened.

She slapped at the holographic screen, also doing nothing. Grumbling, she felt around the outside edges of the little box projecting the holo-panel. It didn't have any usable buttons.

"Not now... not now... Dammit!"

The hatch refused to open. She shoved at it for a moment, punched it a few times, then tried to kick it—a complicated task in a narrow, clear tube. Having zero leverage for a kick, she rammed her shoulder into the hatch. The dull *thud* of her body slamming into thick plastic filled the bathroom. Maybe one of those big military types could break an autoshower open, but a five-foot-nothing sprite like her had no chance. At least, not without psionic Kinetics to make herself stronger.

"What kind of idiot does this?" she yelled at the holo-screen. As much as she hated the idea of falling victim to a virus and paying some criminal actual money, if she had the ability to do it as fast as a NetMini swipe in the moment, she would have. "Who in their right mind has a 'Mini with them in the damn tube?"

After a moment of fuming, she realized over eighty percent of the population had ImDent chips or headware implants capable of functioning like a NetMini for a credit swipe. She shivered at the thought. *I'd rather jump naked into that purplish-black gunk in the Beneath than put metal under my skin.* "Why the heck did bathtubs become a luxury item for the rich?"

She glowered at her naked reflection on the clear autoshower cylinder, imagining Dorian saying something about economy of space making bathtubs obsolete. Tubs took up more room than a round tube only a little bit larger than an adult. Autoshowers let builders cram more tiny apartments in the same amount of space. Plus, people were lazy. Why take baths when they could have a machine clean them while they stood still?

Lashing the machinery didn't help. Despite the freakishly high amount of crazy haunts going on, no spirit locked her in the shower tube, merely the work of a jackass GlobeNet pirate named Plasmahawk. The echo of her rapid, angry breathing surrounded her. The formerly nice warmth of a shower morphed into a damp, sweaty prison. Some diabolical genius figured most people would be way too embarrassed to call a repair technician for help while trapped naked in the shower.

Evan's glowing astral form glided through the wall "Mom, the shower's broken. I can't get out."

"Yeah… same here."

"Some guy's asking for money."

Kirsten rubbed her forehead. "I know. He hacked the tubes. We shouldn't pay him, or he'll keep doing it. Grr. I hate ransomware."

The boy nodded.

"Ugh." She groaned.

"What's wrong?"

"Too damn literal." She punched the locked hatch. "We're *actually* being held for ransom."

"Mom?" Evan scrunched up his nose. "Is it technically kidnapping if we're still at home?"

"Umm." She rubbed the bridge of her nose. Oversleeping. Mashing her foot into something. Nearly falling on her ass. Now, locked in the tube. Too angry, embarrassed, and panicky about being late to think about such a weird philosophical question, she shouted, "Mondays suck!"

Evan laughed.

She squatted, examining the metal floor for an access panel. "If these things lose power, the lock mechanism releases. It's a failsafe."

"Failsafe?"

"Yeah. Means it's an automatic safety feature so people don't get trapped in autoshowers if the building loses electricity." Nothing inside the tube opened to her scraping fingernails. Not a real surprise. Any panels *inside* the chamber would let water get to the wiring.

"Where's Theodore when ya need him, huh?" asked Evan.

"Bite your tongue, kiddo." Kirsten rolled her eyes.

Theodore helped her all the time and *did* have a reasonably good—proverbial—heart, but the man *was* a pervert of the highest order. If he found her locked in an autoshower tube, he'd never simply open it for her without a little teasing. On the off chance he did, she'd never hear the end of it.

"Theodore's out... but..." Kirsten sighed, thinking of Dorian.

Being naked in his presence felt a little awkward since she once had a crush on him. But the military, and by extension the National Police Force, used co-ed shower and locker facilities for over a century. Also, she needed help. Dorian would be totally professional.

Before she thought too much about it—or wasted *more* time—Kirsten closed her eyes and focused on Beacon. *Dorian Marsh, if you're hearing me... could use a little help.* Of course, he couldn't hear her words. Beaconing for a spirit amounted to firing off a flare into a dark night sky, asking a particular spirit to come to her. It might also attract other nearby spirits, but the one she thought of specifically received the strongest pull.

"Ooh. What'cha doing?" Astral-Evan tilted his head.

"Beaconing." She almost asked if they taught him about it in school yet but caught herself. Division 0 only had *one* Astral Sensitive on the West Coast: her. "It's basically sending energy out into the astral world, focused on a specific spirit and asking them to come to you. No guarantee they'll listen, but they'll definitely hear you."

"Cool." Evan smiled. He didn't ask her to teach him how to do it because he assumed—correctly—she would... just not at the moment while trapped inside an autoshower tube. "Be right back." Evan flew into the wall, the silver thread connecting back to his body trailing after him.

Dorian arrived a minute or so after the boy left, stopping short at the sight of her standing in the tube. "Having difficulties?"

"Virus locked me in. Can you turn the stupid thing off?" She slapped the hatch. "I can't get out."

"Ahh. Nasty bit of malware." Dorian stepped closer, crouched, and shoved his hand into the autoshower's base.

A few seconds later, the whole tube went dark, a faint *click* coming from the hatch.

Kirsten pushed it open and hopped out. "Thanks."

"Not a problem." Dorian stood.

The autoshower powered back up. Its holo-panel reappeared, displaying a critical error message, then the system rebooted.

Evan reemerged from the wall. "I'm stuck, too. Can you open it for me, please? Nila's also trapped. Shani's trying to rip the door off with Telekinesis, but isn't strong enough."

"Of course." Dorian coughed, seeming uncomfortable, then followed the floating astral boy into the wall.

He'd been sweet on Nila in life. Barging in on her in the shower as a ghost would be *way* more awkward than helping Kirsten. Grumbling, she grabbed clean underwear from the white box on the wall, pulling them on as she hurried into the bedroom. "Suri, please send a message to Captain Eze. Tell him my shower got hacked and I'm going to be a few minutes late. I'll explain the details as soon as I get there."

"I can explain for you," said her NetMini in an overly innocent woman's voice. "I heard everything."

"Fine." Kirsten waved dismissively, then wriggled into her uniform top. "Sorry. In a mood. Thanks."

"You're welcome," chirped Suri.

"Going to check the building for other victims," called Dorian from the hallway. "I'll catch up as soon as I can."

"Okay." Kirsten stepped into her boots, secured the fasteners, then grabbed her utility belt and forearm guard, carrying them.

Evan darted out of his bedroom, carrying his shoes and backpack, socks hanging from his teeth. They ran down the outer hallway to the elevator. On the ride to the roof, Evan put his socks and shoes on while Kirsten secured her utility belt and forearm guard in place. As soon as the doors opened, they sprinted across the roof parking area to the patrol craft.

Kirsten hit the rapid-on button to skip the usual diagnostics and hurry the power-up process, something usually reserved for responding to emergencies as fast as possible. Evan gurgled at the G-forces of a high-speed liftoff and acceleration. She'd only been stuck in the shower tube for about fifteen minutes, but in order to get to the PAC without being late, she'd need to fly upwards of 500 miles an hour in a straight line, ignoring traffic laws. Not a big deal when responding to an emergency, but against regs in her present circumstances. Division 1 routinely ignored 'trivial' regulations. What would they do? Give *themselves* a traffic citation? Highly doubtful they'd give her one, either, but she still dove down to the fiftieth story and joined the normal flow of hovercar traffic.

"Comm, Captain Eze," said Kirsten.

The dashboard chimed.

Seconds later, Captain Eze's head appeared in hologram at the center of the console. "Good morning, Kirsten."

"I'm sorry, captain. Going to be a little late this morning. I slept right through the alarm and then a stupid virus got me in the shower."

He raised both eyebrows. "Since you don't appear sick, I'll assume you're talking about the Plasmahawk issue."

"Credit Sudzer," grumbled Kirsten. "Did it hit you, too?"

"No, but I received an alert message from Division 2. You aren't the only person affected by it this morning. Seems this virus spent the past several weeks spreading, disguised as a firmware update. Today appears to be the scheduled activation date for a few hundred thousand cases. These things usually go off in batches. Some one day, another batch a week or two later, and so on."

Kirsten repetitively bonked her head backward against the seat. "I feel dumb."

"You shouldn't. It looked like a legitimate update. You'd have to be an engineer for the manufacturer of whatever brand tube you've got to recognize it as fake."

"Even Sam fell for it," said Evan.

"How do you know?" Kirsten glanced at him.

"Because, he didn't warn you about it. He had to have gotten the same update. If he realized it was bogus, he'd have warned you."

She exhaled. "Crap. I need to tell him not to use the tube at his place before he checks it. He showered before I woke up. Why'd it get me and not him?"

"Activation most likely happened at a specific time of day," said Captain Eze. "Things are quiet for the moment, spirit wise. I think they got it all out of their system last week."

She groaned.

"No need to stress about being here at seven on the nose." He smiled. "All the extra time you pulled last weekend more than makes up for being a little late."

"Thanks, captain. Be there soon."

He nodded, then signed off.

Kirsten set the patrol craft to auto-drive to the PAC, then pulled her NetMini out to order breakfast, requesting the delivery bot meet them by the garage entrance. She spent the remainder of the ride filling out an incident report to send over to Division 2 regarding her compromised autoshower.

Eight minutes later, she took manual control of the patrol craft and dove out of the hover lane, flying down toward the access road leading to the underground garage. A few seconds before she touched down on the car's ground wheels, three Division 1 patrol craft shot out of the garage opening, zooming straight at her.

"Gah!" she yelled and mashed the vertical control stick forward, slamming the patrol craft down hard on its belly.

The Division 1 units raced overhead.

"Ow," muttered Evan.

She looked over at him, squished under the console in the space where the passenger's legs are supposed to be.

"I'm okay." Evan gave a thumbs-up. "Just surprised. Not sure why I said 'ow.'"

Kirsten sighed. *This is the Mondayest Monday to have ever Mondayed.*

8

FREE FALL

T he delivery-bot breakfast burrito couldn't hold a candle to her usual from Cabrera's.

She would've ordered from there but didn't for two reasons. One, she refused to give money to Speedy-Nom since they probably tuned their bots to be reckless. Two, the sandwich would be even colder than when Evan ordered for her due to the greater distance between the PAC and the deli.

Considering the way the morning went, she considered having breakfast at all a blessing.

Also, on the Monday from Hell, if she *had* gotten an egg sandwich from Cabrera's, there would've been an emergency dispatch before she could bite into it. She leaned back in her chair, trying her best to enjoy the obviously mass-produced egg-and-cheese burrito. The meat-like substance could've been an attempt at bacon or horribly overcooked sausage.

At least the school didn't give Evan a hard time about being sixteen minutes late.

Cadet Samantha Peña, who lived at home with her parents, also got stuck in her shower tube. Fortunately, her father had been able to call in, requesting Division 2 to un-hack the tube from remote. So, the teacher had no problem believing the reason for Evan's lateness.

Her armband and desk terminal chimed at the same time, but the holo-panel opened on the desk, revealing the face of an Admin cadet. This boy looked about fifteen or so. Despite his youth, he had the poise of experience, not the wide eyed 'what the heck am I doing' stare of a newbie.

"Lieutenant?" asked the teen. "We have a request from Division 2. They're asking for someone to take a look at the wreckage of a hovercar."

She smirked at the half-burrito in her left hand. "Where'd it go down?"

"Don't have that info handy, lieutenant. The wreck is in the lab at the RTC. Sounds like they've run out of ideas to explain why it crashed."

"Oh, not an emergency. Okay. I'll head over there as soon as I can."

He nodded, then dropped the connection.

Yeah. If I'd gotten the real sandwich, Monday would've stopped me from touching it until it got cold.

She neither rushed nor dawdled finishing her breakfast and coffee. Having a few minutes to sit still helped her finish waking up the rest of the way. Though, the longer she sat there, the harder it would be to make her sore body cooperate. So, once she finished the burrito, she picked up her remaining coffee and took it with her to the garage.

Wow. Dorian's still not here... did my entire building get the shower virus? One problem having a ghost partner... I can't vid-call him to ask where he is. But it's not like he'll ever get lost. He can jump straight to the patrol craft wherever it is.

KIRSTEN FLEW IN A PRIORITY MODE TO THE DIVISION 2 REGIONAL TECH Center in Sector 7876.

Investigating a wreck the technicians couldn't get anything from via normal channels didn't require excessive speed while cruising high above civilian hover traffic lanes. However, considering the rampant ghostly activity as of late, she wanted to get this request over with as fast as possible so she'd be available in the event another spirit had a meltdown.

Sitting in ordinary traffic for a two-hour one-way ride left her out of the loop far too long.

Plus, she had an official Inquest active, more legit than driving fast purely to avoid being late. The ride would still take forty minutes, but she used the time to plot the hauntings. Thus far, the surge of agitated spirits appeared in a relatively—compared to the whole city—small region, approximately 300 miles north from the southern edge of West City. With few exceptions, the calls she responded to over the last week and weekend appeared as dots in an area about fourteen sectors across and eleven tall. As each grid sector represented five square miles, she had a fairly big chunk of ground to cover. Something, likely near the middle of the area, had to be agitating the spirits.

Kirsten traced a square on the holo-panel around the plot points, then an X over it, the lines crossing in Sector 2888.

Whatever's stirred up all the ghosts has to be within a sector or two of there. I should swing by once I'm done at the RTC.

Dorian exuded up from the passenger seat, his body glowing blue and transparent for a few seconds before returning to his normal, lifelike appearance... at least to her. Tiny electrical arcs crackled up and down his arms. "What a mess."

"That bad?"

He blinked at the console, thin blue lightning filaments gliding down his face. "Where are we going at 600 miles an hour?"

"RTC techs need help figuring out why a hovercar went splat." She cringed. "Why are you sparking?"

"I spent the past hour siphoning power out of autoshower units." He jammed his fingers into the console; everything flickered. "There we go. Had to offload some energy before I went crazy. PC still had a little room in the capacitors."

She chuckled. "It's so weird you and the car munch on the same food… power."

"I borrow from it often enough. Might as well give back for once. Like I've had way, way too much caffeine. Hate being so jittery. So, again, we're going to the RTC. How is this is an emergency?"

"Normally, it wouldn't be. But after last week?"

"Ahh. You're thinking we might have more issues."

She exhaled out her nose. "Yeah. So, bad?"

"About seventy people stuck in their tubes. Would have been a lot easier if I could talk to any of them. At least eighteen just stood there for a few minutes after I shut the damn thing down. By the way, you might be getting a call from apartment 52-13."

"Oh? What did you do?"

"Woman wouldn't move out of the damn tube, so I punted the hatch open to show her it unlocked. There may have been some screaming involved."

Kirsten facepalmed. "At least I don't feel like such a dumbass for clicking the firmware update if so many people did."

"Yeah, easy to robotically click without thinking. Another thing, the guy in 71-04 has a Nano knife. His wife got caught in the tube, but he sliced it open."

"Civilian possession of Nano knives is out of our jurisdiction. Division 1 problem." She flicked her thumbnail over the grip texturing on the control sticks. "Do you think he's going to stab cops with it?"

Dorian wagged his head side to side while emitting a faint hum of thought. "Ehh, not really. Seemed like more of a scientist-nerd type. Probably bought it because he's got more credits than sense and thinks it's cool. Doubt he's got a permit for it."

Nano knives made her think about Konstantin, which made her shudder. When Nina from Division 9 helped her infiltrate the complex beneath the Senate chambers on the Moon, she'd used one of the synthetic diamond blades to cut her way into a pipe. A knife so sharp even someone as unremarkably strong as her could slice into half-inch-thick plastisteel unsettled her. She didn't want to be near one. While her uti knife did count as a Nano blade, it only had a tiny cutting edge inside a protective shroud to prevent accidental loss of fingers. Just enough to cut seat belts, wires, restraints, or other small things in an emergency. Useless as a combat weapon.

Beeping alerted her to the end of her route approaching.

She slowed gradually from 618 MPH to eighty-five, then pitched the patrol craft into a gentle dive.

West City stretched as far as she could see in every direction, a hint of blue ocean to the west. Dark silver ground between the high-rises gleamed like the protective coating of a circuit board under bright light. Streams of bots raced back and forth among all the buildings in a frenetic rush. From 1,200 feet up, they looked like fleas. At such an altitude, the landscape of tall skyscrapers reminded her of the outer hull of starships from the movies Nicole liked. All metal with random lights, panels, and protrusions everywhere. Real starships didn't have so much crap hanging off them, nor did they bother with lights.

The Regional Tech center stood out as a large X-shaped white building, a mere six stories tall, set like a giant microprocessor chip into the West City Motherboard. She figured the resemblance to electronics had to be more than accidental. Even a non-techie like her saw it.

Out of courtesy, she activated the emergency bar lights while near the civilian hover lane altitude, shutting them off once she dropped under 400 feet. The patrol craft's computer automatically connected to the RTC, announcing their arrival and posting a descent route so anyone else in a hovercar would see their path and be able to avoid crashing. Granted, auto-drive would take over to prevent a collision. True 'accidents' rarely happened with hovercars. They crashed only when someone disabled safety systems and deliberately flew into another car—or something mechanical failed.

Mechanical failure also included—albeit rarely—paranormal situations.

Kirsten thought about the Intera assassin Dorian killed. He'd been chasing them into a black zone, no doubt intending to attack her as soon as he could. Dorian caused the other hovercar's drive system to shut down, and the assassin plunged to his rather abrupt death on the ground. The memory got under her skin, making her squirm in her seat. It didn't bother her *too* much to watch her partner casually kill him. The man *did* intend to murder her, after all. Mostly, it bothered her because if a ghost Dorian's age—not terribly old as a ghost—could take hovercars down at will, it meant other angry spirits could, too.

She swallowed saliva while landing on the RTC's roof. The technicians couldn't determine a reason the car in their lab crashed. Could be, a spirit out there figured out Dorian's trick. A hovercar doing several hundred miles an hour 500 feet off the ground losing all power essentially became a flying coffin.

"Something is bothering you."

"Yeah." She powered the car down and got out. "Remember when you took the Intera guy out of the air?"

He materialized next to her outside. "I do. You're worried another ghost did this?"

"It's a possibility." She shut the door. "How difficult is it? Is it a weird little trick you came up with or could any ghost do it?"

"Any ghost could do it if they took the time to examine the power systems. I've spent a *lot* of time inside a hovercar. The systems have a tremendous amount of electrical power in them. Too much to merely absorb. A microfusion power system can keep an army of spirits caffeinated for a century. Making a hovercar drop like a stone is more complicated than simply draining. You need to draw the power out of the wires feeding the ion thrusters and redirect it into the capacitors, creating a closed loop not connected to the propulsion system."

She whistled. "Sounds insanely complicated."

"It's much easier when you can see the electrical system from inside it." He grinned.

"Yeah, I bet." Kirsten started walking toward the entrance. "So, any ghost your age or older could do it, but it would take them studying the guts of a hovercar for a while?"

"Yes. I don't imagine it would be high on a spirit's list of things to do. In my case, the car is my attachment point."

Whew. Not as bad as I feared. "Okay, good. I don't need to panic."

"Not yet anyway. Let's see what happened here."

A SIX-INCH ORB BOT LED KIRSTEN DOWN A TRIPLE-WIDTH HALLWAY finished in shiny plastisteel.

Overly cool air carried the fragrance of scorched plastic and the subtle flavor of electricity. Garage-sized doors on both sides led to forensic labs used to study large objects—like crashed hovercars. A few exoskeletons stood idle in charging bays between the doors. Several forklift bots crept along, transporting chunks of wreckage or supply boxes. Intermittent brash, bursty screams from high-torque wrenches or other tools made it feel more like she'd wandered into a factory.

Having never visited this wing of the RTC before, she gazed around like Evan at the science center. Some Division 2 techs gave her odd looks, certainly wondering what a psionic would be doing there.

"Can't believe they let those freaks in the NPF," muttered a passing guy in a blue jumpsuit, underestimating the volume of his voice. "They're going to take over the government."

As they passed, Dorian reached out and poked a finger into the guy's coffee cup, chilling it.

Kirsten forced herself to smile pleasantly at the two techs. Once they'd gone far enough away to be out of earshot, she glanced over at Dorian. "He's going to blame me for that."

"Let him. I'll confess."

Imagining the guy's reaction to seeing a ghost appear made her laugh.

The orb bot stopped by a lab entrance the size of three garage doors merged into one. A four-inch thick plastisteel strip—the door— sat flush with the floor, open by means of lowering out of the way. Past it, nine technicians examined the remains of one hovercar and four ground cars. At least, she assumed the mangled metal slab on the middle table to be a former hovercar. It appeared mostly flattened, as though a DS4 military transport ship landed on top of it. The civilian vehicle lacked the armor of a police patrol craft, but still had opaque metal plates for windows with video displays. After multiple fatal incidents involving advert bots during the initial release of hovercars to the civilian market, few manufacturers still made hovercars using glass or plastic windows.

Two of the ground cars had been partially crushed. One's front end crumpled in, the other smashed in from the side. In the farthest recesses of the lab room lay tables of blackened components, the remains of an unknown number of other cars caught in a bad fire.

A moment after she entered, the techs paused in their tracks, looking at her.

"Teela, your long shot's here," yelled the man nearest her.

Better long shot than freak.

"Coming," called a woman from over by the charred bits.

Kirsten waited where she stood, not wanting to accidentally touch anything and contaminate evidence.

A late-thirties woman in a blue Division 2 tech jumpsuit ducked under one of the ground cars up on a lift and jogged over. Her black hair and deep brown skin didn't make her stand out too much, but her metallic gold eyes nearly caused Kirsten to gasp.

"Hi. I'm—oh, crap. Sorry, lieutenant." Teela saluted. "I'm TS2 Randall."

Despite a technical sergeant grade two being equivalent to an E7, Kirsten felt outranked—by experience and knowledge if not pay grade. She returned the salute. "It's fine. Not here to compare pins. Kirsten Wren. Do you mind if I call you Teela?"

"Of course, ma'am."

"It's fine if you want to use Kirsten. Or whatever you're comfortable with." She smiled. "So, what's the situation?"

Teela pulled a small datapad from a thigh holster and stepped closer so Kirsten could see the screen. "Hovercar unexpectedly fell out of the sky three days ago. Citycams caught the accident, but we still haven't been able to explain what happened. C1—that's the hovercar—was cruising at traffic speed of 180 miles an hour when it abruptly went into dead free fall, dropping 500 feet before landing on the two ground vehicles we've designated as C2 and C3 approximately six seconds later. Vehicle C4 had been twenty-six feet behind C3 on the ground, doing sixty MPH. The driver had enough distance to swerve out of the way—but collided with C5 coming in the opposite direction. C5 also attempted evasive maneuvers. C4 struck C5 in the driver's side door, launching C5 off the roadway into pedestrians."

Kirsten and Dorian cringed.

"The drivers of C1, C2, and C3, plus two passengers, died instantly. The occupants of C4 and C5 respectively suffered minor injuries. One pedestrian died as a result of being crushed by C5, three suffered moderate injuries. Another pedestrian suffered a fatal injury from a flying piece of C1, while eighteen others experienced moderate to superficial injuries from airborne debris."

"Ouch," whispered Kirsten. "For what it's worth, I don't see any ghosts hanging around in here."

"Ghosts?" Teela leaned back, eyes widening. "Who said anything about ghosts?"

"I thought you requested me here to help understand why C1 crashed." Kirsten looked over the wrecked cars again, feeling them out astrally. C1, C2, and C3 all had a faint spiritual resonance, proof they'd been in contact with someone at the moment of death.

Teela shrugged. "I just asked for a psionic to help me try and make sense of this. Might as well take a shot at it if you're here. So, we've eliminated mechanical failure or a hacker as the causes. My team's been back and forth over every GlobeNet communication into or out of C1, and nothing looked remotely suspicious. The only damage to the vehicle occurred from impact with the ground."

"All right…"

Teela held out the datapad and played a computer-generated reconstruction of the crash. An amber car-shape labelled C1 flew along in hovercar traffic. The model abruptly fell like a stone, rolling sideways. It flipped over four times on the way down, being almost perfectly upside down when it crushed C2 and C3. C4 swerved around to the left, T-boning C5 and punting it into animated pedestrian models. The video backed up to the moment C1 struck the ground, zooming in on a fragment of metal launching out of the crash and slow-mo showing it flying into the head of a man on the opposite side of the road from where C5 would strike a second later.

"Is it a problem if I touch the car?" asked Kirsten.

"Not at all." Teela shook her head. "We've gotten everything we can possibly find from it already. There's no danger of evidence contamination at this point."

"Okay." Kirsten walked around a bank of diagnostic equipment, stepped over several fat hoses crisscrossing the lab, and approached a wide plastisteel table holding the wreckage.

The four ion thrusters had been removed as well as the ground wheels. Wire bundles stuck out of the mangled wheel cowlings. A jagged, mostly square, hole in the roof resembling a crudely opened can exposed what remained of the driver's seat. About three inches of space separated the cushion from where the roof ended up. Blood saturated the interior.

"Surprised they cut it open to get the body out." Dorian whistled. "They could've merely tilted it up on end and poured him into a container."

Kirsten grimaced. *It's not comforting to say he wouldn't have felt anything. This poor man spent the last few seconds of his life in complete terror. I hope he passed out before he hit the ground.* She rested her hand on the smooth metal to the left of the hole and opened her mind to the astral.

The car gave off a clear imprint of death, which didn't offer any new information. She already knew a man died in the car. No spirits seemed to be attached to it, nor did the metal hold a lingering paranormal presence.

"Dorian, can you tell if a ghost made this crash?"

"Made what crash?" He raised an eyebrow.

Teela blinked.

"The hovercar, obviously." She smirked at him.

He smiled. "This is a hovercar?"

"Was," said Kirsten, playing along.

"Umm, who are you talking to?" Teela looked around. "You have someone on comm?"

"No. My partner's a ghost."

The other eight techs in the room froze, staring at her. She refused to look at any of them, forcing herself to act as casual as if she said she enjoyed coffee.

Dorian walked through the flattened hovercar, stuck his head into a few places, then stood, shrugging. "Can't really tell. But I'd only feel it if a spirit with serious power touched this vehicle. Remember how I explained it before? Maybe they can check the power management system."

"I'm not picking up anything conclusive." Kirsten tapped her fingers on the wreck. "I can ask them to send a clairvoyant. They can sometimes get information from touching objects. My deal is spirits and stuff."

"Darn." Teela exhaled.

Kirsten faced her. "Question?"

"Hmm?"

"Can you tell if the power system did anything strange right before the crash? Such as going in a loop to the capacitors, bypassing the ion thrusters entirely?"

Teela stared at her for a long moment. "How the heck did you know that?"

"She's psychic!" yelled a man on the other side of the room.

Kirsten and Dorian exchanged a glance. She wanted to bonk her head on something but resisted.

"Could be," said Dorian.

"But there's no anger or anything embedded in this car." She looked at Teela. "I've seen a ghost cause a crash similar to this once before. Basically looks like the hovercar shuts completely off in midair and drops like a brick with no power."

"Yeah…" Teela gawked at her datapad. "The diagnostic module recorded a massive influx of power to the secondary capacitor array five-point-five-seven seconds before it was smashed on impact. All four ion thrusters shut off at the same time, but we can't find a reason for it. No hovercar operating system is even capable of processing a command to bypass power around the thrusters, especially while in flight. It's like the electricity itself decided to go where it didn't belong."

Dorian nodded.

"Ugh. You aren't going to like what I'm about to say." Kirsten set her hands on her hips. "I'm going to like it even less."

"Huh?" Teela tilted her head.

"Pretty sure a ghost caused this crash."

Teela started to laugh, but at Kirsten's continued straight face, stared at her. "Wait, you're serious?"

"I am."

"Why are you not going to like it? I thought you said ghosts are your thing." Teela tapped her fingers on the datapad. "How the hell am I gonna log this?"

Kirsten let her head loll back, gazing up at the two-story ceiling of bare metal rafters, powerful lights, and lifting equipment. "Ghosts are going kinda nuts at the moment. Usually, when a spirit gathers enough energy to affect the living, there's a lot of emotion wrapped up in it. They leave an emotional imprint behind whenever they do anything because most ghosts *have* to get emotionally revved up to affect solid objects. I don't feel anything in this wreck. The idea of a ghost killing someone and *not* leaving an emotional residue is terrifying. Means it's probably a sociopath capable of killing randomly without remorse or reason."

"Damn…" Teela whistled. "Lieutenant?"

"Hmm?" Kirsten looked down from the ceiling.

"Don't suppose you guys have any documentation about this phenomenon for me to compare to?"

She winced, but kept a straight face. "Unfortunately not. The other incident of a ghost disabling a hovercar happened in a disavowed sector. I didn't stick around to examine the wreckage."

"Darn." Teela grumbled.

Kirsten looked at Dorian. "Up for a demonstration? If we knew for a fact a ghost did—or didn't—make this car crash, it'll only help us."

"The brass won't take it seriously, but sure." Dorian shrugged.

"Demonstration?" Teela pursed her lips. "Such as?"

"You guys have a hovercar around here you use for testing and such?"

"Yeah."

"Bring it in, hook it up to real time diagnostic monitoring. When you're ready, Dorian will recreate the circumstances of a ghost-induced failure and you can compare the logs to C1."

"Do you have any idea how crazy that sounds?" Teela grinned, a spark of excitement in her eyes. "I love it!"

9

IMMINENT

K irsten's visit to the RTC added another Inquest to her growing collection.

She slouched in the chair behind her desk in the squad room, staring at a screen listing all the Inquests pending completion related to the paranormal surge. Filling out reports had to be the worst part of being in Division 0 I-Ops. Well, second compared to having demons try to bite her in half.

At least it had been somewhat entertaining to crack the worldview of nine technicians. When Dorian made the test hovercar abruptly drop like a brick—all of three inches—they had a little trouble processing what they witnessed. Tara's diagnostic equipment confirmed similar behavior of the electronic systems inside the car at the time... so at least one other ghost out there in West City could make hovercars drop out of the sky on command.

Worse, a ghost who could do so without emotion.

Hmm. She sat up straight and accessed her official logs, searching for the patrol craft's rear camera recording from the day Dorian took out the Intera assassin. Obvious recordings of ghostly or demonic activity usually ended up classified top secret by Command so as not to set off a panic. The video of Dorian causing the hovercar chasing them to crash didn't get classified, since nothing on the camera appeared obviously paranormal, merely a car falling out of the air.

The other car followed them, 142 feet away according to the patrol craft's sensors. For no reason anyone watching the video could understand, the glowing cyan light from the four ion thrusters winked out, causing the car to drop like a brick.

142 feet away. It took six seconds between when Dorian started concentrating and the car shut down. She figured the ghost who caused the crash of C1 had to be either in the car or in another one moving with the same traffic stream. Otherwise, C1 would have gotten too far away from the ghost to suffer a fatal power issue. No reason the ghost couldn't have been *in* C1 at the time. The crash wouldn't exactly hurt them.

"Crap," whispered Kirsten.

"What's on your mind?" asked Dorian, seated behind her at 'his' desk.

She closed the video window. "Just had a bad thought. It's most likely true this crash happened due to the action of a spirit. I'm wondering if we have another big bad nasty running around and their presence is what's stirring up so many other ghosts."

"I haven't sensed anything unusual in the air." Dorian reclined, putting his feet up on the desk. "Maybe it's localized to a small area."

A beep came from the desk terminal along with a pop-up window announcing an incoming call from [CPT Winfield, N – D2IO].

"Eep. What could a Div 2 detective captain want from me?" She eyed Captain Eze's office window, feeling a bit like she ought to have him with her to speak to another captain, but dismissed it as a bit of childish worry. She wasn't an agent anymore. They'd promoted her to second lieutenant, a real investigator—not a kid with a rare, needed ability. She sat up straight and swiped to answer. "Hello?"

The head and shoulders of a black man in a nice blue shirt and neat tie appeared on her screen. Hints of age silvered the sides of his hair. He looked more like a lawyer or business executive than a cop. "Lieutenant Wren?"

"Yes, captain." She saluted. "What can I help you with?"

He returned the salute. "I'm investigating a series of suspicious stock trades involving Lyris Corporation. I understand you were at their main office not long ago, the day before the trades occurred. I'm looking into whether—"

"I stole information?" Kirsten's stomach knotted up.

Detective Captain Winfield smiled. "No, of course not. Your record and psych assessments speak quite clearly as to the nature of your character. It never even crossed my mind you are personally involved. Besides, you arrived days after the privileged meeting ended. I'm calling you to ask if you went there to investigate reports of potential psionic espionage."

"Oh…" She exhaled out her nose. "No, I went there to investigate unexplained thermal anomalies. As you've looked at my record, I'm sure you noticed my specialization is Astral Sense. They wouldn't send me to investigate a telepath illegally mind reading people unless we had a serious backlog."

He chuckled. "All right, then. Just trying to dot all the Is and cross all the Ts."

Oh, crap... "Captain, there's another possibility you probably haven't even considered."

"Go on, lieutenant."

She hesitated momentarily about sharing paranormal stuff outside Division 0, but Winfield *was* a captain and likely had higher security clearance than her. Division 2 still belonged to the National Police Force, after all. Not like she spoke to a reporter. "The incident I investigated occurred in an executive conference room. Their security team recorded a thermal imaging video of the meeting showing a colder region distinctly in the shape of a person who stood there for the entire duration. I'm confident a spirit had been in the room, probably listening to the meeting."

"Assuming this is possible, how does it relate to my investigation?" Detective Winfield gave her the same look most people did when she brought up ghosts. Halfway between laughing and 'go see a psychiatrist.'

"Astral sensitives are very rare. There are only two on record in

West City. Me, and my son. It's a near certainty other people exist in West City who have the ability to interact with ghosts. However, as the 'this woman is nuts' face you're making right now proves, people don't like hearing about ghosts. I'm sure other astrals don't know how to react to their abilities and keep quiet out of fear and wondering if they're crazy. Also, some spirits have ways of communicating with ordinary people."

"What are you saying here?" asked Captain Winfield.

"I think a ghost might have spied on the Lyris executives and passed along vital information to a living person who then either acted on it or sold the information. May I suggest comparing the content of the meeting the executives had at the time of the thermal anomaly with the suspicious stock trades? They didn't let me hear any recordings or tell me anything about what the executives discussed."

Winfield pursed his lips. "Please tell me you're kidding."

"Astrals are super rare, but it's possible. If the spirit is powerful and old enough, he could communicate with a non-psionic person who knows how to use electronics for that purpose. Cybernetic cat ears are sensitive enough to pick them up in a quiet place."

Dorian chuckled. "Most cybernetic ears are able to. You only mention the cat ones because they're visually obvious."

"Shit," muttered Detective Captain Winfield. "Not sure what'll happen if it turns out the meeting you're telling me about *did* contain the information responsible for these trades."

She chuckled. "What'll happen is we'll probably end up working on it together. At least until I figure out why the ghost is involved. It might only be a coincidence."

"Probably is." Winfield wiped his hand down his face while emitting a frustrated noise.

"I'm getting too old for this," said Dorian, attempting to imitate Winfield's voice.

His words matched the detective's facial expression perfectly.

To stop herself from laughing at a captain, Kirsten cleared her throat. "Would you mind letting me know if the information in the meeting matches?"

"All right. I suppose if it does, you will need to be involved. Might take you a bit of work to convince me ghosts exist, though."

She smiled. "Easy. My partner can help convince you."

"You don't have a partner," said Winfield.

"He's not *officially* my partner because there's no current policy for the dead to be on the duty roster."

Detective Captain Winfield stared at her. "We'll cross that bridge if we must. Thank you for your time, lieutenant."

"You're welcome, captain."

The call dropped.

Kirsten collapsed over her desk, head on her arms, feeling as though she melted into a puddle. "Ugh."

"So..." Dorian chuckled. "How does it feel to singlehandedly destroy all faith in the stock market?"

She shrugged, not sitting up. "So a couple of rich people cry into their wine." Memories of being at Konstantin's fancy events killed her appetite for the lunch she missed while at the RTC. "And you're being alarmist. Nothing's going to happen from one detective hearing me say a ghost *might* have spied on a corporation. Plenty of living people spy on corporations all the time and the beloved stock market hasn't eaten itself yet."

"No, but living spies can be stopped. Companies can't do a damn thing about spirits."

"Sure they could." She huffed and pushed herself back up to sit. "Hire astrals to blockade conference rooms before talking about sensitive stuff. But there aren't enough of us, nor enough of a threat of ghost spies, to be worth it."

"At least one." Dorian drummed his fingers on his desk. "We've got multiple ghosts all losing their minds in the same week. Is this a full moon?"

"What?"

He waved dismissively. "Old mythology. People used to believe the phases of the moon affected human behavior."

"Weird." She puffed at a strand of hair hanging in front of her face. "How'd that start?"

"Probably the same way people used to believe a god named Apollo carried the sun across the sky in a flaming chariot… before we understood how planets worked. Though, I suppose if you get enough people convinced of a silly story, it can have a psychosomatic effect on them. They believe the full moon made people act crazy, so some people acted crazy during a full moon."

"Is it a full moon?" Kirsten opened a GlobeNet browser to check. "Nope. Still… *something* has to be responsible for this. I haven't seen such a spike of activity since the Wharf Stalker."

Dorian walked around to sit on the edge of her desk. "You're thinking we've got another spirit of similar power out there?"

"The one who caused the crash, yeah." She opened another window showing the location plots for the haunting calls and pointed at the middle. "It has to be around here, somewhere."

"I hope we're not gearing up for some sort of major event."

She groaned. "Ugh. I really hope not. Let's go scout the area, see if we can sense any—"

An alarm tone rang from her desk terminal and armband.

"Lieutenant Wren." A tween girl's head and upper body appeared on the desk terminal in miniature 3D hologram floating over her armband. "There's a… umm." She glanced to her left, making a 'help' face.

Someone whispered inaudibly over the line.

The girl looked back at Kirsten, her expression urgent. "A 21-47 in progress at Twenty-Nine Palms Mall."

"Rain check the scouting mission." Dorian hopped off the desk to his feet.

"Understood, cadet. On the way."

The girl beamed. "Be safe out there."

SPREE

For the second time in a day, Kirsten flew at 600 MPH, 1,200 feet above the city surface.

"Am I being weird and paranoid, or does it seem like they always have a first-timer working my dispatches?"

Dorian tapped a finger to his chin. "Well, usually, the people you're investigating are already dead, so there's less consequences if a kid messes up. I don't think they mean it as a comment on you, personally. And that kid couldn't have been older than eleven. I didn't think they started them so young."

"Neither did I," muttered Kirsten.

"Had to be her first time in the chair." Dorian smiled. "Adorable. She was so happy when you treated her seriously."

"Yeah, well... I know what it's like to be the kid everyone patronizes."

Nine minutes after leaving the PAC, she reached the edge of a dense smog layer hanging approximately from 700 feet to 1,100 feet, obscuring the ground. Dark grey mist peeled into whorls in the patrol craft's wake, a micro lightning storm of tiny blue sparks flickering within from the ionic discharge. A beep indicated her destination at ten miles out. She slowed down from 602 to 200 MPH.

The sprawling octopusine silhouette of the Twenty-Nine Palms Mall slid into view at the top of the Navcon screen. Wireframe green lines on the windshield traced the outlines of larger buildings so she could see them past the fog. Flying at 1,200 feet allowed her to pass over most of the city's structures, though a handful reached 130 stories.

She dove into the grey, losing all visibility except for the wireframe indicators of solid objects. At 780 feet altitude, streaks of bright colors started whizzing by along with the outlines of orbs and boxes, bots desperately flinging themselves out of the way, likely delivery units going to high-rises around the mall or trying to sell stuff.

The mall might have only been seven stories tall, but it took up nearly an entire five-square-mile sector. Dispatch provided her with a nav pin straight to the location of the 21-47 call. Since the place lacked roof parking for hovercars due to various 'outdoor' venues, she landed in the emergency zone by the entrance nearest the map marker.

Hundreds of people ranging from older teens to late twenties milled around by the doors, most merely hanging out. Few paid much attention to her arrival, unsurprising considering this place's reputation. The Twenty-Nine Palms mall, more so than most physical stores, attracted many of society's lower echelon. Poor people, fringers, off-gridders, gangers, anarchists, and criminals came here as readily as what passed for middle class. Even a few celebrities sometimes shopped here to be 'trendy' or 'cool' considering the reputation of the place.

Conditions—and safety—within the mall improved the higher up one went. The ground floor had all the super-cheap stores as well as frequent shootouts. Division 1 embedded a station in the mall due to the high volume of crime on floors one to three, but couldn't be everywhere in an instant.

The jaded reaction of the shoppers to her presence had the paradoxical effect of making Kirsten happy. Being ignored equaled normal. Much better than feeling like a freak everyone stared at or ran away from.

She didn't dwell on it for more than a second, rushing inside while holding her left arm up to have a waypoint to follow. The small holo-panel floating above her forearm guard displayed a mall map, scrolling with her as she ran like something straight out of the Monwyn games she played with Evan.

This goblin's going to be a bit more difficult to beat.

Another, much smaller, crowd gathered near a food court on the second floor, blocking her off from the spot she needed to reach. Between the electronica music pumped in overhead, the sheer number of people, and the occasional scream, she didn't even bother trying to yell 'Police, stand aside,' and proceeded to push her way forward.

Predictably, the crowd moved her more than she moved anyone. In the tight confines, no one noticed her uniform. After the second creep grabbed her ass, she pulled out her stunrod, fending off a few more idiots by knocking them utterly senseless. A mere tap to the forehead put them down, blue light glowing from their eyes and mouth, for at least ten minutes. Dorian gave one guy a horrible case of brain freeze for attempting to grab the E-90 off her belt.

When someone squeezed her breast from behind, Kirsten thrust the stunrod backward at crotch level. The guy collapsed in a heap, squealing.

Behind him, a teen girl with pink hair gawked. "Oh, shit. Cop! Hey you assholes, move out of her way!"

A small clearing formed around her, the crowd congealing away like a giant mass of gelatin. Most looked at her with 'whoops, sorry' expressions. A handful scowled. Six men and one woman lay unconscious in her wake. Kirsten disregarded them and dashed forward into the food court tables.

Miraculously, not one person sat there eating. Dozens of trays lay abandoned with partially eaten meals still on them. At least half the chairs had been knocked over, some rather far away from tables. A surprising amount of food splattered the floor and columns, one French fry even ended up stuck in an old bullet hole, suggesting it had flown like a missile.

Kirsten stood in the pose of an Old West gunslinger, eyeing the desolate, trashed seating area. Another crowd gathered at the far end of the food court, most holding their NetMinis out, recording video. Scanning the surface thoughts of random people told her many had witnessed trays, chairs, and even tables flying around. One guy had a coat torn off him and hurled at a young woman who'd only been wearing cat ears and a tail.

This ghost has to be at least eighty if they're trying to tell cat modders to cover up. Kirsten shivered. According to Dorian, 'fashion' had become so extreme the only way to push the envelope further involved not wearing clothing at all. Maybe fifty years ago, men and women with the cat (or other animal) mod fetish would draw shocked gasps. These days, people barely noticed them.

She again decided against trying to yell over the music and opened her mind to astral energy.

A sense of a spirit presence gathered near a column a little to the right, maybe forty feet away. Kirsten walked toward the spot, sidestepping to keep some distance between her and a potentially dangerous spirit.

"Yo, this li'l girl's got some nerve," said a deep-voiced man somewhere behind her. "Ain't nuff creds in this whole damn planet get me messin' with no tray-throwin' invisible shit."

Kirsten edged past the column—and locked stares with a little old woman pacing around a burgundy-and-wood antique wingback chair. A physical book with actual paper pages sat on the cushion. Though the woman appeared as ordinary to Kirsten as any living person, she definitely gave off the energy of a spirit. The chair, however, seemed a little too bright, resembling a high-quality hologram an inobservant person might mistake for a real object. She radiated a good deal of anger, but no malice.

"Quiet down, missy!" yelled the old woman, right before swiping a tray from a nearby table and flinging it at her.

Kirsten ducked a gloopy plate of chow mein. "I didn't even say anything yet."

"What's wrong with you people up here?" shouted the ghost. "I'm trying to read and there's so much noise I can't even think! It won't stop."

"Ma'am…" Kirsten stepped closer, so she didn't have to shout. "Is there something keeping you at 29P? There are plenty of less obnoxiously loud places you could go."

The woman hurled an unopened self-cooling soft drink can at her. "Bah."

Kirsten dove to the floor, avoiding the metal canister, which smashed through the window of a boutique clothing store. *Wow. Either she's trying to take my head off or doesn't realize how strong she is.* She pushed herself upright. "Ma'am, if you want quiet, you really shouldn't stay here. If something is keeping you trapped in this place, I can help."

"Darn fool. I came here because it's quieter than where I want to be." The elder glowered at her. "And put on a damn skirt. Those leggings are too tight."

"This place is *quieter*? Where do you usually live?"

"Why are you pestering me?" barked the old woman.

Kirsten tried to radiate as much sweetness as she could. "Are you aware you died?"

"Oh, sweetie, you really ought to stop asking questions like that. You're only making the stereotype worse about blondes. *Of course* I realize I'm dead! I've been dead since 2087!" She threw an empty tray, which Kirsten ducked. "It's been a long damn time. Ain't stupid. You don't think I figured out by now? They built the damn cockamamie thing overhead, which is fine by me. Keeps the damn living people the hell away from my peace and quiet, but now there's the damn racket all the time."

She raised her hands in a placating gesture. "If you tell me about it, I'll do everything I can to make the racket stop. Where should you be?"

"Barstow." The woman folded her arms.

Uhh. Where the heck is Barstow? Gotta be a pre-war name, before sectors. Probably in the Beneath. "All right. I'll go there and stop the racket."

"Why would you bother? You're too damn young to care about us old people."

Kirsten smiled. "I'm a police officer. We still take noise complaints seriously."

"Oh…" The woman's entire attitude shifted from combative to grandmotherly. "Why, thank you, sweetie."

She—and her chair—vanished.

Dorian made odd squeaking sounds, attempting to hold in laughter.

"Other than an old woman being mad enough to throw things, what's funny about this?" asked Kirsten.

"She's upset about her upstairs neighbors making too much noise."

Kirsten started to laugh—but cut it short at the shrill screaming of a terrified child. The crowd at the far end of the food court spun to look behind them. She sprinted past empty tables toward the commotion, reaching the second group of onlookers at the same moment a muscular man in a dark coat appeared on a balcony two stories above, holding a flailing child over his head in both hands. He threw the shrieking six- or seven-year-old girl over the side into a twenty-foot fall heading for plastisteel flooring.

Despite still being almost a hundred meters away, Kirsten strained to run as if she had a chance to get close enough and catch the girl. A blur of neon green and black appeared from the left, intercepting the child before she smacked into the floor. Almost as though he'd teleported, the lanky figure of a seven-foot-tall cyberganger appeared at the end of the blurry trail. Both his legs below the thigh were dark blue metal, the feet presently expanded out to thin struts bearing multiple wheels—a Mishiro booster, essentially ion-thruster-powered roller blades.

His baggy black pants had dozens of pockets, chains, and small skulls. Two steel spikes protruded from where his nipples had once been. A twelve-inch neon green spiky mohawk sprouted from his head with smaller half-inch steel spikes running across his eyebrows. He looked like the sort of freak who'd chase people into an alley and cut them open to see what made them work—only, he cradled the frightened girl after catching her, attempting to calm her down.

Holy shit! What the hell's a street thug doing with speedware? She shook her head, dismissing the question, and kept sprinting over to him.

"Nice catch."

The ganger looked down at her. "Oi. Someone's lookin' for a royal beat down. 'Ere. Take 'er an' make like ya don't see what's 'bout ta happen to that bloke." He handed the girl over.

Another scream came from overhead.

Kirsten looked up the open shaft going from the second floor all the way to the roof, an atrium designed to allow shoppers to easily move between floors. Escalators and elevator tubes surrounded it. Clear barriers on each floor overlooking the wide-open area ought to be high enough for people not to accidentally fall, but a man on the fifth floor had tossed the girl straight over it.

The same guy threw a boy about Evan's age headfirst over the barrier. Kirsten glowered at him—and realized she locked eyes with a ghost.

"Bloody hell." The cyberganger zipped to his left and caught the boy with relative ease, not even straining to absorb the force of his drop.

Dorian rushed up the escalator.

"Hey," yelled Kirsten. "Stay here and play goalie. It's a spirit. You can't kill him. He's already dead."

"Say what, luv?" yelled the ganger. "You off your noggin'?"

Kirsten summoned the lash. "Nope. But he's about to be."

"Oy, brilliant…" He set the boy on his feet.

The kid stared around, disoriented.

Kirsten ran to the nearest tube elevator. The clear plastic pipes contained a constant stream of independent metal discs moving either up or down, essentially delivery bots carrying up to three people at a time. She headed for an upward tube and jumped on the next disc. A frightened man tried to barge in with her when she arrived on the fifth floor, forcing her to knee him in the groin to escape the tube before it whisked her up to the sixth floor.

People screamed and ran in random directions, fleeing from a half-apparated spirit attacking a girl on the older side of teenaged. The muscular ghost had a hold of a short, slender young woman with cobalt blue hair, cat ears, tail—and metal claws sprouting from her fingertips. She shredded at the air so rapidly her arms became a pale haze of motion, though the constant stream of cursing coming out of her did more damage to him than the plastisteel blades. The confused nature of the swearing made it sound as if the girl couldn't see the man grabbing her.

Dorian attempted to wrestle the guy away from the woman—who had to be at least eighteen since she'd obtained cybernetic parts. His effort likely prevented the spirit from tossing her over the barrier into free fall already, though he couldn't quite break her out of his grip. The struggle had already cost the woman her micro-jacket, which lay nearby. The ghost didn't appear interested in damaging the rest of her clothes, a hot pink half shirt and black miniskirt, only throwing her to her death.

At Kirsten's approach, Dorian used a takedown maneuver, flinging both spirit and young woman to the floor. The instant he rolled away from the guy, Kirsten swung the lash. Few things a ghost could do would make her attack without even trying to talk first. Attempting to kill people, especially kids, ranked second on her list—the first being attempting to harm *her* kid.

What the ghost had in strength, he lacked in speed, barely sitting up before the energy whip tore into his quasi-solid body. A visible pulse of energy burst away from him the instant the lash hit him. Kirsten dragged the glowing tendril through him, coiling it back into the air behind her.

He emitted a loud wail of agony—and exploded into a scattering of loose energy blobs.

A sense of a spiritual obliteration chilled her bones. At the same moment, the teen experienced a mild convulsive fit while glowing NanoLED tattoos on her cheek cycled among various cute cartoon characters. Kirsten froze, confused, staring at the dozens of little light flecks fading out one after the next.

"Oookay…" she whispered. "That's two."

"Looked like one to me… or if you're talking about victims, we're up to three," said Dorian.

The teen recovered from her fit, then whirled to face her, claws up. Her pink top had a cartoon of a cute, sedate white cat in the middle, seated in the pose of a meditating monk wearing big headphones. "What the hell was that flash? Is some psionic shithead trying to rip my clothes off? Why did my 'ware just freak the hell out?"

Kirsten shifted her gaze from the dancing light blobs to the young woman. "Please take a few breaths and calm down. You were attacked by a spirit who tried to throw you off the balcony. The force pulling at you was the ghost attempting to pick you up."

"Umm." She fidgeted. "Okay… it did kinda feel like someone grabbed me, but he was like invisible."

She released the lash, allowing it to dissipate. "When the spirit exploded, he caused an electromagnetic pulse strong enough for any electronic devices within about thirty feet to experience a momentary glitch, including your cybernetics."

"Whoa." The girl retracted her claws back into her fingers, then rubbed her face. "I really need to lay off Flowerbasket."

"You didn't hallucinate. Sorry. Can you tell me what you remember?"

"Umm. I was just walking, and it felt like some big dude grabbed me by my jacket and lifted me off my feet. I started trying to claw his face off, but, umm, no dude. Thought it might be one of those people who can move shit with their minds. I got nothin' against psionics, just creeps."

"Sounds like you have personal experience." Kirsten raised an eyebrow. "Is someone using telekinesis to assault you?"

The girl sighed. "I think so, but I can't prove it. This dude who shows up at my work can't handle a Neko wearing clothes, so he keeps yanking my shit off. It only happens when he's there, and he makes faces at me."

"Where do you work?"

"I tend bar and wait tables at That Place With Cats by the Place."

Kirsten chuckled. "You work there and don't remember the name?"

The girl rolled her eyes. "No, it's literally named 'That Place With Cats by the Place.' Jerry used to call it 'That Shithole' but people didn't show up. Then he got the idea to hire a bunch of us with ears and tails, add an army of real cats, and go with a theme."

"There are an astounding number of cat-person themed places." Dorian made an 'I don't understand it either' face at Kirsten.

"Right," said the teen. "This dude Gamedi or something is the creep. Hang on, I took a few pictures to warn the others." She fished a NetMini out of her jacket pocket, tapped the holo-screen, then made a flicking gesture at Kirsten.

Her NetMini beeped with an incoming file.

Kirsten redirected the message to her armband terminal. The image showed a pale black-haired guy wearing a maroon dress shirt and black pants lounging on a mini sofa. Behind him, the décor looked like any other bar-slash-restaurant young professionals might go to, only with a cat theme and numerous actual cats.

"What days does this guy show up?" asked Kirsten. "I'm kinda overwhelmed at the moment with ghost stuff, but I can definitely have someone look into this. If he is using Telekinesis to assault you, it's considered a criminal act."

"Really?" She blinked. "I didn't think cops would do anything about psionic stuff."

"We do."

"Awesome. Really? I can't wait to see the look on this dickbag's face when you guys show up."

"Yeah. Wish I could be there, but... ugh. Running myself thin. Spirits aren't usually this active or I'd look into it myself for you."

"Cool. Umm, so... this ghost?"

"Gone." Kirsten sighed. She didn't *really* regret destroying a ghost who tried to kill random people, but any obliteration bothered her to a point. "Since you sent me the image, I can find you if need be. Shouldn't be much of a need to considering the spirit's dead. Can you think of anyone who might have wanted to hurt you who died within the past six months?"

The girl shook her head. "Nope."

"Okay. Sorry for the disturbance. You can resume the rest of your day." Kirsten looked around at a reasonably calm mall concourse. "Dorian, is there something going on here I'm not seeing?"

"Nothing I can feel."

"Thanks again." The teen walked off, little decorative chains on her heeled boots clinking. Since it appeared calm up here, she jogged to a down elevator.

"Is it me or is the young lady rather casual about nearly being thrown from a two-story balcony?" Dorian watched her walk off.

"She most likely doesn't understand how much danger she'd been in." Kirsten exhaled, then headed for an elevator tube going down. "This is the second spirit I destroyed in one or two hits. First the one at the Funzone, then this guy."

"Definitely strange."

"Both of them"—she hopped off the elevator on the second floor —"attacked kids. Definitely added some emotion to the lash, but hardly the angriest I've ever been. You've seen it react to extreme emotions before, the cord gets brighter and wider. Didn't do it here, but they both obliterated in a single hit. Ghosts new enough for their sense of identity to be *that* weak should not be able to make a cobweb twitch, much less throw people around."

"Hmm." Dorian shifted his jaw side to side while thinking. "Something is going on here we haven't run into before. If you think the spirit responsible for the hovercar crash is the reason other ghosts are going crazy, maybe he or she has some ability to give them temporary power?"

"Umm. Never heard of anything like it before."

Dorian gestured at her. "Like I said… something we haven't run into."

Their conversation about ghosts quieted as they neared the tall cyberganger, a pair of Division 1 cops, both kids who went flying over the barrier, and their parents. The boy held both of his parents' hands, standing between them, still looking freaked out. Next to them, the little girl koala-clung to her father, though appeared outwardly calmer than the boy.

Kirsten approached.

"We don't know for a fact either spirit targeted children specifically," said Dorian, walking beside her. "Might've just been the closest victims. Besides, kids take less energy to throw."

"Not funny," muttered Kirsten.

"Wasn't trying to be. They weigh less."

The cyberganger spoke to the Division 1 cops in a British accent, explaining how he'd noticed the little girl go flying off the balcony and rushed over to help. Neither officer appeared particularly happy to hear him admit to having high grade speedware, but they also didn't give him a hard time about it. Speedware wasn't illegal, but having it tended to cast a cloud of suspicion over a person. Few people spent the hundred thousand or more credits on it purely for personal protection.

Wonder if he's undercover... street punks can't usually afford that stuff.

"Oy, you get the bastard?" asked the ganger, upon noticing Kirsten standing there.

"Yeah. He won't be bothering anyone else."

Both cops went wide-eyed the way people usually looked at Division 9 operatives.

"I didn't kill anyone." Kirsten folded her arms. "The suspect was already dead. A spirit. I'm Div 0, not Nine."

"Ahh," said the officer on the left.

His partner smiled. "Then this one's all yours. Have fun."

The Division 1 officers waved and hurried off.

"Wow. They're not calling you insane." Dorian blinked. "Impressive."

"A pair of Div 1 officers stationed at 29P wouldn't care what kind of crazy story gets them out of dealing with an Inquest. They're happy to believe in ghosts if it means they have one less case to work."

Dorian chuckled.

"Oi?" asked the cyberganger. "Who are ya talkin' to?"

"Another ghost." She took a deep breath and looked at the two kids. "Is everyone okay?"

"Yeah," muttered the boy.

The girl merely stared at her, refusing to let go of her father.

She smiled at the ganger. "Awesome job, man. Okay, everyone please bear with me. I need to collect some basic info. Then I'll answer all your questions."

"Whoa, you believe in ghosts?" asked the ganger.

"You can say that." She chuckled. "Not too often I meet someone else who does until something like *this* happens."

"My dead buddy showed up in my apartment last night, talkin' for hours." He exhaled. "Dude died over a year ago. Thought someone hacked my headware, made me see shit, but he knew things only VB would know."

Kirsten activated the holo-panel of her armband computer and set up two new Inquest records, one for the old woman, one for the child-thrower. "Something around here is causing ghosts to be more active than normal. Still trying to figure out what."

"Wild." He whistled. "So, I'm not nuts?"

"Not at all." Kirsten looked at the parents. "Can you please tell me what you saw?"

Not quite an hour later, Kirsten closed the crime scene.

The cyberganger, Dox, real name Orson Zheng, confused her by acting so completely ordinary despite his augmentations and outlandish outfit/hair. She had little doubt among his people he behaved in a wildly different manner, but she figured he'd still be a decent sort of guy. Being loud and anti-establishment didn't automatically make someone a danger to the innocent. She spoke to him for a while after clearing the other two families to leave.

Unlike most Inquests, there wouldn't be any need for future court proceedings or even contact. She merely needed to collect as much information as possible for the report, then field a barrage of questions. The parents didn't quite appear sold on the idea of spirits but accepted the person who tried to hurt their children had been permanently dealt with.

She added another Inquest for log purposes, regarding Dox's friend VB. Unimaginatively enough, the dead friend got the nickname from being fond of vibro-blades. He died thirteen months ago due to gang warfare, despite not being in a true gang. Dox and his group regarded themselves as 'augmentation enthusiasts.' While they did often gather in groups to hang out, they didn't consider themselves a gang or do anything more criminal than loiter. However, it didn't stop another group from mistaking them for a territorial threat.

Whether or not VB's return had anything to do with the recent spate of hauntings, she couldn't tell... but logged it anyway.

Perhaps overly optimistic, Kirsten headed back outside to the patrol craft. One good thing about most citizens confusing Division 0 with Division 9—no one messed with the car. She hopped in, shut off the emergency lights, and let out a groan of fatigue.

Dorian materialized in the passenger seat.

"Sometimes, I'm really annoyed those two Seraphim didn't give me their PIDs." Kirsten scowled at her NetMini. "It's maddening to have questions no one can answer."

"Welcome to philosophy. Humans have been pondering unanswerable questions for thousands of years."

Kirsten poked the button to power up the drive system. A blast of ion sparks crackled between the thrusters and plastisteel ground, expanding in a cloud around the patrol craft as she lifted off, ascending vertically until reaching 500 feet. "I'm fine with not understanding stuff. It's the people getting hurt part I'm worried about."

"Spirits have an odd way of going about existing. Very few care to understand anything at all about the experience of being a spirit. Many don't even process their reality has changed. Some are endlessly stuck in a loop of repeating the same moment in time until someone like you shows up and communicates with them. Others wander aimlessly."

"Yeah. I know all that." She swung the car around to point in the direction of the PAC, then accelerated.

"I'm saying, not even ghosts understand how ghosts work. You shouldn't feel like you're doing anything wrong here." Dorian scratched at his cheek. "Guess I'm also saying there's no guarantee finding an old ghost and asking them questions would be any help."

A long, frustrated sigh leaked out of her mouth. He had a point. Theodore probably wouldn't understand how such a young ghost could physically touch people. Worse, *her* understanding of the situation had plenty of gaps.

"What if the ghosts aren't new? Is it possible for those spirits to have, I dunno, gotten their asses kicked recently?"

"Anything is possible. Question is, what's probable?" Dorian patted the console. "No spirit with any sense of self-preservation would be caught undead too far from their resting place. I may be more attached than most to this world; however, every time something's handed me my butt on a plate, I've kept my head down until my strength returned."

Kirsten idly tapped her fingers on the control sticks. "Maybe they wanted to be destroyed. But, they would have had no way to know I'd be there."

"Or did they?" Dorian raised the Eyebrow of Dramatic Pause.

"Right." She rolled her eyes.

He pointed at her. "*How* many spirits come looking for you? They've been doing it since you were six. When a spirit wants something bad enough to focus on it, we have this strange way of understanding."

"So, concentrate on wanting to find the reason the ghosts are going crazy." She smirked.

"Already trying. Isn't working too well. Probably due to my lack of emotional investment." He patted her shoulder. "If I needed to find you because of a desperate need to pass along some critical piece of information to my family, I'd probably wander around seemingly at random but run into you."

"Do you think those two ghosts tracked me down specifically to be destroyed in some spectral version of suicide-by-cop? Like, somehow, they knew I get pissed off when people hurt kids so they messed with children on purpose to put me in a state of mind where I wouldn't hesitate?"

Dorian raised a hand. "Merely saying it's a possibility. We already had the old woman at 29P. She's been around for centuries. Her presence could have attracted other spirits. It *might* be pure chance the child-tosser showed up when he did."

"Like the Lace heads of the ghost world, mindlessly violent and don't care if they die." She mulled for a few minutes. "What if they were violent spirits who used so much energy they weakened themselves, or kept getting into fights with other ghosts... and something *forced* them to go crazy?"

"Another possibility."

"Can a spirit overextend? Like if a ghost isn't powerful enough to affect solid objects yet, but something drives them to an extreme state where they strain themselves, is it like burning up their essence to do it, weakening themselves?"

Dorian rubbed his chin. "I haven't pushed myself so far, but you might be on to something here. I doubt it's anything a spirit could simply do whenever they wanted. It would take an extreme situation or external influence."

"Could explain why they both obliterated so fast... they weren't old enough to have the power necessary to touch people and burned themselves out."

"Reasonable as any other idea."

"Hmm." She set the car on auto-drive and leaned back in the seat, eyes closed. "The old woman said she couldn't stand the racket. What could be so bad a 300-year-old ghost floats up from the Beneath to escape it?"

Dorian chuckled. "Have you heard what they're passing off as music these days?"

"I'm serious." She concentrated to make her hand solid to spirits and poked him in the arm. "Some kind of electromagnetic disturbance, maybe? Is someone testing a weird new weapon somewhere and setting off pulses of EM, which are driving ghosts bonkers? Maybe temporarily amplifying them so they can do stuff like older ghosts." She opened her eyes, stunned by a realization. "What if it's *draining* them?"

"Draining?"

She turned her head to stare at him. "New ghosts wouldn't be so casual about throwing people around. They'd be all giddy and impressed with themselves, plus clumsy. Both the ball pit spirit and the thrower ghost behaved like living people in terms of the ease with which they manipulated physical objects—in this case, people."

"Okay… so what are you saying?" Dorian drummed his fingers on the door armrest.

"I'm saying, this phenomenon bothering the ghosts could be a giant *drain* on power. It's sucked up so much of their essence, they're defenseless against the lash."

Dorian's expression shifted to worry. "If true, they would either have to be driven nuts to act irrational or be unaware of their vulnerability. Otherwise, they'd stay in hiding until they weren't as brittle as an origami swan."

"Yeah."

"And if some external force drove them mad, they wouldn't necessarily have the mental faculties to be impressed with themselves for being able to grab people."

She grumbled mentally. The longer a ghost existed after death, the more energy they gathered. New ghosts could usually withstand anywhere from two to four lashes before obliteration. And, until these last two, other spirits she'd been forced to attack always fell into a visibly weakened state where she *knew* one more hit would destroy them utterly. In her mind, she pictured ghosts as accumulating 'armor' the longer they existed. Harbingers could claim a ghost if they didn't have armor—or after Kirsten peeled them out of it. The older the ghost, the more strikes from a lash it took to weaken them.

The ball pit ghost and this one now at 29P had almost been 'wearing' negative armor. Either something drained their essence, or they burned it up overextending… driven into a frenzy by something.

"Curse of Vulnerability," whispered Kirsten.

"Last time I checked, vulnerability isn't a naughty word."

She managed a weak smile. "No, I mean it's like one of the spells from the Monwyn games. Whenever Evan casts it on a tough monster, my arrows do double or triple damage. I was thinking the two ghosts who obliterated right away felt similar. Something made my lash hit them way harder than it ought to have…" She slouched. "Or maybe they simply had their asses kicked earlier."

"Lieutenant," said an adult voice from the console. The holographic head of a young man appeared, seventeen or eighteen. "Are you available to respond to a 21-47 in progress?"

She squeezed the control sticks hard. "Yes. Send me a nav. What information do we have?"

"The call originated from *Kōtō Fune* Sushi."

Kirsten blinked. "The hover boat?"

"Yes, lieutenant. According to my screen, the nav point is in motion."

"Dammit! I love them. The guy's awesome." Kirsten flicked on the emergency flashers and took over manual control. "On the way."

"Copy, lieutenant."

———

A GREEN WIREFRAME BOX APPEARED ON THE WINDSCREEN DISPLAY, targeting a tiny, dark speck in the distance.

The *Kōtō Fune* Sushi Restaurant flew along a regular route spanning thirty sectors, frequenting districts containing dense concentrations of office towers. It happened to be reasonably close to the PAC, which made it a popular target for National Police Force personnel who either started or ended their shifts between three in the afternoon and ten at night—at least anyone who drove a hovercar or patrol craft.

She slowed below 200 MPH. The dark spot on the windshield grew into a shape resembling an ancient Japanese boat, with certain liberties taken for appearances sake. It seemed unlikely the real boats used so long ago had been so fancy or covered in dragons and phoenixes. Two huge ion thrusters at the back end emitted a sedate cyan glow, nudging the bizarre craft along at about twenty miles an hour—a veritable stationary object compared to hovercars and bots.

As she so often did when in the mood for dinner, Kirsten pulled the patrol craft up alongside the forty-foot flying boat. Hideo Koizumi, the chef-owner, and his two sons ran around the open part of the mid-deck chasing a manic-eyed man who kept grabbing random objects or food and throwing them overboard. The Koizumis didn't react to the spirit, only objects moving around.

"Oh, come on," yelled Kirsten. "That's sushi abuse."

"Sushi is food abuse," muttered Dorian. "The ghost is performing a public service."

She ignored him and pushed the door upward. "Dorian, take control. Get as close as you can."

"Got it." He melted into the seat. Seconds later, the patrol craft drifted toward the sushi boat.

Kirsten grabbed the 'oh shit' handle above her on the left and faced out the door.

"You're not seriously considering jumping?" asked Dorian via the speakers.

"Not if I can avoid it, no." She cupped her hands around her mouth. "Hey, you. Ghost. Stop messing with Mr. Koizumi!"

The three men on the boat looked at her. The ghost paused to glare at her, about to chuck a wad of fish over the side. A long, olive-drab coat and frumpy clothing gave him the aesthetic of an off-gridder, though he lacked the disheveled hair and layer of dirt.

Mr. Koizumi recognized her right away and waved. "Miss Wren! You are here? I am having some difficulties at the moment. Police will be here soon for the ghost."

She pointed up at the emergency lights on the roof, which saturated the boat in rapid flashes of intense azure.

"Oh!" Mr. Koizumi smacked himself on the head. "Something is wrecking everything."

The spirit shrugged and proceeded to raise his arm as if to throw the fish—which one of the sons tried to hold on to.

"Yeah, you." Kirsten pointed at him. "Why are you messing with the Koizumis? Knock it off."

"Fuck off," said the ghost. He let go of the fish, causing the younger man to fall on his ass, and picked up a stack of disposable bento boxes.

"Need to get a little closer, got a reach of about fifteen feet," said Kirsten before shouting, "Last warning. I'd rather help you, but you have to stop destroying stuff."

The spirit set the bento boxes down, picked up a handful of fish slices, and hurled them at her.

A piece of tuna sashimi hit her in the forehead with a wet *slap*—and stuck. Another bounced off her chest before falling into her lap. Several flew past her, two sticking to the inside of the passenger window.

Dorian's grumbling came from the car's sound system. "It's going to smell like fish in here for weeks."

She peeled the tuna from her forehead and tried to toss it back onto the boat, but the wind caught it, making it fly off to the left. *Oops!* A small piece of fish falling from 500 feet overhead probably wouldn't hurt too much if it hit someone. Annoyed, she pointed at the spirit and concentrated on pulling his hand away from the refrigerated display case of fish.

This ghost resisted more forcefully than she expected, but only due to the previous two aggressive ones being so weak. He growled, attempting to reach for a wad of whitefish, though his hand remained frozen in midair as if held in a vice.

"Stop wasting food!" yelled Kirsten. *I feel ridiculous.*

Snarling, the ghost faced her again, his eyes manic. He stopped trying to grab fish; the sudden release of tension made her rock back in the seat. Kirsten sat back up to the ghost trying to grab a large knife. Mr. Koizumi screamed like a father defending his child and pounced the instant the blade twitched, pinning it to the cutting surface.

Grr. This ghost is an idiot. She concentrated on the last, projecting the energy cord out as long as she could. "Need another foot or two closer."

The patrol craft drifted left, almost bumping against the large sushi boat.

She clutched the overhead handle tight, leaned forward, and whipped the lash at the spirit. The last four inches or so snapped through his back, tearing a gouge in his spectral essence as if he'd been grazed by a laser sword—only without all the blood and smoke. He screeched in pain, body twisted up on his toes, left arm flapping. The eight-inch wound shrank closed, shimmered, and once again took on the appearance of an undamaged coat.

"I don't want to harm you, but you have to stop vandalizing this boat!" yelled Kirsten.

"Gah!" shouted the spirit. He whirled, staring at her with an almost 'what the hell am I doing here?' expression. Before she could say anything more, he blurred into an energy smear, rocketing off toward the ground.

"Okay… what the heck?" Kirsten released the lash, leaning out of the patrol craft enough to watch the luminous streak vanish into the plastisteel sidewalk below.

Mr. Koizumi approached the edge closest to her, leaning on the railing. "You are watching something fall? Did you knock him overboard?"

"In a manner of speaking. The spirit is gone. Sorry about all the mess."

"It is not your fault." He smiled. "Thank you for saving my best knife."

"You're welcome. Didn't really want it embedded in my face."

"Agreed. That would have been worse than losing it." Mr. Koizumi exhaled. "So, we really had a spirit on the ship?"

"Yes." She shifted ninety degrees to her right, sitting normal in the seat again. "One sec." After closing the door and opening the armored window, she described the ghost's appearance. "Does he sound familiar at all?"

"No." Mr. Koizumi shrugged. "I have no idea why he would bother us."

Disappointed, she nodded though *did* feel a little better her favorite sushi chef hadn't made enemies of a spirit. She collected the rest of the tuna out of the patrol craft and handed it over. "Almost done, just need to go over some basic questions for the report."

He tossed the fish bits in a de-assembler. "It's almost dinner time. Care for your usual?"

"Are you sure it isn't a bad time? The ghost made a big mess."

"My pleasure. The least I can do."

Mr. Koizumi started putting together her usual order of sashimi while she asked the standard post-incident questions. Two other hovercars plus a Division 1 patrol craft pulled up at the boat to order while she monopolized Mr. Koizumi's attention. One of his sons scrambled to clean up, the other stuck his hands in a sanitizer field before working on incoming orders. Eventually, Kirsten had dinner for herself and Evan sitting in the back, and another Inquest on the pile of Inquests pending final reports.

The chefs waved as she pulled away from the sushi barge.

Dorian appeared in the passenger seat as soon as she took flight control back. "Something doesn't make sense."

"A lot of this doesn't make sense."

"Why did that man scream like someone tried to steal his baby when the ghost went for the knife?"

She sighed. "Nothing unusual there. Some of those professional sushi knives can cost thousands of credits."

"Who'd pay thousands of credits for a plain knife?"

"They come straight from Japan and are extremely sharp."

Dorian gave her side eye. "He should use a vibro-blade. Much sharper and a tenth the cost."

"If they tried to cut sushi with a vibro-blade, it wouldn't be sushi anymore. It'd come out cooked. Those things get ridiculously hot. What the hell is going on?"

"It's not a full moon." Dorian leaned back in his seat. "Let's check over records. Maybe someone disturbed an old mausoleum."

She exhaled, lips fluttering. "Wouldn't the spirits all be going after the people who bothered them?"

"Probably, but you don't have anything else."

"I do. Sorta. There has to be something at the center of where most of these attacks are occurring. And the old lady mentioned a loud racket. Maybe it'll be obvious?"

"Maybe, but when do you ever get so lucky?" He chuckled.

She smiled to herself, thinking of finding Evan and meeting Sam within months. "Happens sometimes."

11

THE WARLORD

Never in Kirsten's life did she imagine she'd find herself in a blue cheongsam, running around ancient ruins while sword-fighting ninjas.

However, she presently ran up a stone path somewhere in a rural area of China—as it would have been about a thousand years ago. The men who showed up occasionally to kill her didn't act like ninjas. She only thought of them as such due to their faces being covered. Not only did masks make it less obvious she fought the same person over and over, it also made it easier to kill them.

Despite knowing she participated in a virtual reality simulation, it still took her a while to find the nerve necessary to stick a jian into an apparently living person. In the Monwyn games she played with Evan, the sim didn't convey how it really felt to slice or stab into beings of flesh and bone. The few times she'd been stuck at too close range for Asara's longbow and had to use the elven longsword, stabbing creatures reminded her of slicing cake.

Here, in the Division 2 training area, not only did the Chinese jian sword seem heavier than Asara's fantasy weapon, the simulation let her feel every grind of blade on bone or the variations in squishiness depending on where she stabbed or sliced. It took some work to ignore being squeamish about it.

Part of her wanted to ask Gabriel to turn sensation off. She never expected to use a sword in a fight with an actual person. If the blade had to come out, she'd be dealing with ghosts, abyssals, or demons at a point where she'd become too exhausted to use the lash. Division 0 had a few astral sensitives in decades before her, but none had any means of fighting supernatural entities other than astrally binding a physical weapon—like a sword. Ballistic firearms didn't do anything to ghosts unless each individual bullet was astrally bound. Guns barely irritated abyssals. No one had any data how They Who Always Were reacted to bullets, but she figured 'true demons' would laugh at them.

If the day came when Evan found himself officially part of Division 0, his only recourse for dealing with dangerous supernatural beings would be a sword—or perhaps a laser. The reason Zeroes carried energy weapons instead of physical firearms like other police divisions was due to a Tactical officer fifty-some-odd years ago accidentally discovering laser weapons disrupted spirits.

Granted, it would take something like fifteen to twenty hits from an E-90—the most powerful handgun-sized laser available—to disrupt a spirit's essence as much as one swipe from her lash. An astrally bound sword would likely be weaker than the lash, but far better than a laser except for the obvious handicap of having to be close to the angry ghost.

I just know they're going to pressure him to sign up... and he's going to. He wants to help people. She took out her worries over Evan's future health on the next 'ninja' to spring out from behind an old stone column. Gabriel still had the sim running on a low skill setting. She ran the training course today mostly for acclimating to the feel of using a sword in 'real' fights, as opposed to sparring with Gabriel, not to push her to the limit of her skills.

Yet.

Eventually, every 'ninja' would be a serious challenge to beat. Today, however, she defeated them easily. The ones who came right in, she'd wait for them to swing, parry, then counterattack. If the man hesitated, she'd sometimes initiate, but usually let them make the first move.

The earlier he starts, the better he'll be able to defend himself.

She begrudgingly decided to bring the subject up with him. Naturally, she expected the fantasy-obsessed boy to *adore* the idea of learning sword fighting for real. He'd much prefer magic, but alas, spellcasting only existed in video games.

Another man shouted a war cry as he jumped from the bushes, sword over his head.

Kirsten ducked under his initial swing, slashing him across the knee. The man fell over, spinning to slice at her as he went down. She darted forward, avoiding the attack, and kept going. Gabriel would probably have wanted her to finish the guy off, but despite him being entirely made of ones and zeroes, she couldn't 'kill' someone not presenting an immediate threat.

The meandering stone path up the side of the hill led past multiple smallish clearings littered with the rubble of collapsed stone huts. Each platform, much like a video game, had a somewhat more skilled opponent compared to the basic guys attacking her on the trail. Kirsten fought her way to the edge of the sixth clearing. Past it, a straight uphill path led forty feet to the final 'palace,' a red-painted wooden structure surrounding a square area more like a dojo than the residence of a king.

The warlord waited inside, wearing a ridiculously elaborate outfit, arms folded, frowning imperiously at her. Not exactly realistic for him to stand there watching her fight his minions, but she didn't run this sim to learn how to fight six people at once. Even Gabriel said the best way to win even a three-on-one when swords are involved is to haul ass—or pull out a gun.

She knew as soon as she entered the sixth small clearing, two men would rush at her from behind the ruins of a small stone building on the left. This would be her fifth attempt to get past them. The first try, they overwhelmed her right away without her even scoring a hit on one. Subsequent attempts progressively improved. The last two tries, she took one guy out but 'died' to the second man as soon as she lowered her defenses to attack his partner.

Maybe I'll try focusing on defense this time. Wait for them to make an error?

As soon as she stepped forward, the men, one wearing blue, one green, appeared and charged.

Kirsten darted left, dodging the green man on the right while parrying the other guy's downward chop. Green spun around behind Blue, leaning into a thrust at her face, which she deflected using her blade. Blue slashed at her leg. She managed to reorient her jian fast enough to block while backpedaling.

"Every opponent has a pattern," said Gabriel's voice from everywhere. "Before you can get past any defense, you must find the holes in it."

Easy for you to say from up there. Fortunately, her defenses felt noticeably better, coming from reflex and training rather than her trying to remember a specific single technique. She weaved back and forth between the two men, entirely focused on defending herself. In a real fight against two living people, she'd already have used Suggestion to make them stop. One of the other trainers, Mina Hong —who mostly administered urban assault scenarios—made no secret of her irritation at 'Division 0 prima donnas' who thought their psionic powers ought to work in the computer. She'd apparently had an argument with Officer Solomon, and Kirsten caught the fallout of her opinion on Zeroes.

Fortunately, Kirsten didn't need to go through her urban assault and tactics course.

The two swordsmen kept pressing their attacks. The *clank-clank-clank* of swords striking swords echoed over the beautiful mountainside. It didn't take long for her to make one tiny error and suffer a painful slice to the arm, rapidly leading to two more slices and a fatal stab to the chest—which didn't hurt at all.

To prevent mental trauma, any killing blow came with cartoonish video game sound effects.

Kirsten reappeared at the bottom of the mountain and sighed at the jian in her grip. "I'm never going to get past those two. Do I really need to do this again?"

"Of course you don't *need* to." Gabriel's chuckle rolled overhead like thunder.

She squeezed the sword's grip. "Okay. I'm just frustrated. Not gonna give up."

"Hang on. Let me modify the sim a little."

Kirsten shook her head. "I've been stuck on this same fight for five sessions. It's not going to help me learn if I cheat."

He remained quiet for a moment.

A little Chinese girl in a fancy pink-and-red gown appeared at the curve in the trail ahead, fleeing from two men chasing her. Upon spotting Kirsten, she shouted, "Help!"

Another man sprang out of the weeds, grabbed the girl off her feet, and sprinted up the path, carrying her.

"Not going to cheat," said Gabriel. "Merely give you a little motivation."

She closed her eyes. "Is the kid really necessary? This isn't funny."

"Not meant to be."

"Help!" shouted the distant child.

One thing about a virtual course, she didn't genuinely tire from all the fighting, so didn't need to take a rest break. She did, however, stand there for a moment listening to the child voice repeat her call for help every twenty seconds or so, trying to convince herself a genuine little girl had been kidnapped by an evil warlord. It didn't take too much for her to get into it. The Monwyn games had a few 'save the child' side quests, and she'd become entirely engrossed in the story there. Granted, those had been way more immersive, as she'd often run several quests for the family prior to something happening. Gabriel just kinda threw this kid in here. Having a bandit literally jump out of a bush and grab some kid before running 'off-screen' like something from a 350-year-old side-scrolling video game had been so silly it made her want to laugh more than help.

Deep breaths. There's a kid in trouble.

She opened her eyes and marched forward.

With each nameless thug she sliced down, she thought her way deeper and deeper into the false reality, making up a storyline to go along with it. The girl was the daughter of a beloved king, kidnapped by the man's sociopathic younger brother who wanted to take the throne. This sim didn't have any real story, merely a bunch of fights for training purposes... but making stuff up helped from a motivation standpoint.

Having done the scenario now six times, the first two small clearing 'bosses' went down easy. She stormed up the next section of path, crossing swords with an opponent every thirty meters, though no fights lasted more than seven seconds. All the while, the kidnapped princess shouted for help—as if Kirsten might forget she existed if she didn't keep yelling.

Focused on the need to rescue the girl, Kirsten fell into a rhythm with the swordplay, seizing openings she'd have passed on before, attacking more aggressively.

In a mere twenty minutes, she found herself at the edge of the sixth clearing again. From there, she looked up the straight incline at the palace. A red-and-gold octagonal 'birdcage' with decorative Chinese woodwork hung from a chain at the rear of the structure, behind the warlord. The princess sat inside it, gripping the bars.

She appeared far too calm, but then again, hadn't been programmed to be a kidnap victim.

Kirsten looked away from the girl and thought about Seneschal the abyssal threatening Evan. The simulated 'ninja' became abyssals in her head, the girl in the birdcage a stand-in for her son. She charged into the sixth clearing, darting left as she had the past three times, and parrying Blue's overhead chop. Green spun around to come at her from behind the wall; however, instead of running past the wall into his attack, she pushed through the block, yanking her jian down and slicing Blue's thigh. She caught his wrist in her left hand, finishing him with a thrust to the chest before Green could finish coming around the wall. The ancient stone barrier had given her a precious three seconds of one-on-one.

Undeterred by the death of his companion, Green rushed in,

slashing at her neck. Kirsten blocked, maneuvering to counterattack, but ended up thrusting down left to parry a rapid reversal strike. They crossed swords four times in three seconds, blinding glints of sunlight flashing from the steel. Green scraped his jian off hers, dropping into a spinning low slash at shin height.

Kirsten jumped the blade while thrusting hers down into his chest —killing him.

Slightly winded, she faced the path up to the 'palace.'

"Help!" shouted the princess. "I can't get out."

Both dead guys faded away.

After a few seconds of staring at the warlord, imagining him to be Seneschal, Kirsten ran up the trail. The warlord drew a jian from his belt scabbard, waiting for her to enter the 'arena' inside the red wall. Kirsten charged straight at him, taking the first swing as soon as she got close enough.

He parried in a smooth, clean motion, setting up for a counterattack he had to abort due to the speed with which she recovered. Her downward chop stalled against his blade, inches from his face. He emitted a low grunt, shoving her backward off her feet. Kirsten rolled left, avoiding a stab he sank into the dojo floor. He wrenched the sword out and stabbed at her again, forcing her to keep rolling while he stabbed the floor again and again—until she got the idea to kick his leg out from under him.

The warlord and Kirsten scrambled to their feet at the same time. She feinted a strike, but he didn't fully fall for it, so she didn't risk attacking. He teased a few fake high thrusts, then committed to a low slash. Kirsten parried, tried to force her way past his defense, and ended up on her butt again, due to a major disadvantage in physical strength.

Roaring, he lunged, grabbing his jian in both hands for a powerful overhead cleave.

She leapt between his legs to dodge, landing flat on the ground behind him as his blade sank into the woven mat. Kirsten scrambled around onto her knees fast enough to slice the inside of his leg before he could turn. She ducked his imbalanced retaliatory slash, then sprang to her feet, thrusting the blade up into his chin—out the top of his head.

The warlord fell over, dead.

"You saved me!" said the girl. Her cage popped open all by itself— and the world faded out to pure white light.

12

INTENTIONAL MALFUNCTION

The horrible glare dimmed to the ceiling of the virtual training center ceiling lights.

Kirsten scooted forward, pulling her head out of the giant interface machine—basically a 3,500-pound senshelmet. The military tech came close to the same realism possible by a direct brain connection via M3 interface jack. So deep, in fact, if someone pulled their head out of the bowl at the top of the bed before the sim disconnected them, they could suffer almost the same effect as an M3 plug being yanked out—basically a bad seizure with vomiting, severe headache, and a decent chance of brain damage.

Of course, no one told her this until she'd already used one more than a dozen times.

She now understood why the beds had straps. Unlike an M3 jack, these units didn't block communication between the brain and real body. Someone doing acrobatic maneuvers in the sim had a roughly ten percent chance to sit up or roll around in the real world and break connection.

Gabriel walked over and undid the Velcro bands holding her legs while she wriggled her arms loose. It didn't take much effort to get out as the safety straps were designed to stop accidental motions, not keep people prisoner.

"You *had* to throw a child into it?" She grumbled, only half pretending to be annoyed. "Feels like you're exploiting a psychological weakness."

"Don't think about it as exploiting. People who are fighting for *something* always have an advantage over those who have less or nothing to lose." He gestured at the ceiling. "You remember the basic tactical course in the academy, right? People fighting to defend their homeland routinely outperformed invading armies or mercenaries, even when the invaders had the advantage of better training and better equipment."

"Yeah... I know." She sat up, grabbing her face in both hands. "Still messes with me how I feel tired after these courses. And I'm sweating for real."

"Well, you were twitching a lot on the last fight." He smiled. "Nice job by the way."

"You nerfed them, didn't you?"

He held up both hands. "Swear. Only thing I did was drop in Royal_Child_Female_118 and slap together a few lines of script. It looked like you were holding back. Just needed a bit of motivation."

"I don't think I'll ever end up in a sword fight against living people." She spun sideways, letting her feet dangle. "The simulation is so realistic it felt *wrong* to kill them."

"Ya never know." He winked. "The crazy stuff you deal with, you might just end up invading an ancient Chinese palace someday."

Kirsten rolled her eyes. "Yeah, sure."

"Heh. Don't be so quick to dismiss the idea. Not many people have the nerve to jump off the eleventh floor."

"Don't remind me. And the guy had like *ten* hand grenades on his chest. I'm still not even sure why I jumped. Falling to my death would've taken longer than blowing up. Didn't even think, just leapt. Only survived due to a luckily timed advert bot going by." *And maybe a little help from a Seraph.*

"That's how you stay alive in a sword fight. Or a hand-to-hand fight. Don't waste time thinking too much. It will all start to feel natural and instinctive before you know it. Looked like you were almost there in the last two matches."

"Maybe. I kinda psyched myself up a bit too much. Knowing this is a sim has me thinking of it like a video game. In a real situation, I'll have all the motivation I need."

He smiled. "Yes, knowing you can't get back up after death to try again is great incentive not to let them stab you."

"Sure is. Okay… shower time." She plucked at her sweaty blue jumpsuit.

"All right," said Gabriel. "Nice run. See you in a few days and we'll throw some more time at jiu jitsu."

She hopped off the bed. "I can hardly wait."

"Don't sound so excited." He winked at her before walking off.

Despite being in love with Sam—and Gabriel having a wife—she watched him for a few seconds. Admiring beauty hurt no one. Gabriel Silva had the physique of a Greek god. Well, maybe a minor one. Geeball players often turned themselves into monstrous piles of muscle, but her trainer hadn't taken it anywhere near as far. She also kinda liked long hair on a guy. Made him look like a warrior or something from the Monwyn world.

Kirsten headed out of the simulation room to the locker/shower area midway down the next hall where she'd stashed her uniform and gear. Two other women and three men stood by lockers, stripping in preparation to shower. Two people used shower tubes, another six by the benches in the middle of the room changed between Division 1 uniforms and training room jumpsuits.

No one paid much attention to her beyond a casual glance, acknowledging her existence. She kicked off the thin sneakers, stripped the jumpsuit off and stuffed it into the laundry chute before hopping in an available shower tube. Warm soapy water hit her like a full-body muscle massage. Despite her actual body being Velcro-strapped to a bed the entire time, the simulation's extreme realism made her feel as if she'd hiked up the mountain six times. A few scrapes on her knuckles and shins where she'd hit the ground still hurt, even though her skin hadn't been damaged in the real world.

A second after the autoshower switched to rinse mode, a holographic woman in a Division 2 dress uniform appeared standing outside the tube. The vacantly happy expression made no secret of her being a dispatch doll.

"Lieutenant Wren, 21-49 in progress. Your presence is requested immediately."

Kirsten shouted, "Shit!" and mashed the emergency-stop button. Code 21-49 meant a ghostly manifestation presenting an imminent threat to life. A non-psionic saw a ghost, knew it to be a ghost, and the spirit tried to or had killed someone. Dripping wet, she rushed to her locker and scrambled into her underwear, uniform pants, and top as fast as she could move.

Carrying her utility belt, arm guard, and boots, she ran down the hall to the elevator. Knowing it wouldn't give her enough time to put anything more on—only going down one floor—she didn't bother trying. The instant the doors snapped open, she sprinted out of the Division 1 wing into the common area, crossing to the Division 0 wing, heading straight to motor pool.

Dorian already had their patrol craft online, having pulled it up right to the door into the garage, her door open and waiting.

She jumped in, tossed her stuff on the passenger seat, then yanked the door down while simultaneously accelerating. Dorian activated the emergency lights and transponder. The gull door sealed, emitting a faint pneumatic hiss. She activated hover mode before reaching the ramp out. The gate opened in response to the car being 'Code 3,' allowing her to hit 160 MPH still inside the garage.

Once she leveled off at 700 feet, ten stories above civilian hovercar traffic, she lined the car up with the direction indicator pointing to Sector 3181, then let go of the sticks. "Dorian, take it for a bit."

He disappeared.

Kirsten pulled her boots on, smacked all the fasteners closed, attached her belt, then clamped the armored bracer around her left forearm. The screen popped up indicating a missed emergency notification as well as two calls from Captain Eze. According to the active dispatch details displaying on a mini terminal next to the Navcon, she headed to an Ancora Medical facility.

"Oh, no," said Kirsten. "Comm, Captain Eze."

The captain's holographic head appeared over the middle of the console. "Wren... I see you're already on the way. What happened? You didn't answer earlier."

"Was in the shower after sim training."

"Ahh." He nodded once. "I should have guessed due to your wet hair."

His mentioning it made the water soaking into the back of her uniform shirt colder. "Did you try to call me about this dispatch or something else?"

"The dispatch. They escalated it as a 21-49 and you weren't responding to a page."

She relaxed a little. At least she didn't have *two* problems to deal with. "I'm on the way to Ancora. What happened?"

Captain Eze heaved an inaudible sigh. "A PR rep from Ancora contacted us, requesting assistance. She didn't provide many details beyond saying a patient has been killed and her people are blaming a ghost. The woman made it abundantly clear she thinks they're insane, but the entire surgical team—including a doctor—had the same story."

"Wait, killed?" Kirsten's heart sank into her gut.

"Unfortunately." Captain Eze bowed his head. "Miss Ishikawa didn't hesitate in conveying her complete skepticism."

Kirsten frowned. "So why she'd call us? Not like they have to cover their backside legally. No one takes ghosts to court."

"Won't stop someone from *attempting* to sue them."

She grumbled. "I'm three minutes out."

"All right. Stay safe, Kirsten."

"Thanks. I will try." She exhaled out her nose.

He only used her first name when worried about her. Most likely, his overprotective side came out. 21-49 calls were highly rare, but she'd dealt with multiple paranormal entities capable of killing people before. As long as she didn't find an abyssal at the med center, she should be okay.

KIRSTEN DOVE THE PATROL CRAFT IN HOT, KICKING UP A HUGE BLAST OF cryonic fog and ion sparks.

As if expecting her to ram the giant hovercar straight through the doors of the emergency entrance on the roof, people scrambled for cover. She decelerated hard, stopping to a hover five feet away from the door, sliding sideways to land on the sidewalk so she didn't block arriving MedVans. Dorian shut down the drive system as she leapt out, then followed her, not bothering to run around people. Shivering visitors, patients, and one orderly in their wake, shrieked as if doused with ice water as he phased through them.

A head-sized floating orb bot zoomed over to her, a prim-and-proper voice calling out, "Excuse me? Are you the police sent here about the unexplained event?"

She wanted to ignore the bot but facing a sea of clueless faces and the urgency of a killer ghost, she forced herself to stop. "Yes. Where is the ghost?"

"I am unable to comment on the location of any unexplained phenomena. However, I am here to escort you to the scene where numerous staff members have indicated they observed one."

She fought the urge to yell at the bot, merely thrusting her arm forward. "Lead the way. Is it true a patient is dead?"

"As a non-sentient artificial intelligence assistance unit, I am unable to comment due to issues of patient confidentiality. The medical technicians in the procedure room we are going to will be able to provide this information."

"This is why we have so many gangs." Dorian waved dismissively at the bot. "Each one of those machines is someone out of a job."

Kirsten decided not to start a political debate with him in the middle of a 21-49 scene, jogging after the flying ball in silence. It led them down a series of hallways to an elevator, then another series of hallways plus two security checkpoints it breezed by without engaging the security staff.

At long last, the bot entered an incredibly long, shiny white corridor. Forty doors, twenty per side in a staggered pattern, led to procedure rooms containing medical tanks and their associated computer systems. Padded benches lined the walls between the doors, all empty. The scenery reminded her of the hall where she sat waiting for Brooke while the medics tried to detox the Lace out of the eleven-year-old. Up to forty people could be floating in breathable gel, with only a few ones and zeroes standing between life and death. It didn't take much energy for a ghost to drain power from nanobots. Even a relatively young spirit could easily kill someone undergoing a precarious enough surgery.

Shit. If there's a killer ghost down here...

The relative lack of chaos came as both a relief and a shock. On one hand, the quiet meant the spirit didn't continue on a rampage. Unfortunately, it also offered her little clue where to go—and seemed altogether wrong in the wake of a death.

"Almost there, officer," said the bot.

She didn't feel like arguing over her rank with a robot, so ignored it. To most civilians, every member of the NPF was 'officer.'

It stopped at the seventh room on the left. "Here we are. Feel free to go inside."

As if I'd wait. She waved her armband at the ID reader, invoking a police override. The door slid to the right, emitting a soft whirr. All the chaos she didn't see in the corridor went on inside the room. Two women in white jumpsuits argued over the idea of ghosts being real. Another woman and two men in light grey jumpsuits went around examining display terminals as well as the insides of three refrigerator-sized computer cabinets.

Strong residual spirit energy hung in the air, though the room contained no ghosts other than Dorian. She reached out with her mental feelers, sensing a handful of distant spirits elsewhere in the hospital, though none matched the energy in this room. Much like how dogs could identify individuals via their noses, different spirits' energy *felt* unique.

No real surprise a hospital had a handful of resident ghosts.

The most prominent source of paranormal energy came from the medical tank at the far end of the room. A clear cylinder three times the width of an autoshower spanned between a pair of thick metal platforms, one on the ceiling and one on the floor. Within the peach-hued gel floated the nude body of a Hispanic man, his abdomen open, intestines unfurled into the fluid. Except for being dead, he appeared reasonably young—late thirties perhaps—and in good condition, meaning not like an off-gridder or fringer who spent years away from medical care or good hygiene practices.

Beside the med tank, a black woman in a blue Division 2 jumpsuit crouched over a portable terminal connected by wire to the tank's platform base. The sight of a crime scene technician already here shocked Kirsten into staring for a few seconds in disbelief. For her to be here already must mean Division 0 never received a call until well after Mr. Mendoza died. Someone— probably a brand-new Admin cadet—punched in the wrong code or got confused when told a person had died. 21-49 meant an *active* scene where a ghost was about to kill someone or had killed and still rampaged. *This* scene was more of a 21-60, an observed spirit manifestation where someone died, but the ghost had already left the area.

Dorian approached the tank, tracing his fingers over the clear cylinder at heart-level to the dead occupant.

"Tech?" asked Kirsten, approaching the tank.

The Division 2 tech peered up from the holographic screen, went wide-eyed at the sight of her, and sprang to her feet, saluting. "Lieutenant."

Kirsten returned the salute, eyeing the woman's nameplate, which read Kelly, T. beside the rank logo for Tech First Class, an E5. "No need for excessive formality at a crime scene. Can you tell me what's going on here? They said we had an active spirit manifestation likely to cause harm."

"I'm glad you're here, lieutenant." Tech Kelly exhaled hard. "Psionic stuff freaks me out. I can concentrate again with you here."

Dorian raised an eyebrow at her. "She's afraid of you but calmed by your presence?"

"Have you found anything yet?" Kirsten set her hands on her hips, failing to hide all the annoyance in her tone.

"Oh! Sorry. I didn't mean it like that." Tech Kelly waved rapidly in a 'no no no' sort of way. "I get just as rattled when there's a bad guy running around with a gun and I don't have one. Psionics are cool, just not when people use 'em bad. When the other two Zeroes were here, I didn't have to worry whatever did this might come back.'

"Other ones?" Kirsten blinked.

"Yeah. You're the third Zero here. Initially, Ancora thought they were hacked. After my team couldn't determine what happened to the machines, we figured it had to be a psionic messing with the computers. You guys sent a pair of Tactical officers first. One just kinda stood there looking useless while her partner walked around touching all the machines. He said he felt 'weird energy' in the air but couldn't tell what made the machines freak out. He didn't think a psionic person did it, but he did keep insisting this room 'felt weird,' like a haunted place. When he started talking about spooky stuff, the medical techs and doctors mentioned seeing a ghost appear."

She exhaled. "Right. So, they sent for me."

"How come?" asked Tech Kelly.

"I'm an astral. Everything no one else can explain ends up on my desk." Kirsten read over the Inquest file on her armband's holo-panel. It had no record of any other Division 0 on site. *Guess Tactical made a separate Inquest, or maybe the dispatcher screwed up and started a new one instead of tagging me in the existing one. Dammit!* Her stomach sank at the thought Mr. Mendoza had been dead before she even heard about this incident. The 21-49 code kicked her straight in the adrenal glands, making her worry she had to haul serious ass to stop a pissed off spirit from killing someone.

"What exactly happened here?" Kirsten looked around at everyone.

"Sorry, lieutenant." Tech Kelly pointed at her terminal. "The deceased was undergoing routine surgery to remove several tumors from his lower intestine. For reasons we haven't been able to determine, the nanobots went crazy and ate millions of holes in him. Can't see them without magnification, but he's a sponge. All of his blood leaked out into the b-gel. Heart couldn't pump anything because of the damage. Multiple organ failure. Nerve damage. Brain damage."

The female medtech approached, no trace of fear in her at all. A few strands of her blonde hair escaped the sanitary bonnet, proof it had been quite crazy in here. "I saw the ghost. So did Dr. Nash."

One of the women in white jumpsuits, the one with grey hair, nodded.

Kirsten peered up at the medtech's emerald green eyes. At five foot even, she'd long ago accepted going through life looking up at people, but *women* didn't usually make her feel so tiny. This one even had an inch or so of height on Dorian. "Do you mind if I peek at your memory of it?"

"Go right ahead." The tech, Michaela Skye according to her badge, smiled. "I know the drill. The other guy already did it."

Dorian moved on from the tank, checking around the large electronics cabinets.

Grr. Should be in the Inquest already. They didn't even link it. Kirsten smiled, then established telepathic contact with Michaela.

The woman's memories showed her standing by a console, monitoring the performance of 'nanobot squads' attacking three tumors within Mr. Mendoza's large intestine. The doctors manually controlled other nanobots removing more delicate fibrous extensions of the tumor tissue where it had migrated into the liver. Since she'd already uploaded the procedure to the system, Michaela mostly stood there watching in case something went wrong.

A sudden sense of dread came out of nowhere, making Michaela feel as though she'd die if she didn't run out of the room right away. She started to take a step but couldn't bring herself to leave a patient. Despite shaking, she gripped the side of her terminal and held on, refusing to run. Jake, one of the other techs, screamed and fainted.

Soon after, the overpowering fear abated, and she caught a flicker of light in the corner of her eye. Michaela glanced away from her large holo-panel toward the tank, at a fist-sized light orb hovering roughly where Dorian had touched earlier.

What the heck is that? whispered Michaela's voice in her mind.

She worried a severe electrical problem in the machinery had released ball lightning. However, before Michaela could call attention to the orb, it flickered into the form of a transparent, somewhat muscular man. From behind, she couldn't really guess his age, but the grungy dark yellow jacket and pants gave off a construction worker vibe.

"Hey!" shouted Michaela. "Who are you?"

The grey-haired woman—the only doctor in the room at the time —plus the other two medtechs all looked over, noticed the spirit, and jumped away in shock. Various alarms went off on the terminals, flooding the room in red light. Though the spirit hadn't appeared to have done anything, the medical tank systems went haywire.

Michaela looked back at her terminal, noting readouts showing the nanobots haphazardly perforating biomatter at random, drilling holes and destroying tissue without regard for where. The terminal disregarded her attempts to shut them down, throwing connection errors or 'command not recognized' errors for several seconds before simply dying to a black screen.

The doctor shouted about the 'red button' not working.

More alarms went off as Mr. Mendoza's heart stopped

Michaela stared transfixed at the spirit. Another, much smaller light orb shot out of the tank, zooming into the wall. The ghost collapsed back into a glowing orb before zooming straight down into the floor.

Kirsten released her telepathic link. "Wow. This one's been around a while. Tech Kelly, please send me any video feeds of this room during the event." She tapped at her armband terminal, entering notes on the Inquest file.

The woman nodded. "Will do, lieutenant."

"What do you mean by 'been around a while'?" asked Michaela.

"You saw him appear in front of the tank as a transparent apparition. I'm not entirely sure why he bothered to manifest at all, but a spirit capable of being seen by normal people so clearly is fairly powerful."

Tech Kelly stood and walked up to her. "Lieutenant, I've run multiple diagnostic tests on the system. Overloaded capacitors, broken connections, and some dead sub-boards. None of the damage would have caused the nanobots to malfunction. It's commensurate with a power surge. The logs are full of error messages indicating the nanobots failed to respond to control input, right up until the whole thing fried. At first, we thought it might have been the work of a hacker, but Ancora is surprisingly intelligent—all the tanks are on a closed system. None of these systems involved in nanosurgery have direct access to the GlobeNet."

"They did it to avoid lawsuits," muttered Dorian. "There is ghost all over this machinery."

Kirsten glanced at him. "I'm assuming you mean metaphorically and a spirit didn't explode."

"Yeah." Dorian gestured at the big computers. "Feels like he blew them out intentionally. Pure damage. Not trying to use the computers to get to the nanobots."

"He wanted to stop the medical team from saving the guy." Kirsten rubbed the bridge of her nose, angry at circumstance because she hadn't gotten here in time to save him.

"I know that face." Dorian patted her shoulder, his touch manifesting as a chilly spot. "You're wondering who tagged this as a 21-49."

"Yep." She let her arm fall to her side and looked at the doctors. "Have you already given statements to the other Division 0 officers?"

The grey-haired doctor, Vivian Nash according to her badge, nodded. "Yes. I spoke to them already. Don't your people keep notes?"

"Of course we do." She forced a smile. "I'm on the investigation side, the tactical team has a separate report. Due to a minor miscommunication, they sent me in on an emergency call as if the spirit was still running around attacking people. Didn't have time to read on the way here."

Dr. Nash's expression softened. "I see. Do you need me to go over it all again?"

"No, doctor. If the other team already interviewed you, it won't be necessary." She glanced at the other doctor.

"Dr. Kumar wasn't here during the event," said Dr. Nash. "She's been trying to convince me I hallucinated the spirit."

"I'm sure she thinks she saw something." Dr. Kumar smiled. "Probably a trick of light created by the equipment shorting out or perhaps a psionic projecting an illusion into her mind."

"All right." Kirsten glanced over at the medtechs. "I'm not here to change what anyone believes about supernatural phenomenon. The evidence here is enough for me to conclude a spiritual presence caused this malfunction and death."

"Hah." Dr. Nash pointed at Dr. Kumar. "Told you."

Dorian walked in through the wall. "No signs of other tampering in the area, or the suspect ghost."

"Were the adjacent rooms in use at the time of the attack?" asked Kirsten.

"One moment." Dr. Nash took a NetMini from her pocket, tapped at the screen for a moment, then pointed at the wall. "Yes. To the right. They reported no issues."

Kirsten sighed hard, tapping her foot. "A spirit targets this patient specifically, kills him, and leaves right after."

"Sounds like revenge to me. Or an assassination." Dorian gestured a thumb at the corpse. "I'd have asked the guy who'd want him dead, but he isn't around."

Doesn't feel like Harbingers showed up here. "Maybe he chased the killer, wandered off, or transcended right away."

"Pardon?" asked Dr. Nash.

"Sorry. I was talking to my partner." She smiled. "Would you mind sharing whatever information you have on the deceased?"

"Your partner's not with you?" Dr. Kumar tilted her head.

Dorian turned partially transparent, indicating he'd manifested. "I'm right here, doctor."

Dr. Kumar's face paled.

Kirsten smirked at him. *So much for being the smiling face of psionics. We're not supposed to shatter people's worldview.* She caught herself about to chuckle at the doctor's shocked expression and looked at the dead man to stop herself. "What is the official cause of death? Electrocution?"

"No." Dr. Nash poked a few buttons on her NetMini's holo-panel, sending Mr. Mendoza's PID over. "The electrical surges didn't reach the breathable gel. Mr. Mendoza experienced multiple organ failure and severe, rapid blood loss due to millions of micro-perforations all throughout his body. His central nervous system suffered extensive physical damage from the nanobots as well."

The ghost made the nanobots tear him apart from the inside out. She squirmed at the thought. *Poor guy. Hope he didn't feel it.* "Thank you, doctor."

Her armband beeped the alert tone.

"Lieutenant Wren," said the voice of a younger girl. "There's a 21-49 in progress! One dead, at least two people in immediate danger, including a child."

Kirsten wanted to scream 'are you sure it's a 21-49 this time,' but settled for simply yelling "Shit!"

Everyone stared at her.

"Gotta go." She pointed at Tech Kelly. "Please gather the contact information for everyone in here at the time of the event and send it to me."

Before the tech could answer, Kirsten raced out of the room.

CODE 21-49

K irsten screamed in her mind out of frustration—for not having the ability to teleport.

It didn't matter teleportation only existed in video games. Not being able to instantly arrive at the place where a ghost—theoretically—threatened lives, drove her to the edge. Somehow, despite the overwhelming urgency ruling her brain, she managed to remember the way back to the hospital entrance without making an error.

She jumped into the patrol craft and executed an emergency liftoff procedure.

The car shot straight up as if by rocket engines, people nearby stumbling toward it from the rapid updraft. Dorian phased through the door an instant before she accelerated as hard as possible. Her body squished into the seat. The patrol craft went from a hovering standstill to a hair under 600 MPH in seven seconds. Considering its size and the weight of its armor, capability to hit such speeds—much less accelerate so fast—often drew shocked gasps from civilians.

Sport model hovercars could go supersonic, though doing so inside the city would usually cause someone to lose their license, have the car confiscated, and could include a minor prison sentence. It didn't matter the police patrol craft couldn't catch them; the city had enough transponders to identify the car and driver. The police merely found them after they landed.

In the moment, however, Kirsten would have sacrificed the armor to push the speed up past Mach 1.

"Dispatch," yelled Kirsten. "Talk to me. What's the situation?"

The head of a maybe-thirteen-year-old girl in an Admin cadet uniform appeared in hologram over the middle of the console. "We received contact from a Suri linked to the NetMini registered to a woman named Johanna Beck. It said a ghost invaded their home, tried to kill the woman's eleven-year-old daughter, and probably killed a repair technician. According to the Suri, electromagnetic fluctuations are still going on at the address."

"Dammit!" yelled Kirsten.

The hologram girl shrank back.

"Sorry. Not you. General frustration." She flattened out of the climb at 1,800 feet, well above even the highest buildings in West City so she could fly in a straight line directly at the waypoint. "If you've got the Suri on the line still, what's the current status?"

"Standby." The girl looked to the side. "Suri, what's going on now? Are Mrs. Beck and her daughter okay?"

Kirsten shifted her gaze down from the holographic teen to the Navcon. The waypoint led to Sector 2655, a 'theme' development of residential housing where single-family homes existed in a recreation of pre-Corporate-War suburbia. Unfortunately, a single family occupying the land footprint equal to a hundred vertically stacked apartments ended up making those houses prohibitively expensive in a city trying to cram as many people into as small an area as possible. People who could afford them didn't want to live there because the homes were too 'common.' Though a handful of people at the upper end of middle class opted to live there, many of the houses sat empty, due to the financing companies taking so long to start lowering the prices for some reason. They'd become more affordable, but anyone living here would *not* be hurting for money.

The thought of Henry Motte, the old ghost who lived in a similar neighborhood, brought a tear to her eye. The old guy had been nice. She felt horrible for having to send his son off with a Harbinger… but Albert killed people. At least he showed some remorse at the end and went willingly, unlike every other spirit she'd ever seen a Harbinger take.

Wonder what happens to spirits like him?

"Lieutenant?" asked the teen from Dispatch. "Suri says she has no idea about the daughter, Tamsen, since the child is upstairs. Mrs. Beck is unconscious on the floor next to the NetMini in the downstairs living room. Suri called us on her own. She also hears two men talking at the back end of the house."

"Understood. Let the Suri know I'll be there in about three minutes." Kirsten shifted her jaw side to side. *Weird hearing a girl her age refer to 'the child' upstairs.*

"Copy, lieutenant. I'm monitoring your ID for this incident. Dedicated mode."

Wow. This kid's on point. Better than the older boy. "Thanks, umm…"

"Rosana Najafi, lieutenant."

Kirsten nodded once at the hologram. "Thanks, Rosana. Glad to have you over my shoulder."

The girl grinned, saluted, and vanished.

"They get younger every call." Dorian shook his head. "The mix up with the 21-49 at the Ancora facility is the exact reason they need to train dispatchers *before* they take calls. Not *while* they're taking calls. And good grief, let them grow up first."

Kirsten exhaled. "For the most part, I agree. But Rosana's like a prodigy or something."

"Until she sees something so horrible she ends up hiding under her bed for months."

"She's not an astral." Kirsten squeezed the control sticks so hard her hands hurt, trying to force the patrol craft to fly faster from sheer desire. "And psionic crimes tend not to be too disturbing visually."

"Pyrokinetics on a bender can get pretty messy." Dorian glanced over, one eyebrow up.

"Fair point."

TWO MINUTES AND THIRTY-NINE SECONDS LATER, THE 'SUBURBAN' district came into view.

A two-sector area, ten miles north-south, five miles wide, resembled a pit surrounded by hundred-story residence towers. From 1,800 feet in the air, it looked like a scale model a high school student might make for a history project on pre-war living. The sprawling development contained hundreds of freestanding houses, each with a backyard, attached garage, and front lawn.

As a child living in the Beneath, Kirsten saw lots of similar houses, only they'd been abandoned for centuries. Back then, she'd wondered what the world would've looked like before the metal plates covered everything. Flying to this place full of rare greenery amounted to walking into her daydreams.

Alas, she couldn't spare more than a few seconds of wandering thought.

The waypoint led her to a beige house on a street lined with similar houses, each one slightly different in design but functionally identical. A white hover van sat in the driveway behind a Halcyon-Ormyr Puma, a small black hovercar in the 'sporty luxury' category.

Disregarding anything but the need to get inside the house as fast as possible, Kirsten landed on the front lawn, throwing up a spray of grass, dirt, and shredded flowers. At the sight of the front door already open, Dorian blurred past her, racing into the house before she even shut the drive system down.

Kirsten shoved the door out of her way, ran a few steps, then jumped the three porch stairs, summoning the lash on the way into the living room.

A woman lay on the floor behind a large sectional couch, long light brown hair splayed on the rug. She bled from a cut above her left eye, but otherwise had no visible injuries.

"Hello, lieutenant," said Suri from the NetMini on the floor a short distance from the woman's right hand. "Thank you for helping my family."

"Is the ghost still here?" Kirsten crouched, checking the woman's vitals. The rudimentary medical scanner in her armguard didn't sound any alarms, so she calmed, considering Johanna Beck unconscious but in no immediate danger.

"I am still detecting electromagnetic disturbances," said Suri.

Straight ahead, an archway led from the living room to a dining room. Another doorway at the far side of the dining room opened to a darkened space with hints of furniture visible. Whispery voices grunted and shouted as though someone watched a martial arts holovid with the volume almost off.

Dorian's on him.

Kirsten sprang upright, about to run toward the spectral brawl—but stopped short at a child's voice wailing from the top of a staircase at the right side of the living room. Though the scream had a strange, distorted quality, "someone help me" came through loud and clear.

She couldn't risk a child's life to lessen the chances of a ghost escaping, so she diverted to the stairs, trusting Dorian to handle the specter. Continued screaming led her down the upstairs hallway to the third door on the right. Kirsten rushed over, raising her arm to lash the crap out of whatever spirit threatened a child—but stopped in stunned shock at the sight waiting for her.

A tween girl treaded water inside a flooded autoshower tube, only twelve inches of air at the top. She struggled to stay afloat, appearing exhausted and about to run out of energy.

Upon seeing Kirsten, the girl screamed, "Help! I can't get out!"

What the hell? I've never seen a tube fill up with water before... they're not supposed to be able to.

"Don't be afraid. This light can't hurt you." She swiped the lash at the autoshower just in case ghostly influence kept the girl inside, but it passed through with zero resistance.

"Ack!" yelled the girl. "What is that?"

Kirsten released the lash and hurried up to the tube. "A weapon that only hurts monsters. Tamsen?"

"Yeah. Please let me out of here. I've been stuck in here all day."

"*All day?*" Kirsten blinked. "Calm down a bit, okay? You don't need to thrash around. Just float. Maybe step on the handrail to keep your head up."

Tamsen fumbled around with her feet until she found the railing, then braced her hands against the tube walls. She didn't need to tread water at all to keep her face above the surface. She clung in place, long mouse brown hair fluffed out around her in the water, giving Kirsten a sorrowful, pleading stare.

The control screen, unaffected by the water due to being a hologram, displayed the Plasmahawk ransomware, only it demanded Ͼ200,000. Kirsten gawked. *Two hundred grand? What the f—oh... damn virus must demand a percentage or something.* It only asked for Ͼ5,000 from Kirsten. She could've paid it without feeling *too* much pain.

One look into the terrified girl's huge blue eyes tempted her to enlist Theodore's help in tracking down Plasmahawk. Maybe she would—after the present ghost craziness stopped.

Kirsten grabbed the handle, but the hatch refused to open. No surprise it had locked, thanks to the ransomware. Whirring pumps and the motion of the child's hair suggested the tube still tried to flood all the way, but it must have a failsafe drain preventing it from doing so.

"It won't open," said Tamsen. "I've been kicking the stupid hatch since six this morning."

"What?" Kirsten shook her head in disbelief. "You've been trapped in the shower tube for almost *nine hours?*" *I'm gonna slap her mother.*

"Yeah." Tamsen sniffled. "Mom leaves for work before I got up. The school called her when I didn't log in. She came home because I didn't answer my 'Mini. She tried getting me out but couldn't do it, so she called a repair guy. He never showed up. Mom started screaming like a half-hour ago. That's when the shower filled with water. I screamed, but Mom's ignoring me. What's going on? Why are the police here?"

Kirsten pressed a hand to the tube, opposite the girl's. "There's a dangerous ghost here. It's why the tube's flooded. I'm honestly not sure how it did that. I've never seen a shower fill up with water before."

"A ghost? Are you serious?" Tamsen pointed at the control screen. "It's some stupid hacker."

"A hacker locked you in, but the spirit made it flood. I can get you out of there, but I need my partner to do it. Can you hang on for a little while longer?"

Tamsen whined. "I dunno. It's so cold my legs are numb. And where's my mother?"

"Your mom is okay, but she passed out. She's not ignoring you."

The girl shivered. "Mom? She's hurt?"

"She'll be fine. I promise." Kirsten contemplated putting a hole in the autoshower with the E-90, but the laser would likely pass through without damaging the clear barrier.

"Am I locked in the shower with a bad guy in the house?"

"Just a ghost. Not a living bad guy."

Tamsen made a face half terrified, half calling her crazy.

Kirsten kicked the hatch, again contemplating using the laser pistol to take out the metal parts keeping it sealed. Sure, a few hundred gallons of water would flood the house, but the girl would be out—assuming the laser didn't reflect weird and hit her. She bit her lip, unwilling to chance it. "Hang on. I'll be right back."

"Hurry!" yelled Tamsen.

"I will."

Kirsten forced herself to leave the kid trapped in the bathroom and rushed downstairs. She leapt over the sectional rather than waste the three seconds to go around it, then darted down the hall toward the dark room. An annoyed man stood in the middle of a room containing various Monwyn and sci-fi props mounted on the wall, a giant holo-bar screen, and two computer desks, one full sized, one smaller covered in girly stuff.

The man gave off an obvious sense of being a spirit. An ordinary shirt and pants made him look like the sort of guy who spent most of his time sitting around at home watching holovids or logged into virtual reality games. Strong arms suggested he formerly worked a physical type job, though he had a bit of a belly, which backed up her assumption of a stationary home life.

He frowned at her. "Little late."

Kirsten summoned the lash. "Let Tamsen out of the tube, right now."

"Whoa." He blinked, raising his hands, staring at the scintillating bright energy cord. "You can see me?"

"Obviously." She narrowed her eyes. "Let her out."

The guy waved in a 'hold on' gesture, then pointed at the floor behind the larger desk. "Not me. I came here to open the damn shower."

Kirsten circled to the side, not fully trusting him despite the weakness of his presence—until she went far enough around the desk to see a corpse on the floor. Despite the dead body wearing a totally different outfit than the ghost—brown utility coveralls instead of casual clothes—she had no doubt the ghost belonged to the remains right in front of her. A patch on the breast of the coveralls bore the name Kenton Macy beneath 'TMC Onsite Repair.' *Shit. He's a victim.* It momentarily impressed her he'd been able to alter his latent self-image not to appear exactly as he'd been dressed when he died, but he likely hadn't done it on purpose. How his spirit appeared represented the truest sense of how he thought of himself.

She lowered the lash. "Sorry. Thought you were the other ghost."

"Nah. Some cop ran in and dragged the guy out the wall into the backyard."

Kirsten glanced at the back wall, above the smaller computer desk loaded with cute mini-dolls and little unicorn toys. Grunting and cursing like two men having a brawl came from the backyard, but again sounded much quieter than it ought to have.

"Craziest shit I've ever seen." Kenton raked a hand up over his head. "I get here to fix a stuck shower, right? Goin' absolutely freakin' nuts with this ransomware bullshit these past couple a days, right? Soon as I walk in the door, crap starts flying around the living room. The woman who requested the repair is running around in circles. Some kid upstairs is screaming her head off. I see a dude hiding in the back—this room—and he don't look like he belongs in here. So, I get in his face and he shoves his hand *into* my chest. Like the dude isn't even solid. Felt like he stabbed me with a damn giant icicle. Next thing I know, I'm standing here looking down at my dead ass body."

"Crap," muttered Kirsten.

Kenton smirked. "Little bit of an understatement."

"Yeah." *Shit.* She squeezed her fists tight. Spirits who could stop a living person's heart at a touch were the sort of spirits who often had a small conga line of Harbingers following them around waiting for the first chance to pounce.

"So, this guy was about to do the same thing he did to me to the woman out there, and probably attack the kid upstairs, too. No way could I take a dude that big, so I tried to keep his attention on me. Figure I'm already dead, right? What worse could he do ta me? I kept jumping in front of him, trying to get in his way. Mostly went right through him, but he eventually got pissed and started chasing me instead."

"Nice job. You probably saved both their lives. Wait here. I'll help you as much as I can once things settle down."

"Where am I gonna go?" Kenton flapped his arms in frustration.

She sighed at him. "I'm sorry."

A door to the right led to a tiny hallway with a bathroom and laundry room opposite each other, the end open to the kitchen. She hurried into the kitchen, hunting for a door out to the yard. She made it halfway across the room before catching a glimpse of motion behind her—a large figure raising a reassembler unit in both hands as if to bash it over her head.

She whirled around, slicing the lash at the spirit's chest.

Evidently not expecting her to see him, the big guy made no effort to dodge. The energy whip tore a gash across his ethereal substance, making his whole body flicker transparent for an instant. The momentary loss of solidity allowed the reassembler to drop straight through him to the floor. He stood there, bewildered, hands still up as if holding it.

Kirsten swallowed hard, more than a little intimidated by his appearance. The top of her head barely came up to the middle of his chest. Two of her together wouldn't be as wide as his shoulders. The man's shaved-bald head bristled with tiny cybernetic implants around the crown and clustered at his temples. His enormous, square jaw appeared to be entirely plastisteel—as did his teeth—both eyes mirror-silver orbs. He wore a voluminous black trench coat open, revealing numerous weapons, hints of an armored vest, and boots heavy enough to kick a dent in a cyborg's leg.

She froze in fear, her mind jumping back to the day mercenaries tried to kill her. This guy didn't look familiar personally, but he *had* to be a hired killer. Or *was* a hired killer at some point, the sort of paid enforcer who'd think nothing of drowning a tween girl in an autoshower tube to send a message to a rival corporation.

The spirit's confusion at being seen wore off at the same time Kirsten got over the shock of his appearance. Merely a spirit. Nothing she couldn't handle. Even if the dude had been alive, Suggestion or Mind Blast didn't care how big or augmented someone was. In fact, the more electronics crammed into a brain, the better for her. The further from human a person became, the less defenses they had against psionic attacks.

He pulled a giant handgun out from under his coat.

Kirsten snapped the energy whip at him again, the cord reacting more to her desire than the physical motion of her arm. It swiped through his arm and shoulder, deflecting the 'shot' off to the side, a glob of spirit energy zooming harmlessly into the wall. The appearance of a ghost's attack meant little insofar as power went, merely a representation of the spirit's former life and preference. Whether this guy shot her using a ridiculous hand cannon or punched her, it would have the same effect.

The older the spirit, the more it hurt.

He recoiled from the lash, twisting away to the right while thrusting his left hand at her chest. Kirsten 'caught' the incoming hand using her psionic power, holding him back. His massive physical strength meeting her astral power ended up being a roughly even contest, except for her body weight. The spirit pushed harder, shoving her in a standing slide across the kitchen until her back hit the fridge. With nowhere to go, the pressure on her mind increased. She snarled, refusing to let him freeze her heart to a stop. Glowing fingertips teased at the air less than an inch from the fabric of her uniform.

Dorian stumbled in through the wall, as disheveled as if he'd been run over by a PubTran bus, his expression radiating a sense of 'oh, F this guy.' He raised an E-86 handgun and fired. Rather than the green laser it should have made, it launched a small white bolt of spectral force into the assassin's back.

The big man grunted. Spots of neon green light appeared at the core of his mirrored eyes, intensifying as he pushed against Kirsten's power. Instinctively, she kicked at him, but may as well have attempted to punt a hologram. Making herself solid to spirits would definitely backfire on her when dealing with a man this size. To have any chance at a contest of strength, she had to rely only on her mind.

"I really don't like this guy," said Dorian, firing again and again into the spirit's back.

"Who sent you here?" yelled Kirsten. "Why this house?"

The assassin pushed harder, lifting Kirsten off her feet; she slid up the fridge, knocking magnets to the floor.

Thinking of Tamsen stuck in the tube upstairs gave Kirsten a burst of desperation. She mentally shoved at the ghost, knocking him back a step, and dropped to her feet again. He stopped reaching for her, grabbed a kitchen chair, and swung it. Kirsten dove to the floor; the chair smashed into the fridge, denting it.

"Die..." rasped the assassin, in a voice too deep to have ever been human.

"Nah. I'll pass." She swiped the lash at him, raking it across his legs at knee level.

He staggered to the side, waving his arms for balance and moaning.

Dorian shot him once every four seconds, hitting every time but seemingly not bothering him much.

"Irritating," grumbled the assassin. He spun blurry fast, driving his fist into Dorian's face.

Kirsten screamed in anger at the sight of her partner's head distorting into a four-foot smear of vaguely Dorian-shaped ectoplasm. The rest of him followed it, flying into the wall out of the room. She slashed the energy whip down the assassin's back again, burning a two-inch deep trench from shoulder to ass. Ghostly essence wafted into the air like smoke.

The spirit, his expression manic, lunged at her.

Kirsten ducked the huge fist flying for her face, jumped back from the left cross, and scrambled out of the way of an attempted tackle. She rushed a hasty swipe of the lash across his side as he rounded on her again. The assassin drew his hand back. She jumped to the right to avoid the punch—stopping short with a scream when he grabbed her by a fistful of hair.

The assassin lifted her off her feet by her hair, swinging her up in an arc before walloping her face-first into the stove. Bright lights flashed in her vision on impact. He mushed her cheek into the smooth, glass cook surface. It took Kirsten half a second to realize what her face touched—and notice the heat building up.

Too much like Mother.

An eruption of fear and rage exploded inside her. She grabbed the front of the stove and shoved, jerking her head away from the cooking element before it could heat up enough to burn her. Mother only used it on her hands, never the face. Consumed by pain and wrath, Kirsten thrust the lash like a spear into the assassin's chest, impaling him, the cord as thick as her arm, nearly twice its usual width.

Wheezing, the spirit let go of her hair to grab at the wound—his fingers scorched as if he'd clutched a laser sword.

Roaring in anger, Kirsten yanked the lash out, swung it up behind her, and brought it down over his head. The strike split the spirit in half to the midpoint of his chest, leaving a disoriented, drunken expression on both parts of his face.

He wheezed, "What are you...?" and pulled himself together.

She swung the lash again, having gone well past any attempt to be gentle. While she still tried to find the good in every spirit, she doubted this one had any left to reach. At the same instant the lash struck the spirit's shoulder, a barrage of shiny silver kitchen knives flew at her.

A wide carving knife stuck in her left thigh, another in her right forearm. One bounced off her left forearm guard with a *clank*. A steak knife stuck into her left shoulder. Two went over her head, a third slicing her ear as it passed.

Shocked at the sudden pain, Kirsten looked down at herself, horrified at the sight of multiple metal handles sticking out of her. The assassin slugged her in the side of the head, launching her into the front of the stove. She bounced off and hit the floor, fires raging in her muscles from the angry knives.

The kitchen spun.

Kirsten pushed at the floor, struggling to move before the ghost finished her off.

He looked up at the ceiling, grinned, and walked out of the kitchen.

No! No damn way! Shaking from pain, Kirsten pushed herself up from the floor. Her left leg didn't want to cooperate. If she tried to bend her knee, it would collapse, so she kept the leg stiff and hobbled after the assassin. Dorian's pained moan came from the computer room.

As expected, the giant ghost walked toward the stairs. Leaving her alive long enough to know she failed to stop him from killing Tamsen would be his twist of the knife. She'd spend the rest of her ghostly existence carrying the guilt.

Kirsten refused to let him win. She refused to allow him to hurt an innocent. Faster and faster, she hobbled across the dining room, waving her arms to keep from falling over despite the knives sticking out of them. The assassin paused by Johanna Beck, peering down as if contemplating killing her, too. He glanced up, starting to laugh, but his mirth turned to fear the instant he realized she didn't lay helpless in the kitchen.

"You don't belong here," rasped Kirsten before swinging the lash with all the energy she had left.

This time, he tried to jump back, but underestimated her reach. The energy whip crashed down onto his chest, swatting him flat to the floor and setting off a reverberating thunderclap audible only in the spirit world.

Suri—in Johanna's NetMini—screamed. The living room holo-bar turned on and off multiple times. Two lights exploded.

The assassin groaned and started to sit up.

Kirsten walloped him again.

And again.

A brilliant white flash exploded from the point where her energy whip hit the spirit. Screaming, he reached at her, his human form losing cohesion, collapsing into a melty blob of textures and color.

Her third attack drained her to the point her legs gave up. She swooned to the floor, still struggling to raise her arm for another strike. A strong sense of ominous doom saturated the house. Kirsten stopped trying to force herself to move.

"Thanks… he's all yours," she whispered.

Vaporous blackness welled up from the walls, spilling into the living room. The inky fog rose into the shapes of nine Harbingers. The assassin struggled to roll over onto all fours, despite his substance having the integrity of molten cheese. Two Harbingers drifted close by Kirsten, the icy chill of their passing relieved her pain like ice on a burn.

Damn… I didn't even have to call them. This guy's a real prize.

The assassin roared in protest, scrabbling futilely at the rug as the Harbingers dragged him down under a mass of shadowy, clawed apparitions. His scream faded into the distance.

"Rosana, are you still listening?"

"I'm here, lieutenant," said the girl's voice over comm. "You dropped offline for a few seconds, but you're back."

"Need a medical team on site. The woman took a nasty hit to the head. Site is secure."

"Copy. Medical team on the way."

Kirsten rolled gingerly onto her back as the roiling mound of shadows sank into the floor. She fished out a pair of stimpaks, flicked the yellow safety caps off the business ends, then grasped the handle of the big knife stuck in her thigh.

Okay. Deep breaths. I can do this. Can't possibly hurt worse than anything demons have done to me already.

She clutched both stimpaks together in her left hand, stabbing them into her thigh while simultaneously yanking the knife out. Surprisingly, removing the blade didn't hurt anywhere near as much as she expected it would, probably because it hadn't wedged in bone. Bloody foam seeped up from the hole, but the area soon deadened to a cold numbness and the tingle of working nanobots.

One by one, she removed the other knives, administering a stimpak shot by each one.

"Ugh." Dorian groaned in pain-slash-fatigue, stumbling over to her. "Sorry it took me a bit to recompose myself… are you okay?"

"Been worse. Been better." Kirsten stuck an empty stimpak into the holder. "Worried about you."

"I've never been knocked loopy before as a ghost. Son of a bitch was strong."

Kirsten took another stimpak out and administered it to Johanna's arm.

Six seconds after the soft hiss of the autoinjector, the woman's eyes snapped open. The small cut above her left eye sealed. Johanna sat up fast, looked around, and shouted, "Tam!" before realizing Kirsten sat next to her. "Who are—?"

"Mom!" screamed the girl from upstairs.

"Tamsen's fine. She's still in the shower tube, but unhurt. Gonna get her out in a sec." Kirsten peered up at Dorian. He looked reasonably intact, but still as though he'd been run over. No trace of the assassin or any Harbingers remained, so she made herself solid to spirits. "Can you help me up? My leg's still on strike."

Dorian took her arm and pulled her upright.

Johanna scrambled to her feet but swooned and had to grab the sofa to keep her balance. "What are the psionic cops doing here?"

"I called for help," said Suri from the NetMini on the floor. "It's good to see you are okay."

Kirsten put a hand on the woman's arm. "The spirit gave you a nasty hit to the head. Medics are on the way to check you out. Please have a seat for now. Let me go up and get your daughter out of the tube first, then I'll answer all your questions."

Johanna kept a grip on the sectional as she maneuvered around to the other side and sat on it.

"Dorian, need you upstairs." Kirsten limped to the stairwell, cringing at the pins-and-needles effect of the nanobots repairing deep muscle damage. "Hate knives... hate knives."

He followed her up to the bathroom.

Tamsen still stood on the handrail inside the autoshower tube. Her lips appeared blue and she shivered so hard she seemed likely to lose her balance and go under at any moment. At the sight of Kirsten walking in, she perked up a little. "W-w-what happened?"

"The spirit didn't want to leave. I had to kick his ass."

"Heh." The child emitted a shivery chuckle. "Can you please get me out of here?"

Kirsten nodded. "Dorian..."

"Huh? My name's Tamsen."

"Dorian is my partner. He's a ghost, but a nice one."

The girl stared at her. "Umm, okay. Whatever. If it'll get me out of here, I'll believe you."

"This virus is getting out of hand," said Dorian.

"Tell me about it. Poor kid's been stuck in there all day. Have you ever seen a tube flood before?"

"No. They aren't supposed to be able to." Dorian crouched by the base platform and stuck his hand inside. "Interesting. There's a force squeezing the drain hose shut, but the seal isn't perfect."

"Whoa, seriously? I thought it had a failsafe to prevent flooding all the way."

Dorian shook his head. "Alas. No. The pressure from an eight-foot-high vertical column of water is more than the ghostly force on the hose can hold back. He *tried* to flood it all the way, but the plastic hose isn't capable of making a seal against this much pressure."

Bastard... Kirsten shuddered at the thought of what almost happened here.

"One... second..." Dorian grunted as if attempting to lift a heavy object. He appeared to be struggling to pull something out of the floor beneath the tube. After a few seconds, it gave way and sent him spilling over backward.

The water level in the tube began to go down, about an inch every twenty seconds.

Dorian got back up and thrust his hand into the tube base again. "Sec. Turning off the water."

"Run some warm… she's freezing."

Tamsen shook her head. "I've had enough water."

A *clonk* came from beneath the floor. The water level dropped faster, about an inch every five seconds. As soon as it became low enough for the girl to stand on the floor and keep her head above water, she jumped down off the handrail. Kirsten plucked a towel from the wall. Once the water drained completely, Dorian fiddled with something in the base, turning on the hot air dry cycle. Tamsen's hair blew straight up over her head. She clung to the handrail, seemingly adoring the cyclone of hot air. A few minutes later once she appeared dry, Dorian drew all the electrical power from the unit, shutting it down and freeing the safety lock from the hatch.

Tamsen shoved the hatch open and rushed into Kirsten's waiting towel. "Holy crap. I thought I was gonna be stuck in there forever."

"Stupid virus got me too the other day." Kirsten wrapped the towel around her. "There are medics on the way. They're going to check your mom out and should probably have a look at you just to make sure."

"What happened to my mom?"

"The ghost hit her on the head. She's a bit dizzy, but awake."

Tamsen ran out, clinging to the towel.

"Poor kid's going to be afraid of shower tubes for the rest of her life. Lucky they have a tub in here." Dorian brushed at his sleeve, his uniform rearranging itself back to perfect order. The electricity he'd absorbed from the machinery did more for him than a stimpak to a living person.

Kirsten suppressed a shiver. The idea of drowning in a locked tube had never occurred to her before. She considered requisitioning a

Nano knife to hang in her autoshower at home, just in case, but those blades frightened her more than the one-in-a-trillion odds of some other spirit plugging the drain during a ransomware attack. Besides, if she cited fear of being trapped in the shower as her reason for wanting one, they'd probably double her sessions with Dr. Loring. "What idiot thought it a good idea to make the hatch lock?"

"Safety feature, I suppose. The spray ring could cause serious injury if it comes down on an arm or leg sticking out the opening." He shrugged. "You could probably trace back the origin of why a company does anything to a lawsuit."

Shaking her head, Kirsten headed out of the bathroom and went downstairs.

Tamsen sat beside her mother on the sectional, clinging and shivering.

The stimpaks had mostly done their work, reducing the pain of Kirsten's injuries to annoying more than crippling. She limped off the stairs and approached the two. "Please don't go into the back of the house for the time being."

"Why not?" asked Tamsen.

Johanna's expression said she knew the repairman lay dead in the other room. "It's fine, hon. Just stay here with me for now."

Kenton's ghost walked in. "Umm, hey cop lady. What in the absolute fuck was all the black stuff?"

She glanced at him. "The universe has trash collectors. They came for the guy who killed you."

"Ack!" Kenton backed up a step.

"Don't freak out. You're not even an hour old yet as a ghost and have no defense against them. If they wanted you, you'd already be elsewhere." Kirsten returned her attention to Johanna. "Short explanation, you were attacked by a fairly powerful spirit."

The whirring buzz of a hover vehicle arose outside.

"Ahh, medics are here," said Dorian.

"You look much better." Kirsten smiled at him.

At the *whud* of van doors and footsteps approaching the house, Tamsen gasped and blushed, clutching her towel as if she'd only now realized she had nothing on under it. The child made an 'oh well, they're doctors' sort of face and decided not to move.

Kirsten went to the room where Kenton lay dead while the medics checked Johanna and Tamsen over. "Rosana, please send a medical examiner team. One deceased."

"Copy, lieutenant. On the way."

"Impressive," said Dorian. "She didn't question why you weren't requesting a crime scene unit and going straight for the ME."

Kirsten opened her armband terminal and added notes to the current Inquest file. "Kid knows her stuff. D2 CSI isn't going to find ghost fingerprints. Kenton, still here?"

"Yeah." He appeared beside her.

"I'm sorry to tell you this, but you've died."

He chuckled. "Yeah, kinda figured that out, what with my dead body lying on the floor here."

"You have a couple options. For the first few hours, you're likely to feel tethered to your body, unable to go too far away from it. Eventually, your remains will be cremated unless you happen to be rich."

"Nope. My butt's headed for an urn." He shrugged.

"Once they're done with your body, you might feel the urge to linger around here—the place where you died. You also might feel a pull back to where you lived, or the urge to go through a silver doorway."

"If you have no particular desire to stick around, I hear the doorway's nice." Dorian smiled.

Kirsten crouched to scan the PID from the NetMini in the body's pocket. "If you need me to pass any information or messages on to living relatives, I'd be happy to. There shouldn't be any need for revenge or justice here as the entity responsible for your death is about as punished as it's possible to be for a spirit."

"You sent him to live with my boss?" Kenton laughed.

Kirsten chuckled. "Worse. Probably."

"Corporate managers might actually be more evil than Harbingers." Dorian snickered.

"Harbingers aren't evil. They're only doing a necessary job."

Dorian held his arms out to either side. "They're made out of the very fabric of infinite suffering."

"You *have* met my boss." Kenton laughed. "Err, former boss. He's probably going to want a coroner's note to prove I died or he'll dock my pay for not showing up."

"This guy should do stand up." Dorian pointed at him.

"Nah, I can't handle crowds. Wouldn't have a ghost of a chance."

Kirsten groaned. "You seem to be taking your death in stride."

"Ain't like my attitude will change what happened." Kenton offered a 'what can ya do' shrug. "People are scared of death on account they think it's the big end. Never expected I'd still exist somehow. It's kinda cool."

"A future *Kind*." Dorian chuckled.

"Well, if you ever need me to pass on a message for you, let me know. Otherwise, I need to finish up here."

Kenton grinned. "Don't suppose you'd tell Mr. Quaid to suck a fat dick for me?"

She clenched her jaw.

"Just kiddin'. You look way too sweet and innocent to say anything like that." He winked.

"You could always haunt him yourself." Dorian raised both eyebrows.

Kirsten elbowed him in the side. "Don't corrupt the newly dead."

"Lieutenant?" asked a woman.

She turned to find one of the medtechs standing in the archway, Patel, R according to her nameplate. "Yes?"

"Mrs. Beck and her daughter are fine. We treated the child for minor hypothermia and gave her mother something to help with the dizziness. She has a mild concussion, but should be okay if she avoids another bump to the head and tries to stay off her feet for a week or so."

"Great. Thank you."

The woman leaned closer. "Are you all right? Seems you suffered some injuries as well."

"Ghost threw a whole block of kitchen knives at me. A few stuck. Stimpaks seem to have done the trick."

"You'd best let us have a look since we're here. Could be nerve damage."

"Okay. Sure."

She followed the woman out to the MedVan parked beside her patrol craft. Johanna remained on the sectional, though Tamsen had vanished, likely having gone upstairs to change. Kirsten climbed into the back of the MedVan and took a seat while the woman checked her over with a scanning unit. The stimpaks hadn't quite repaired all the damage, only constructing a basic tissue lattice to hold the wounds closed.

A medical examiner van landed on the road behind the driveway. A short, black-haired woman in a blue jumpsuit emerged from it. She continued staring at her NetMini while walking around to the back of the MedVan, then looked up from the holo-panel at Kirsten. "Lieutenant Wren?"

"Yes."

"Alana Chang with the ME's office."

"Wow."

Alana tilted her head. "Wow?"

Kirsten blushed. "Sorry. My boyfriend's named Chang too."

"Ahh." Alana laughed. "There are quite a few of us. So, I hear you have someone needing a ride in our limo."

While the tech administered several nanobot injections to finish mending the knife wounds, Kirsten filled the ME agent in about the body in the back room.

"You're saying the killer is a ghost?" Alana blinked in disbelief.

"Yes. You'll most likely find some manner of inexplicable damage to his heart and he has no external wounds."

Alana shrugged. "Sounds like a heart attack, but you guys are up to your eyeballs in the weird stuff so I'm not going to question it. All right, as soon as you're done with recording the scene, we'll get him out of here."

"Great. Just be a moment in here."

"Going as fast as I can," said the medtech.

Kirsten tried to relax despite the sensation of stuff moving deep inside her muscles. "Take your time. Excuse for me to rest a bit."

About ten minutes later, Tech Patel finished.

"Thanks. Not sore now." Kirsten rubbed her thigh.

"Stimpaks are basically a bandage good enough to let you survive the trip to a real medic." Tech Patel smiled. "I also gave you an immune booster in case the knives had any nasty stuff living on them."

"Again, thanks." Kirsten stood, waved, and headed back into the house, Alana Chang following.

Tamsen—now in a purple top and jeans—sat beside her mother. The Becks watched Kirsten and Anna head to the back room. Kirsten took a series of photos and some video documenting Kenton's body, then made an 'all yours' gesture at Alana, who went outside to collect a gurney and her partner who'd been goofing off in the van, playing a video game on his NetMini.

Kirsten approached the sofa. "Almost done here. Just a few questions for you."

"I'm sorry," said Johanna.

"There's nothing you need to apologize for." Kirsten blinked.

Johanna opened her mouth to speak, paused, then exhaled. "Until today, I didn't believe in anything supernatural and thought psionics were all dangerous. I'm apologizing for being an idiot."

"Thanks. Not easy to have your world turned upside down."

"Being picked up, thrown around, and choked by something I couldn't see, then having an onyx egg fly off the table and hit me in the face all by itself sure did it. Thank you for stopping whatever it was from hurting my daughter." Johanna looked down. "Tam said it tried to kill her, too. And I saw that poor man drop to the floor, clutching his chest."

Not wanting to talk down at them, Kirsten sat on the sectional as well. "The spirit who attacked you did attempt to harm your daughter." She explained the blocked drain, trying to make it sound like it couldn't possibly happen again, adding some self-deprecating humor about ending up locked inside a tube herself thanks to the same ransomware. "I normally ask people who've been attacked by spirits if they've been directly or indirectly responsible for any deaths, but this guy was a ghost long before you were born."

Alana and her partner went by, pulling a hover-gurney bearing Kenton's remains. His ghost followed, waving at Kirsten.

Johanna fidgeted. "I'm a graphical artist for Bloodbath Entertainment. I draw and animate a lot of dead bodies for video games, but I've never hurt anyone for real."

"The spirit had a rather distinctive look." Kirsten made eye contact with Kenton, nodding farewell. "The sort of people shady corporations hire to hurt people. Any chance you or your spouse—if you're married—might have gotten on the bad side of someone with the resources to want retaliation?"

"Not that I can think of." Johanna shrugged. "My wife Arielle is a programmer. She's good, but not exactly a phenom companies would literally kill to keep or poach."

Hmm. The old lady mentioned a racket. Could the same thing have driven this spirit mad?

Kirsten nodded, adding to her notes. "Strange question. Have you heard any strange noises lately?"

"Only the ghost voices today."

"Ghost voices?" asked Dorian.

Kirsten repeated his question.

"The guy who tried to kill me making all sorts of roars and grunts."

"Oh. Nothing else, like a maddening constant racket or noise?"

Johanna and Tamsen shook their heads.

"Well, maybe if you count the music my daughter listens to."

Tamsen shot her mother a 'really?' smirk.

Kirsten chuckled, taking it as a joke. "Okay, so no reason you can think of for a spirit to want revenge on you."

"None I can think of." Johanna fussed at her daughter's hair.

"All right. I understand. The ghost who attacked you felt fairly old, at least forty years or more as a spirit. Highly doubtful he came here for revenge."

Johanna managed a weak smile. "Not unless my parents handed me a gun when I was a newborn."

"We're basically done for now. I don't have any more questions for you. If you need anything or have any questions for me, please reach out to Division 0 and I'll get in touch with you as soon as I can." Kirsten stood. "For what it's worth, the spirit who attacked you is gone for good."

"What about the repair man?" asked Tamsen. "Is he gonna haunt us?"

Kirsten tilted her hand back and forth. "It's possible. Some spirits are drawn to hang around the place where they died. But he's not a bad guy. He'll also be too weak to really do anything anyone could notice for years. *If* he decides to hang out here."

Tamsen nodded.

Johanna blushed.

If you feel watched during intimate moments, call it in and I'll come back, said Kirsten telepathically.

The woman seemed to relax. "All right. Do ghosts watch people all the time? And, umm, did you read my mind?"

"No." Kirsten smiled. *The look on your face said it all. And yeah, it's pretty common for spirits to be around watching people. This city has a lot of ghosts, but very few wander away from their homes.*

"All right." Johanna wobbled up to her feet and shook Kirsten's hand. "Thank you for what you did for my daughter and me."

Tamsen stared gratefully over the pillow she cling-hugged, too choked up to speak.

"You're welcome." Kirsten shook Johanna's hand, smiled at Tamsen, and let herself out.

She paused at the edge of the porch, noting a small group of neighbors watching from across the street, no doubt curious at the spectacle of several emergency vehicles at the house. One older woman appeared distinctly unhappy. It struck Kirsten as suspicious enough to peer at the elder's surface thoughts. She considered complaining to the NPF about parking their vehicles on the lawn, as it violated homeowners' organization policy.

"Oh, you have *got* to be kidding me... Are people really that petty?" Sighing, she shook her head and walked to the patrol craft. "So why would a cybered-up enforcer be here?"

Dorian appeared beside her. "Corporate assassins don't usually take contracts *after* they're dead."

"I'm thinking about Mr. Mendoza. Looked like an assassination. This felt like one, too. Except, there's no reason for him to attack Mrs. Beck and her daughter."

"That we know of. And... interesting theory." He pursed his lips. "Was this guy the same one who attacked Mendoza?"

She got into the car and pulled the door shut, waiting for him to appear in the other seat. "Different spirit. This guy was a lot stronger."

"Any theories yet?"

"Still working on it." She powered the car up. "We should probably get out of here before the homeowners' organization rep complains."

"Let her. Bet if she does, Division 5 will have an A3V parked on her front lawn in twenty minutes."

Snickering, Kirsten lifted off and plotted a Navcon point for the PAC.

PHANTOM MOTIVES

After a shower and a trip to the quartermaster for a new uniform, Kirsten sat at her desk, staring up at the ceiling. She dreaded starting anything, fearing as soon as she got thirty seconds into any sort of research, report-filing, or investigation, another alarm call would come in.

For a few glorious minutes, she sat in total calm.

Frazzled… but calm.

She leaned forward in her seat and fired off a request to Captain Eze, asking him if he could do anything to get Division 2 to commit more resources into finding Plasmahawk. Tamsen Beck being locked in a shower tube for nine hours infuriated her far more than the ransomware affecting her personally.

"Dorian? Did the Mendoza case feel like an assassination to you?"

"Hmm. An unknown spirit entered the Ancora Medical facility, targeted Elan Mendoza, and left without attempting to do anything else. I can see how you're thinking it might be an assassination considering all the crazy spirits we've been seeing lately."

She spun in her chair to face him. "Exactly. If it had been another ghost coming unhinged, they would've been going after everyone or trying to do as much damage as possible. The Mendoza ghost appeared calm, the exact opposite of manic or rampaging. I hate to say it, but the big guy at the Beck's house also didn't feel like he'd been driven out of his mind."

"If the spirit *did* target Mendoza on purpose, they would've had to wait for him to be vulnerable in a medical tank."

"Not necessarily. The tank might've only provided a conveniently easy way to do it."

Dorian tapped a finger to his chin. "Did you consider this spirit might have wanted to kill only one person and just happened to pick him randomly from everyone who happened to be in a tank at the moment?"

"Yeah. I've considered it. Still, I can't shake the feeling the ghost went after Mendoza on purpose."

"A cop with a hunch." Dorian laughed.

"Well, I *am* psychic." She laced her fingers behind her head, smiling.

"Didn't realize you were clairvoyant."

"I'm not." She stretched her legs out, a minor twinge of pain stabbing her where the knife had been. "But spirit stuff is different. The ghost at the Beck house *looked* like an assassin. I checked Johanna and Arielle's records for anything suspicious. Nothing there even close to turning either of them into a target. They work for a video game company. I can't explain why the ghost attacked them specifically—but he didn't feel like the others, going randomly nuts. It's bothering me."

Dorian twirled a light pen around his fingers. "All right, well… let's look at this under the theory the ghost who attacked Elan Mendoza killed him specifically."

Kirsten spun back to her desk and logged into the terminal, digging through Elan Mendoza's files. By some miracle, the surge of haunts took a break. Forty minutes later, she'd exhausted all available online paths to investigate his background. The man didn't appear to be anyone overly important in a political or business sense. He worked as a director-level manager at Naturahealth Pharmaceuticals, part of their client services group. Such a position wouldn't have given him access to any valuable company secrets, nor made him the sort of employee some corporations would rather assassinate than allow to work for a competitor.

Scouring his company records failed to suggest any connection to deaths where a vengeful spirit might have come after him. Sure, Naturahealth had its fair share of lawsuits when its products hurt or killed people, but Elan Mendoza didn't design drugs or medical devices. He managed a group of mid-level managers who oversaw the team responsible for maintaining account relationships with doctors and hospitals who purchased Naturahealth products.

Nothing in his work records came close to suggesting a motive for anyone wanting him dead.

She moved on to his personal files. A six-year-ago divorce brought up the possibility the ex-wife had a grudge. The woman lived far to the north, almost at the outskirts of the city's official footprint, beyond the end of the city plates. It looked like a wonderful place to live, on natural ground surrounded by snowy pine forest … if not for the constant worry dangers from the Badlands would wander by. Everyone who lived there, including children, tended to carry guns all the time.

"Call me crazy, but the risk of being randomly mauled by a canid mutant in my backyard is *not* worth having a private home on actual ground." She fidgeted.

"Agreed," said Dorian. "And where did that come from?"

"Mendoza's ex-wife. She lives way up north. I don't see any contact between them for at least four years. Don't see her randomly hiring a psychic medium to convince a ghost to kill him."

"It sounds so silly when you say it that way."

She laughed. "It does… Hmm. Did he have any secrets?"

"No idea."

"Not asking you. Just asking." She chuckled while activating an AI deep dive of his NetMini activity.

Nicole and Corporal Forrester entered from the right, both covered in pink, blue, and green slime studded in multicolored dots.

Morelli snickered.

Kurosawa and Montez, the two other I-Ops people in this squad room, also laughed.

"What happened to you two?" asked Montez.

Nicole held up a middle finger, marching across the room to the hallway on the left, heading for the showers.

"Telekinetic tantrum at Flavor Rainbow," said Forrester. "Ten-year-old brat had a meltdown and lost his damn mind. Didn't realize he was telekinetic, so when shit started going crazy, it scared him, too, making it worse. Ice cream, smoothies, and sprinkles flying everywhere. Samir's going to be cleaning our PC for the next two hours."

Kirsten chuckled.

Nicole and Forrester vanished into the corridor on the left.

I should take Ev and his friends to one of those places for ice cream sometime.

"Analysis complete," said a nondescript male voice from the terminal.

Kirsten leaned forward, opening the results. Elan Mendoza's NetMini activity didn't trip many red flags for potential illegality except for one orange entry: The Cat House. He'd never called the place, though he did spend a rather significant amount of time there, third most time in the same place after home and the Naturahealth office.

"What the heck is The Cat House?" muttered Kirsten.

Morelli cracked up.

"It's an older term for brothel," said Dorian.

She sighed at Morelli, then tapped the link in the log of Mendoza's NetMini locations. "Not *a* cat house. *The* Cat House. And good grief, another cat themed place?"

Dorian chuckled. "I told you, they're everywhere."

The Cat House had a file in the Division 2 system associated with numerous investigations into organized crime. This, of course, made Kirsten think about the Syndicate. She disliked the way the NPF handled them, something of a tentative truce. While it did—mostly—stop the Syndicate from attacking police officers, it also permitted them to get away with various crimes. She didn't think a literal war between the Syndicate and the National Police Force could possibly end in any way other than the annihilation of the criminals. Though, any such war would undoubtedly drag many civilians into the chaos.

According to the official report, The Cat House operated as a casino-slash-bar as well as a brothel. Prostitution, in general, didn't bother Kirsten as much as the association between the Syndicate and prostitution. Selling sex had been technically legal for centuries. Much like low-grade recreational chems, the police didn't bother to enforce the laws against it unless they had some other motive. 'Other motives' often took the form of pressuring informants, retaliation for grudges, or in some cases, pulling minors off the street protectively. A person still had to be over eighteen to work as a prostitute. Some shadier places tried pulling an end run around the law by sending their sex workers to Reinventions, genetic surgery shaving a few years off so they *looked* sixteen or occasionally even younger. Kirsten shuddered at the thought. However, a person surgically de-aged below eighteen legally counted as a minor again.

Some people often got mistaken for being under eighteen even without fakery—case in point: Kirsten. This muddied the waters and created enough doubt for scumbags to slip through the cracks. The mere thought of it made Kirsten want to storm in the place and mind-read everyone to verify age. Having an association with the Syndicate worried her the worst rumors might be true. In some dark corners of the GlobeNet, people whispered the girls working in Syndicate brothels didn't do so of their own free will. Some even threw the word 'slave' around. However, if anything like that happened, it probably went on in colony settlements, or Mars. Not Earth—at least not in West City.

Elan Mendoza being a fan of The Cat House definitely piqued her suspicion. It meant he possibly had dealings with the Syndicate, and anyone who had frequent contact with them stood a higher than normal chance of ending up on the wrong side of an assassin.

"Maybe he made an enemy there?" Dorian leaned close to read the screen. "It's a casino. If Mendoza ended up owing money, they might have coerced him into killing someone to break even. There's a motive for revenge."

Kirsten leaned back in her chair, rubbing her forehead. "The ghost of someone Mendoza killed couldn't possibly have gotten strong enough to kill him already. He started frequenting this place six years ago."

"Right after the divorce, most likely." Dorian wiggled his finger at the terminal. Another window popped up with the official GlobeNet site of The Cat House.

"Ack!" Kirsten reached to close it but hesitated when he held a hand in her way. "What are you doing? They're going to think I'm a pervert."

Morelli, Kurosawa, and Montez all looked at her.

"You are conducting an investigation"—Dorian smiled—"and have a perfectly legitimate reason to investigate the place."

She sighed. "Dorian's controlling my terminal. Not me."

The Cat House GlobeNet 2D site depicted a pair of nude women with cat ears and tails perching on pink cushions on either side of the page content. She didn't even want to imagine what their in-net presence looked like, for anyone using a senshelmet or M3 head jack. Kirsten rolled her eyes. From the look of it, most of the people who worked there sported feline body modification. They also advertised themselves as a 'cat lounge,' meaning *actual* cats roamed all over the place—available for adoption. She decided not to go any further into the site and closed it. Except for being only a bar (and not a casino/brothel) 'That Place With Cats by the Place' hadn't been as original as the owner thought after all.

"It's a bit of an outside shot, but I suppose it's possible Mendoza got on the Syndicate's bad side." Dorian folded his arms.

"Are you suggesting they somehow hired a ghost assassin?" Kirsten stared up at him in disbelief. "Why would a spirit still work for them? Not like they need money."

Dorian shifted his jaw side to side. "No, not the Syndicate. They have plenty of resources to eliminate people in-house. Maybe the spirit used to be an assassin who died thinking he owed them something, so he's stuck being unable to transcend until he settles the debt? The guy on the sushi boat seemed to come to his senses when you smacked him once. This dude kept trying to kill you after multiple hits. Makes me think he wasn't being driven mad by some outside force."

"Sure… a Syndicate assassin isn't going to transcend, at least not to anywhere nice."

"Hmm. True." Dorian paced. "Though, you're assuming they know this. Death doesn't come with a user's manual. Being stuck here with unfinished business can become all consuming. A spirit might not even be able to think about anything else or the consequences."

She grumbled.

Dorian returned to his desk. "Also, maybe the ghostly presence at the hospital had been a fluke and the Syndicate took him out via hacker. Could be, the ghost merely sensed someone about to die and went there to watch."

"Now you're messing with me. You and I both know how it felt in there. Plus, D2 couldn't find any evidence of a hack."

"Div 2 couldn't. Have you asked Nine to check it? Syndicate has some serious hardware. They might've been able to get in undetected." He smiled. "Of course, 'hacker' is quite likely going to be the official explanation for when Command decides not to believe you about a murderous ghost working as a Syndicate assassin."

She groaned and bonked her head on the desk. "Do you think it's just another spirit going nuts? Something is driving them wild and amping them up."

"Possibly."

Kirsten stood. "I'm pretty sure this is desperation pretending to be thoroughness, but I'm going to go check the place out."

"You realize, you're going to come home with three cats."

"I am not." She sighed at the ceiling.

"True. You collect children, not cats."

She stuck her tongue out at him.

"Every time you find a kid in need, you want to bring them home. This time next year, you'll have Rafael sharing a bunk bed with Evan.

Adoptable cats are going to give you the look and you'll start collecting them like you do kids."

She bit her lip, guilty for having been tempted to take Rafael in, too. "Stop. I have my son, and I don't 'collect kids.'"

"Only teasing." Dorian patted her on the shoulder. "Your heart is too big for this world. It kills you to see kids having a life as bleak as the early part of yours. Nothing to be ashamed of."

She looked down. "Thanks."

"But you can't take them all home. The underwear machine will burn out. Especially with boys."

She snickered.

"Oh, just wait until he's a teenager. You'll go to pick up a stray sock and cut your hand."

Kirsten glanced at him. "What? That doesn't make any sense at all. How would I cut my hand on fabric? And what does Evan being a teenager have to do with the sharpness of socks?"

"Huh?" asked Kurosawa.

She gestured at Dorian—who no one else in the room could see —"He just said when my son's a teenager I'll cut my hand picking up a stray sock."

Kurosawa, Montez, and Morelli burst out laughing, making her feel clueless.

Kirsten tapped her foot. "Is someone going to explain why that's funny?"

"Can't do it." Dorian patted her on the head. "I don't want to be responsible for corrupting the innocent."

The other three laughed far too hard to speak—they all found excuses to be busy when she asked them for an explanation.

Grumbling, Kirsten trudged off toward the garage.

15

THE CAT HOUSE

Many things in life fell under the heading of 'extremely bad idea'—like walking into a Syndicate-run casino-brothel in full Division 0 uniform.

Any cop entering such a place would likely cause a shitstorm, but a psionic cop would set off a nuclear shitstorm. *Maybe* the Syndicate would regard her like many grey zone and black zone fringers, figuring she had 'psionic shit to do' and would leave them alone, so they left her alone. More likely though, some paranoid underboss would assume the government sent her in to telepathically spy on them.

Which, technically speaking, she intended to do. However, in spite of her feelings about the Syndicate in general, her goal had nothing to do with shutting them down or even causing trouble. She only wanted to investigate any potential connection between them and the death of Elan Mendoza. Of course, if she discovered any of the prostitutes to be held against their will, she couldn't simply leave well enough alone.

After submitting a notification to Captain Eze of her plan, Kirsten flew home to her apartment and changed into civilian clothes. The most outlandish outfit she owned wouldn't raise a single eyebrow in a place where nude cat-modders pranced around. She went a little retro with a neon-green half shirt, black jacket and black mini-skirt. Since she didn't have any, she ordered a pair of neon green boots, short topped with half-inch heels. A delivery bot arrived with them in four minutes.

So backward. A damn pair of shoes gets here faster than the police could. She put them on, stood, and sighed. *If we rode delivery bots, we'd get there faster.*

She stuffed her E-90 in a purse, since the size of the weapon made it impossible to conceal anywhere on her person under clothes. *Maybe I should ask Nicole to come along for backup. Nah, she's worse than I am. She* will *take ten cats home. Besides, I'm not going in there to do anything other than look around.*

Following normal traffic rules, it took a little over a half-hour to reach the place. The sector didn't quite qualify as grey, but it came close, mostly containing residence towers built on top of commercial properties. An overriding sense of grunge clung to everything, including the pedestrians. Her patrol craft—hell, any hovercar—stood out here like a sore thumb. The black Halcyon-Ormyr sedans and a few sleek hoverbikes parked on the roof of the building where The Cat House occupied the first three stories had to belong to Syndicate bigwigs, being the only other hovercars in sight.

Kirsten overflew the place, landing four blocks away in a deserted section of alley. If not for having Suggestion and an E-90 on her, she'd never have set foot in an area like this alone. The fermented stink of rotting biomatter, urine, and chemicals smacked her in the face when the door opened. Even the cryonic fog wafting out from under the patrol craft seemed unwilling to touch the ground here. She coughed, trying to take air in small sips, and got out. Some places in the city offered far worse smells than this, though it didn't make breathing here pleasant.

"Shall I keep an eye on the PC or go with you?" asked Dorian.

She looked back at him. "Can you stash it on a roof somewhere safe and catch up? I'd feel better having you with me in there."

"Yeah, give me a moment." Dorian's expression made no secret he much preferred to be with her. He melted through the door into the car, which promptly took off.

Kirsten cringed from the tingly electrified blast of air, shielding her eyes until the patrol craft flew off far enough for the downblast to stop. *So strange not wearing the uniform. Guess I need to get out more.* The alley didn't look remotely safe, so she headed out onto the street and started walking toward The Cat House. Pedestrian traffic here seemed an even mix of lower-class normal people and those likely to be in gangs. Despite wearing a miniskirt and half-shirt, she felt like a prude compared to the amount of skin some showed. A few even wore transparent clothes.

In order to be 'cutting edge,' fashion had two directions to go in: bizarre or extreme. One guy had a thing around his neck so similar to the appearance of a toilet seat ring she nearly laughed at him. Another woman wore a jacket with puffy shoulders large enough to hide toddlers in. The pedestrians around her not trying to stand out or announce gang affiliations tended toward plain and drab in their wardrobe. Compared to them, *she* felt a little conspicuous in neon green, but preferred no one noticed her.

Dorian appeared beside her half a block from The Cat House.

She smiled at him and kept going.

The place didn't have a line, though two large guys stood on either side of the front door like guards protecting the gates of a medieval castle. She'd been spending so much time with Evan in the Monwyn games, it struck her as strange they didn't have halberds or plate armor. The thudding of an electronica beat inside the place seeped out onto the sidewalk by the entrance.

"Hold up, hon," said the guy on the left when she tried to go in. "Gotta be twenty-one. Try again when you're old enough to have boobs."

Kirsten bit her lip. If she had Nicole's personality, she'd have flashed him to prove she had them. Of course, her friend's top half didn't disappear under a semi-baggy jacket and shirt. While she frequently got mistaken for thirteen or fourteen, no one mistook her for a pre-teen. This guy meant it as an insult, not a mistake. She frowned. "Funny guy. I'm twenty-three."

"Yeah, sure, kid." The other bouncer laughed.

She glanced back and forth between them, concentrating on both men. "*I'm twenty-three.*"

The brief glow in her eyes reflected back at her as two tiny points in the void of the men's sunglasses. They stared at her in derpy silence. Ignoring them, she walked between them at the automatic doors, which slid open, revealing a short hallway decorated in dark blue and blacklight. On the left, a skinny young cat-eared woman wearing a black lace bra stood behind a coat and weapons check desk, regarding her with moderately bored disinterest. Holographic signs on the walls warned rather colorfully any weapons found inside would be inserted in random body cavities.

"You could've shown ID." Dorian chuckled. "Though, I agree. Much more satisfying."

"Showing ID would be the same as walking in here in my work clothes."

He pursed his lips. "Ahh. Yes."

Kirsten considered complying with the house policy about weapons but decided not to for several reasons. One, showing a laser pistol would cause a stir. Civilians couldn't own them without holding a bounty hunting license. So, someone waving an E-90 around would either be a bounty hunter, law enforcement, or military intelligence, none of which would be popular guests at a Syndicate casino-brothel. Secondly, while businesses had the right to demand civilians check weapons at the counter, they had no legal standing to disarm a member of the National Police Force. She wouldn't get in any trouble if someone caught her with it inside, at least not trouble in a legal sense.

If she got in the other sort of trouble, she'd rather have the E-90.

She glanced at the Neko girl on the left, unable to help herself but skim the woman's surface thoughts. Mostly boredom. Contrary to Kirsten's expectation, she didn't think about trying to escape or being afraid for her life. Even the most broken captives still thought about their situation, so this woman had to be a legit employee. Also, her cat ears somewhat picked up Dorian's voice, but due to the music, she didn't recognize what she heard.

Dismissing the girl as a non-issue, Kirsten went through the next pair of doors into a massive room taking up almost the entire footprint of the ground floor, except for a small private area, likely for offices and bathrooms. Staffed game tables filled most of the right side. Banks of electronic gambling machines sat all the way in the back against the wall. Three women and three men, all with cat ears and tails, danced nude on six tiny stages arranged around the gambling area. Employees running the card tables and roulette wheels also had cat ears, though they wore fancy suits or gowns.

The rear left third of the room contained numerous small tables, the bar, and an area where about seventeen young women and four young men—all Nekos—lounged on various divans, sofas, and padded chairs. She assumed it the brothel part of the business due to their skimpy or nonexistent attire and the way they kept trying to catch the eye of people nearby. While most acted relatively normal as prostitutes went, a few took the cat thing *way* too far, licking themselves or crawling around on all fours.

She started to cringe, totally unnerved at the sight of people acting like animals, until she noticed a few of the catgirls appeared to be on leashes. Concerned, she made her way toward the bar, intending to skim their surface thoughts. Her heart rate increased, hands sweating. If she'd found kidnap victims, her information gathering mission just changed into something potentially over her head.

Dozens of actual cats wandered around, climbed carpeted sections of wall, or draped themselves on small elevated platforms. The few cats she came close to stared at Dorian, making faces like they'd just huffed hard on a Flowerbasket inhaler. Any second now, they'd get the zooms and go racing around.

Once she came within about a hundred feet of the prostitutes, she began surface thought reading, starting on the four leashed women. Much to her relief—and unease—they didn't mind, wearing the collars as part of their 'character.' Two utterly adored being tethered to the wall, unable to escape on their own. One worried the mechanism wouldn't auto-release if the fire alarm went off but got a nervous thrill from the risk.

Ugh. What is wrong with people?

Relieved her mission would not turn into a wild shootout with Syndicate thugs while trying to rescue trafficked women, Kirsten let a long breath out her nose. As far as she could tell from the surface thoughts she could understand, all worked here willingly, and got paid a decent amount considering the niche kink of finding people with cat mods willing to be sex workers. About half of them thought in Russian or German.

"So weird," whispered Kirsten.

"'Weird' could be referring to far too many different things in here for me to have a clue what you mean." Dorian whistled.

She faced away from the prostitutes. "Why would they pay a premium to hire Neko modders as prostitutes? It's not exactly uncommon."

"Most of the cat people are new-agey nature children, not sex addicts. They have some nonsense about clothing being the prison of a society they reject, getting close to the natural world... or something along those lines. They tend to get pissed off and violent when people automatically equate nudity with sex or them being promiscuous."

She blinked. "How do you know so much about them?'

"It's common knowledge. Their social movement is covered in school around the same time as the Marsborn political issues."

"Oh." Kirsten slouched. "I don't remember."

"Well, they did kind of fast track you to get out the door at sixteen." Dorian gave her the pitying look she disliked so much, not for his sympathy but for it reminding her she once needed pity.

"Still don't get it. What is the attraction to people with cat ears and tails?"

Dorian shrugged. "I have no idea either. Think it started in Japan centuries ago. It's hardly the strangest kink out there though. Some guys get off on bots."

"Sex bots are way less rare than cat people."

"No, I mean like orb bots. Box bots, the little tank tread ones, too. Saw a guy grinding away on an orb bot once."

Her jaw dropped open. "Seriously?"

"Yeah. The most disturbing part was the little ball repeating 'help me' in a toneless voice."

"Stop." She rolled her eyes. "You're messing with me."

Dorian shivered. "Okay, the bot wasn't begging for help, but otherwise, I'm being serious. There are some times when having the ability to walk through walls is a true curse."

"Wow. Do you ever wonder if the human race has gone past the point of being worth saving?"

"Plenty of times." He winked. "But I know you don't."

She chuckled.

"I mean, you don't even understand how someone can cut themselves on a sock."

"Are you seriously not going to explain it to me?"

He shook his head. "Nope."

"I'm not a little girl."

"Yes, I am aware."

Grumbling, she resumed scanning random people's thoughts.

From the bartender, she learned The Cat House did not, in fact, belong to the Syndicate, rather, a cybergang known as the Silicon Knights. She'd heard of them only in passing and knew little other than they acted more like a rogue corporation than a literal street gang. Most of their crimes happened online rather than in alleys, mostly prostitution, data piracy, and other tech related criminal activities.

The Cat House, unlike the gang, had legit books and operated on the level.

She took her NetMini out, brought up Elan Mendoza's ID photo, and approached the nearest employee, a cat-eared man wearing only jewelry, carrying a tray of drinks from the bar over to the casino area. Kirsten approached, him, refusing to look down.

"Excuse me."

He paused, smiling at her. "Oh, hi there."

"Ever see this guy?" she showed him the photo and peeked at his head.

The man had a 'he kinda looks familiar' reaction, but couldn't put a name to the face.

"No idea. I see so many people here it's hard to keep track. Maybe I saw him, but he doesn't stand out."

"Thanks."

He walked off, tail swishing.

Kirsten spent about twenty minutes intercepting table servers, showing the picture, and checking surface thoughts. Most had some degree of recognition to Elan's face, but didn't know much about him. She approached a woman who looked like a living shadow: unnatural ink black skin, black hair, black fur on her cat ears and tail. The only color on her came from her metallic gold irises and a thin gold anklet.

"Aren't you adorable?" purred the woman. "Sit wherever you like. You don't need to ask to be seated."

"Have you seen this man?" She held up the picture.

The woman remembered seeing him frequently over by the prostitutes and also in the gambling area, but never spoke to him. She frowned, having unpleasant thoughts toward anyone who would partake of prostitution or be one. The harsh opinion surprised Kirsten into stunned staring, given this woman traipsed about naked and worked in a brothel. A slight mental push wanting to understand the contradiction made the answer reverberate in the woman's mind. She didn't work *for* the Silicon Knights, she was a full member of the gang. In addition to waiting tables, she had combat grade speedware and claws, thus served as security. People here knew her as 'Silo,' pronounced like the first part of silhouette.

"He's been around a lot. Usually upstairs with a working girl or over there losing money." Silo gestured at the casino tables. "Mind if I ask why you're looking for him? You a PI or something? The guy can't be your father."

Kirsten laughed. "No. But he knows or knew my father. Hoping he might be able to help me find him."

"Aww. Sad. Sorry." Silo made a pouty face at her. "I hope you find him. You are twenty-one at least, right?"

"Yeah, I'm twenty-three."

"Damn, girl." Silo looked her over. "You get a thing done?"

"Nope. Just six years of malnutrition early in life."

Silo sighed. "Sorry ta hear it. Hope you find your father. And I hope he's got a good damn reason for disappearing on you."

"Thanks."

The woman glided off toward the casino area.

"I'm astounded you managed to lie so smoothly." Dorian made a fake scolding face at her.

"Fear is a strong motivator. Trying not to need the big stick."

He gave a thumbs up.

Kirsten's NetMini rang. When she swiped to answer, Samuel Chang's holographic head appeared in miniature.

"Hey, Sam. What's up?"

"Umm..." He looked around. "Interesting place. Are you okay?"

"Fine, just trying to find information on a case. A dead guy I'm investigating came here a lot."

"I'm sure he did," muttered Dorian.

Kirsten gasped.

"Following up on Mendoza?" asked Sam.

"Hang on. Let me go somewhere more private." She hurried to the bathroom and took a seat on a mini sofa right inside the door, close to the sinks. "Okay... yeah, I am. Any good news?"

"Well, I didn't see any evidence connecting him to any sort of shady dealings with other corporations. In my opinion, no one would've gotten rid of him to protect secrets. However, his NetMini account had terabytes of photos, all showing the same Neko woman. Couldn't find her in the system by a face match, so she must be either off-grid or undocumented."

"What do you know about Silicon Knights?" whispered Kirsten.

"Makes sense. They run numerous brothels and are known to import women from overseas, forcing them into prostitution."

"Forcing?" whispered Kirsten, eyes widening.

"In a manner of speaking. They tell the women the UCF considers prostitution highly illegal and will put them in jail for decades or deport them if they're caught. As far as I know, they don't physically hold any woman captive, just keep them too scared to leave. One sec." He looked off to the side, his face tinted blue in the glow of a nearby holo-panel. "Ten to fifteen percent of the prostitutes in their organization are in that situation. According to Division 2's file on them, the rest are simple employees, treated well. More than well, actually. About the worst thing they do to their prostitutes is keep sending them to Reinventions to stay between eighteen and mid-twenties."

"Except for a small chance of death, it doesn't sound *too* bad." Dorian shrugged. "Assuming they could quit if they wanted to. Plenty of rich women stay twenty-one for decades."

Kirsten had mixed feelings, but none strong enough to set off a war with a hacker gang. "This girl Mendoza liked, can you send me a picture of her face? Don't need the rest of her."

"Sure, easy." Sam smiled. "Sec."

Her NetMini beeped.

"Sent."

"Thanks, Sam. Anything else I should know?"

He grinned. "Yeah. I love you."

"I love you, too, Sam."

"Want to grab dinner later?"

"Sure, if I can. Spirits have been insane. It's a near-constant series of calls."

"Wow." He blinked.

"Hey, can you do me a small favor? See if you can find any references to a strange noise with paranormal overtones Ran into a spirit earlier who blamed a loud racket for driving her nuts."

"No problem. I'll let you know as soon as I have anything."

"Thanks!" She kissed the hologram, then hung up.

A new email from Sam contained a picture of a young woman somewhere between nineteen and twenty-two. Long, powder-blue hair framed a delicate face as unnaturally white as Silo was black, perhaps a Marsborn. The girl's ice-blue eyes seemed a little bit oversized, likely making her appear younger or more vulnerable than reality. Fur on her feline ears matched the color of her hair. At least one of the women she'd seen lounging over by the bar had blue hair.

Kirsten left the bathroom and made her way across the club to the area where the prostitutes relaxed. Only one had powder-blue hair— one of the girls wearing a leash—though three others rocked cobalt or midnight blue. Steeling herself for the inevitable assumptions about her strangers would make, she entered the prostitute area and approached the girl from the photo.

Mendoza's favorite companion wore nothing other than the plastisteel collar connecting her via a six-foot chain to the wall. After years of mixed showers at the PAC, being around nude people didn't bother Kirsten *quite* as much as it would have otherwise. Honestly, the chain embarrassed her more than having men's junk waving hello at her.

The woman forced a smile. "You're cute, but I don't do girls."

"Not a problem. Didn't come here to hire you. Is it okay if we talk for a minute? I'm Kirsten."

"Clover," said the woman, sitting up on her divan. "Sure, I'll talk all you want until I need to work."

Standing over her felt rude, but sitting on a padded bench frequented by naked people didn't appeal either. Still, she had a skirt between her and the seat, and skirts could be washed. Kirsten gingerly eased herself down to sit on the edge of the divan next to Clover.

"Sorry, gotta ask." Kirsten gestured at the collar. "Why are you wearing that?"

Clover fidgeted at the chain. "It turns me on. Tells customers I'm a bottom."

Huh? Bottom? Kirsten tried not to look as clueless as she felt. If she really wanted to know, she could ask Dorian or Sam later.

"Also makes me harder to kidnap," said Clover.

"Are you seriously worried about someone grabbing you?"

Clover laughed. "No, it's a joke. Almost all of us have claws."

A slender cat-eared man crawled over, sniffing at Kirsten's boot. She cringe-smiled, more than a little freaked out at him. Sensing her unease, he 'dropped character' long enough to give an apologetic shrug, then crawled away.

"Umm…" Kirsten pulled Mendoza's picture up again. "Do you know him?"

"Oh, Elan? Yeah. He's a nice guy. Got some problems though. He's into the boss for a lot of credits. Great in bed, not so great at the games. Last I talked to him, he wasn't feelin' so hot. Had indigestion. I kept telling him he should go to the doctor and get checked out."

Dorian's eyebrows went up. "Gambling debt is a motive. Pretty bad one though. Dead people never pay back what they owe."

And why would a ghost care?

"Any reason you can think of someone might want to hurt him?" asked Kirsten.

Clover leaned back, the shiny silver chain draping over her chest. "Nah. The guy didn't have enough motivation to do anything people would get pissed at him over. Wife left him a few years ago and it kinda broke him. Like half the time he hires me, we don't even do it. Just wants to, yanno, spend time with me."

"I'm not sure whether to think it tragic or pathetic," said Dorian.

Clover's ears twitched, as did the ears of a few other prostitutes.

Kirsten smirked at him. *Poor guy.* "He sounds real lonely."

"Yeah, he is. He's either at work, here, or sleeping at home. Dude practically lived in this place… until the boss kinda got mad at him."

An actual cat trotting along on an elevated, carpeted walkway attached to the wall stopped short and hissed at Dorian before zooming off the way it came.

Clover's surface thoughts matched what she said. She'd started off thinking the guy a sad case, happy to take his money only to sit there with him, but he'd ended up feeling a little like a friend. She considered him good in bed, even though it annoyed her he didn't like using handcuffs or leashes on her. Kirsten squirmed.

Am I too innocent or is this entire city full of perverts?

"Thanks. Oh, umm…" Kirsten lowered her voice to a whisper. "Do you think the boss here might want something bad to happen to Elan?"

Clover shrugged, thinking of the name Carlos Bennett. She couldn't completely dismiss the idea he'd arrange the death of someone who pissed him off but didn't think Elan had done anything bad enough to deserve it. "I dunno. I only stick my nose in places attached to people, not in the boss' business."

Kirsten smiled, then stood, happy to cease touching the furniture here. "All right. Thanks."

"How do you know Elan?" asked Clover.

"I don't really." She looked down. *Unless I force or trick my way in to see the boss, I doubt I'm going to learn anything else here.* "I'm investigating suspicious circumstances surrounding his death."

"Oh, no..." Clover covered her mouth, tears gathering in her eyes. "He died? How?"

Guilty at the woman's emotional reaction, Kirsten sat again. "He was in the middle of surgery when the tank malfunctioned. Ancora Medical is still trying to determine what happened." *Shit. Silicon Knights are professional hackers. Is it possible they're good enough Division 2 missed them? But a ghost was there... dammit! More questions than answers.*

Overcome, Clover grabbed Kirsten in a hug and cried on her shoulder. She tried not to notice the woman had nothing on and patted her reassuringly. While the girl sobbed, she made eye contact with the other women whose surface thoughts rattled around in other languages. One by one, she telepathically said, *Prostitution is not illegal in the UCF. You won't be deported.*

A few made 'holy crap' faces.

Kirsten smiled to herself. Maybe they'd run away if they truly didn't want to be working here. She resumed debating if a ghost killed Mendoza randomly, on purpose, or if the spirit presence had merely been a coincidence while top tier hackers turned the medical tank into a killing machine.

A faint tingle spread over the side of Kirsten's head; she recognized a surface thought read in an instant, snapping her gaze to the obvious source: a thirtyish man in a black suit. He stood out because no cat ears broke the shape of his perfect flat-top afro. One blue orb earring appeared suspiciously like a communication device.

His surface thoughts contained curiosity about people using—or intending to use—psionic abilities to cheat at gambling, as well as confusion at why she'd be looking for Elan Mendoza.

Scanning for cheaters? asked Kirsten telepathically.

All casinos employ telepaths to screen for cheats. Sensed another psionic nearby, but you don't seem to be here for gambling.

I'm not.

Surprise flickered across his expression in response to her thoughts. *Division 0? What are you doing slumming around a place like this? Got a thing for catgirls?*

Kirsten rolled her eyes. *Probably doesn't look it considering I've got one draped on me now, but no. Not here for catgirls—or catboys. Not even really concerned with what your bosses are doing. Looking for reasons a ghost might have killed Elan Mendoza and left a trail of paranormal breadcrumbs back to Carlos Bennett.*

The telepath stifled a laugh. *Ghosts?*

Kirsten held onto the thought the Silicon Knights killed Mendoza via hacking, but a ghost happened to be there at the time, and he's trying to lead her to Carlos Bennett.

His grin fell flat. *Oh, my. You* are *serious... ghosts exist?*

"Thanks." Clover let go of the hug. "Sorry for falling apart on you like that. Not sure why it hit me so hard."

"Because he was your friend, more than a client."

"Yeah." Clover wiped her eyes. "Hope you find who killed him."

"Trying to…"

"You aren't like a weasel from Ancora trying to pin it on someone else so you don't get sued, are you?" Clover's ears rotated back in the posture of an angry cat.

"Nope."

Dorian leaned close to Clover's right ear. "She's about as opposite of weasel as one can get. We're Division 0."

The woman's ears snapped up, her eyes huge. She leapt to her feet, scrambling away from Dorian until the leash jerked her to a halt. "Who said that?"

Other prostitutes and the bartenders looked over, concerned.

Mental snickering filtered into Kirsten's mind. The telepath appeared amused at Dorian startling Clover. The man couldn't see him normally, only via her surface thoughts.

"I heard him too," said a woman in a heavy Russian accent, her pink cat ears pivoting like small radar antennas.

"No one you need to be afraid of." Kirsten smiled. "But if you're afraid of ghosts, you might not want to tie yourself to the wall anymore."

"Ghosts?" Clover blinked, tugging at the collar. "Are you being serious?"

"Nothing to freak out over… mostly."

"Is Elan a ghost? Can you talk to him?" Clover rushed back to her and grabbed her shoulders.

Kirsten's brain seized at the unexpected direction the conversation took. Eager excitement didn't happen often when someone found out ghosts existed. "I'm not sure if he's hanging around as a ghost, but yes, I can talk to spirits. Technically, anyone can talk *to* spirits. Hearing them reply is the tricky part."

"If you see him, please tell him I know why he got into so much debt, and he didn't have to do it. I'm sorry for not seeing it before."

"Seeing what?" Kirsten tilted her head.

"Elan was like forty. He told me he'd fallen in love, but I'm only twenty. Felt icky to be with a guy old enough to be my father, yanno?"

"Quite," said Dorian.

Kirsten exhaled. "Yeah, I understand."

"Elan wanted to go to that place where they could make him young again, but it cost so much. He kept playing games here trying to get the money… but he always lost." Clover slouched and slumped to sit on the divan.

"If I see him, I will tell him. But you shouldn't feel like you did anything wrong. You didn't drive him into debt."

Clover sniffled. "Thanks."

Idiot, said the telepath. *There are better ways to accumulate wealth than gambling.*

"Take care of yourself. I'll let you know if I find him."

"Okay."

Kirsten walked out of the lounge area, approaching the telepath who leaned on a column near the middle of the room, between two blackjack tables. Once again, she stood face to face with someone a full head taller than her.

Division 0. Interesting.

She offered a hand. *Yes. Lieutenant Kirsten Wren.*

He shook. *Rone Coombs. What's your endgame here?*

She raised an eyebrow. *Why are we speaking telepathically when we're this close?*

Secrets stay quiet. I'm psionic before I'm a Silicon Knight. Figure we should stick together. Hope you return the favor.

As long as you don't use psionic abilities to break the law.

Rone smiled. *The Cat House is a completely above-board operation. My role here is technically enforcing the law, hunting for cheaters.*

Fair point. Kirsten surveyed the various gambling stations. *Never did see the allure of betting credits. Too easy to lose.*

True. The games are stacked in favor of the house by design. Odds favor the establishment. So, Mendoza?

Yes. Did Bennett want him dead, or is the ghost I'm chasing trying to make your boss look bad?

Rone glanced around as if searching for eavesdroppers. *Yeah. Off the record, Mendoza was on the list. Not sure exactly what went down, but Bennett definitely put money on someone taking him out.*

Kirsten gawked. *Whoa, you're freely admitting it?*

Telepathic conversations aren't admissible. Besides, you don't look dumb enough to make trouble.

She bristled at the veiled threat but contained herself.

Oh, not me. I don't make trouble for anyone. Only thing I do here is catch cheaters. Just sayin'.

How much did Mendoza owe? The man worked a fairly high-level position at a pharmaceutical company. He had money.

Don't know exact numbers. It had to be at least a couple million. People don't end up on the list for less.

"Ouch," muttered Kirsten. *Okay, do you have any idea how Bennett could have hired a ghost to kill someone?*

Rone laughed. *You really do have some wild shit in your head. I'd call you nuts for believing it but the other cop I thought you were hallucinating scared the shit out of Clover, so I guess he's really there. Either way, the boss is a couple layers removed from me. All I can say for sure is Bennett put Mendoza on the kill list for not paying back his debts fast enough, and likely didn't think he would ever pay back. Don't know if someone acted on it yet or what. If the dude died because of us, some freelancer must have figured out a bizarre way to get the job done.*

The idea of someone sending ghosts to do hits didn't seem *too* out there. Technically, Kirsten could do it. Anyone capable of speaking to ghosts could ask them to do things. The part where the idea broke down came at the reward phase. She couldn't think of anything a ghost truly needed from the living aside from passing information. Problem being, any ghost old enough to be able to kill the living would certainly not have any immediate family left alive to send messages to.

Perhaps a ghost might desperately want to be allowed to inhabit a living person's body long enough to taste food again, but such a triviality didn't seem worth it to request an assassination. Even the dimmest-minded ghosts understood dark acts would make it impossible for them to transcend, and too many dark acts got the Harbingers sniffing around.

Granted, a ghost as old and potent as the one she fought at the Beck house wouldn't be worried about Harbingers randomly grabbing them. Something would have to drain their energy and weaken them sufficiently first, and as far as Kirsten knew, no one else in the world had figured out the Astral Lash yet. Theoretically, anyone who happened to have Mind Blast and Astral Sense could do it, but both of those powers were quite rare, Astral more so than Mind Blast. One person getting both had worse odds than winning the lottery.

Well, perhaps not quite as bad as a lottery win.

Do your people ever go after anyone on the list directly?

Rone shook his head. *Never. We try to keep things as clean as possible.*

Whenever blood gets spilled, there's always at least three layers of separation. If a hacker offed Mendoza, it wouldn't have been one of ours. You'll have to start checking freelancers if you really want to figure out who did it. Be careful though. Some of those fixers have black market shit in their head. Telepathic feedback crap.

I'll be careful. Thanks.

You do that. He grinned. *And we never spoke.*

Kirsten nodded goodbye, then walked to the exit, laughing at the technical truth of Rone pointing out they didn't 'speak' to each other. Also, the surrealness of having such a candid non-conversation with a guy working for organized crime tinted the entire experience as a weird dream. Her exchange with him felt more like employees of rival corporations griping about the higher-ups over lunch than a criminal openly admitting to illegal activities.

Even stranger than a ghost killing someone for a contract.

"What happened there?" Dorian jogged up beside her.

"I'll explain in the car." She went outside, ignoring the two bouncers yelling at her for sneaking inside. At the curb, she raised her left arm—and stared at her bare skin for a few seconds, wondering why no holo-panel appeared. "Crap."

Dorian cackled. "You left your WDT in the PC. Want me to get it?"

"Still have a NetMini. Don't *need* a wearable duty terminal." She fished it out of her purse, opened the link to the patrol craft, and requested it auto-drive to her location.

The two bouncers at the door kept giving her dirty looks. She smiled at them, watching their expressions go from sneering annoyance to confusion, to 'WTF' when the large all-black Division 0 patrol craft landed behind her, close enough for her hair and skirt to flutter in the downblast of the ion thrusters.

"Told you guys I'm over twenty-one." She waved at them and got in.

Dorian manifested in the passenger seat. "Being active duty Division 0 does not necessarily prove someone is over twenty-one."

"Touché." Kirsten pulled the patrol craft skyward, the door sinking closed with a soft hiss. "Touché…"

16

TOO MANY UNKNOWNS

Seventy-eight minutes after leaving The Cat House, Kirsten flopped into the chair behind her desk.

Two back-to-back 21-47s had come in, both within twenty miles of Sector 2888, the area she'd calculated as the epicenter of the 'ghost storm.' At least being on the small side let her change into her uniform relatively easily in the patrol craft on the way there. Both spirits had been more mischievous than dangerous, making noise, breaking things, and generally acting like drunk college students at an off-the-rails party. The first guy ignored every attempt she made to talk, behaving as though he had earbuds in at max volume. When he caused a PubTran kiosk to explode, showering people with sparks and shattered glass, Dorian grabbed the guy and slammed him into the side of a building—as much as a ghost can be slammed into a solid object.

As soon as Dorian shook him, his entire demeanor changed from limitless drunken energy to a bewildered stare. He'd said, "Damn music" and dove into the ground, seeming angry.

The second call came in before they even made it back to the patrol craft. A 'wailer' as Kirsten unofficially called them, created a scene in a residential apartment tower. The ghost of a young-twenties woman parked herself in the landing of the stairway between the second and third floors, wail-crying like she'd recently witnessed her entire family murdered. Her clothes looked quite dated, a T-shirt with the faces of two men above the words 'Tears for Fears,' jeans, strange sneakers with strings hanging off them, and lots of bracelets.

She'd been cautious, since the spirit gave off serious energy as if quite old, sitting there and trying to talk to her. Nothing she did got the ghost's attention. Eventually, the spirit looked up from her sobbing, made a 'what am I doing here?' face, and walked off. Kirsten asked her what happened to make her cry so hard, and she mumbled something about a song hitting her real hard.

Kirsten added two more Inquest records to the ever-growing pile, one for each 21-47.

Lacking the motivation to finish the reports, she drummed her fingers on the desk. Her mind wandered from feeling horrible for the crying ghost to utterly freaked out at Clover *enjoying* being chained to the wall by the neck to imagining Evan would be working on cit points at the moment, cleaning classrooms. He'd gotten a ton of them for trying to 'free' Abernathy, the old ghost who'd been haunting the PAC for years. Upon learning the man's brain sat in the Archives, he assumed the spirit needed help. Unfortunately, the kids broke a statuette containing a poltergeist and made a bit of a mess. Evan demanded to be given Shani's allotment of citizenship points since she wouldn't have participated if he hadn't begged her to. To Kirsten, it seemed like they gave him too much for what amounted to a well-intentioned accident. Kids who'd done bad things purely for fun because they enjoyed doing bad things didn't get hit so hard with points. Evan not complaining at all about it bothered her the most.

He's not still terrified they'll make him go back to the dorms, take him away from me, is he?

At least he'd stopped panicking over his grades. For the first few months, the boy thought if he scored anything less than perfect, they'd punish him by not letting him stay with Kirsten. She folded her arms on the desk, rested her head on them, and tried to cry without making any noise. Anger sometimes made her cry, too. These tears came from her feelings toward Evan's bio mom.

"You're going to have a rough time convincing Div 2 to pursue any sort of official investigation of Carlos Bennett for Mendoza's death," said Dorian.

"I know." Kirsten managed to keep emotion out of her voice.

"What's bothering you?" A chill seeped into her left shoulder.

"This? Just rage tears. Pissed at Evan's mom."

"You're angry at yourself?"

Kirsten barked a laugh, then sat up. "No, the other one."

"She's not his mother, and you shouldn't waste energy being angry at someone who's going to end up dead in a year or two, anyway."

"What?" Kirsten blinked at him.

"Overdose, random shooting..." Dorian waved randomly. "Something's going to happen."

"Now you're making me feel guilty for not commanding her to get help." Kirsten squinted. "Hey, wait a sec. Isn't that woman incarcerated now?"

Dorian paused in thought. "Oh, you're right. Still, she'll most likely serve two out of seven and be right back in the same situation soon enough."

"Cheerful today." She groaned and poked a finger into her desk terminal's intangible screen, staring at the information on Elan Mendoza. "How hard can it be to convince Div 2 the guy running The Cat House ordered a hit on a man who owed them money?"

"If you had some evidence more compelling than your hunch a *ghost* somehow pulled a contract hit on him."

"Damn. We don't even really know for a fact the ghost did it."

"I'm curious why Mendoza's spirit didn't stick around."

She narrowed her eyes at Dorian. "Maybe he did."

"Going to go hunting again? They probably haven't cremated him yet. I doubt you have the stomach to lop off a finger and use it as a focus."

"Ugh. No. I don't have to track him down if he's *willing* to talk to me." Kirsten took a deep breath, closed her eyes, and concentrated on Beacon, calling out into the aether for Elan Mendoza.

A few minutes later, she sensed another astral presence nearby, and opened her eyes.

The naked, slime-covered form of Elan Mendoza stood beside her desk, his facial expression holding the perfect mix of desperation and discomfort for a guy who'd been stuck outside for days wearing nothing more than medical tank gel.

"Ack!" Kirsten jumped away, grimacing at his dangling intestines. "I forgot about where you were when you died. Was *not* prepared for the visual."

Dorian whistled. "Come on, man. Pull yourself together."

"Did you just do something?" asked Elan. "All of a sudden, I get this strange urge to come here."

"Yes. I've been investigating what happened to you and running into a wall." She explained being an astral sensitive who can see and speak with ghosts, and how Beacon was the paranormal equivalent of paging a ghost over a PA system.

Elan paced, his guts swaying around his legs like a macabre skirt. "A ghost killed me, no doubt. Dude was standing right in front of me when I slipped out of my body. He made this face at me like I annoyed him and walked away. Tried chasing him, but I couldn't go too far away from my body."

"Did you recognize him?"

"No." Elan shook his head, then looked down. "Am I going to be stuck like this forever?"

Kirsten hunted down the list of Inquest files and opened the one for Mendoza's death at the Ancora Medical building. "A ghost's appearance is entirely based on what we call 'latent self-image.' Ninety-five percent of ghosts initially look exactly as they did at the moment of death. For some, it's hard to change due to the emotional trauma of being killed. Ghosts who die naturally have an easier time. All you have to do is think really hard about your appearance to change it, but it's not as easy as it sounds."

Elan kept staring down at himself. Some of his intestines quivered.

"You don't recognize the ghost who killed you. Did you kill anyone or were you possibly indirectly involved or responsible for any deaths?"

"Not without some weird butterfly effect shit." Elan chuckled. "Like if I took a parking space someone else wanted, and they had to go six spots over, then got mugged and killed."

"What does that have to do with butterflies?" asked Kirsten.

"She never took philosophy class." Dorian smiled. "Don't mind her."

Kirsten smirked at him. "Anyone you can think of who might want you dead or who would gain from your death?"

"Fred Ruiz is probably going to get promoted into my old job, but it really isn't likely he'd kill me to get the promotion."

"Ex-wife?" asked Dorian.

Elan slouched, heaving a despondent sigh; his guts hung lower. "No. She wouldn't want to kill me at all. Leaving me alive hurt more."

"Ouch," said Dorian. "Bad marriage?"

"No, it was great. I still love her." Elan looked down. "She wanted a kid or two. I didn't. So, she left."

Kirsten added notes. "What about Carlos Bennett?"

"Uhh… you know about him?" asked Elan, making a face like a boy caught grabbing cookies before dinnertime.

"I do. Also met Clover."

Elan fidgeted. "Yeah, I guess Carlos was upset with me for not paying him back fast enough. It's possible he might have wanted me dead or roughed up. Stupid of him to kill me though. Now I can't pay him anything."

"Were you going to?" asked Dorian with a hinting smile.

"Yeah… eventually. Once I uhh, dealt with some stuff."

Kirsten looked up from the screen at Elan. "Visited Reinventions?"

"Wow. You really did talk to Clover."

"Yeah. She was pretty upset to learn you died. I think she liked you a lot more than she admitted. Also asked me to tell you she's sorry for making a big deal about the age gap."

Dorian chuckled. "She *should* make a big deal about it."

Yeah. Almost as bad as me having a crush on Dorian. She chuckled to herself, thankful to have gotten over it. *He died at thirty-six, so a fourteen-year age gap... plus being a ghost. Mendoza and Clover have twenty years separating them. Definitely creepier. Maybe not as creepy as a girl who had a thing for a ghost, though.*

She let out a long, slow sigh.

I'd just been lonely, needed someone—anyone—to want to be with me.

"You think Bennett sent the ghost to take me out?" asked Elan.

Kirsten shook off her somber thoughts, leaning back in the chair. "Do you know for a fact Bennett did it?"

"Not exactly," said Elan, "but there's no one else who'd want me dead and I didn't recognize the ghost at all. Never saw him before."

"Possibly random?" Dorian tapped a finger at his chin. "Could some aggressive spirit have been roaming the building looking for a vulnerable person in a med tank?"

"I suppose it's possible." Kirsten came close to screaming in frustration but kept an outward calm. "Doesn't really work for me, though. The report I got from Ancora showed eleven other patients in mid-surgery at the time, four of whom were involved in procedures more critical than removal of intestinal tumors. Brain surgery, two heart surgeries, and a liver regeneration. Killing any of them would've been much easier. Why did this ghost only attack Elan?"

"I'd like to know that, too." Elan folded his arms.

"Oof," said an elderly voice. "Talk about swingin' in the breeze... Son, you're taking it too far."

Kirsten pushed off the desk, rotating her chair around to face the voice.

Abernathy.

"Everyone's a comedian," muttered Elan. Again, his dangling intestines quivered.

The old man gave a wheezy laugh.

"Abernathy? Do you have any ideas?" Kirsten gave him a brief explanation. "Why would a seemingly random ghost attack him?"

"Nothing random about it." Abernathy leaned on Dorian's desk. "A spirit looking for a random victim would have stopped at the first possible target. From any direction into the surgical area, he had to go past other people to get to this guy... unless he came straight up from below the city. Hmm." The elder scratched his head. "Maybe he *did* come straight up. Guess it ain't proof he ignored other victims to go for him. Oh, well. Theory sounded good at first."

Dorian glanced at the old man. "If the ghost *did* come up from below, directly into Elan's room, it could also suggest the attack had been deliberate. What is the connection between this ghost and Elan? If Carlos Bennett is involved, how did he manage to hire a ghost to assassinate someone?"

"Ooh, interesting theory." Abernathy's eyes gleamed. "Been a while since I've been involved in an investigation."

"Eww," said Evan.

Kirsten twisted to her right.

The boy, eyes glowing bright white, entered the squad room, backpack over one shoulder. Shani trailed after him. He grimaced at Elan Mendoza in far too casual a way for a ten-year-old seeing a man's guts hanging down to his knees.

"Don't eat too many hot peppers, son." Abernathy winked at Evan. "Or this happens."

Evan made a flat face in response. The words 'not funny' practically scrolled across his forehead.

"Who are you talking to?" whispered Shani.

Evan spun to face her. "Don't look. He's kinda scary. You'll get bad dreams."

"Okay." Shani evidently did not peek at Evan—or Kirsten's—surface thoughts, as she didn't shriek in disgust.

"Abernathy," said Dorian, "why don't you take Elan, go snooping around Bennett's office, and see if you can find anything linking him to the attack?"

"A capital idea!" Abernathy thrust a finger into the air. He tried to grab Elan's hand, but slipped away, staring at breathable gel glooping off his fingers. "Son, you need to work on your manifestation. C'mon."

The two ghosts headed off into the wall.

Dorian patted Kirsten on the arm. "Go on. Take the kids home and decompress. You're already here late."

"All right." She locked the terminal screen. "You realize what you just did, don't you?"

Dorian feigned innocence.

"You sent Abernathy to a place full of cats."

"So?" asked Dorian.

"I'm talking about the actual cats. It's going to be a bloodbath."

Dorian cringed. "Oops."

17

THE WORST POSSIBLE TIMING

The constant, dull thrum of electronics filled the patrol craft, slightly louder than the whirr of hovercars in the traffic lane outside.

Concerned at such quiet inside a vehicle carrying a seven- and ten-year-old, Kirsten peered back at the kids. Evan appeared to be asleep. Shani had her nose in a datapad, the glow of the screen in the dimness making her look as if she told ghost stories around a campfire. She watched Evan breathe for a moment before facing forward again. Sitting in a quiet patrol craft while auto-drive carried them along at traffic speed amounted to staring at a hypnotist's watch.

Burning off citizenship points didn't involve any truly heavy work, mostly wiping desks, sweeping floors, sometimes organizing shelves. Basically, boring tedium. Sometimes, the kids helped clean up the mess of projects, parties, or events.

He tries so hard.

Six minutes away from home, an alarm tone came from the console. A brown-haired, vaguely Hispanic looking woman appeared. A line of text at the bottom read [A-SPC Wiley, T.] The shock of having an actual adult, someone in Division 0 Admin with an E4 rank, working dispatch stalled her mute.

"Lieutenant Wren," said Specialist Wiley. "We have a 21-47 in progress. Your presence is required at the Mayoshi Technologies building in Sector 3150."

She grabbed the control sticks and squeezed them hard. "Uhh, copy, Dispatch."

"Is something wrong, lieutenant? You don't sound very confident."

"I've got my kid with me as well as another." She bit her lip. Shani hanging out with Evan late at school meant Nila had to be stuck at a crime scene somewhere. *Maybe I could drop them at Sam's?*

"Just go," said Evan.

"What?" Kirsten stared back at him.

He pointed at the dispatcher's hologram. "She said 21-47. Those aren't too bad. Just go. I promise we'll stay in the car unless it's dangerous not to get out."

Dorian appeared in the passenger seat. "I realize we start cadets off on the young side, but these two are still a bit small."

"Wouldn't stop Burkhardt from sending them into the field if they were powerful enough," deadpanned Kirsten. "If he knew about me when I was ten, he'd have sent me into the field. Maybe not given me an E-90 yet, but I'd have been activated."

"He's a butthead," said Evan.

Kirsten chuckled. "Don't repeat that out loud at school."

"Willow said they want her to sign up 'cause she's like real advanced with Pyro." Evan swiped his hair off his face. "She can do stuff Shani's mom can't even do."

"Nuh uh!" yelled Shani. "Willow's cool, but she's just a kid."

Evan looked at her. "Can your mom stand in fire and not burn?"

"I dunno. Who *does* that?" Shani scrunched up her face. "Why would she even try?"

"She didn't want to. Bad people tried to hurt her," said Evan.

"Oh." Shani cringed guiltily.

Dammit. It could be another wailer, something harmless. "Okay, fine. But you two are to stay in the patrol craft."

"Yes, Mom," said Evan. "Only reason we'll get out is if something bad happens inside the car."

"Wiley, confirm. We're en route." Kirsten turned on the emergency lights and audible warning system. Multiple cars up ahead swerved or dipped as their drivers panicked at the sudden presence of police lights behind them and a siren noise coming from their sound system —at least until she pulled up out of the traffic lane and accelerated around in a turn.

Specialist Wiley appeared confused. "We? You're including the children?"

"No, my partner. Dorian. Check my file."

"Never gets old." Dorian chuckled.

"People not believing in you?"

"No." He pointed at the disturbed hovercar traffic. "People jumping when the lights come on."

"You enjoy scaring people? Sounds like someone's been a ghost too long." Kirsten shook her head, though chuckled.

"Look at it the other way. Once they realize we're not after them, they feel great." He gestured at the 'window' to his right. "Besides. We did them a favor. Helped them stay awake. You know, I bet in the days before hovercars existed, people used to daydream about how thrilling and exciting it would be to fly to work every day."

"Few things are as boring as sitting in a hover lane for half an hour with nothing to do but wait for the car to finish driving itself where we want to go."

"Those people agree with you. Wouldn't have swerved if they'd been on automatic." Dorian whistled innocently.

She rolled her eyes and accelerated toward the nav point.

"Mayoshi Technologies owns an entire century tower in Sector 3150," said Evan. "The company started in Japan but they have offices in the UCF and on Mars. They make cosmetic cyberware, mostly cat stuff."

Kirsten groaned mentally. "What are you doing?"

"Bored," said Evan. "Looking on the GlobeNet. Since we're going there, you might wanna know."

"I wanna get cat ears like her," chimed Shani, pointing at the screen of Evan's datapad.

"Why?" asked Kirsten, still baffled as to what could possibly make anyone want big floppy ears or a tail.

"They're cute." Shani laughed.

Dorian shrugged. "I don't get the appeal of it either."

"Mom?" asked Evan.

Kirsten braced for an awkward question, dreading he looked at a picture of a naked woman with cat ears. "Yes?"

"Why do they call them century towers? Are they a hundred years old?"

Relief rolled off her in waves. "Oh, umm. Most are even older. I think they call them that because they made so many identical buildings all exactly a hundred stories tall. Most of the residence towers are essentially the same inside."

"Century tower sounds cooler than 'hundred story high-rise,'" said Dorian.

Evan laughed.

Kirsten set the patrol craft down on the roof of the Mayoshi Technologies building.

A scattering of hovercars remained in the parking area, which took up the entire roof plus one story down except for the small structure near the middle housing the elevators. She shut the drive system off and got out, hesitating at the idea of bringing the kids with her to an active scene. Still, they'd been through worse already. Evan had a front-row seat to Seneschal and his friends trying to kill her—and smashed one himself using the patrol craft.

Shani hadn't been involved in anything demonic, though she had evaded a bunch of gang punks angry at Evan for humiliating them. Sitting in the back seat of an armored PC while she chased a nuisance ghost shouldn't be too dangerous.

"I'll be back as soon as I can. Call me if anything weird happens."

Evan puffed out his chest. "Call me if you need backup."

Dorian laughed.

Sighing, Kirsten shut the car door and jogged to the elevator. "What, no welcoming committee?"

"It *is* oddly quiet here." Dorian slowed, looking around at the roof.

"Dispatch," said Kirsten, triggering a soft beep from her earpiece. "What's the situation at the Mayoshi building? Looks quiet."

"The caller mentioned bots going crazy, but the line dropped before they gave much detail," replied Specialist Wiley.

"How did this end up coming my way? There are a hundred explanations for bots going nuts other than a ghost."

"Umm." Specialist Wiley hesitated. "The video call made it kinda obvious. An apparition appeared behind the woman who called and physically dragged her away from the terminal."

Kirsten and Dorian exchanged an 'uh oh' glance.

The elevator door opened, revealing a small Japanese woman in an all-black security uniform curled up in a ball, trembling, shielding her face with a short vibro-sword. Blood smeared the wall behind her from a relatively minor injury to her left arm.

"Hey…" Kirsten rushed into the elevator and crouched beside her. "You're okay now. It's gonna be all right."

"I've never been shot at before," said the woman in a voice far less emotional than she appeared to be. "The dead are here."

"Drawing a sword is perhaps not the wisest response to gunfire." Dorian gestured at the handgun on the woman's belt.

Kirsten examined the woman's arm. A few inches below the shoulder, she'd suffered a grazing wound. Despite having a stimpak case on her belt, she hadn't used one. *She's in shock.* "Look at me."

The woman made eye contact.

"You're safe now. The spirit can't hurt you while you're with me. I'm Kirsten. Tell me your name."

"Satomi." She swallowed. "Satomi Ito. Security officer. You're the psionic cops?"

"Yes."

"Oh, shit. Finally." Satomi uncurled, sitting slouched on the floor of the elevator, almost falling over sideways. "I'm so happy to see you."

Distant rapid gunfire went off far below.

"Idiots," said Dorian. "Are they really trying to shoot a ghost?"

"What's with the sword?" Kirsten gestured at it.

Satomi looked at her like she asked why the sky appeared blue. "It's a restless spirit. Everyone knows guns aren't effective. Swords can hurt them since they channel a person's inner energy into the attack. I read online. Even you guys carry swords."

"Sometimes. Not sure how effective they are without astral binding, but probably better than a gun on a spirit. What can you tell me about the situation downstairs?"

"I saw the ghost on the security system. He appeared in random rooms, going up or down a dozen floors in an instant."

"On camera?" asked Dorian, eyebrows up.

"Did he show up on normal video or only thermal?"

"Both." Satomi winced, finally appearing to realize she'd been hit. She pulled a stimpak out of her belt case. "Didn't see a face. Looked like a shadow on the display. Security bots went nuts, started shooting randomly at everyone."

"Shit," muttered Kirsten. "How many dead?"

"I don't know. We tried to shut them all down, but some wouldn't deactivate. The orbs spun in circles, firing constantly like they weren't trying to hit anyone on purpose, just do damage to the building."

"Where's the shooting coming from now?" asked Kirsten.

Satomi pushed herself up to stand, staring into space as if reading a nonexistent video display, probably cybernetic eyes or an optic nerve interface. "Fifty-eighth floor offices."

Dorian poked the button for the elevator.

"Whoa. How did you do that?" asked Satomi.

"My partner is a spirit."

Satomi looked at her. "Oh. Cool."

"Yeah, he is. Literally." Kirsten whistled.

Dorian shook his head.

Seconds after the elevator passed the fifty-ninth floor, a bullet punched a hole in the door. Kirsten and Satomi flattened themselves against the sides. Two more shots holed the doors before they slid open, letting smoke in. Rapid gunshots continued in the corridor, like someone firing a handgun as fast as they could click the trigger.

Dorian, standing there in the open, raised an arm.

A metallic *thud* followed, along with the cessation of gunfire.

"Orb bot. It's down," said Dorian.

Kirsten peered around the side of the door into a hazy, smoke-filled hallway. Small flecks of glass and metal debris sparkled atop blue grey carpet. Continuous swearing in a man's whispery voice came from the vicinity of two small fires burning about fifty feet ahead. She couldn't make out much visually due to the smoke but sensed a ghostly presence about where the grumbling originated.

"Stupid, useless piece of shit, come on," grumbled the ghost.

Satomi followed her out of the elevator, clutching her small sword in both hands. The woman still appeared frightened, but a surface thought scan revealed she felt safer near Kirsten than alone in the elevator, even if it meant approaching the angry spirit.

Having an adult not only happy to see a psionic but regard her as a 'protector' offered a welcome change from the usual fear, suspicion, or derision she so often faced from the general public. Satomi's comment about swords implied a level of familiarity with spirits. Sadly, the woman had no psionic talents.

Kirsten advanced down the corridor, not bothering to pull the E-90 out, keeping her hand free for a lash if needed. Dorian walked on her left, Satomi on the right but mostly hiding behind her. As she drew closer, a human figure appeared out of the smoke, kicking at a dead orb bot the size of a gee-ball. A white shirt and nice pants gave him the look of corporate management. Grey had started to seep into his brown hair, whitening patches above his ears.

"Junk. Why do they buy such junk?" grumbled the ghost.

"Hey," called Kirsten. "I need you to calm down, okay. Tell me what's going on."

The ghost glanced in their direction for a moment, but resumed abusing the non-functional orb bot.

"Yes, I can see you." Kirsten edged closer. "I'm talking to the spirit kicking the bot."

He glared at her. "The damned thing stopped working."

"I shut it down." Dorian walked toward the man at a fast, deliberate stride. "Can't let you throw bullets at people."

The ghost glared at Dorian, raised his fists over his head, and let out an enraged scream.

Fire sprinklers went off, spraying frigid water everywhere. Kirsten tensed, stunned by the shock of a sudden, icy shower.

Satomi shrieked, arching her back.

Dorian leapt at the spirit, who dove into the floor to avoid the tackle. Dorian chased.

Kirsten sighed, not bothering to try shielding her face from the downpour. "This is going to be one of *those* ghosts."

A moment later, Satomi reached both hands up, parting the hair away from her face like a theater curtain. "The spirit's on the forty-second floor."

"How do you know?"

"Jun in the control station sees them on thermal. Your partner and the bad spirit are fist-fighting in the break room. Another orb is shooting up the cubicles down the hall from them."

Kirsten nodded, and ran to the elevator. *At least it's not raining in here.*

Satomi rushed after, yelling at someone to turn off the fire system.

They exchanged a glance. Satomi hit the button for the forty-second floor. For a brief moment, a sense of camaraderie came over Kirsten, being with a fellow member of the Short Girl Society, or the Five-Oh club as Nicole called it. Her friend thought it hilarious since Five-O had been an old slang term for police and Kirsten happened to be exactly five feet tall.

"How many are wounded or dead?" asked Kirsten.

"158 people suffered injuries. Somehow, no one died." Satomi reached out at thin air as if pushing buttons on a giant computer screen.

Kirsten squirmed at the thought of the woman having cybernetic implants in her head or eyes. "I don't think the ghost is trying to kill anyone. He's having a meltdown."

"Yes. I think you are right." Satomi nodded. "The shooting started in crowded offices but aimed high. He's destroying computers, furniture, and expensive equipment."

"Satomi?"

"Yes?"

"I'm going to send you a telepathic image, okay?"

"Sure."

Kirsten concentrated on the image of the spirit, projecting it into the woman's mind. "Do you recognize him?"

"Wow. He looks like a normal person. Is he the ghost?"

"Yes. They look ordinary to me. If I couldn't sense their energy, I'd never know they were ghosts just from looking at them."

"That's pretty cool. The apartment where I grew up was haunted, but the ghost was nice. Little old lady, just lonely. Umm, no, I don't recognize him. You think he used to work here?"

"Possible. Last time I had to deal with a ghost shooting up a corporate office, he'd been upset with the company and came back for revenge."

"Checking."

The elevator doors opened.

Kirsten ran into a deserted hallway. Traces of blood spattered the walls here and there. Smashed windows, broken electronics, and a few burning bots cluttered the corridor. It appeared the company had evacuated everyone already. Distant gunfire led Kirsten through a series of hallways and security doors—most of which lay in shattered pieces. She stopped short at a flurry of sparking ricochets hitting the floor at an intersection.

Back pressed to the wall, she edged up to the corner. Bullets continued to hit the floor less than three feet away from her. She didn't like her odds of hitting an orb bot, but still drew her E-90 as well as NetMini.

"Suri, link and display."

"You didn't say please," replied the AI in a somewhat whiny tone.

"Not now, Suri. Bullets are flying."

"Okay… okay…" The AI overacted a sigh, then opened a holo-panel above the device showing the view from the E-90's optical sight.

Kirsten stuck the laser pistol around the corner, watching the floating screen above the NetMini. Another twelve-inch orb bot floated in the middle of the hallway about forty feet away, spinning in circles while firing at nothing in particular. Experienced soldiers often struggled to shoot orb bots out of the air, but this one sat still in midair.

She lined up the crosshairs on the holo-panel and clicked the trigger.

A dark azure beam flickered in the thin haze of smoke from the ballistic propellant. Tiny spurts of molten metal shot out from both sides of the bot, which promptly thudded to the ground and caught fire. A hundred feet down the hall, a small flame indicated where the beam hit the wall.

Satomi stared at the E-90 the same adoring way Shani stared at unicorn toys.

She holstered it, stuffed the NetMini back in its clip on her belt, and rushed into the hall. "Thanks, Suri."

The NetMini chirped happily.

"Thirty-eight!" yelled Satomi.

Kirsten looked at her.

"They went down again. This way!" Satomi ran off.

Kirsten followed her to another elevator. Heavy, thudding gunfire echoed up from below, growing louder as they descended four floors. The doors parted to another hallway hazed with smoke and dust from pulverized drywall. She winced at the loudness of the machine gun and intermittent explosions. Dorian ran across the corridor from right to left, about a hundred yards away. Seconds later, the 'manager ghost' dashed left to right, Dorian right behind him.

A footlocker-sized bot backed out of a doorway on miniature tank treads, still offloading bullets from a long-barreled machine gun into the room. Kirsten pulled the E-90 and shot the security bot repeatedly until it stopped firing and burst into flames. The relative quiet in the absence of gunfire felt like a hug from the universe.

The manager ghost again darted across the hallway, Dorian right behind him.

Kirsten sprinted after them, passing a large room of shot-up computer components. Satomi stopped at the door, peering in while she likely reported the fire to the security over her implanted comm. At the first intersection, Kirsten cornered to the right, following the sounds of a brawl to the third door, which led to a large room of cubicles.

Dorian and the manager spirit tumbled over each other on the floor. Her partner had the advantage in training, but the ghost made up for it with greater physical strength. He slipped away and started to lunge to his feet. Dorian sprang after him, jumping on his back, taking him to the floor again.

Grumbling, Kirsten summoned the lash, swiping it at the manager ghost in an underpowered strike, hoping to slap reason back into his mind rather than tear him apart. The energy cord scorched a burn trail up the ghost's chest and over his face.

He screamed, pawing at the spot; the distraction enabled Dorian to get a better grip, though pain compliance grapples didn't work too well on ectoplasm.

"Fuck's sake!" shouted the manager ghost. "Don't do that!"

"Stop running around blowing shit up!" Kirsten pointed the lash at him. "What the hell is wrong with you?"

"I'm angry!"

"Obviously." She stared at him. "Why?"

The rage somewhat melted out of his expression. "I dunno. I'm just pissed off and want to mess shit up."

"Did you used to work for Mayoshi?"

"No, I hate mayo. Mustard all the way."

"Guess not." Dorian dragged the guy upright, still holding him.

"Since when do the damn cops care what the hell ghosts do?" grumbled the spirit.

"Since you endanger people's lives." Kirsten walked right up to him.

He squirmed, instinctively trying to retreat from the energy cord. "What's up with the glowing death noodle?"

"It's a weapon I really don't like having to use." Kirsten paused, watching the mild slice in his ectoplasmic form seal up. "Ghosts don't go to prison. If I can't talk them down or solve their issues, and they remain a threat to people…"

"Okay, okay." He held his hands up. "I get it."

Satomi ran in the door. "Whoa. He's right in front of you."

The manager appeared as solid as any other living person, so he couldn't have manifested to the living. Whenever a ghost did so, Kirsten's perception of them changed to ghostly transparency. She eyed the other woman, peeking at her surface thoughts. Satomi saw a light orb hovering where the manager ghost stood.

"Yeah. Give me a moment." Kirsten looked back at him. "Why are you tearing this office apart? Grudge?"

"Nah. I died long before this place went up. Just got so angry I needed to vent."

"What made you so angry?"

He grabbed his hair in both hands. "The noise. The damn noise…"

"This again," said Dorian.

"Are you in control now?" Kirsten focused on his essence. Alas, he didn't feel familiar, though seemed to be much older as a ghost than Dorian.

"Yeah. It's stopped." He eyed the lash. "Is that thing necessary?"

"As long as you stand here and talk to me, no. I noticed you didn't kill anyone even though you could have."

The ghost gestured at the cubicles. "Yeah. Just breaking stuff to blow off steam. Not here to hurt anyone."

Dorian let go. "There are plenty of places you could've gone off without so many people in the way."

The spirit blinked at him. "What part of irrational anger includes having the reasoning capacity to select a safe place to destroy?"

Kirsten almost laughed. "Okay. What's your name?"

"Nikolas Platt. With a k. N-i-k, not c-h." He grumbled. "People misspelled it constantly before I died. I'm not dealing with it now."

"Fair enough. Tell me about the noise. Maybe I can help."

Nikolas again grabbed his hair in two fists. "It's incessant, like bugs under my skin. Gets into my head. Usually, I walk off before it drives me nuts. Tried to ignore it today, but it invaded my head. Made me so damn angry."

"If you tell me what the noise is, I'll try to stop it."

"Won't stop," yelled Nikolas, sounding manic. "Makes me feel things. Sad. Angry. Wild. I hate it. I hate it so much and it just won't stop. Dragged me here. Don't remember picking this place."

"Easy…" She released the lash and raised her hands in a comforting gesture. "Calm down."

Nikolas let go of his hair, his arms falling at his sides. He had the expression of a confused puppy who didn't know why the human yelled at him. "Aethervein."

"Sorry, what?" Kirsten blinked.

"Aethervein," muttered Nikolas—before disappearing.

"Shit," whispered Kirsten.

"Hey, the light orb shot into the floor." Satomi pointed.

"At least we stopped the rampage." Dorian whistled while surveying the room. "Going to be interesting watching the insurance company try to wriggle out of paying this claim."

"Yeah." Kirsten faced Satomi. "Please let your manager know Division 0 will need to document the effects of this attack."

Satomi nodded. "Okay."

"Dispatch, Wren. Site secure. Need an Admin team here to document the damage. It's a bit much for me to do alone and I've got two kids in the PC. Can't leave them up there for hours."

"Acknowledged, lieutenant," replied Specialist Wiley. "Standby."

"Did you say children?" asked Satomi.

"In Division 0, 'take your kids to work' day occurs randomly, sprung on us at the worst possible time." Dorian flashed a cheesy smile.

"I'm the only astral on the West Coast. Was on my way home for the day when the call came in." Kirsten rubbed her forehead.

"Ahh." Satomi winced. "Ouch. Rough. I got the okay to send you video from our security systems. We have seventeen areas of damage throughout the building in varying degrees of severity."

"Great. That'll be a big help." Kirsten pulled her NetMini off her belt on the way out the door. "Might as well start with the server room over here."

KIRSTEN PUSHED THE ELEVATOR BUTTON FOR THE ROOF.

She'd briefed the five-person Admin team, giving them instructions to capture photographs and three-dimensional enviro-scans of all the areas affected by the manifestation. Tomorrow, she planned to return and interview people herself, but for now, she couldn't make Evan and Shani sit in a patrol craft all night.

A cool post-sunset breeze flooded the elevator as soon as the doors opened. Weak lights on knee-high posts provided the bare minimum of illumination needed for people to locate their hovercars. In addition to the area being mostly empty, snap-flashes of blue from the patrol craft's bar lights made its location rather obvious.

"What the heck is Aethervein?" Kirsten stepped out of the elevator, heading for the car.

"Either a drug, a gang, or a band." Dorian shrugged. "Nikolas mentioned music, so I'm going to assume it's a band."

"The old woman from 29P mentioned music, didn't she?"

"Technically, she said 'racket,' which I believe is 'old person' for music." Dorian chuckled. "Think some kids are blasting music too loud somewhere?"

"Doesn't sound plausible."

"I've heard some people complain about music being so loud—or awful—it could raise the dead. Never expected it to be literal."

"Bad," muttered Kirsten past a smile.

Dorian jumped at the patrol craft, but rather than go into it, he bounced off the armored shell with a dull *thud*. "Ouch. Aww... what the hell?" He slapped the door.

Laughing, Kirsten opened her door and peeked in at the kids. They sat in the back seat, clinging to each other, both seemingly frightened. Bots shooting at the car wouldn't have scared him.

"Mom!" yelled Evan, scrambling into a hug.

"What made you blockade the PC?"

"There's a bad spirit trying to hurt us."

Shani trembled. "It's *really* scary."

"He's gone."

Evan jumped back, pointing. "Behind you!"

The look of pure fear on her son's face caused her brain to summon the lash as a subconscious reaction. Kirsten whirled around and locked stares with a scrawny, vaporous apparition of pure darkness creeping up behind her. Shadowy claws on oversized hands, long, distortedly thin arms, a 'hooded cloak' shaped head, and nothing but a cloud where legs should be pulled a single word to the tip of her mind.

Wraith.

18

NO TRUE QUIET

F ew spirits embodied wickedness in the way wraiths did.

Kirsten swiped the lash at it without hesitation. The wraith zoomed backward, circling to the right and attempting to get to the patrol craft. She snapped the energy whip in its path, again driving it back.

Shani squealed.

Kirsten spun to look at the kids, fearing a second wraith. Evan had climbed out of the patrol craft. He stood right outside the door, smearing blood from a cut on his hand over the blade of the sword she kept stashed between the front seats. Spectral light glowed from the red stain, seeping into the metal.

Dorian fired his E-86 at the wraith, launching pulses of spirit energy rather than a laser beam. The first one hit it in the chest, the next two missing as the creature raced around in a circle, faster than a human could run, going around to the passenger side.

It fiended to get at the kids like a Lace head chasing a fix, though appeared somewhat torn between them and attacking Kirsten. She jumped up onto the hood and ran to the other side, swinging the lash up into the wraith's path, warding it off.

Hissing, the wraith raised its claws, caught in a mental battle between its need to attack the innocent and its fear of the energy radiating from her weapon. Dorian ran to the back end of the patrol craft and resumed shooting.

The wraith rushed straight toward Kirsten, giving a keening wail.

She snapped the lash at its vaporous body, meeting about as much resistance as swinging a sword into a standing column of water. For an instant, the inky darkness obscured the intense glow. Despite the relative insubstantiality of the hit, the wraith went flying off to the side, out of control. Kirsten chased after it, striking again and again, missing by mere inches each time as the shadow outpaced her.

Grr. Damn thing! She pushed herself to run even harder.

The wraith abruptly reversed, flying straight back at her in an instant. She shrieked in surprise, crossing her arms over her face. A blast of arctic ice washed over her, but the wraith kept going. Teeth chattering, she forced herself to turn, watching the dark spot rush headlong at the kids.

Evan gave the sword to Shani and ran to the side, waving his arms. "Hey. Here! Leave her alone. Get me. I can't hurt you."

"No!" shouted Kirsten.

The wraith veered to the right, following Evan.

Kirsten struggled to make her frozen legs move. Screaming like a Vakken Shield Maiden from the Monwyn world, she charged after the wraith despite knowing she'd never get close enough to strike before it reached her son.

The sword flew in from the side, swiping through the wraith, peeling a six-foot trail of shadow in its wake out of the creature's body. Shani waved her arm around, the sword swerving and dipping in response. The wraith looked down at itself, then turned its hood toward her.

Shani screamed in terror; her concentration on Telekinesis shattered, the sword clattered to the rooftop.

Dorian jumped in front of the girl and shot the wraith in the face, sending a small puff of black vapor out the back of its hood. Shani burst into wailing tears, calling for her mother. The wraith started to turn back to Evan, but upon seeing Kirsten coming, whirled to face her—too late.

She swung the lash into the wraith's torso, commanding the energy cord to coil around and around, holding and crushing the abomination like a hand squeezing an egg. The wraith flailed its shadowy arms, twitching and convulsing for three seconds before exploding in a flash of extreme cold.

The interior of the patrol craft went dark. Hundreds of post-mounted lights on the roof parking area shut off.

Kirsten stared at a scrap of ectoplasm writhing on the rooftop, a glowing pale-grey lump of snotlike ooze. She approached the fragment of a once-human consciousness, so consumed by malevolence they'd become a wraith. Similar to a poltergeist, they lacked full sentience, a mindless entity driven to destroy life. The amount of life energy they could absorb from a child tempted them like irresistible candy. Naiveté, idealism, and hope attracted them as well.

She felt no need to bother Harbingers for such a creature.

One final swat with the lash splattered the oozeling into a blast of ethereal smoke. The sense of obliteration passed by, this time without guilt of any kind. She'd destroyed a basic elemental form of evil, a dangerous creature, not a living soul.

Where the heck did a wraith come from out here?

Lights on the waist-high posts lining the parking rows flickered back on. Her NetMini beeped while rebooting, as did her armband terminal.

Musical jingles came from the direction of the patrol craft. She looked away from the splat mark at the car. A pair of advert bots hovered by Evan and Shani, each one surrounded by a dozen holo-panels showing toy ads.

Kirsten sighed and released the lash.

At least Shani no longer appeared ready to wet herself, instead gazing up in awe at the toys on the screens in front of her.

Evan mostly ignored the bot, staring at Kirsten.

She walked up to him, eyeing the sword in his hand. He must've run to grab it after Shani dropped it. "Why?"

"Just in case I had to stop it from hurting Shani."

"Why not get back in the car and put the Blockade up again?"

Evan shook his head. "Takes too long. It would'a got us if I tried."

She pulled him into a hug. "You know I don't like it when you cut yourself."

"Yeah. But it's already gone." He held his hand up so she could see it.

His stomach growled.

The advert bot bombarding him with toy ads switched to food, mostly fried things, nuggets, and so on.

"It's damn unnerving how they know people are hungry." Kirsten couldn't help but feel hungrier for looking at the tempting pictures. "Thanks, but we have food at home."

Both bots drooped, attempting to convey sadness.

"Shan, you okay?" Kirsten brushed a hand over the girl's head.

"Yeah. It made me super scared, but it stopped. Just a mind trick." She ground the toe of her sneaker into the roof. "Prolly gonna have a nightmare anyway, even if I know it's a lie. I saw you splat the bad ghost, so I'm not scared of it now."

Kirsten ruffled her hair. "Good. Okay, you two. Hop in. Let's go home."

"Are you gonna get squeezy later?" asked Evan.

My kid was five feet away from a wraith he taunted to come after him. "Yeah."

"Cool." He climbed into the patrol craft. "Me, too."

Kirsten got in, set the car to auto-drive home, and created another Inquest file to log the encounter with the wraith. Details in the report for this and Nikolas going on a rampage could wait. "Bleh. I'll finish them later."

"Not like you have any idea who that was or why they showed up here. Nor will anyone, ever." Dorian shivered. "Hate wraiths."

"Yeah." She stared out the windscreen at the stream of hovercar traffic ahead of them, the sea of taillights mesmerizing. "You think the wraith might have heard this 'noise' the other ghosts are talking about?"

"No clue."

"Do you hear any noise?"

Dorian looked around. "Only the constant advertising jingles. And I do mean *constant*. There's no true silence left in the city."

"The Beneath," said Kirsten in a soft, wistful tone. "It's quiet down there. I used to be able to hear water dripping… of course, I had a plastic bag for a dress and didn't know if I'd eat any given day."

"I'm sure it's quiet in the Badlands, too, but I'm not going to live out there to get away from advert jingles."

Evan and Shani hummed the music from the Kwik Kleen ads.

Dorian fake moaned in agony. "On second thought…"

The kids laughed.

Kirsten closed her eyes, too choked up to speak at seeing them happy so soon after being near a wraith. *Kids can't imagine what it really would've done to them. Why did it show up here? The one time I'm reckless and bring Ev—no… he's been with me before and no wraith showed up. It would've been here, anyway.*

Kirsten ended up fixing dinner for Shani as well, since Nila *still* hadn't returned from her call.

A few texts conveyed she probably wouldn't be home for a while, dealing with a bunch of psionic gang thugs and a hostage situation. After dinner, Evan and Shani cuddled with her on the sofa, both letting their guard down and clinging. The wraith had scared Evan worse than he'd let on. He needed some 'squeezy time' as he called it. Kirsten happily obliged.

When Sam called, Kirsten apologized for missing a chance to have dinner, but he already knew she'd been sent on a dispatch. They talked a little about work, mostly 'the noise.' He mentioned some obscure references to unexplained 'hums' some people reported hearing in certain places, often attributed to aliens or secret government projects. No concrete information existed about what caused the phenomenon. He also mentioned ELF sound, or extreme low frequency. Theoretically, exposure to ELF could trigger feelings of dread, anxiety, or panic in humans and had been cited as the reason some areas seemed 'haunted.'

Of course, neither aerial hums nor ELF sound explained the sudden severe surge in paranormal activity.

Later, after a Monwyn movie, Shani borrowed one of Kirsten's T-shirts as a nightgown. Kirsten crawled into bed with a kid under each arm, neither one of them wanting to be alone after meeting a wraith.

Kirsten didn't mind.

She didn't want to be alone either.

19

PLASMAHAWK

The following morning, Kirsten spent two hours at the Mayoshi Technology office.

She ran on four hours of sleep, three triple espressos, and a mocha latte. Both kids had nightmare issues, waking her up—unintentionally—multiple times. Kirsten didn't blame them, though by the time the alarm went off, she despised wraiths. The child who lived in a house she'd responded to last year with a wraith in it refused to even go inside, clawing the hell out of her mother when the woman attempted to carry her closer to the building.

Considering neither Evan nor Shani ran screaming at the mere presence of a wraith spoke volumes of their bravery. She couldn't fault them a nightmare or four. Conjurations of the mind often proved far scarier than anything in reality.

Still, it made for a rough night. Nila hadn't gotten back home until three in the morning. She'd be collecting the kids after school today as they'd given her the day off to make up for last night.

It astonished her the number of people at Mayoshi who'd seen Nikolas appear. She assumed he'd manifested on purpose to scare them out of his way so he could tear up inanimate objects. The handful of executives she'd briefed on the events of last night appeared relieved the company hadn't been targeted specifically, though expressed dismay in terms of liability. This, of course, meant she would likely wind up in a courtroom at some point within the next six months trying to convince a judge ghosts existed when Mayoshi sued their insurance company for refusing to cover the damage.

She returned to her desk in the squad room a little after eleven and collapsed in a heap.

The clock jumped twenty minutes in an instant.

Kirsten snapped awake and sat up fast, looking around in hopes no one noticed she'd passed out. Dorian's soft snickering came from behind, but no one alive appeared to catch her. She probably wouldn't get in trouble for taking a quick nap—after all, they had a barracks room specifically to allow people to catch a few Zs on long shifts. However, it would look bad for someone to be asleep at their desk if a high-ranking officer happened to come by.

"Hey, Dorian?" She twisted to look at him. "You know the guy in Sam's office who puts all that stuff around his computer to ward you off?"

"Yeah." He grinned.

"Does any of it really work?"

He raised an eyebrow. "Why? Getting tired of me?"

She frowned. "No. Absolutely not. Just wondering if there's a good luck charm or something out there to give me some breathing space. We've had more 21-47s in the past three weeks than the entire previous year."

"You're exaggerating a little. We usually average one every two weeks."

"Still. I can't even take a breath before another one happens." She swung back around to face her terminal. "At least there's some information now. What the hell is Aethervein?"

She ran a GlobeNet search, taking a few tries to get the spelling right.

According to the Net, Aethervein was a relatively new band who'd released their first album about a year ago. In a short time, they'd amassed a fair amount of fan pages and message forums. Kirsten poked a link, starting playback on a track titled, 'The Halls of Introspection.' Dreamy electronica underscored a female voice singing in tones rather than words.

"This sounds like the sort of music people on Flowerbasket get high to," said Dorian. "Mellow, spacey, repetitive."

She tapped her finger on the desk, listening. "It's not bad."

"No. Not remarkable either. There are a ton of groups out there like this."

"Would you call it noise?"

Dorian chuckled. "No. This would put ghosts to sleep, not drive them into a destructive rage."

"Time to abuse police privileges."

"How so?" asked Dorian.

She cracked her knuckles. "Nikolas said Aethervein when I asked him about the noise. There has to be some connection. So, I'm going to find who's in this band and go talk to them."

"It's not an abuse of police privileges unless you're a fan and only using your access so you can meet them."

"Well, considering I *just* found out about them yesterday and they're connected to multiple open Inquests, I think I'm safe." She accessed the government database, pulling up the official registration for the band Aethervein.

Her NetMini rang, playing the ringtone associated with her personal PID rather than the Division 0 one she gave out to people involved in paranormal events. Off the top of her head, she could only think of five people she'd given the PID to: Evan, Sam, Nicole, Nila, and Captain Eze. This caller didn't display any identity information.

"Suri, log this connection and send it to Div 2 if it turns out to be suspicious. Please."

"Okay," chirped the AI.

She answered. "Hello?"

A relatively generic brown-haired Caucasian anime cartoon man appeared, obviously an avatar. "Oops. I may have the wrong number. Are you the one who deals with ghost problems?"

"Yes. Who is this and how did you get my PID?"

The cartoon man grinned so hard his nose disappeared. "Excellent! Wow, I was expecting someone older. Are you eighteen yet?"

She frowned. "If you're hitting on me…"

"No. Promise. Just kinda wrong asking a kid to visit a bad area."

"I'm not a kid, and you haven't told me who you are or how you got this PID."

A sweat bead the size of a potato appeared at his left temple. "Ehh, I'm good online. Doesn't really matter."

"You're a hacker." She rolled her eyes.

"Someone's got a fan club." Dorian winked.

Kirsten sighed.

"Hacker… whatever. I've been called worse. Look, I need your help. Some super crazy shit is happening. This dude is appearing out of thin air, breaking stuff. Been hearing demonic laughter, breathing, footsteps, swear something straight-up grabbed me by the neck. Shit's been thrown at me. I've been pushed at windows and stairs. Even had a power cable try to stab me in the eye."

"Wow. Wonder what he did to piss off a spirit." Dorian whistled.

"Can you help me?" asked the guy. "I found a spot where the attacks have more or less stopped, but it's not a great area. If I stay here, the locals are going to be a problem. If I leave, the ghost is going to kill me."

"Not a great area sounds like black zone," deadpanned Kirsten.

"Must be a *really* horrible one if a ghost won't go there." Dorian chuckled.

"Where are you?" Kirsten pushed the Aethervein lookup aside and brought up a sector map along with another lookup window. "And who are you?"

"I'm a quarter mile away from the southern border of Sector 1509, near the eastern corner."

She scrolled the sector map to 1509. Sure enough, it had been blacked out of the system due to 'extreme danger of violence.' 1509 sat on the edge of the city by the ocean, close to the southern end of the elevated city plates. The actual ground under the city in the same region had once been called Long Beach, part of Los Angeles.

"Full of Angels…" Kirsten tilted her head side to side. "Gang issues?"

"Not so sure." Dorian walked over to stand beside her. "The Angels prefer civilization. Can't sell chems if there aren't people around with credits. 1509's most likely collecting random miscreants, crazy augs, and possibly some small self-contained gangs who don't leave the area."

"Great…" She grumbled.

"Hey, kiddo," said the hacker. "I'll pay you fifty grand if you get this thing off my ass."

"I'm not a medtech. Don't do moles."

He laughed. "Seriously. Fifty grand if you can stop this… whatever it is from killing me."

"Have you killed anyone or been responsible for any deaths in the past twenty years?" asked Kirsten.

"If I have, it's been an accident. Took a bot or two out of the sky. It's *possible* they crashed into someone, but I doubt it."

"I need to know what I'm getting into. What the heck is your name?"

"Max Buffer," said the hacker.

"Wow. Look, dude. I'm blonde, but I'm not *that* blonde. I know what a buffer is, and you're about to max out my patience buffer. Aren't you hacker types supposed to be egomaniacs? Proud of your accomplishments? What's your handle?"

Dorian chuckled.

"It doesn't ma—AAAH—ter." The animated head whipped to the side, screaming from a mouth big enough to swallow a watermelon whole. "Holy shit… uhh, okay. Fine. I'm Plasmahawk."

Kirsten scowled. "What are the odds?"

"Probably not too bad considering he's likely hacked at least half the city's shower units. I imagine quite a few people want this guy's head on a plate."

"I meant what are the odds *this* guy calls *me?*"

"There didn't seem to be any other option for seriously dealing with an angry spirit." The huge sweat bead reappeared on the anime figure's head, along with a cheesy smile.

She locked her desk terminal. "Okay. I'm on the way. And you don't need to pay me."

"Excellent." He grinned. "Head to the southeast corner of Sector 1509. Once you're close enough, I'll send a waypoint to your 'Mini."

"Sounds like a trap." Dorian put a hand on her shoulder. "Why doesn't he send it now?"

"All right." Kirsten ended the call. "Suri, please package the entire recording up and send it to my official inbox, copy Div 2 and Sam with a request to verify the origin."

"Okay," chimed the NetMini.

"He's not sending me the waypoint now because he's afraid we'll roll in with a Division 6 assault squad to arrest him. If he sees too many of us coming for him, he'll take his chances with the ghost. If it's only me, he'll show me his front door."

"You're going, aren't you?" Dorian folded his arms.

"Yeah. Can't let a ghost kill someone, even a jackass like Plasmahawk." She fast-walked to Captain Eze's office. "Cap?"

He looked up from his terminal. "Good afternoon. What's on your mind?"

"You know the guy with the autoshower ransomware? Plasmahawk?" She tapped her NetMini. "He just called my personal PID asking for help. Looks like he has a ghost trying to kill him. Sounds fairly serious. He used the word 'demonic,' but it's unlikely an abyssal."

"What makes you so sure it isn't?" asked Captain Eze.

"He lived long enough to track me down and call me." Kirsten rested her hands on her hips.

"All right. You know where this man is?"

"Generally. Sector 1509. For some reason, the ghost is leaving him alone wherever he is now. I'm guessing he's found an old bit of sanctified ground or someplace where the energy is off-putting to spirits. He's going to send me a more exact waypoint when I get closer. Can you put a tac team on standby in case I get in over my head with the locals?"

"You don't want to lead a team in?"

"He'll spook and not send me his location if he sees a whole team coming."

"Depends on how scared he is of this ghost." Dorian tapped his foot. "He did tell you his name rather than risk you not going."

She looked at him. "Yes, but giving me his name makes him *more* likely to be afraid of a team. If we didn't know who he was, he wouldn't be worried."

Captain Eze leaned back in his chair, lips pursed. "All right. I trust you'll be as careful as possible. I'll have a tactical unit shadowing you from a distance."

"Thanks, captain." She smiled and hurried out.

Dorian jogged after her to the garage.

THE SEVENTY-FIVE-MILE FLIGHT SOUTHWEST TO SECTOR 1509 FROM the PAC took a hair over eleven minutes.

To avoid having crazy cybergangers shoot missiles at the patrol craft, she decided not to fly directly into the black zone and circled around to approach from the southeast, cruising in over the grey Sector 1458. Based on the appearance of the buildings and general conditions at ground level, she kept flying west into Sector 1457, directly south of the 1509 black zone. From the air, the demarcation between grey and black took the form of a rapid decline in the integrity of high rises, and a near total lack of surviving glass in the windows. Within Sector 1509, the city looked like it had suffered a nuclear war, only with slightly less melting of the plastisteel structures. Destruction had, as it invariably tended to do, crept past the arbitrary square boundary of a grid sector on all three sides. The western border of 1509 had nowhere for the blight to creep, being the edge of the city plates overlooking the ocean.

It seemed unlikely fish in the area overindulged in cybernetics and did chems, but she'd seen weird things before.

She descended between rows of filthy high-rise buildings, skimming along about fifty feet above the traction-coated plastisteel roads. Wrecked cars, burn barrels, barricades for gang warfare, and the occasional working land vehicle went by below. People who stayed in grey zones typically didn't shoot at police on sight but could become dangerous if provoked. Enough time spent in the armpit of civilization, a person stopped caring how much trouble they got into.

A street a little over a mile from the start of the extreme decay finally offered enough open space to set down. Due to all the junk in the roads, only small ground cars could navigate here. The spectacle of a police patrol craft drew hundreds of curious locals out of various shadowy holes. Faces peered at her from high rises. Filthy kids dangling on fire escapes watched her go by. Vagrants emerged from alleys and trash bins, drawn by the unusual sound of ion thrusters.

"Are you sure this is a good idea?" asked Dorian.

Kirsten frowned at a pack of pre-teens sitting with their legs through the bars of a fifth-story patio. "What are children doing here?"

"Living... sort of. We're not in the black zone yet."

She extended the ground wheels and set down in the middle of the road. "I'm not *too* worried. Street punks don't usually mess with Zeroes. You know that. Div 1 always gives them a hard time. We don't."

"Right. Shall I fly the PC to 1406?" He pointed at the closest non-grey sector. "If I don't, you'll come back to a bare frame. They'll steal the armor right off it."

"You are exaggerating, but better safe than being grilled by an inquiry board over losing a PC."

He chuckled. "If we were Div 1, I'd make a joke about them being more upset at us risking the PC than your life, but we're not."

"Div 1 isn't *that* jaded."

"My dear sweet ingénue, they're *all* that jaded. Division 0 people are simply harder to replace."

"What did you call me?" Kirsten shot him a sideways glance.

"An innocent, naïve young woman."

She sighed at the dashboard and pushed the door up. Even expecting it, the stink made her cough. Sector 1457 smelled like the drain pipe out of a Division 6 locker clogged up with charred roadkill.

A few hundred people, most of whom peered at her from windows overhead on both sides of the street, stared at her in curiosity. The patrol craft lifted off again, throwing a scattering of blue sparks across the ground.

Beep.

Her NetMini received an incoming directional ping, similar to how various common dating apps allowed people using it to find each other when close. Keeping a wary eye on her surroundings, Kirsten crossed the street, heading down a debris strewn sidewalk. A single police officer showing up in a grey zone stirred curiosity more than anything. Locals would react to a larger group by fleeing or possibly becoming violent, but only if they overdid it on chems. Sector 1509 hadn't been the site of any military attempt to retake ground from the undesirable elements, so the denizens lacked access to abandoned heavy weapons. It didn't prove no one had anti-armor rockets or explosives, however. Cybergangers frequently got a hold of illegal weapons on the black market and ended up hiding in disavowed sectors, confident the police would never go after them there.

For the most part, it proved true. Pursuing a suspect into a black zone required almost as much effort as overthrowing the government of a tiny Third World nation. The cost involved in mobilizing a large Division 6 assault—or sending in active military personnel—far exceeded the presumptive value of capturing a criminal. Plus, as Captain Eze told her on more than one occasion, conditions in these places amounted to worse than prison—mostly because more people would actively be trying to kill them at any one moment and no one brought them food at regular intervals.

Off-gridders and fringers stared at her as she walked among them. A few had cybernetic arms, eyes, or legs, though none wore the insignias of an organized cybergang. She scanned the surface thoughts of anyone who gave her a bad vibe. Most were confused at seeing *one* cop so close to a black zone. Once they realized the significance of her uniform, people mostly retreated behind a wall of fear toward psionics. One guy with red cybernetic eyes thought she looked like a fourteen-year-old. He argued with himself over the urge to help her 'get out of the bad part of town.' He'd picked up on her being psionic by the Division 0 uniform but didn't completely trust she wouldn't 'freak out' and melt his brain. Still, his protective urge surprised her, even if being mistaken for a kid annoyed her.

Guess it doesn't really bother me too much, or I'd go to Reinventions. They could make me taller, give me bigger boobs, curvier hips. She mentally stuck out her tongue at the idea. *What a waste of money. How many people could eat for the cost of vanity?*

A wiry man stepped in front of her. Metal lens eyes sticking a few inches out from his face whirred, focusing down at her. Spikes covered his giant metal shoulder pads, almost as sharp as the spiky blue hair sprouting from his scalp. She peered up at him, disturbed at the realization the shoulder pads appeared to be screwed into his flesh.

"Police ain't allowed here," growled the augmented thug.

"Says who?" asked Kirsten.

His iris lenses widened, whirring faintly. "The hell you think you're talkin' to?"

"An idiot with too many microchips where brains should be." She frowned. *"Go away."*

Everyone within thirty or so feet able to see the glow in her eyes fell silent.

The aug twitched, a line of drool rolling over his chin. His iris lens eyes snapped shut for a millisecond in a simulation of blinking. Two seconds later, he strode off in a random direction as urgently as if he had ten seconds to get to a toilet before his ass exploded. People continued gawking at her.

She checked the waypoint on her NetMini and resumed walking.

Telempaths have it easy. A little radiant fear keeps the morons away. They don't have to kill anyone in places like this.

Amazingly, she passed a few shops and food vendors still in operation despite being a quarter mile away from a black zone. *Even the violent idiots need to eat.* She couldn't decide if the people running businesses here qualified as brave, foolish, or desperate. Food served by a person behind three-inch-thick bulletproof armored glass had to be the sort of stuff one ate when choices ran out.

People thinned out block after block. Eventually, after she'd gone a few cross-streets into the official black zone, she felt like the lone survivor of the end times, wandering between collapsing high-rises. A brownish-grey 'sand' formed from the long-ago crushed remains of a million windows, decorative siding fallen from the sides of buildings, destroyed furniture, machinery, and various chemicals crunched under her boots. The sediment gathered in windblown piles against wrecked cars or the sides of buildings.

Proximity to the ocean lent a noticeable salty flavor to the air. Old street signs scattered around on the walls or stuck to the sides of ruined cars hinted at an open access to the Beneath nearby. Someone in the area had evidently developed a fondness for scavenging stop signs, one-way signs, rectangular green street name signs, and so on. Even a few ancient license plates hung from walls like ornaments.

If anything existed akin to a sense of nostalgia for a place one hated and feared rather than looked fondly back on, Kirsten experienced it. The trappings of three centuries ago everywhere brought her back to the two years she'd spent living in the Beneath as a child. Other than a few fond memories of nice ghosts looking after her, she mostly had horrible memories of being down there. Near starvation, running away from crazy tribals or the Discarded, sleeping in trash, hoping no one found her before she woke up, struggling to find food. Worst of all, the man who took advantage of her when she'd been twelve. In a strange way, she considered him responsible for her present life. She would never credit the man who coerced her into having sex for food as any sort of savior, but if he hadn't terrified her enough to flee to the surface, she'd have stayed down there, grown too big to fit through the pipes, and spent the rest of her—probably short —life living like a wild creature.

In him, she had finally encountered something scarier than the worry Mother would find her if she returned to the city above.

Kirsten squeezed her hands into fists, stuck trying to figure out how she'd react to running into him again. *I'm way too damn nice. I'd only arrest him. Bleh. Captain Eze is right. Being down there is already prison. Besides, he's gotta be dead by now.*

Another beep came from the NetMini.

Kirsten paused in front of a collapsing hundred-story former residence tower. According to the red triangle on her NetMini, she'd arrived at the place where Plasmahawk waited for her. Telepathy wasn't her strongest ability, though she rated higher in it than Mind Blast. Granted, she hadn't gone through a re-evaluation after the fiasco at Konstantin's mansion where she'd gone on a Mind Blasting spree. She closed her eyes and opened her thoughts, searching via Telepathy for any living minds within whatever range she had.

Astral Sense let her pick up the presence of ghosts out to a few hundred meters in all directions. Using it frequently from age six to ten, and damn near constantly from ten to twelve, resulted in it testing at a high rating when Division 0 first found her. After years of handling haunting cases, she'd only gotten better. Psionic powers grew like muscles. The more one used them, the stronger they became.

She'd never tested the limits of her telepathic range but assumed it far shorter than her astral. It ought to at least be enough to check the first room inside the building for an ambush. Sensing no one alive, she rested her hand on the E-90 and approached the entrance.

The lobby of the old apartment building appeared to be the site of a bomb blast. No sign of any desk remained, the entire space charred black. Someone had painted a twelve-foot-wide pentagram in the middle of the room, circumscribing it with unusual symbols. She recognized a few of them in the sense of having seen them before, but not what they meant. The remains of candles, dead rats, and a few human bones lay in the center of the five-pointed star.

If the room had a paranormal presence, it lacked the energy to be noticeable over her ambient nervousness. Despite having confidence in her Suggestion ability, she didn't enjoy being alone in a disavowed sector. Most cops dreaded black zones due to heavily augmented, insane people who would laugh off most department-issued sidearms. Cyborgs didn't worry her. Androids, on the other hand, did. They didn't have biological brains to use Suggestion on. On the plus side, the chances of encountering an AI robot in a black zone amounted to nothing. Such beings didn't have any need to hide from the law in slums.

She cautiously approached the ritual circle. "Wonder if this is why the ghost is avoiding the place. It's definitely not sanctified ground."

"Heh. This place is more like the opposite of sanctified," said Plasmahawk, his voice the same as what had come out of her NetMini earlier.

Kirsten looked up and left at the hallway going deeper into the building.

A mid-twenties guy leaned against the wall, hands in the pockets of loose lavender slacks. He wore a strange coat, much longer in back than front, made of blinding, sparkly purple-pink material likely visible from low-Earth orbit in the right lighting conditions. Other than his bizarre outfit, he looked unremarkable. Late twenties, brown hair, pale like he rarely went outside. A few blinking lights behind his left ear flickered between blue and green. Dark circles under his eyes indicated he'd not been sleeping well recently.

"You're younger than I expected," said Kirsten.

"Hah. What were you hoping to see?"

"Dunno. Bird made out of plasma?" She shrugged.

"We're not online. My avatar is a beautiful hawk." He un-leaned from the wall and approached her. "I appreciate you taking the risk of coming out here."

She dove into his surface thoughts, still suspecting a trick. Surprisingly, he had no intention to do anything to her at all and genuinely appeared frightened of a spirit. He did, alas, wonder if she might be fifteen and felt guilty for dragging her out to a black zone. The concern didn't impress her, not after meeting Tamsen who he'd been responsible for trapping in an autoshower tube for most of a day, never mind likely thousands of other people.

"Yeah, so I have no idea why the damn thing didn't follow me here." He kicked at the circle. "Think it's this?"

"Might be, but this circle doesn't have much energy to it."

Plasmahawk pointed back over his shoulder. "Maybe down the hallway then. It's quite creepy in the courtyard."

"This place has a courtyard?"

"Yeah. The building's a square, open shaft up the middle. Probably did it so more apartments had outside windows."

Curious, Kirsten approached the hallway, advancing about halfway down toward a set of smashed metal-framed doors, beyond which lay an overgrown mass of bushes and trees—a giant flower box left out of control. As soon as she saw the enclosed garden, a familiar heavy sense of gloom settled over her. Something out there stared back at her.

Not *something*… the Abyss.

"Oh. Now I understand."

"Are you mind-reading the trees?" asked Plasmahawk with a bit of a chuckle.

"No. There's a breach out in the courtyard. It's a place where Harbingers come across." *And probably other things if they can find it or have the power to.* Kirsten backed up. "The spirit going after you is pretty dark if it's afraid to get close to a breach."

"Damn thing sure seemed evil." Plasmahawk whistled. "I mean, do nice ghosts try to stick a 48-kilovolt wire up a man's nose?"

Yeah, said Dorian's voice in her imagination. *The mean ones aim for other openings.*

Kirsten shuddered. "I wouldn't imagine so. Unless you killed them. Desire for revenge can twist a person, or ghost."

He shook his head. "Nah. I deal with data and credits. Violence isn't my thing."

"Right. So, where's the ghost?"

"Not here. Doesn't come here."

"Yes, we've established that. Unless you want to spend the rest of however long the spirit's going to be after you hiding in here, we should go to where the spirit is so I can deal with it."

Plasmahawk scratched his head, then spent a moment fussing at his long hair. "All right. You're sure you can handle it?"

"Assuming you haven't managed to summon and annoy an elder demon, yes."

He stared open mouthed. "Are you telling me demons are real?"

"In a manner of speaking, yes. Actual occultists call them 'They Who Always Were' to avoid unwanted associations to religious mythology, though, classical descriptions of demons are close enough to the truth."

"You've seen these things?" He continued gawking.

"Twice."

"And you beat them?"

"I'm still standing here, aren't I?"

He whistled. "But you're so small."

"Physical size doesn't matter. The absolute biggest, strongest human alive would have better chances punching a power loader unconscious than surviving a fistfight with one of those things."

"I don't think I'm being chased by something that... horrible." He smiled.

"Good. What's he or she look like? Did you see it?"

"Just a shadow. Seemed like a man. Saw it out of the corner of my eye a few times right before something heavy went flying at my head."

Mendoza seems to have been targeted by a ghostly assassin. This guy set off the Credit Sudzer virus. I'm sure it pissed off some people in high—or low—places enough to put out a hit on this guy. Could it be the same ghost?

"So, Plaz..."

He smirked.

"How many times did the spirit attack you, and were all the attacks in the same place?"

"Umm, over a dozen. Maybe twenty. And the damn thing chased me halfway across West City."

Wow. "Did you get the feeling he's specifically coming after you?"

Plasmahawk made a pinchy gesture. "Just a little. I'd make a joke about a greedy ex-wife's lawyer, but I've never been married and I'm not rich enough to bother with. But you get the picture. Guarantee we're away from this place less than fifteen minutes and he's going to be trying to kill me again."

"All right." She opened her armband terminal and created an Inquest record. "What's your real name?"

His surface thoughts gave away the answer as soon as she asked: Anson Edwards.

"Daz Raines."

She typed both names into the file. "Okay, Daz. If you want to be rid of this spirit, you'll have to dangle yourself as bait."

"What if it won't come after me while you're around?"

"If this spirit is as dedicated to killing you as you think, he won't hesitate. Unless they take the time to hunt down someone capable of helping them, most spirits are pretty shocked to run into someone who can see them."

"Hope you can do more than see them."

She smiled. "Yes. I can keep you safe."

"Okay, follow me."

Kirsten nodded, focused on his thoughts. He'd become nervous having such close contact with the police, so wanted to return to his place, grab his hacking gear and a few credsticks, then burn out his less portable computers to destroy evidence. If she succeeded in getting rid of the ghost, he planned to hop on the first shuttle to Mars and lay low for a while.

Dorian entered via the street-facing door, stopping short a few steps in, wide-eyed. "This building is definitely something unusual."

"Breach in the courtyard," said Kirsten.

"Yes, I mentioned." Plasmahawk—aka Anson—smiled.

"No wonder this guy is safe here." Dorian clenched his jaw, steeling himself.

"Talking to my partner. He's a ghost, too."

Anson eyed the room warily. "In here? Why's this place not keeping him out?"

"He's not dark enough to be afraid of the entities who might emerge from the breach."

Dorian held a finger up. "I'm dim enough to be mildly concerned about the entities who may emerge from the breach. Still not completely convinced they've forgotten about me."

"Well, stop feeling so satisfied about those summaries you carried out."

"K… remember the spirit who threw the two little kids off the fifth floor at 29P?"

She glowered at the far wall. "What about him?"

"How you felt when you blasted him out of existence? Same thing. I only summaried bastards who hurt kids… or women. The Harbingers are the ones who need to revisit their policy. Some people *should* be killed."

"Maybe, but you came too close to enjoying it."

"I enjoyed taking people like that off the street so they couldn't hurt anyone else. Wasn't the killing I liked. I'm thinking they're confused. Notice how they always give me this look like they aren't sure what to make of me?"

"True…"

Anson puffed air past his lips. "Whoa. You sound pretty close to nuts. Or are you on an implant call?"

"Ghost. Right next to me." Kirsten rested her hands on her hips. "Should I recall my car?"

"Nah. My place isn't too much of a walk. C'mon." Anson went over to a door marked 'employees only.'

"Are we going to regret this?" asked Dorian.

"Nah." Kirsten followed him. "But I might go through a stimpak or two."

20

SPIRIT IN BLACK

Anson cut across the maintenance office to a stairwell, taking it down to a room of old electrical equipment.

Rats scurried for cover as he entered an aisle between hundred-year-old capacitors and electrical boxes. Kirsten followed, gingerly stepping past accumulated junk and broken tech parts. Anson opened a submarine-hatch style door at the rear end of the room, entering the city plate. Kirsten concentrated on Darksight, pushing her visual perception halfway into the Astral Realm. The darkness around her brightened to a wavering sepia-toned version of reality. In a place like this, rarely disturbed by people, even the random junk sat in the same place long enough to develop an astral echo.

"Just like a hacker to ignore the law," said Dorian. "The door is clearly marked 'official use only.'"

She stifled a chuckle.

Due to the city plates' interior holding the city's sensitive parts—fiberoptic data cables, power lines, water and sewer lines, and so on—only authorized personnel were supposed to have access below the surface. This explained why the official entry hatches all had code locks. However, many buildings, especially older ones, had doors out of their basement levels like this where anyone could enter the plate interior.

Almost makes it pointless to lock the hatches. Anyone who really wanted to get down here to tap a data line or do bad stuff is going to get down here.

"Don't worry about all the stories," said Anson in an overly confident tone. "No mutants here. Just BS to scare people."

Seriously, he thinks I'm going to be afraid of the basement? "Did you know thousands of ghosts live in the Beneath? There are also numerous feral villages as well as roving bands of brain-damaged crazies, The Discarded. Rumor has it they're cannibalistic."

Anson stumbled over a piece of scrap. "Did you say cannibals?"

"Never spent enough time near Discarded to ask them. They usually ran away from me."

"Afraid of you?" He chuckled. "Why?"

"Look back."

He peered over his shoulder—and walked straight into a support column while staring at her eyes.

Dorian laughed.

Anson swung around the pole, clinging to it—almost hiding behind it—staring at her. "Why are your eyes glowing?"

"Relax. It's a simple trick to see in the dark. Discarded run away from anyone with light coming from their eyes, even cybernetic ones, too. Something in their mythology about the great destroyer."

"Probably androids or whatever the government sent down there to clear out the Beneath years ago, ran out of funding, and never got around to doing again."

She grumbled. Discarded might be dangerous and crazy, but they didn't deserve to be exterminated like roaches. Underneath the tattered rags and face-wraps were humans—more or less. Anson resumed walking, glancing back at her every so often to marvel at her glowing eyes. He eventually reached a crossing passage half the width of a standard corridor. Pipes ranging from one to six inches in diameter ran along both sides, as well as under the metal gridding serving as a walkway. They followed it for a few minutes before Anson took a left into a short alcove.

He crawled into a hole in the side of a huge pipe at the end.

"Are you sure we couldn't have taken a car here?"

"Yes. It's not much farther, and there's no good place to land near my apartment. A whole bunch of not-very-nice people around it."

Kirsten crawled into the pipe. Thankfully, it didn't contain any muck, merely dust. "You're clothing is kind of loud for someone who lives in a grey zone."

"Dress for the job you want, not the job you have," said Anson, his voice echoing. "Eventually, I will have a fancy apartment in a fancy part of the city."

"I'm sure," muttered Dorian.

Kirsten grinned.

She could've done without the view of Anson's sparkling ass for sixteen minutes, though considering a crawl down a pipe below the city surface could easily have resulted in an encounter with 'the muck,' she tolerated an excessive amount of fake plastic gemstones.

One of these days, I'm going to take a sample of that crap to the lab and figure out what it is.

Merely thinking about the black, sticky, tar-like substance made her skin crawl. It somehow turned whatever fabric it touched permanently purple, took forever to scrub off skin, and smelled like a mixture of chemicals, fermented raspberries, and poop. Her last encounter with it involved full submersion in a pit she didn't notice until stepping into it, mistaking it for solid ground. Peeling her uniform off ripped out most of her body hair, perhaps the least fun thing she'd ever done to herself.

Anson reached another hole in the pipe, this one on the top, and stood before climbing out. Kirsten hurried after him, pulling herself up into a room loaded with trash, mostly one-gallon white plastic canisters and random papers.

Wow. This is like a slum version of a ball pit.

Anson waded through the shin-deep garbage to the only door, going through it into a large room containing tools, workbenches, and four non-functional multi-armed robots dangling from the ceiling. Half-built food reassemblers and dishwashers piled up in one corner. Anson strode across the repair room to another stairwell, which led up one level to a barren plastisteel hallway. No longer in the darkness of the city plate interior, Kirsten shut off Darksight.

While he headed left, she paused to glance in the other direction. The end of the corridor on the right opened into a lobby where grimy windows looked out on a street. They'd likely emerged in another apartment building out of the black zone, but still deep in the grey.

"Almost there."

She turned to the left again, noting Anson had gone most of the way down a relatively long corridor past various doors. She hurried after him to a rightward bend. The instant she rounded the corner, a strong residual paranormal energy washed over her. "Whoa."

Anson paused to look back. "Whoa? I hope that's a good 'whoa.'"

"I'm feeling energy left behind by the spirit who tried to hurt you." She opened her mind to astral energies, searching around, but only picked up Dorian as an active haunt in the vicinity of her range. "And it's not the same ghost as Mendoza."

"Who the heck is Mendoza?" asked Anson.

"Another case. I was talking to my partner."

Okay, so different spirits. Not an assassin ghost taking contracts. She continued looking around while following him past first floor apartments.

Anson stopped by a pair of Epoxil faux wood doors etched in ornate dragon carvings at the end of the corridor. Despite being on the ground floor, it looked like an expensive apartment, or maybe an event space. Two seconds after he typed a code into a panel on the wall, the doors gave a loud *click*. He pulled them open and stepped past them.

"Behold my palace." Anson held his arms out to either side, gesturing at marble columns, half-size statues of men and women posing in the manner of Greek nudes, multiple long cafeteria tables loaded with dozens of strange machines, all connected via glowing blue fiberoptic wiring. Floor-to-ceiling bookshelves encircled the room. The back corner, walled off by teal medical privacy screens, contained a bed. A small kitchenette near the barrier had a reassembler, small table, and industrial-sized refrigerator.

"What is all this?"

"Ninety-year-old computers." He laughed, patting one of the devices, about the size of a double-thickness briefcase. "I've got fifty of them interconnected into one processing unit. They run software so antiquated modern defenses can't counteract it. "These machines pre-date holographic display screens. Fairly remarkable."

"That's a word for it." She whistled.

"I mean, old tech isn't remarkable on its own... old tech in pristine condition working perfectly is." He gestured at the ceiling, made to look like an ancient 'tin ceiling' covered in decorative patterns. "This entire building is mine. Impressive, right?"

Dorian poked at a glowing fiberoptic cable sticking up from a computer box. "Considering anyone might kick in the door at any time and shoot him... if he's squatting here, he's overpaying rent."

"Anson?" Kirsten trotted up behind him as he prepared to sit at a workstation.

"Hmm?" He peered at her, casually at first, then went wide-eyed upon realizing she'd used his real name.

"Don't delete anything." Her eyes flared white for a second.

He stared into space.

Leaving him to chew on her Suggestion, she walked around the outer edge of the room, between bookshelves and the tables of computers. It had to be an event hall. No apartments consisted of a single windowless space this large. Whoever designed this building went out of their way to make it look old as hell. Computers aside, the décor reminded her of an old holovid she'd watched as a teen in the dorms, supposedly set in the year 1940. Especially the creepy cherub-angels on the ceiling.

"Thought he was under constant attack," said Dorian. "Suppose it's Murphy's law."

"Oh, the ghost will be here soon. I just have to... Umm..." Anson stared at the keyboard. "Wanted to do something, but... oh, hell. Am I having a stroke?"

"No." Kirsten smiled to herself. *I'm preserving evidence.*

A few minutes later, the corner of the room across from the only door in or out took on a sinister feeling. It somewhat reminded her of the dread Harbingers cloaked themselves in, only much weaker. The fancy Epoxil doors slammed.

"Shit!" shouted Anson. "It's here!"

"I know." Kirsten focused on the corner radiating bad energy. "Stay close to me and don't panic."

Anson scrambled out of his chair and ran up behind her. "Too late. Already sorta panicking."

A muscular, bare-chested man emerged from the wall in the corner, his skin black as ink, his eyes glowing crimson. Waist-length black hair and baggy pants lent an almost samurai-like quality to his appearance, though he didn't carry any visible weapons. Thin dark red lines, tribal tattoos, decorated his arms and chest. The 'dread' definitely came from him, but he didn't give off abyssal energy.

Other than a general building panic, Anson didn't react to the man's appearance, continuing to look around at the entire room, on guard for something to go flying at him. Dorian tilted his head in the manner of a confused dog.

Just a ghost... but fairly dark—or he's using something like telempathic fear.

"Hello, tall, dark and shirtless," said Kirsten. "Any chance you feel like talking here or are we going straight to the bad part?"

The spirit walked out of the corner, drifting to his left, approaching the end of one of the long tables, his stare fixed on Anson.

"Huh?" Anson looked around nervously. "Who are you talking to?"

"Your ghostly friend." Kirsten edged to the right, keeping herself between the ghost and Anson.

Dorian circled around behind the spirit. "I don't think he's in the mood to talk."

"Why are you trying to hurt this man?" asked Kirsten, in as forceful a tone as she could manage without yelling.

The ghost picked up an electric screwdriver.

At the sight of the apparently free-floating tool, Anson screamed and ducked under the other end of the long table.

"Don't." Kirsten summoned the lash.

He shifted his gaze onto her.

"Tell me why you want to hurt him." She advanced. "There is no need for us to do anything more than talk. Maybe I can help you."

No trace of emotion showed on the spirit's face. They stared at each other for a few seconds before his glowing red eyes brightened. He threw the screwdriver at her face. Kirsten expected the throw, not the speed. A slightly too-slow duck saved her from having a screwdriver impaled in her cheek, but the spinning tool hit broadside over the top of her head. Dazed, she fell on her ass, rolling onto her back, cradling her skull in both hands.

Ow! Crap, that hurt!

The odd *pew* sound of Dorian's 'E-86' went off twice before the pain in her scalp lessened enough she could uncurl and move. Anson screamed an instant before a heavy, jangling *crash* shook the floor. Fortunately, her vision didn't blur, nor did she feel overly dizzy. Kirsten shifted to her knees, grasped the table edge, and pulled herself upright.

Dorian fired another spectral bolt from his E-86, which passed less than a foot away from Kirsten's face.

She whirled to watch where it went; the projectile narrowly missed the red-and-black spirit who retaliated by launching an apparent fireball from his palm. Though it looked like magic, his attack amounted to the same ghostly ability Dorian used to simulate a laser pistol. The phantom white fireball whizzed by her at roughly the same distance as the false laser bolt.

"Eep!" Kirsten scrambled to the side, running at the spirit. "Okay, this guy's into Monwyn a little too much."

He pivoted and threw another fireball at her.

She dodged left, but the head-sized orb of ghostly flames swerved after her, hitting her in the gut hard enough to lift her off the ground and throw her over the table. Kirsten somehow managed to land on her feet, staggering two steps before swooning down on one knee, unable to breathe.

Regardless of what a spirit's attack looked like, they almost always hit as a blunt impact. Dorian's 'laser,' this spirit's 'fireball,' a ghost she ran into her fourth week on active duty who threw 'knives'… all felt as if she had an Intera enforcer tenderizing her with his knuckles.

This ghost's fireball packed a wallop, about how she expected it might feel to get run over by a pro gee-ball player. One good thing—the phantasmal nature of the attack softened the blow. Had a physical fist hit her, something vital inside would likely be bruised or bleeding.

Dorian shot at the spirit, forcing him to run around the outside of the room to stay ahead of successive shots.

"Ooh, I'm really not liking this guy." Kirsten wheezed, coughed, and forced herself upright.

The dark spirit stopped running long enough to grab one of the nude statues and hurl it at Anson. The hacker saw it coming and fast-crawled deeper under the table, avoiding the several-hundred-pound artificial rock smashing one end of the table. The other end kicked upward, flinging three computer cases a short distance into the air. They crashed down in a heap, somehow not breaking.

Kirsten ran around the tables, circling toward the spirit, lash held high.

He threw another spectral fireball at her.

Rather than try dodging a guided missile again, she stopped short and focused her astral power on it, opposing the incoming spirit energy. With a grunt, she shoved the fake fireball to the side, blasting a computer case to bits as if it had been shot by a cannon.

Damn, this one's on the old side, too.

She ran at him again.

Evidently deciding she got too close, he ran—way faster than any human could hope to move without speedware. *Grr. Not fair. He doesn't weigh anything.* She pumped her arms, trying to squeeze as much power as she could out of her leg muscles.

Dorian clipped him with a well-aimed leading shot, knocking the ghost into a sideways stumble. He spun into a fireball throw at Dorian. She swung the lash; he zipped out of the way a second before the tip made contact. Kirsten chased him around the room for several minutes, unable to get close enough to swing again. She deflected three more ghostly fireballs, each one tearing up bookshelves where she redirected them. Dorian dodged about half of the ones the spirit threw at him. Despite both ghosts suffering numerous hits, all the computer equipment in the room offered a ready source of energy. Compared to the lash, the ghosts' attacks in a room with so much electricity amounted to two men beating each other over the head with pillows in a stimpak factory.

Again, the spirit projected a sphere of spectral flame at her. Kirsten focused on it, stopping the projectile in midair twenty feet away, anger and frustration giving her the edge. She shoved it back at him, throwing it a bit wide and high to the right. His shock at her stopping the attack dead halfway between them gave Dorian a clear shot.

The 'laser' blast hit the ghost like a hard punch, knocking his face to the side.

Kirsten sprinted hard, trying to get close enough to hit him.

Snarling, the spirit launched another fireball at her.

Desperate to end this before her legs melted into jelly, Kirsten fell into a slide, trying to go under the ghostly orb while rounding the lash over her head. The fireball missed her by an inch or two, dissipating into the floor the same instant the energy tendril sliced across the spirit's chest. Her extreme frustration manifested as a significant power boost, setting off a loud *boom* when the lash made contact.

The strike launched the ghost backward into the air. He flew most of the room's length in under a second before smashing into the crumbling wall beside the fridge. The force of his impact knocked over the privacy screens surrounding Anson's 'bedroom' and lofted a billowing dust cloud. Two points of red light flickered within the haze. Kirsten held her breath and ran at him, starting another swing before she got close, hoping to catch him again before he zoomed away.

"Wait," rasped a startlingly deep voice. The dark spirit emerged from the fog, hunched over, one hand up in a defensive gesture. Glowing spectral blood dribbled from his mouth.

She aborted her attack, but kept the lash poised.

"Careful…" Dorian ran over to stand beside her, tiny sparks crawling over him.

"Talk." The ghost struggled to straighten his posture. His cold, glowering demeanor had softened to a more human expression, less like a killer android.

Oh, sure. Now he wants to talk. She didn't bother trying to pretend she'd run herself nearly out of breath. "What are you?"

"I am Dacre," said the spirit in a faint French accent.

She blinked. "Never heard of them."

"It is my name." Dacre gave a wheezy chuckle. "I am a spirit, like the one next to you."

"Did you take tattooing a bit too far in life?" asked Dorian.

Dacre smiled. "No. I made myself like this in death because it looks cool."

Whoa. Unusual for a ghost to alter their appearance cosmetically. He really is into Mon—no, he died long before they made it. "Okay, so you're kinda old as a spirit. I was pretty frustrated, but one swipe of the lash shouldn't have hammered you so hard your entire personality changed."

"My mind is now clear." Dacre attempted to smile, though glowing red eyes made the gesture sinister.

"Why are you trying to kill Anson?"

"Did he trap you in a shower tube, too?" asked Dorian.

Dacre gestured at her. "Another person who can see me forced me to hunt this man."

"What?" Kirsten blinked. "Forced you?"

"Yes. And now, I hunt them instead." Dacre bowed his head—and vanished.

"Grr!" Kirsten looked around, sweeping the area psionically for any signs of spirits. She sensed a few loitering on the upper floors of the building, but none potent enough to be Dacre. "Why do they do that?"

"Do what?" asked Dorian.

She whirled to face him, allowing the lash to retract into her hand. "Say something important and shocking, then disappear before I can ask them more questions."

"How should I know?"

"You're a ghost."

"Have I ever done the cryptic poof to you?"

She folded her arms, grumbling. "No."

"The man dresses up like a wizard from the game your boy likes. He probably loves acting mysterious."

"Not helping." Kirsten strode over to where Anson hid under a heavy desk. He hadn't connected any interface cables to his M3 port, so she felt reasonably confident her suggestion—plus his terror during the ghostly attack—stopped him from wiping out his files. "The ghost is gone. He won't be back."

Anson crawled out, stood, and dusted himself off. "Are you sure?"

"Yes." She grabbed his arm and threw him forward, bending him over the table while plucking binders from her belt. "Anson Edwards, you are under arrest for data crimes. You have the right to remain sil—"

"Are you serious?" yelled Anson, a bit of a laugh in his voice, pulling away from her.

"*Don't resist.*" She locked his hands behind his back while he lay motionless. "Quite serious. Your virus got my shower, trapped my son in a tube, too… and you almost killed a little girl."

"Not *that* little." Dorian tilted his hand back and forth. "Most eleven-year-olds would hate being called 'little girls.'"

She gave him side eye.

"What? No way. It can't possibly hurt anyone. Not even from starvation. If they don't pay in twenty-four hours, it gives up and unlocks."

"To be fair, a ghost made it worse." Dorian held up a finger. "Tamsen wouldn't have been in any danger if the tube hadn't flooded."

"Still," muttered Kirsten.

"Exactly *how* did my virus almost kill a child?" Anson struggled at the binders.

"The autoshower she was trapped in flooded and she couldn't get out."

"Impossible. They can't flood. No autoshower tube made has a drain block feature." Anson shook his head, struggling harder. "Are you seriously arresting me after I called you for help?"

"I am. We're already here and I can't simply *not* arrest a fugitive."

"But this is a black zone." Anson flashed a weak smile.

"The law doesn't stop working here because it's not on the Nav. It just takes way more motivation for the police to come after someone."

He rolled his eyes. "But you're ignoring the spirit of it. Rules, yanno. Unwritten code between cops and people who bend the law."

Dorian shrugged. "You might have been able to talk her out of it if not for the kid almost drowning in a tube."

She sighed at him. "Plenty of kids, and adults, got trapped in shower tubes due to his virus."

"Yes, but you didn't see them all in person. Seeing a terrified child gets you."

"What?" Anson looked back and forth between her and Dorian's general location. "What is your ghost friend saying?"

"He's overestimating my willingness to let people who break the law get away with it. We found a child stuck in a tube who almost drowned in it after being trapped for nine damn hours. Do you have any idea how scary it is for a kid to be trapped in a confined space for hours?"

Anson threw his head back in a dramatic sigh. "Oh, please. I didn't target children."

"You didn't program the virus to skip them either." She tugged at his arm. "Come on."

He set his heels, not moving. "Autoshowers do not have cameras here."

"Huh? *Here?*" She stopped pulling on his arm and stared, aghast. "Saying 'here' implies they have cameras somewhere."

Anson shrugged. "Japan."

Dorian chuckled.

She narrowed her eyes at him. "Why is that funny?"

He patted her on the head. "You are too sweet."

"It's a fetish thing." Anson twisted his right hand around, trying to slip out of the cuffs. "People set up GlobeNet channels and sell videos of themselves in the tube."

"I don't wanna know." Kirsten pinched the bridge of her nose.

Anson grinned. "Want to hear the weirdest part?"

"No, but you're going to tell me anyway, aren't you?"

"The ones with the least—or no—sexual overtones make the most money. Vids of people showering like they're not being recorded sell the best."

She sent a 'help me' look at her partner.

Dorian grimaced. "Weird, but quite tame compared to what people *could* be into."

"Okay, enough." Kirsten again tried to drag Anson toward the door.

"It's illegal for manufacturers to put cameras in autoshower units here," said Anson.

"Damn right it is. Stop resisting." She tugged on his arm again.

"No way for me to tell who the occupant is. I thought about hooking into the weight sensor, but only the expensive ones actually measure the user's weight. Most simply return an 'occupied' code over forty pounds."

"They're not going to send a crime scene team out here." Dorian looked around. "You're going to need to lug all this stuff out of here yourself."

"Not everything. Only evidence. The electronics."

"Shit!" yelled Anson.

"What?" Kirsten jumped.

"I, umm. Would you mind letting me log in real quick? I need to email my parents."

She frowned. "Nice try. You can wipe your systems out after they copy them."

He groaned, slouching.

"C'mon. Let's go. Your new bed's going to be much safer—and less smelly—than this place."

Anson offered a sheepish smile. "How about a hundred grand?"

"My partner thinks I'm too nice. I'm going to pretend you didn't just try to bribe me because I'm sure you meant it as an inappropriate wiseass joke."

He sighed—and tried to run.

Kirsten swung him around by her grip on his arm, directing him into the table. He collapsed bent over it. She climbed half on top of him and pulled the stunrod off her belt. "Does Japan have fetish vids about one of these going into a body cavity?"

Dorian cackled.

"Uhh…" Anson shivered. "Do you want me to seriously answer that?"

Her stomach did a backflip. "Ugh. I may be small, but I am still strong enough to drag you out of here unconscious. Would you rather deal with the legal system or another contract killer?"

"*Another* one? Are you saying someone paid the ghost to kill me?" He lifted his face from the table to gawk at her.

Dorian whistled. "Probably autoshower manufacturers. How many people ended up afraid to get back into one after this? Or sued them."

"It's a working theory. But the amount of people you pissed off, someone else is going to find you."

"Entire point of living out here." He sighed.

"I can't explain how it happened, but the spirit said a living person made him come after you. Sounds like a contract to me."

He smiled sheepishly. "I'd rather take my chances here."

"*Walk with me,*" said Kirsten, her eyes glowing white.

Anson stood.

She glanced at Dorian. "What are you laughing at?"

"Hearing you threaten to stuff a stunrod in a body cavity is hilarious." He snickered. "You'd never do anything of the sort."

"Yeah, but he doesn't know that." She frowned, dragging Anson to the door.

21

EMPATHIC HARMONICS

K irsten got lucky, and not in a 'spending the night with Samuel Chang' way.

Her luck involved a NetMini call to him instead. Division 2 didn't need to physically take possession of all Anson's hardware. He walked her through connecting to a 'target' site so the techs in the police lab could locate the private network and copy it. The process proved surprisingly fast, allowing her to get back to the patrol craft before her 'sit still' suggestion wore off.

While her Inquest concerning Anson involved the ghost, she had no jurisdiction over the non-paranormal, non-psionic hacking crimes. She handed him off to Division 1 upon arrival at the PAC, but remembered the 'net lore' about how deep hackers can hold grudges. Unbeknownst to the Division 1 officers in the room, she telepathically warned him to forget she existed. Any attempt at revenge for arresting him would result in 'hundreds' of spirits who like her paying him a visit. Again, she'd never ask any of the ghosts to hurt him, but he didn't need to know that.

Judging by how pale he turned, she figured no need to worry about him coming back to haunt her.

She fell into her chair in the squad room a little after three. Evan would be out of school already, probably working on citizenship points. Any day now, he'd be done with them. She called him to check up. Sure enough, he did chores in an empty classroom. A quick 'where are you and are you okay' call from his mother wouldn't get him in trouble, so she didn't keep him on the line despite wanting to.

Her attention returned to the search she'd started earlier in the official database regarding Aethervein. According to the copyright registration, Aethervein was the product of one person—not a band. The PID record of a twenty-year-old named Marley Santiago popped up in a sub panel. She looked as though she tried to look closer to sixteen or seventeen between her fashion choice and widening her eyes for the photo. She had on a white-and-pink sweatshirt, heart earrings, and appeared to be wearing pale pink contacts. Marley dyed her shoulder-long hair red on the right, pink on the left, leaving a two-inch-wide snow-white strip between the halves. Tri-color hair didn't even rate in the top fifty weird fashion quirks of notable musicians, but the overall aesthetic made her look like a high school kid unable to decide between counterculture or hypercute aesthetic.

Nothing Kirsten could find on the GlobeNet about Aethervein included any pictures, likenesses of Marley, or any fictional band members. Even her 'official' page didn't list anyone as being 'in the band.' It almost seemed as if the woman wanted to portray 'Aethervein' as an entity unto itself, perhaps an AI or alien.

She poked the file on Marley.

The woman had no criminal history, not even a tag for shoplifting or possession of recreational chems. Cops rarely bothered with most common ways people got high. A record of a chem-related arrest most times meant an underage teen's parents asked the cops to bring them home. Past eighteen, though, the police had better things to do than drag an adult who hadn't committed a crime somewhere they didn't want to be.

Marley, however, appeared genuinely clean. Her file indicated she lived in an apartment in Sector 2980.

"Okay, Marley… when a ghost says your band's name as a response to 'why are you going crazy,' means I gotta talk to you."

Kirsten pulled up the NavMap to set a waypoint to the woman's address, and stopped short, staring at Sector 2980—right in the middle of the circle of excessive hauntings. She'd estimated the center at Sector 2888, two spaces to the left. The poltergeist she'd responded to not too long ago went nuts in Sector 2838, the adjacent sector to the south of the one Marley lived in.

"Oh, crap."

She re-plotted all the haunts connected to open Inquests. Sure enough with only a few outliers, they formed a ring around Sector 2980, not *perfectly* at the center, but close enough. Some of the attacks happened quite far away, such as the Beck house—140 miles west from Marley's apartment. Or the attack at the Ancora Medical facility where Elan Mendoza died, over 260 miles northwest. Anson's black zone hideout in Sector 1509 plotted 201.8 miles away to the southwest.

All the distant attacks kinda felt deliberate. The ghosts were different there... Dacre said someone forced him to. Could she be sending spirit assassins out? Maybe the random crap going on around her is a side effect?

"If she's somehow able to make spirits do things for her, a few hundred miles isn't a big deal." Kirsten rubbed her chin, staring at the dots much closer to the woman's apartment. "Doesn't make sense."

"Hmm?" asked Dorian, walking up beside her.

"Look at this." She pointed out the ring of plots. "They're all generally surrounding the place where Marley Santiago lives."

"Who?"

Kirsten gestured at the other holo-panel displaying the band registration. "She is Aethervein. Nikolas mentioned her, or at least the band when I asked him about the noise driving him crazy angry. The part I'm having trouble understanding is, if this woman is somehow influencing ghosts to do things like contract killings on Elan Mendoza and Anson Edwards, why would she be sending spirits into a frenzy right around where she lives?"

"I can think of a few theoretical reasons." Dorian sat on her desk. "One, she is unaware Division 0 has the ability to react to ghostly manifestations and thinks she's completely undetectable."

"Okay."

"Two, whatever she's doing might be unintentional."

Kirsten peered up at him. "How does someone unintentionally send a ghost to assassinate a specific person? *Twice.*"

"You're assuming someone wanted Anson dead."

She folded her arms, leaning back in her chair. "He trapped like forty-three percent of West City's population in their autoshowers. There are probably a million people who want Plasmahawk dead."

"True." Dorian chuckled. "I meant actually putting out a contract, not merely wishing pain on the man. We know Carlos Bennett added Mendoza to a hit list, but there's no concrete proof anyone figured out Plasmahawk is Anson. And even if both of them ended up on an assassination contract, it wouldn't prove the ghostly attacks happened because of it. It's your theory."

"Explain how Dacre was so fixated on Anson? Chased him for miles until he got lucky and found a Breach."

Dorian shifted his jaw back and forth in thought. "Still could be Anson was the first person Dacre ran into after that woman did something to agitate him."

"If he was simply agitated and looking to kill someone, why would he chase the guy across the city? He would've passed thousands of other potential victims. Also, he said someone ordered him to hunt the guy."

"K, you are well aware of how some spirits become obsessed with things. He might have become frustrated at Anson escaping and literally could not think of anything else other than killing him until you slapped sense into him."

"Grr." She glared at the map plots. "It doesn't add up. Some of those ghosts are going too far to be random, and if she's doing it on purpose, it makes no sense to cause so much activity in an area around her. It's practically a giant neon arrow pointing us right to her."

"So, let's follow the arrow." Dorian slid off the desk to his feet.

She smiled. "My thoughts exactly."

SECTOR 2891, ONE SQUARE EAST OF 2890, SHOWED UP IN THE NAVCON as 'greying.'

It hadn't officially been classified as a grey zone, but then again, no black zone had formed here yet. One sector east, 2892, qualified as 'dark grey,' on its way to becoming a black zone. Though it hadn't collapsed to the point the police abandoned it, the violence in 2892 had gotten so bad the surrounding sectors already started to show the effects of decay before it had gone fully black.

Kirsten flew into Sector 2890 from the west, thus avoiding going over the worsening area. However, Marley's apartment sat near the eastern edge of the sector. In maybe another ten years, 2892 would go completely black and take the sectors around it firmly into the grey.

"Maybe the local district governor will attempt a police surge and take the city back?" asked Kirsten.

Dorian chuckled. "The Moon might also have a baby. But, if they're up for reelection, maybe."

"I hate that."

"Blight?"

She frowned, guiding the patrol craft lower and hitting the button to extend the ground wheels. "No. I hate how politicians only help people in their districts when they need votes. Why do politicians only do good things when it somehow also benefits them?"

"Because they're politicians. People who do nice things because they're nice things never run for office."

"So cynical. It can't be true. There *have* to be some people out there who run for office because they want to help people." She landed on the road about a half mile from Marley's apartment building, since the Navcon indicated it didn't have rooftop parking.

"Okay, perhaps I am exaggerating a bit. Idealists *do* run for office, but they rarely get elected."

"Don't people want to vote for someone who will help them?"

Dorian nodded. "Oh, yes. They do. Problem is, even here in the UCF, there's a power structure at play. The rich, corporations, career politicians… they don't want anyone outside their club having enough power to rock the boat. When a politician comes along who is more concerned with the wellbeing of the general citizenry at large rather than merely towing the party line and keeping things comfortable for the upper classes… they never quite seem to make it."

"Assassination?" Kirsten gasped.

"No. Ever wonder how when a group is running for a district governorship or a senate seat, the popular one is never the final nominee? The power structure weeds out the idealists and the nonconformists long before they can be a threat."

"I hope you're being cynical." Kirsten stopped for a red traffic signal, six blocks from Marley's building.

"Be nice if I was. They only get away with it because most people are so disconnected, overworked, exhausted, and flat out apathetic they don't care what the people at the top are doing. I think the last senate primary for my district before I died, something like thirty-eight percent of the eligible residents voted. Most ignored it or didn't even know about the election."

She whistled. "How the heck can people not know?" The signal went green. She looked around to make sure no idiots decided to disregard traffic laws, then accelerated. "I mean, seriously."

"Virtual reality. People go to work, come home, and lack the energy to do much more than plug in and forget the real world until they pass out."

"I don't know what to say."

"No real need to say anything. And you really shouldn't think about it too much. You'll only get depressed when you realize there isn't anything you can do about it."

"Dunno." Kirsten parked in front of the building. "If it really is as bad as you say, it's like a whole bunch of gas hovering over the city. I may be small, but every explosion starts with a tiny spark."

"So you're going political crusader now?" He phased through the door to the sidewalk.

She got out, glancing over the roof at him. "Nah. I'm up to my eyeballs in ghosts. But I'm not going to accept it's impossible. It's only impossible when *everyone* gives up."

The door sank closed as she walked around the front end of the patrol craft. Four ad-bots zoomed over to her but appeared confused as to what products to hawk. A second later, the bots all bloomed into flowers, metal orbs surrounded by holographic screen petals displaying food.

"Oh, dammit. I missed lunch again." Too fast to think about it, she pointed at a chicken Caesar salad wrap.

One bot did a victory shimmy while the other three spammed her with drink ads. Purely because their artificial sad act worked on her, she ordered a green iced tea from another bot. Four minutes later, two separate delivery bots arrived with her late lunch.

Kirsten sat on the hood of the patrol craft, eating her food and watching people go by. Most had some visible electronics grafted onto their heads somewhere, tiny blinking lights or little silver M3 ports. A mental sigh slid across her mind at feeling like an outsider. Society moved onward and upward, merging with technology, a world she wanted nothing to do with. Even if implants didn't have a negative effect on psionic abilities, she still wouldn't want anything inside her she hadn't been born with. Her mother didn't want her. Society didn't really want her, either. But Evan did. And so did Sam... and Nicole, and most of Division 0 even if having Mind Blast kinda creeped them out.

Kirsten smiled to herself. *I'm thinking of it backward. I reject normal society, not the other way around.*

So what if she lived as an anachronism.

"Dorian?"

"Hmm?"

She finished chewing her last bite. "Did you ever see that vid *Technocracy Fall?*"

"Yes. Had to watch it in school, like almost everyone."

"Do you think I'm the barefoot girl in a white dress sniffing the single flower growing up from a crack in the plastisteel street?"

"She wasn't real... merely a product of Gerald's imagination. It's why no one ever tried to talk to her but him, and how her dress remained immaculately white despite the overwhelming grime of the city."

"Beside the point. I mean, like… everyone here has at least an M3 port. Am I stupid for not getting one? Should I have been born 200 years ago?"

Dorian smiled. "Well, you do have one thing in common with Anastasia. You are a spot of purity in this place."

"I'm not innocent." She looked down.

"I don't mean it like that. Your soul is pure. After everything you've been through, your metaphorical dress is still immaculate."

She chuckled. "You really think so?"

"You aren't at all cynical, so yes." He playfully punched at her shoulder, imparting a faint chill. "Try to hold on to your idealism. We don't have enough in this city and people try to kill it whenever they see it."

"I'm kinda hard to kill. Ask Konnie."

Dorian snickered.

"Ready?" Kirsten slid off the patrol craft.

"Of course. So what are you expecting?"

Kirsten headed for the building, dropping the containers from her lunch in a nearby trash bin. A few locals gave her odd looks. At first, she thought they stared at her for being a cop in this part of the city, but their surface thoughts contained shock at someone actually using the trash bin.

Too stunned to formulate a response, she entered the building. One bit of good luck in this investigation—Marley Santiago's apartment was on the ground floor. No stairs or deathtrap elevators in the way.

She headed down the hall straight ahead to apartment twenty-eight, almost at the end of the hall.

"Hmm." Dorian kicked at a piece of trash in the hall, making it twitch. "No one would ever suspect a famous musician would live in a dump like this."

"Correct. She isn't very famous." Kirsten pushed the doorbell. She didn't have any solid justification to barge in, merely suspicions.

"Who the heck are you?" asked a woman's voice from the panel below the doorbell button.

"Kirsten Wren, Division 0, National Police Force. I'm looking for Marley Santiago."

"There's a zero?" asked the woman.

"Yes."

"Not sure I believe you. Can you have a normal cop show up and verify? Just trying to be careful."

"Can you see me?" asked Kirsten. "Do I look like someone who's trying to trick their way into your apartment?"

"People have cyberware. You could be like a cyborg ninja or something who can throw cars. Even if you're small."

Kirsten sighed. "I could override the lock with a police code. Will that prove I'm legit?"

"Won't using an override set off an alarm all over the building? Lock everyone in?" asked the woman.

"You've been watching too many movies." Kirsten chuckled. "It'll log the entry, but no alarms. No one is locked in. That's a whole separate process, not merely using an override code on one door."

"What do you want with me?" asked the woman, likely Marley over the chirps of a NetMini. A GlobeNet welcome jingle followed.

"Hoping for some answers to some really confusing questions. Or maybe you can't answer them and I at least know I'm in the wrong place."

"Welcome to the National Police Force public GlobeNet portal," said a soothing female voice inside the apartment.

"Oh, shit. There *is* a Zero. You're psionic."

"Correct."

"You're not a crazy fan?"

"I am not a crazy fan." Kirsten smiled. "I've only listened to one song of yours, but okay, it's pretty good."

"You're being generous," said Dorian.

Kirsten gave him a 'not now' look.

The door slid to the right, vanishing into the wall.

Marley Santiago looked pretty much the same as her ID photo except for clothing. Same three-color hair, same pale pink irises. She still wore a sweatshirt, only this one didn't have white-and-pink alternating rings down the sleeves, being solid pink with a cute white cat face on the chest. The legs of her baggy white sweatpants mostly covered her bare feet.

For the second time in a week, Kirsten ran into someone who didn't make her feel tiny. Marley had only about an inch of height on her.

"So, umm... why do you want to talk to me?" She leaned a little into the hallway, looking around. "C'mon in. It's way creepy out there."

"Thanks. I've just got a few basic questions."

Kirsten followed her into a living room so cluttered it seemed as though six teenage girls shared it and expected their mother—who didn't live there—would pick up after them. Holographic posters decorated most walls, mostly faeries, flowers, rainbows, unicorns, or cute cartoon versions of characters from pop culture. Six miniature waterfalls made from what appeared to be stacked stones, probably fake, stood around on shelves or tables. The biggest, a five-foot-tall ivy colored 'stone wall' took up one whole corner. It used holographic water, likely due to its size. A fruity-berry smell clung to the sofa and carpet, testament to frequent Flowerbasket or Placid Rain use going on here.

She totally looks like the kind of girl who'd inhale Rain all the time. Kirsten learned about the chem in the dorms, mostly as a warning from the staff, when she'd been about fifteen. Within forty seconds of inhaling it, the user fell into a state of mellowness, awash in feelings of positivity and contentment. Unfortunately, they became so mellow, their body tended not to move for up to an hour. Someone taking it on purpose enjoyed the ultimate chill out, but it left them vulnerable to assault since they'd be functionally paralyzed. For this reason, most of the street chemists who made it added overwhelming grape, cherry, or mixed fruit flavors to prevent sneaky dosing of an unwilling person.

Dorian walked in behind her, whistling. "She's lived here for years and still expects her mother's going to swoop in clean up?"

"Ugh, not again." Marley fidgeted, staring at the doorway.

Kirsten raised an eyebrow. "Not again?"

"I'm just having one of my anxiety attacks. Sometimes, I get scared and stuff for no reason. It feels like someone's watching me when there's no one around. Even if I'm alone. I'll be sitting in my studio all by myself and out of nowhere, I'm a little kid afraid of the monster under the bed. So annoying. Been happening to me ever since I was little."

Curious, Kirsten peeked at the woman's surface thoughts.

Normally, making a telepathic connection also came with a mild sense indicating whether a person had psionic ability. If a person had weak abilities, they might not be apparent without a deeper telepathic dive. However, when Kirsten linked to Marley's brain, a mild storm of tingles went off in her sinuses. This girl *definitely* had psionic abilities. Despite the distracting urge to sneeze, Kirsten managed to read confusion in her surface thoughts as to why Division 0 would bother with her as well as genuine fear reminiscent of how she used to feel at home, dreading Mother would come looking for her.

"Umm, Marley?" asked Kirsten in a hesitant, soothing tone. "Do you realize you're psionic?"

"Me?" She laughed, glancing briefly in Dorian's general direction. "You're kidding, right?"

"I'll take that as a no." Kirsten bit her lip. Her suspicions regarding Marley's involvement in the storm of hauntings shifted. She changed modes from interviewing a potential suspect to wanting to help a psionic who had no idea how to use her abilities.

Dorian walked over to a corridor leading deeper into the place.

Marley's laugh shifted tone from genuine to uneasy and petered out. "Seriously, you gotta be confused."

"How long have you been living here?" asked Kirsten.

"Almost two months." Marley raked her fingers through her hair, again glancing vaguely in Dorian's direction. "Used to live in East City, but my ex-boyfriend went super psycho when I tried to break up. Wouldn't leave me alone. He snuck into my place and sat in the ventilation duct, watching me work on a new track. Goes completely crazy and tries to kill me. Well, kill *us*. Said if he couldn't live with me, he didn't want to live."

Kirsten winced. "I'm sorry…"

"Not your fault." She rubbed her hands up and down her arms, eyeing the big waterfall—where Dorian stood.

Two months… the spike of hauntings is only two weeks old, but if she is somehow connected, it explains why it never happened before. "You keep looking at specific spots. Does it feel like where the sense of fear is coming from?"

"Yeah. Like the monster is watching me."

Dorian smiled. "No one's ever called me a monster before."

"Marley, I'm not sure how you made it to age twenty without realizing it, but you have psionic abilities. It's the reason you've always felt something watching you, an eerie presence nearby. You are sensing my partner, Dorian. He's a ghost."

"Hey," said Marley in a dazed, sleepy voice. "I'm the one on chems. You shouldn't be talking about seeing ghosts."

"How much do you know about psionics?"

"Umm, not much. I heard they exist… and some people don't like them." Marley shrugged. "You're the first one I ever met and known about, but I got nothin' against anyone. We're all on Spaceship Earth together, part of the same breathing world."

Dorian made a face at Kirsten. "Been here two months? I think we solved the Flowerbasket shortage."

Fighting the urge to laugh, she stepped closer to Marley and cleared her throat to regain seriousness. "Is it okay if I take a deeper look to see what kind of abilities you have?"

"Are you going to tell me why you're interested in me? You said you're not a crazy fan, right?"

"I'm not a stalker fan, no."

"What are you going to do?" Marley dazedly scratched her head.

"Look into your thoughts. It will only take a moment."

Marley flapped her arms in an 'okay, whatever' gesture.

"All right. Just try to relax and stand still."

"If I relax any more, I'm gonna fall over." Marley giggled. "You interrupted me when I was about to start writing a new track. The Rain's gone to phase two."

"I've never tried it. Don't know what you mean." Kirsten rested her hands on Marley's shoulders and stared into her bright pink eyes.

"Means I'm still one with the universe but I can move."

Kirsten initiated telepathic contact, again suffering a strong tingle in her sinuses. *Must be from the Placid Rain...* It both surprised her— and kinda didn't—to find the woman also possessed Astral Sense, though felt quite a bit weaker at it than hers. Evan likely had a higher rating, but the boy *had* been practicing lately—not to mention frequently used Astral Projection before she found him. Marley also showed signs of having weak Telepathy. By far her most potent ability was Telempathy. Considering Kirsten didn't have Telempathy at all, her being able to sense it meant the woman had a strong rating.

She burrowed deeper into older memories, unable to find even one case of Marley using her psionic abilities intentionally. Based on hundreds of 'fear attacks' starting around age five, Kirsten figured Marley had been aware of ghosts nearby but didn't understand what she felt. Everything inside the woman's head appeared somewhat blurry and indistinct, another likely effect of the chem. One curious theme repeated in her thoughts: whenever she sat at her equipment making music, Marley experienced a near transcendental sensation. It reminded Kirsten of how it felt to astrally project with the added sensation of being surrounded by rainbows and riding a wave of emotions from dozens of other people. This woman performing in front of an audience gave her a high ten times stronger than any chem on its own.

Kirsten dropped the telepathic link, finding herself holding onto Marley's shoulders to stay upright. "Whoa."

"Yeah, whoa." Marley giggled again. "You made me feel dizzy."

Something she'd read about Aethervein clicked in her head. *People who go to concerts* adore *her. Fans hearing it only online aren't as enthusiastic. She's a telempath...* "Marley?"

"I'm still here." She grinned. "At least, I think so."

"Try to focus. You are a psionic, strongest in Telempathy, but I'm also seeing Astral Sense and Telepathy in there, too."

Marley blinked. "Am I in trouble?"

"No. You haven't done anything intentionally wrong. But I'm starting to maybe understand what's going on… and also getting more confused."

"How can you understand and be confused at the same time?" Marley laughed.

"I'm curious as well." Dorian folded his arms.

"You have some seriously devoted fans out there."

Marley nodded. "Yeah. Some are wild. I've had people offer to give me their children."

Dorian whistled.

"What?" Kirsten gawked.

"Yeah, like they think their kids will be *sooo* happy living with me or they're like totally in love with me they want me to have their most precious possession. Not like a kid's a possession, yanno? Just a saying."

"Right… and the fans who only hear you online aren't as nuts."

Marley nodded.

"Oh, shit," muttered Dorian. "She's an empath."

"Exactly."

"Huh? I didn't say anything." Marley looked sort of at Dorian again. "You talking to your ghostie?"

"Yes. Ooh. Idea. Quick experiment." Kirsten concentrated on Marley's thoughts and telepathically sent how it felt to concentrate on basic Astral Sight years ago when she needed to 'turn on' the ability to see spirits.

Marley made a cross-eyed face and nearly collapsed to the floor. Probably would have if not for Kirsten holding her up. "Ooh, that felt weird."

"Try to think exactly the way I just sent to you. One of your abilities is called Astral Sense. It's *super* rare. There's only like three of us in West City. You're relatively weak at it yet, which is why you need to concentrate on wanting to see spirits."

"You're teasing me. I... umm." Marley looked down. "Thought I saw the ghost of my brother once when I was little. He's a lot older than me and got killed."

"Sometimes ghosts can appear to you when they want. Please try what I showed you."

Marley looked up, making a concentration face.

"She's either going to turn it on or need new pants," said Dorian.

About two minutes later, Marley's eyes glowed bright pink—she screamed, grabbing Kirsten, hiding behind her. "There's a man in here!"

"It's Dorian. He's been here the whole time."

Marley peered around Kirsten. "He doesn't look like a ghost."

"When we use Astral Sense to see spirits, they appear exactly like a living person... assuming they don't have visible wounds. If you see a ghost who appears ghostly, it means they've manifested."

"Manifested?" Marley blinked at her.

"Projected themselves into the physical world so anyone can see them. Not all ghosts can do it. They start off real weak after death and need years to build up energy."

"Oh."

"She got the hang of it rather fast." Dorian clapped.

"Well, I *did* telepathically show her exactly how to do it. Much more difficult to talk someone through it."

"Wow. I really am Psionic." Marley picked up a small mirror from the floor. "My eyes are glowing."

"Yes. It's normal for using Astral Sight."

"Yours aren't."

Kirsten chuckled. "I basically lived with Astral Sight on continuously for two years, so it kinda stuck. I see ghosts all the time now. *Can't* turn it off."

"Wow. So how did you find me?"

"Most of what I do with Division 0 is handle cases involving ghosts. There have been a *ton* of spirits causing trouble lately, all around this area. You're living at the center of a spirit hurricane. Some of the spirits I had to deal with complained about 'the noise.' Another said 'Aethervein' when I asked him what the noise was."

"Everyone's a critic." Marley stuck her tongue out. "My music isn't noise. It's deep and emotional. Trancelike. No screaming... well, only one track, but that one's all about being angry."

"Are you thinking what I'm thinking?" asked Dorian.

"I can't read your mind, but I believe so." Kirsten took a deep breath.

"This is so weird. I like legit heard him talk." Marley walked over to Dorian and poked a finger through his chest. "Wow. He's cold."

Dorian appeared about to make a wiseass remark but held it back —likely because Marley could hear him.

"Remember me saying I understood but also became confused?" asked Kirsten. "You are what we call a telempath. You also have telepathy, but it's way weaker than your empathy. Telepathy is sending thoughts—words or images or ideas—to someone else's mind."

"Okay," said Marley.

This is telepathy.

Marley gawked. "How did you talk and not move your mouth?"

With Telepathy. Kirsten smiled. *Sending words into someone else's mind is the second most basic use of it.*

"What's the first?"

"Reading surface thoughts, knowing what someone's thinking in the moment." Kirsten rested a hand on Marley's shoulder. "Tele*mpathy* is similar to Telepathy, except instead of words or ideas, you read or send pure emotions. You can tell how someone is feeling or forcibly change their emotions if you want to."

"Whoa. Really? I never did anything like that." Marley fidgeted. "Why is... His name's Dorian, right?"

"Yes," said Dorian.

"Why's he scary?"

"He isn't. Anyone with any psionic ability feels weird when they're around ghosts or other paranormal beings. You feel scared because you don't realize what the sensation is and your mind's giving it meaning based on uncertainty."

"Okay, so does that mean my random anxiety attacks aren't really anxiety attacks at all but ghosts being close to me?"

Kirsten nodded. "If what you're calling 'anxiety attacks' are more like feeling watched, nervous, and a little on edge, then yes. Actual anxiety attacks are much more severe."

"Wow." Marley blinked. "Lots of ghosts kept being around me."

"Yes. They can sense people who are astrals, and probably hoped you could talk to them."

Marley gazed into space. "Trippy."

"Okay, so, hear me out. You didn't know you were psionic, so you couldn't have intentionally or consciously used your abilities. However, the subconscious mind isn't limited by awareness. I think you subconsciously use your telepathy abilities whenever you are creating or performing music. You infuse actual emotions into the people listening to you or radiate them around you."

Marley trembled.

"What's wrong?" Kirsten took her hand.

"Couple days ago, I was kinda pissed off. The distribution company said some bullshit about my music not having 'wide enough appeal,' which is their sneaky way of saying it's not basic enough to make tons of credits. They don't understand music *at all.* Just want the same generic crap everyone else is putting out there. Like music, for me, is a total emotional journey into another place, a higher state of being where me and the audience just like... you know, share this prismatic transcendence."

"Riiight..." Kirsten tilted her head.

"I got pretty pissed off at the company. Pissed off is kinda rare for me, since I'm like way mellow most of the time. I decided to make a song about how much greedy people suck. It's angry, not like most of my stuff. But I'm a critter of emotion, so I ran with it. Same day I wrote the song, the cops came to this building seventeen times."

"Nikolas…" Dorian raised an eyebrow. "Guy was overcome with anger. Mindlessly trashing everything in the building."

Kirsten checked her terminal. The same day she got the call about Nikolas, Division 1 had eighteen separate calls to this building for assault, fighting, two attempted murders, and various noise complaints related to people screaming at each other. "Wow. Damn. Okay, Marley? This is where you get to see me bend the rules."

"You do it so rarely." Dorian rolled his eyes.

"Hush, you." She smirked. "Division 0, in general, bends this rule all the time."

"Uh oh." Marley took a step back.

"When you're performing music, you subconsciously use Telempathy, projecting the emotion you're feeling out into the world. The reason Div 1 showed up here so many times that day is because you made everyone in the building as furious as you were."

"Umm…"

"Relax." Kirsten smiled. "No one died. Bending rules, remember? You didn't do it on purpose. Psionics are in a delicate place as far as society is concerned. If the people in this building understood what happened, they'd make life rough for you."

"Just a little," whispered Marley. "I'm sorry… I had no idea."

"Kirsten, since my terminal's only as good as my memory… pull up our file on Placid Rain. I'm tempted to think there might be something relating it to Telempathy."

She accessed the Division 0 database. Sure enough, the file record indicated a person on Placid Rain frequently experienced an increased level of potency in Telempathy—but also a significantly decreased resistance to it. Not necessarily a problem unless two empaths got into a bigger brain contest.

"Could explain her range and power." Kirsten rubbed her sinuses. "And the tingling."

"What?" asked Marley.

"Do you always take Placid Rain before performing?"

"Yeah. It helps me get into the right head space. Makes me feel like I'm becoming the music, floating out into the universe with it."

"And it may also be lubricating the mental pathways, making her unable to stop herself from radiating." Dorian tapped his foot. "Still doesn't explain why she's making ghosts go haywire."

Kirsten held her arms out to either side. "That's the part I don't understand. Telepathy and Telempathy don't work on spirits."

"Neither does Mind Blast, but you can lash," said Dorian. "Maybe she has some undocumented power symbiosis?"

"Feel like being a guinea pig again?" asked Kirsten.

"As long as she makes it stop before I do anything harmful or too embarrassing."

Kirsten looked at Marley. "How am I feeling right now?"

"I dunno."

"Seriously. Concentrate on me and think about wanting to know what my emotions are." Kirsten prepared herself for something psionic, but not having Telempathy, had little to no defense against it. If she sensed things going out of control, she'd need to erect a Mind Block fast.

"Umm…" Marley stared at her, eyes still glowing from Astral Seeing. After a moment, she cringed. "Are you like so frustrated you want to scream but you're kinda also like 'aww, lost kitten.'"

"Yeah, pretty much." Kirsten smiled. "You just read my emotions."

"You think I'm a lost kitten?" Marley set her hands on her hips.

"Well, you *do* dress like a fourteen-year-old obsessed with cute. And… I expected to find an outlaw psionic driving ghosts crazy on purpose. Once I realized you might be doing things unintentionally, my mission here changed."

"Gotcha. And yeah, I like cute. It's part of the whole Aethervein persona."

"Can you read Dorian's emotion?"

Marley focused on him. "Is he about half bored to tears, half scared like a monster's waiting to ambush him, and half heartbroken?"

Dorian stiffened. "Close."

The astonishment of someone apparently getting Telempathy to work on a spirit left Kirsten speechless. She figured his fear of monsters came from his worry Harbingers might not have gotten over their interest in him. Heartbreak? Easy—Nila. Maybe his family, too. Any telempath could claim to pick up sadness on a ghost and be right nine times out of ten... except maybe if they read Theodore. Some spirits adored being ghosts.

"Okay. I'm no longer confused," whispered Kirsten. "I've gone to awestruck."

"Now you sound like one of my fans." Marley laughed.

"It's unusual to be able to affect spirits with mind-related psionic abilities." Kirsten whistled.

"Might not be." Dorian rubbed his chin. "Astrals are incredibly hard to find. It's not as though we have a large sample size to study in order to understand what they're capable of. *You* can't use Telepathy on spirits. Doesn't mean it's particularly rare."

"Hannah—Division 0's East City Astral—can't do it either. And she's at the peak of psionic power. Wait, I think she's fourteen now, but still at the top of the curve."

"Whoa, you guys hire kids?" Marley whistled.

"Only in rare situations like astrals." Kirsten sighed. "Command thinks dealing with ghosts is tame and easy, harmless."

"I'm guessing by the way you said that, it's anything but."

Kirsten scratched the back of her head, laughing cheesily. "Yeah, kinda. But I've been finding the crazy stuff. Demons... *Ghosts* usually are fairly tame."

"Don't wanna know." Marley held her hands up.

"Okay, so... I understand now." Kirsten grabbed Marley's hands together. "There have been a *ton* of ghosts going bonkers around here for the past two weeks. I think you are playing your music here, maybe writing new songs, and when you get super into it, you start letting your emotions radiate out into the world. It's affecting living people *and* ghosts. Only, it's having a crazy powerful effect on spirits."

"Oh, no..." Marley looked down, her expression as somber as if she'd been told her parents had been killed.

"What's wrong?"

"Are you going to tell me I can't make music anymore? I'd die..."

"No. I'm sure you'll be able to control it with a little practice. I can help you with Astral stuff, but Telempathy is out of my reach. We have people who can help you learn how to use and control your abilities. You can even still use them when you do concerts, but you will have to disclose to the audience they'll be experiencing telempathic mood tweaking."

Marley brightened. "Seriously? It's legal?"

"As long as people know what they're getting, yeah. Not much different from taking mood altering drugs willingly. Gets a bit complicated if you're doing it intentionally without telling anyone. However, up until now, you didn't know."

"Is it true you guys make every psionic join?"

"We ask, but it's not required. You'll need to register, but it's for your protection. We'll help you determine what abilities you have and help you understand how to use them for free. Might be some testing involved since astrals are rare and you seem to be able to use Telempathy on spirits. The research helps you, too."

Marley grinned. "Wow, you feel like a kid getting birthday presents. Okay, since you're like totally posi-vibing, let's do it. Can I go now?"

"She likes helping people." Dorian patted Kirsten on the shoulder.

"Umm, is it against the law for me to do the empathy thing on people to see how they feel?" Marley kneaded her hands together.

Kirsten shook her head. "Reading emotions is okay. Changing them on someone is not so okay, unless you're doing it in self-defense."

"How can tweaking someone's emotion be self-defense?" Marley blinked, confused.

"Someone's trying to attack you… make them terrified so they run away."

"Ahh. Cool. I can do that?"

"Most likely. Telempathy is not my area of expertise." Kirsten opened her armband terminal and started another Inquest file, plus a registration process form. "If you're serious about wanting to go meet some people right now, we can definitely do it."

"Cool. And wow. I guess this is really why my fans are so loyal—and oh, shit..."

"What?" Kirsten looked up from the screen.

"Did I drive Zenn crazy? I didn't know I could do any of this..."

Kirsten pondered. "You said he was stalkery and possessive?"

"Totally." Marley grabbed two fistfuls of her hair. "Like insanely."

"But he didn't really go off the deep end until he was spying on you while you played music."

"Right..." Marley let her arms drop at her sides. "Oh. Umm. So you think the music affected him?"

Kirsten tapped a finger on her forearm guard. "It's hard to say without examining him. If he'd previously heard your music, it's possible he became addicted to you in the same way your fans do. His obsession could be ordinary crazy, or conditioning as a result of repeated exposure to your subconscious power."

"Wow. Seeing her in concert has to be better than most chems." Dorian chuckled.

Marley grinned. "I'm usually high on stage, so yeah. It's a trip. I'm as rainbowed as everyone listening. Have you ever tasted colors?"

"No," said Kirsten and Dorian simultaneously.

"You're missing out." Marley winked.

"Not my scene."

Dorian nudged Kirsten. "She's the good girl."

"Yeah, pretty much. Not gonna argue since he's right." Kirsten shrugged. "Before we go, let me try and teach you how to Blockade. If you can do it, you can shield your apartment so you stop whacking a ghostly hornet's nest every time you compose or practice."

"Okay..." Marley twirled around twice, then stopped short. "Umm, am I in trouble?"

Kirsten resumed typing into the registration form. "No, not yet. You haven't done anything deliberately wrong."

"You are lucky." Dorian pointed his thumb at Kirsten. "After the week you've given her chasing ghosts all over the city, any other cop would have found everything they could to charge you with."

Marley laughed nervously. "Umm, sorry. I didn't know."

"It's okay. I believe you." Kirsten smiled.

"What's this blockade thing?" asked Marley.

"Let's go to your studio, which I assume is a fairly small room… and I'll show you."

"This way." The girl hurried off down the corridor.

"Think it'll work?" asked Dorian in a low voice.

Kirsten exhaled. "I really freakin' hope so."

22

MOMENTS OF HAPPINESS

P ale orange light from the Comforgel pad saturated Kirsten's bedroom.

She lay awake, staring up at watery patterns crumples in her bed sheets cast around the indistinct shadow of her body on the ceiling. The constant din of hovercar traffic outside lulled her into an almost meditative state.

For the first time in her life, she couldn't fall asleep due to an *absence* of anxiety.

Two weeks of back-to-back 21-47 calls all traced to one unwitting psionic throwing raw emotion into the world. Not everything made complete sense, but she had to admit the notion of a single ghost, much less two, working as a contract killer exceeded even her limit of stretching plausibility. Maybe if the same spirit had attacked Elan Mendoza and gone after Plasmahawk, she'd have more doubts. Despite not seeing the ghost at the Ancora Medical building, they'd left enough of a residue in the room for her to tell it hadn't been Dacre.

She couldn't come up with much of an explanation for how Marley's psionically amplified music sent at least two ghosts off like guided missiles after specific people. The attack at the Beck house appeared completely random. Neither Johanna, her daughter Tamsen, nor the woman's wife, Arielle, had done anything to make them a target as far as she knew. It had to be simple coincidence for agitated ghosts to attack Mendoza and Plasmahawk, totally unrelated to them both likely being in the crosshairs of assassins.

"People can act weird when their emotions go out of control. Why not ghosts?"

She imagined Dacre or some other ghost gliding by close enough to Marley's apartment, getting caught in the storm of her music, and zooming off in a random direction before attacking like a drunk guy irrationally furious at a PubTran kiosk. The old woman she'd asked to leave the Twenty-Nine Palms mall food court had to 'live' in The Beneath. Perhaps her old house sat directly—or almost directly—below Marley's building. No way could the actual music have penetrated twenty-five meters of city plate and been audible all the way down on the natural surface… but the psionic radiance must have carried it like radio waves transport sound.

Marley's power obviously didn't work over electronic transmissions, or the people listening to her music via the GlobeNet would have also experienced the emotional effects. She'd never heard of anyone being able to use psionic powers over a Vidphone call or via NetMini. Then again, no one should be able to effect spirits with Telempathy, either. Maybe a powerful enough Technokinetic might develop a symbiotic power to use abilities like Telepathy on someone via video call someday. She shivered at the thought of mind-reading over unlimited distance.

If anyone ever manages to do that, Division 0's going to keep them under constant surveillance. Wouldn't be surprised if C-Branch tries to get them.

"The crazy surge is over…" She exhaled hard and closed her eyes.

Being excited at the hope of a boring day tomorrow seemed odd, but also awesome.

Faint giggling came from the hallway.

Kirsten opened her eyes to glance at the clock: 2:07 a.m.

Why is he awake at this hour?

She closed her eyes. Evan giggled again.

Most parents would get annoyed. Kirsten didn't have much of a reference for how a mother *should* be. Her mother became annoyed over *any* sound, even during the day. Nocturnal giggling would have earned serious punishment. Not like Kirsten would have ever giggled as a child, not after age six when the ghosts started showing up asking for help. She didn't blame the spirits. If her parents had been normal, it wouldn't have been a problem. Even if they'd abandoned her at the Division 0 dorms for being psionic, she'd have eventually been able to laugh again before she grew up. But no, she had to get the psychotic religion-obsessed mother who thought everything she didn't like came from some made up Devil, and everything she didn't like could be cured by pain and cruelty.

Evan's mother had been horrible to him, too. Unlike hers, the woman didn't actively torment him. She ignored him, laying around the house high all the time, and usually naked. Her boyfriend took care of the physical abuse. Evan probably didn't giggle very often at home either.

Hearing the boy sounding happy now made her cry tears of joy. She didn't even mind him being awake so late.

Evan giggled again.

Curious, Kirsten peeled the sheets away and got up. Her long sleep shirt draped around her knees as she crept out into the hallway, sneaking up to his room.

"... fell out of the tree with a crashing *bang*, sending all the chipmunks running off screaming," said the voice of Kirsten's father. "Ice cream went all over the place, one scoop landing directly on the blue rabbit's head."

Evan laughed.

Kirsten crept closer, peeking in the door.

Her dad sat on the edge of the Comforgel pad, holding a datapad, no doubt open to a children's story. Despite the millions upon millions of video games, holovids, and other interactive media, enough people still enjoyed reading for writers to keep making books. Also, no one ever 'played a bedtime video game' to their kid. She couldn't tell if he held a real datapad, or the device manifested as a projection of his spiritual being.

Kirsten pressed a hand to her chest at the base of her neck, choked up. She vaguely remembered her father reading to her once or twice. After the ghost stuff started, Mother forbade her from almost everything remotely fun, nice, or possessing an ounce of warmth. The woman thought punishing her continuously would appease the man in the sky she worshiped so he'd 'fix' Kirsten back to normal.

Dad defied her a few times, but Mother could hear mice fart at a hundred paces. She always caught Kirsten whispering to ghosts, begging them to go away and not make her mother angry. Of course, she heard every time Dad read her stories. He probably gave up on it because he knew she punished Kirsten for it the next day.

Her father made silly faces while narrating the voices of different characters in the story. Being a ghost, he could make his voice do things a living person couldn't. Evan stared at him, utterly enthralled.

Watching her father be silly to amuse Evan stole the breath from her lungs. Such a special moment, seeing the boy she'd found in such horrible conditions grinning and bright-eyed like any ordinary child who'd never had to wonder if they'd live to see the next day. She couldn't have even whispered, too overcome with happiness for her son.

Faint whirring near the floor attracted her attention briefly to a silver disc bot making its way along the corridor, scrubbing the carpet. When it reached the square of dim light coming from Evan's bedroom, it paused, rotating as if peering into the room. She imagined the cleaning bot being happy to see Evan full of joy, too, though in reality, it likely sensed the unusual electromagnetic presence of Dad and didn't know how to react.

Not wanting to ruin the special moment, Kirsten watched in silence for another minute, then carefully backed away and returned to bed. She pulled the sheets up to her chin, sighing at the ceiling. It finally occurred to her she didn't feel the least bit jealous.

Kirsten closed her eyes.

It's okay, Dad. I was terrified of her, too.

THE DREADED ALARM WENT OFF AS IT TENDED TO DO EVERY WEEKDAY morning.

Going from bed to autoshower to kitchen went by as such an automatic process Kirsten felt as if she'd teleported straight from bed to standing beside the counter trying something new: pancakes. Okay, so she cheated buying premixed liquid in a squeeze bottle. Anyone— even her—could cook pancakes when she only needed to squirt the beige goo onto a warm, flat pan. After the first charcake, she realized she needed to flip them over.

Evan murmured something unintelligible behind her.

She peered back over her shoulder.

The boy, eyes closed, walked naked out of the hallway into the kitchen and approached the reassembler.

"Forget something?" asked Kirsten.

Evan stood in front of the 'sem for a moment, swaying as if about to collapse at any second. "Mmm."

"Ev?"

He murmured a non-word while fumbling around blind for the buttons on the 'sem.

"What?" She flipped the sixth pancake, having gotten the hang of cooking them.

The reassembler beeped and whirred to life.

Evan continued to stand there, eyes closed.

"Go get dressed, hon."

He wiped a hand down his face, then yawned. One eye popped— halfway—open. "I fell asleep in the shower tube. I'm having a caffeine emergency."

"You're too young to be caffeine dependent." She scooped the pancake out of the pan, set it on the stack designated as his, and squirted another portion of batter into the pan.

"Nmmn." He opened the reassembler after a minor amount of fumbling around, grasped the cup which had appeared inside it, and sipped.

"Are you just going to stand there in your birthday suit drinking coffee in front of the reassembler?"

"Uh huh." He sipped more coffee. "Sorry. Caffeine emergency."

She chuckled. Only because she knew he'd been up *super* late did she not panic.

Evan took a few more sips, less and less time between them. He opened his left eye, yawned again, and set the cup on the table before trudging back down the hall.

Should I have interrupted them and told him to go to sleep? She bit her lip, second-guessing her skills at momming a child. *Nah. He'll learn.*

Thud. "Ow," deadpanned Evan.

She snickered. "Be careful!"

"Oops," said Evan in complete seriousness.

She felt ninety percent certain he joked, and smiled.

Nah, I did the right thing. Can't shut down moments of happiness, not even for bedtime. We all need them whenever we can find them.

23

DAMAGE

E van smiled in his sleep, out cold in the passenger seat on the flight to the PAC.

Pancakes had been a big success. Neither of them finished, since Kirsten underestimated how filling they would be. Hopefully, the leftovers would keep in the fridge until dinner time. After an uneventful flight in, she carried Evan to the school entrance in the Division 0 wing before waking him up.

He hugged her, yawned again, and stumbled off to class, looking way too much like a small version of an office worker on a Monday after a long weekend. She watched him until he vanished behind the curve of the hallway. Thinking about her dad reading to him kept a smile on her face the whole way to her squad room.

Dorian, already at his desk, looked up from the holo-terminal, smiled at her, and resumed reading. Perhaps one might consider it progress no one in the squad room thought it weird anymore whenever his terminal activated seemingly by itself.

She flopped in her chair, grabbing her stomach in both hands. *Oof. Pancakes are awfully heavy. Shouldn't eat so many.* Groaning, she leaned forward and logged into her desk terminal, looking forward to a calm day spent in the PAC. As the only astral sensitive Division 0 had in

West City, Command preferred to keep her on standby in case something paranormal happened. They didn't want her bogged down on a case any other psionic investigator could deal with while a spirit wreaked havoc.

Predictably, due to the often infrequent nature of hauntings, this made for long hours sitting around the PAC feeling like a lazy freeloader. However, for at least the next week, she wouldn't mind the idleness at all.

Two new emails greeted her as soon as she logged in. The first came from the Admin section containing the registration info for Marley Santiago. The woman tested at a grade 3 rating for Astral, surprisingly high for someone who never consciously tried to use it. Kirsten suspected Marley had at least a grade 2 since she'd gotten Blockade to work.

She's probably been using it subconsciously for a few years.

The evaluators down in the lab agreed with Kirsten's theory of subconscious radiance into her music, most likely empowered or uncontrolled due to her frequent use of Placid Rain. Oddly, despite her impressive grade 5 rank in Telempathy, Marley struggled to use it actively. The passive evaluation rated her at a five, but active testing resulted in scores closer to someone with only a grade 2—if that— power level. However, when they had her demonstrate it in tandem with playing her music, she had most of the medical wing feeling mellow and 'at one with the universe.' As of yet, they hadn't determined if the power difference came from lack of trying to use her abilities on purpose or if she had some mental hang up where she could only truly use them at their full potential while engrossed in performing or creating music.

Either way, it meant two things: Marley didn't intend to make ghosts go crazy, and the storm of crazy ghosts would stop. Between her now being aware of what she did, plus having the ability to Blockade her studio, her abilities wouldn't leak out and drive spirits over the edge. People living in apartments close to her would continue to feel her music, but with training, she might be able to control it more.

The second email, alas, made her fake cry.

"Darn. Not again."

Dispatch sent over a 20-04 call, a low-priority investigation request from a construction site in Sector 4858.

"Didn't we already fix this?"

"What?" asked Dorian.

"Another ghost causing trouble."

She sighed at the screen. The construction site being upwards of 200 miles away from Marley's apartment weakened her hopes a spirit agitated by Marley's power had gone so far afield to mess with workers. Of course, multiple other events happened well away from the ring of hauntings centered on her.

At least a 20-04 often ended up being relatively tame. The code meant someone reported observed paranormal activity such as objects moving or strange sounds, but nothing actively went on at the time the call came in. Consequently, it became a low-priority email request and not an alarm beeping right to her NetMini.

If nothing else, it gave her an excuse to continue hiding from the mountain of Inquest files she still needed to finish filling out reports for—her least favorite part of a job she never asked for. Kirsten generally loved being a Division 0 I-Ops officer, but she'd never *asked* for it. They dropped it on her. Having a near irreplaceable skill gave her a fair amount of bargaining power. She might be able to demand an end to reports but couldn't bring herself to seriously consider it. All cops had to do reports. Even if no one else *could* handle spirits, she didn't consider herself better than anyone or worthy of being above tedium. Tedium came for everyone.

And most cops tended to procrastinate on reports.

Smiling, she locked her terminal and stood. "Let's go check it out."

"Situation?"

"Construction site supervisor reporting a bunch of 'spooky things' going on. Didn't give much detail over the vid, but I'm guessing it's going to be tools moving around or disappearing, maybe people seeing shadows. Machinery turning on or off, you know, the usual stuff."

Dorian cracked his knuckles. "Ahh. A good normal haunting."

She exhaled hard. "Here's hoping."

———

A BLUE HOLOGRAPHIC FALCON THE SIZE OF A SMALL PRIVATE AIRCRAFT flew in lazy circles around a skeletal high-rise, projected from an orb bot.

Kirsten steered the patrol craft into a leftward descending curve, flying in a wide circle around the construction site.

Rising spars on the topmost floor suggested the crew had no intention of stopping at sixty-five stories. Thus far, only the first fourteen levels had outer walls, the rest of the structure remained as a simple stack of floor slabs open all the way through, supported by a grid of interior pylons. Bots of various sizes glided or drove around doing spot welds, transporting materials, or scanning. A scattering of people also roamed the wide-open floors, some controlling bots, others running wires, working, or standing around apparently doing nothing.

"Weird. Bit early to take breaks, isn't it?"

"Hmm?" Dorian glanced over.

"There's one or two people on every floor among the workers who are just kinda standing there doing nothing."

"Oh, they would be the supervisors."

She chuckled. "Seriously?"

"Could be safety watchers, too."

"What the heck is a safety watcher?"

"People who stand around watching other people and bots work to make sure they're being safe."

Kirsten blinked. "What do they do if someone's not safe?"

"Yell at them. Maybe throw a helmet."

She rolled her eyes. "You always tease me."

He snickered. "Okay, fine. Don't believe me."

"Don't they use the bots for scanning, like to check safety stuff? They really still hire people to do it?"

"Union rules."

"Wow. Is that good or bad?"

"Good, I suppose. It's a job for a living person on Earth. Less people ending up in gangs. You know what's worse than a desperate person?"

"Dare I ask?"

"A desperate person in a society where everyone has guns." Dorian brushed at the same piece of lint he always dislodged from his sleeve, and always reappeared. "You know they do it on purpose. The government, I mean. They stopped regulating firearms because they *want* the undesirables to handle population control on themselves."

"So pessimistic." She shook her head, more disgusted at the idea he came closer to being right than not.

Numerous signs and banners on the building-in-progress bore the same falcon logo as the giant hologram beside the words 'Peregrine Fabrication Services.' A few large piles of debris sat at one end of the border defined by the fence surrounding the site, no doubt remains of whatever building stood here prior to this project.

Century towers usually lasted for a long time, but they still eventually degraded to the point replacing them turned out to be cheaper—and safer—than repair. However, except for bad areas where neglect hastened the process, few buildings ended up being replaced out of need. More often than not, property changed hands, and someone wanted an office where a residential tower had been, or a residential tower where a commercial building or parking deck stood.

She didn't even bother trying to understand why people would tear down a perfectly usable building. It *had* to be cheaper to modify an existing one, right? Kirsten never got along well with math, and economics fried her brain worse than a stunrod to the nose.

A decent amount of open space at the southeast corner of the yard contained a handful of hovercars, parked as far as possible from danger while still being on the property. They all likely belonged to managers, supervisors, or inspectors. 'Bot wranglers, electricians, plumbers, human labor, and others most likely took PubTran cars to the work site—or walked if they could get a hotel room close enough.

Billowing clouds of grey dust exploded off the plastisteel ground when she brought the patrol craft in for a landing, likely dirt from the building they tore down before starting on the new one. She'd once heard somewhere the average century tower had something like 500 pounds of crud in the ventilation system.

She opened the door to the flavor of dust and metal in the air. Coughing, she tried to breathe through her nose as much as possible.

A fortyish woman in dark green coveralls, armored boots, and a hard hat walked up to her. "You must be from Division 0."

"Yes. Good morning. Kirsten Wren." She offered a hand.

"Sharla Ward. I'm the site supervisor for day shift. Mero told me he'd had enough of the weird shit and called you guys. He's the night supervisor."

"You're working around the clock?" Kirsten gazed up at the massive structure, finding it far more imposing from the ground.

"Nah. He's more security than operations. His crew watches over the place to keep curious locals out when it's dark. Guessing you're going to ask me what kinda stuff's happening to make us call you."

She smiled. "Wow, you're psionic, too? You totally read my mind."

Sharla laughed. "Started off as nothin' real bothersome. Workers reporting their stuff wasn't where they left it. Bots acting odd for no reason. Didn't think much of it initially. Figured maybe a prank. Then one of the guys said he saw a shadowy figure staring at him on the second to top level, which, uhh, would'a been the thirty-fourth at the time. After the ghost stories made the rounds, everyone and their mother started reporting hearing footsteps, feelin' like someone was standin' right behind them. They'd turn, no one there. Had about fifty some odd reports of workers being grabbed, pinched, or squeezed— mostly women. Hell, the invisible man copped a feel on me once."

Kirsten bit her lip. *Sounds like Theodore is bored.* "Did it feel like an invisible person grabbed you?"

"Not really. Was on my way to the car after end of shift. Just handed things off to Mero. I open the door and a cold hand clamped onto my tit. Straight to skin, like I didn't have on a safety vest, these coveralls, or a shirt. Only lasted a second or so, but damn it kinda got me."

Dorian frowned. "Death can be a pervert's paradise."

"Yeah, sounds like a ghost messing with people." Kirsten cringed as a huge, flying bot went overhead in a roar of ion thrusters. It lugged a bundle of pipes up to the sixty-eighth (or thereabout) floor.

"He's doing more than messing. It's gotten worse the past few days, which is why Mero and I decided to call it in without telling the project manager. He doesn't believe in weird stuff. Wouldn't want the bad publicity. Anyway, we had three bots fry themselves so bad they had to be scrapped. One took out a column on the fifty-first, which we had ta replace. Workers reported being shoved when they got close to the edge or something dangerous. Last straw was, couple days ago, we had two guys fall straight off the sixty-third."

Kirsten gasped. "Oh, no…"

"*Walls* might help with that," said Dorian.

She gawked at him. "I don't believe you."

"It's true," said Sharla.

"Sorry, I'm a ghost. All my humor is *dead*pan."

"Not you. I believe you." Kirsten sighed out her nose, then stared at him. "People died! You can't joke about it."

"Umm…?" Sharla tilted her head. "Are you okay?"

"Yes. My partner has a horrible sense of humor. He's a ghost."

Dorian raised an eyebrow. "I didn't technically make a joke. This is presently a seventy-and-a-half story building, and it has walls only on the first third. Why do they wait so damn long to add the walls?"

Sharla grimaced, looking around uneasily. "He's here now?"

"Yes."

"What did he say?"

"He's wondering why so many floors don't have outer walls."

"Easier for the bots to get in and out, transporting materials." Sharla pointed at hoverbot almost as big as a car lugging a stack of drywall up to the twenty-sixth, the lowest level lacking walls. "Once we get all the wiring, piping, interior walls, and other major stuff finished, then they cap the outsides. More efficient."

Kirsten nodded. "I suppose that makes sense. How did the two men end up falling?"

"Officially, worker carelessness. They got too close to the edge and tripped. But it's all bullshit for the insurance company. Everyone near 'em at the time they fell said it looked like someone or something threw them. I heard Upton was more than fifteen feet away from the edge and went literally flying like someone hit him with a running tackle. Steve was a bit closer. You ask any crew member near the upper floors, they'll all tell ya the same story. He floated up off his feet a couple inches and went flying like a cyborg picked him up. But nothin' there."

"So much for a mischievous haunt." Dorian frowned. "I don't think this is related to Marley. Slow escalation demonstrates more of a calculated plan, not a spirit driven nuts by music."

"All right. Anything else?"

Sharla thought for a moment. "More of the usual stuff. Noises at night. People seeing a figure lurking in dark places, an' so on."

"Okay. I'm going to look around, see if I can find any residual traces of the spirit."

"Hold on a sec. Let me get you a hard hat." Sharla held up a 'wait' hand, then ran over to a portable office trailer. She returned in a few minutes, handing over a white helmet bearing a Peregrine Fabrication Services safety logo. "Here ya go."

Kirsten thought it flimsier than psi armor, but still put it on, mostly because she didn't have psi armor with her and didn't feel like driving the 237 miles to the PAC to get it.

Sharla accompanied her on a tour around the work site. Over the next hour and forty-eight minutes, they visited multiple spots where unexplained events had been included in reports. Kirsten interviewed various workers, hearing more stories of being grabbed or pushed, having tools go missing, construction materials flying at their heads, and bots going crazy. Descriptions of physical contact remained consistent: men reported aggressive shoving or tripping while women relayed sexual groping and grabbing. All the events followed an escalation path from annoying to risky to deadly... except the perverted groping. None of the women reported being shoved at the edge of the structure or touched in a way likely to cause physical injury, though the strength and inappropriateness of the contact escalated along with the violence elsewhere.

After touring the fifty-ninth floor, they stopped to catch their breath—Dorian notwithstanding—by the elevator, a no-frills device consisting of a red plastisteel mesh cage with ion thrusters, essentially a delivery bot for carrying people. About twenty workers and sixty bots of varying types and sizes worked around them, creating so much buzzing, whirring, and banging, she had to yell to be heard.

"It's almost as if the ghost is trying to make your people leave the site," shouted Kirsten. "Everything going on here fits the pattern for an angry, territorial haunt."

"A few have." Sharla nodded. "Stacie, one of our bot technicians, told me she got goosed by an icicle. She demanded to be transferred off this site or she'd quit on the spot."

Kirsten squirmed. "Don't blame her."

"Theodore's move," said Dorian.

"He's hardly the only spirit capable of doing it. And he's definitely not the type of ghost to throw random innocent construction workers off a high-rise." Kirsten grumbled. She'd found multiple pockets of residual spirit energy, but none had enough potency to give her a sense of the spirit's identity, or 'fingerprint' so to speak.

Sharla laughed. "If I believed in such things, I'd swear KHI hired a damned voodoo witch doctor to mess with us."

"KHI?" asked Kirsten.

"Oh, sorry. I'm used to dealing with people in the business. KHI is Kalis Heavy Industries, another construction company. They're bigger than us and on the shady side. They put a bid in on this job but didn't get it. Things got kinda heated. Word is, they made a veiled threat to the bosses if they didn't pull out and let KHI take this project. It's most of the reason Mero and his team are here at night."

"You think the other company would sabotage this site?" Kirsten opened a sub-window on her screen, accessing the police record for KHI.

"The bosses sure do." Sharla grumbled. "Not directly, of course. KHI contracts out. They have a bit of a reputation. Everyone on my crew checks every piece of equipment twice for bombs or malware each morning. Sometimes, they even pay gangs to come in and do damage. Almost feels like the strange stuff going on here is because they hired a damn witch doctor to curse the place." She chuckled. "Good thing I don't really believe that, or my ass'd be gone already."

The sub-screen on Kirsten's armband terminal filled up with thousands of Division 1 Inquests alleging KHI illegally arranged property damage, intimidation, sabotage, and so on at various construction sites. Somehow, the vast majority of the Inquests ended up closed as 'inconclusive' for lack of evidence. Not one had any links to Division 0 for 'paranormal oddities.'

Kirsten furrowed her brow at the implication of a spirit trying to drive everyone away from a construction site after a rival company threatened them. She'd seen plenty of spirits protesting changes in their environment by creating disturbances similar to the activities going on here. Some spirits *hated* construction, especially when their former home had to be demolished first or altered. One sour old man kept pushing people—including a small boy—down a new flight of stairs the family added to their home because he didn't like them changing 'his' house. Occasionally, spirits experienced an alternate reality based on their memories, but sudden, severe changes—like a new high-rise going up—could disrupt their ideal reality and trigger hauntings.

The pranks, groping, pushing, and two deaths here most likely resulted from a ghost who objected to the demolition of the prior tower. Before Elan Mendoza's death, the two situations would never have come close to appearing related. Also, Dacre, the spirit who attacked Plasmahawk, claimed someone *forced* him to do it. She'd initially thought Marley's uncontained psionic-charged music threw him into a frenzy out of his control. Frustratingly, ghosts didn't always speak plain truths.

"Dorian?" Kirsten glanced at him but ended up watching two men working near the edge a distance behind him. This high up, the lack of walls around the outside of the building resulted in a significant crosswind ripping through the building. Even though both workers had safety harnesses on, she couldn't help but worry.

"Hmm?" asked Dorian.

She shifted her attention back to him. "Do you think when Dacre said someone forced him to attack Plasmahawk, he meant specifically him or someone forced him to be violent in general and he chose a victim at random?"

"I had been taking it the same way I believe you did... Marley drove him crazy and he couldn't stop himself." Dorian paused to watch a large bot rumble by, transporting a stack of metal struts. "Are you wondering if it might have been less than random?"

Sharla took a NetMini from her pocket, opened the holo-panel, and tapped at it.

"Think about it... someone wanted Mendoza dead, and a ghost attacked him. There's a real good chance someone wanted Plasmahawk dead, and a ghost attacked him." Kirsten gestured at Sharla. "Now she's talking about a contested bid against a rival construction company known for retaliating illegally. There's tons of Inquests, but nothing came our way."

"Hang on..." Sharla looked up from her NetMini. "Do you seriously think they somehow sent a ghost after us?"

Kirsten swiped a hand at the holo-panel, closing it, and let her arm hang limp. "They don't seem to have ever done anything like it before. But, could be, it's simply not been noticed. It's too early to say one way or the other if they are involved."

"How do you prove something like this?" asked Sharla.

"Usually... we don't. Most times—" Kirsten jumped, startled by a sudden spike in paranormal energy; she looked up at the bare metal ceiling covered in dangling wires and half-built ventilation ducts. "Most times it never gets to court. Judges don't like psionic issues to begin with, because they can often be difficult to prove to people who don't have telepathy. They like spirits even less. Umm, we have a guest."

"What?" asked Sharla.

"Above us." Kirsten eyed the elevator shaft, despite not trusting it in the vicinity of an angry ghost. If a spirit killed the ion thrusters, the mesh cage would fall straight down the shaft. She didn't exactly love the idea of climbing several stories up a metal ladder in a vertical shaft either, but it beat free-falling inside a cage. "Ghost."

Sharla hit the call button for the elevator.

A surge in paranormal energy came from above, along with—possibly—a man screaming. Given all the construction noise, she couldn't be sure. Kirsten started to step out on the ladder, but froze at the sight of the red mesh box racing upward. Deciding against testing how much room the shaft had between elevator cab and wall, she jumped back.

The floating metal box bobbed into view, hovering in front of them on the fifty-ninth floor. Only route selection programming kept it within the walls of the future elevator shaft, a large bot flying up and down a vertical corridor formed by square holes in each floor slab.

Against her better judgement, Kirsten got in when Sharla slid the cage door open.

Dorian cheated—floating straight up through the ceiling.

"Which floor?" asked Sharla, sliding the grate closed. "And why do you look scared?"

Ghosts love to drain electrical power out of things like this, said Kirsten via Telepathy. *Don't want to free-fall.*

Sharla jumped back against the elevator wall, wide-eyed.

Sorry. Using Telepathy so the spirit doesn't hear me and get the idea to kill the elevator. And I'm tired of yelling over the noise.

"Uhh, okay. Whoa, trippy. Is this what it sounds like to get a call with a headware implant?"

Kirsten shrugged. *Don't know personally, but some people have said so.*

"Seventy!" shouted Dorian from above.

Kirsten typed '70' on the keypad inside the elevator, requesting it go to the second floor down from the present top of the structure. Roughly two-thirds of the seventy-first story's floor had been installed, making the seventieth the topmost complete story—at least in terms of having a surface to walk on. The mesh cage lurched upward, stationary to full speed in three seconds. Fortunately, after riding it up and down with Sharla over the past almost two hours, she expected the hard acceleration and didn't end up on her ass like she did the first two times.

The sixtieth-through-sixty-ninth floors shot by in a blur. Plastisteel mesh offered no protection from the veritable tornado inside the box. She cringed, hoping her hair clip would withstand the abuse. Weightlessness came on for a few seconds as the elevator slowed rapidly upon reaching the seventieth floor. She rose up on her toes, not fully leaving the ground before gravity returned to normal. Sharla pulled the manual door aside. Kirsten squeezed through before it opened all the way, eager to get out of a potential deathtrap.

Once on solid footing, she looked around for the ghost she sensed.

Three times the amount of workers scurried about on the seventieth compared to the fifty-ninth, most of them focused on assembling the floor of the story above this one. Car-sized bots on huge rubber wheels trundled around, transporting huge squares of plastisteel into position before lifting them into place to form the 'slab' for the seventy-first story. Smaller bots zipped back and forth on the floor, scanning and checking joins. Sharla had earlier explained they needed to be absolutely sure a slab met all quality checks before building higher than one level up. Since it appeared the seventieth floor still had auditing to undergo, they couldn't start on the seventy-second.

Dorian hid behind a column, pointing.

Kirsten jogged over to him, not bothering to be sneaky. Dorian had a reason to hide, as ghosts easily recognized each other as spirits. Most didn't realize Kirsten could see them until she did something to prove it.

A large-framed man, his pale arms studded with black metal circles—some manner of long obsolete cybernetic implant—stood with his back facing them near the south edge of the seventieth floor, watching a group of four workers adjusting the position of a plastisteel square they planned to raise to become part of the seventy-first floor. Despite the size and apparent ponderousness of the bot, it appeared capable of making millimeter adjustments to its position.

The man's brown brush cut, his overall size, and stance, gave Kirsten the impression the spirit had been military in life, or at least pretended to be. Some mercenaries acted the part even if they'd never served. The old cyberware—she'd never seen anyone with rows of one-inch discs up the backs of their arms before—suggested he'd died over a century ago. She didn't worry about it, though. Cyberware didn't do anything for ghosts. He'd kept it purely out of latent self-image.

He also felt familiar.

This is the ghost who killed Elan Mendoza. He's not upset they tore down the old building.

"Bet he's gonna push someone off," said Dorian. "Altitude is the easiest way to kill here."

"It's the same guy from Ancora!" yelled Kirsten.

The ghost kicked a tool, sending it rolling to within a foot of the edge.

One of the workers chased it.

Wait! shouted Kirsten telepathically into the head of the man jogging after the tool. *Stay away from the edge or you're going to die!*

"Gah!" yelled the worker, stopping short.

Kirsten ran in a straight line at the ghost, the wide-open floor devoid of any walls or obstructions beyond support columns, bots, tool carts, and workers. Dorian circled wide to the left, keeping pace with her. The ghost showed no sign of noticing or caring about her running toward him. She leapt a floor-scanning disc bot, unfurling the lash from her right hand. The brilliant blue-white energy cord trailed after her, seemingly floating on the wind. She didn't often go straight to attacking spirits, but a spirit who had already killed three people wouldn't be in the mood to talk. She also didn't want to lose him. He could drop straight down through sixty-nine floors and be long gone before she even got to the elevator.

The ghost spun to face her, no doubt sensing the energy in the lash. Despite being seconds from killing a man, his expression held little discernible emotion—at least, until he saw her. His eyebrows crept up a little.

Kirsten whipped the energy cord around in a wide arc, swinging sideways at chest level. The ghost dove at the floor, sliding under the lash. Dorian crashed into him at a full run, knocking the bigger man into a logroll, tumbling with him. She snapped the energy whip to the right and down, its long reach allowing her to land the last two feet of it into the murderous spirit's back.

The man howled in anguish as the energy strand sliced through him, leaving an inch-wide gap in his body from armpit to the middle of his back. Glowing white spectral essence lined the sides of the wound rather than gore. Still screaming, the man attempted to push himself up, his right shoulder grotesquely rising into the air away from the rest of his body.

Being a ghost, his essence coalesced whole by the time she ran up to him, coiling the whip for another strike.

"Fuckin' hell that hurt," wheezed the ghost.

For no reason Kirsten quite understood, she hesitated. Something about his demeanor had changed, though she couldn't pinpoint exactly what. The shimmering glow of the lash painted long, twitching shadows on the floor from the vertical columns around her. All the workers had gone silent, staring at her.

Dorian grabbed the spirit from behind in a technically perfect compliance hold, though the size difference in the men made it appear somewhat comical, like a little dog atop a German shepherd.

Kirsten couldn't explain why she aborted her swing, so raised her arm again.

"Hold the fuck on, kid. Don't do that shit again." The big ghost held a hand up as if to block. "You broke it."

"Kind of the point," muttered Dorian.

"Broke what?" asked Kirsten.

"Whatever made me want to do this."

"Let me guess…" Dorian smirked. "The noise."

"What noise?" asked the ghost.

Kirsten walked around in front of the man so she could see his face. "I know you're the one who killed Elan Mendoza at the Ancora Medical building. You killed two people here already. Why?"

"Another breather sorta like you forced me to do it." He rubbed the spot where the lash hit him. "Son of a bitch… stings. But it gave me my thoughts back."

He doesn't look like a robot anymore. Dacre did the same damn thing… soon as I hit him, his expression changed to human. "What did this person do?"

Construction workers gathered in a semicircle around her, whispering amongst themselves about the 'glowing noodle,' wondering what it might be.

"He told me to come here and 'do damage' until the company abandoned the site. I couldn't think about anything else until you zapped me."

Kirsten lowered her arm, letting the lash coil loosely around her boots. "How did he make you do this?"

"This dude with glowing eyes walked up to me, said 'stand still,' and I couldn't move. Then he holds up a screen with a map. Tells me to go here and do damage until they abandon the place."

Dorian whistled. "What are the odds we've found *two* more astral sensitives?"

"I've been saying for years we're not as rare as Command thinks. It takes a certain kind of experience for someone to realize they're an Astral to begin with… and most of them probably think they're insane. Society, generally, doesn't believe ghosts are real. There have to be more astrals around, but they're unknown, even to themselves."

"The dude who sent me here figured it out," muttered the big guy.

Kirsten thought about wanting a Harbinger to check this spirit out. She tried not to 'summon' them the way she'd done before in a 'I need you now' mindset, attempting more of a polite request if they had a moment to spare. *Dacre must have run into the same guy. Marley didn't affect either of these ghosts. Dammit! No wonder some of the events happened so far away from Sector 2890. Only the agitated spirits around her apartment reacted to the music. Shit! Does that mean Johanna Beck was targeted on purpose? What the heck for? She might be in danger still.*

"All right." Kirsten glanced around. "I'm inclined to believe what you did to Elan Mendoza and the two men here wasn't of your free will... but I need to make sure."

"Swear, kid." The antique soldier held a hand up. "I didn't wanna do it."

"I'm not a kid." She sighed, gesturing at Dorian to get off the guy. "If you're telling the truth, it should be obvious in a moment."

The large ghost rose to his feet, rolling his right shoulder around. "What did you do to me? My damn chest still hurts."

"It's a weapon." She glanced down at the lash. "Drains energy. Not permanent."

Dorian smiled. "Unless she hits you with it too many times, then it's fairly permanent."

A pool of black vapors bubbled up out of the silver metal floor beside her.

"What the fuck is that?" The ghost took a step back, glowing orange crosshairs appearing in his eyes.

"Little overkill?" Dorian blinked.

"Three people are dead," said Kirsten. "I want to believe this guy but—"

"Lennox," said the ghost. "Name's Lennox Beake."

The black, vaporous form of a lone—somewhat small—Harbinger emerged from the plastisteel, its head nearly as tall as the ceiling.

She peered up at its sparkling metallic silver eyes. "Thank you. I don't trust myself not to be too optimistic. Is Lennox responsible for those three deaths? Do you want him?"

"Oh, what the shit is this?" whispered Lennox.

The Harbinger gazed at the spirit for a moment, then shook its head before pointing at him, then down to the side.

"He's okay, but you want the guy who forced him to kill?"

The Harbinger nodded once.

Eek. The guy's alive. I can't go execute someone... but I don't think the Harbingers will mind waiting for him to die. Not like they're in any hurry. Kirsten dispelled the lash, smiling. "Thanks. Sorry for bothering you."

It peered down at her. Despite having nothing even remotely close to facial features beyond its two scintillating eyes, it gave off a sense of not minding—then sank into the floor. Wispy trails of inky black smoke withdrew along the seams between square plastisteel tiles, following it out of sight.

"Freaky," whispered Lennox. "So... what happened here?"

Kirsten set her hands on her hips. "I'm still fuzzy on the details, but it looks like there's another Astral Sensitive out there who managed to find a way to mind-control ghosts. The same man ordered you to kill Elan Mendoza?"

"Yeah." Lennox nodded. "I barely even remember doing it."

Dorian whistled. "We're going into strange territory here."

"You heard him say what I did, right?" Kirsten rubbed her temples. "Another live person *ordered* him to chase Peregrine Fabrication off this site—and kill Elan."

"I heard it but I'm not sure what to make of it." Dorian nodded. "Using Suggestion the way Marley can use Telempathy on ghosts?"

"Suggestion doesn't work on spirits."

"Have you ever tried?"

She locked stares with Dorian. "*Quack like a duck.*"

He blinked. "Why would I do that?"

"See? Doesn't work. Spirits don't have brains. There's nothing for me to connect to... but." Kirsten waved a hand around. "Evan is an astral and he can't do the lash."

"No Mind Blast," said Dorian.

Lucky kid. She forced a smile. "Yeah."

"Umm, what the hell is going on?" asked Sharla, walking up to Kirsten. "Did you find the ghost?"

"Yeah. He's right here." Kirsten looked back toward Lennox— who'd vanished. "Or was. Dammit!"

"What now?" Dorian leaned back.

"He poofed before I could ask him where the hell this dude is." She grumbled.

Dorian plucked the same lint ball off his arm. "You heard the man. This other astral merely walked up to him. He probably doesn't even know where the man lives."

She made herself solid to spirits and leaned against him. "Not fair! Ghosts are just supposed to know stuff."

He laughed.

"Hello?" asked Sharla.

"Yeah…" Kirsten exhaled, un-leaned from Dorian, and walked over to her. "The spirit attacking your people is gone. This sounds crazy, even to me, but I have a theory someone on the living side arranged for the harassment. Probably KHI, but the odds of me proving it are extremely low. At least, proving it in any way a judge won't laugh at. However, I'm going after the guy who sent the ghost here."

Sharla whistled. "Well, damn. I guess it's better than nothing. Didn't really expect you'd like 'arrest' a ghost or anything. But you got it to stop? That's the important part."

"There's a chance the same person might send a different ghost here once he realizes the last one is gone. If anything else paranormal happens, call it in." Kirsten accessed her armband terminal. "Need to collect a few more bits of info for the report and I'll get out of your way."

"She loves reports." Dorian grinned.

Kirsten gave him epic side-eye.

24

CORPORATE LEVERAGE

Kirsten leaned against the door of the patrol craft, gazing up at a tower of gleaming naked plastisteel.

The construction workers had been a little reluctant to accept all the ghostly weirdness would stop right away. Calling a Harbinger here had likely not been the smartest thing, as it made bots and electronics on every story below her go haywire in a spectacle ten times more obvious than anything Lennox did. She didn't exactly consider it lying to tell them the mass disturbance had been part of her removing the ghost from the property. Generally, she tried to avoid talking about Harbingers to normal citizens. She'd already exceeded her monthly allotment for shattering people's worldview.

Technically, the disturbance *had* been part of stopping Lennox, if indirectly.

Dorian constantly called her 'too nice,' which he meant as a compliment. However, she knew full well she often let people—and ghosts—slide on certain things. Three murders, she couldn't simply ignore, so she *had* to know for sure Lennox didn't bear responsibility. It encouraged her to learn the Harbingers' view on crimes of compulsion aligned with Division 0. If a person used Suggestion to force someone else to murder, the law considered the psionic responsible for the death. Apparently, the Universe felt the same way about this man who could control spirits.

Lennox describing how he'd been forced to do things sounded rather like Suggestion, but it didn't prove anything. Astral Lash wasn't truly Mind Blast, but some wholly other thing somehow related to her having both powers. She thought of it as an entirely separate ability, not her Astral Sense letting her use Mind Blast on ghosts. Were that the case, she'd merely stare at ghosts and give them nasty headaches.

She couldn't even explain why it took the form of an energy whip. Maybe it came from something she'd seen in a holovid somewhere as a teen and forgot about except at a subconscious level. The first time the lash came out had been a manifestation of fear. She'd been fourteen, not activated as an agent at the time, but Division 0 brought her to a scene to act as an interpreter between a spirit and the people living there—only the ghost turned out to be malicious. When the specter, a barely human shaped monster with giant needle-like teeth and hollow black eyes, grabbed her, she screamed, wanting it to get the hell away from her—and blasted it with blue-white energy.

Maybe Tactical Officer Yanez, who'd escorted her there, calling it 'lashing out' helped her form it into a literal lash. Of course, Yanez seeing her wield an actual weapon conjured of pure psionic energy against a ghost was largely responsible for the Command Council activating her two years later at sixteen when the Wharf Stalker happened.

She didn't want to be special. Having more astral sensitives around would be awesome. Not every ghostly weirdness would land on her desk. She could help on other cases without feeling as if she ran the risk of failing to respond fast enough to something critical. Alas, Marley had no interest in being a cop, and the guy sending ghostly assassins after people wouldn't get the chance to. People who used their powers to commit murder—especially contract killings—weren't asked to join.

Division 0 could brush aside killing in some circumstances, such as self-defense or accidental eruptions of power. It would take a truly extreme situation for Command to give someone a pass on deliberate murder.

Someone can mind control ghosts... She fidgeted, trying to process the idea. *Oh, shit. The spirit watching the board meeting... the insider stock trades. There's no reason for a ghost to care about money—unless he was ordered to spy.* Kirsten ran her hands through her hair, neatening it and re-clipping it up off her shoulders. If Burkhardt learned of a person who could turn ghosts into weapons, spies, or assassins, he'd probably lose his mind. Generally, Kirsten tried to think of the government in a positive light, but even she accepted they occasionally did highly shady things. Most of that came from C-Branch, military intelligence. If *they* found this guy...

The spirits don't deserve to be turned into guided missiles. C-Branch won't even think of spirits as people. Hell, they barely think of people as people—assets.

"What the heck am I going to do here?" whispered Kirsten.

"About?" Dorian appeared beside her.

"If I arrest this guy, Burkhardt might turn him into a weapon. What if C-Branch gets him? I can't kill the guy. I can't ignore what he's doing." She hung her head. "Every decision here feels like it's the wrong one."

Dorian rested a hand on her shoulder, chilling it. "The actions of others don't reflect on you. This guy's a killer. You have to bring him in. Whatever happens after we get him isn't your fault. And you know Director Carter would never let Burkhardt abuse something like this. She's almost an older version of you after the naïve idealism has been squeezed out of her."

"You make it sound inevitable."

"Not intentionally. Only a special sort of person can grow old in this world and cling to the hope people are inherently good. Maybe you can. Director Carter surrendered a little to pragmatism."

Kirsten folded her arms. "They're going to want to study him like they did me. Maybe even worse because he's got military and intelligence applications."

"Ghostly assassins aren't practical. C-Branch has living people, synthetics, dolls, and bots far more deadly and useful than an unwilling spirit."

"What about spying? Remember the Lyris Corporation boardroom?"

Dorian blinked. "You're thinking it's the same guy?"

"Why else would a spirit care about information valuable to stock traders?"

"All right, spying maybe... but Astral Projection is no different. And far more reliable than a spirit *forced* to do it against their will."

She took a deep breath. "Okay. You're right. I'm being melodramatic. Everything I'm worried about them misusing this guy for, we can already do."

"That's the spirit." He smiled.

"Ugh. There's my cue. Time to leave."

Kirsten pushed off the door and turned to grab the handle, but stopped, staring over the patrol craft's roof at the ghost of a Chinese man sprinting into the construction yard heading right at her. He appeared dressed as an ordinary office worker, but she tensed up at his expression of urgency and panic. Only a few situations could make ghosts appear frightened: the sight of a Harbinger, being close to obliteration, or having a living relative in imminent danger.

"They always seem to find you when they need help," said Dorian.

"I don't mind." She let go of the door and hurried around the back of the patrol craft as the ghostly man jogged up to her.

"You're the one..."

"If you mean the person who can see and talk to spirits, yes." Kirsten focused on his essence. His energy was unfamiliar, but reasonably strong, not a recently killed spirit. His office casual outfit gave off little indication of age. It didn't look obviously outdated, so he most likely had been dead less than thirty years.

He kept staring downward, catching himself, and making eye contact again. "They said you can help."

"Is someone related to you in danger?"

The spirit shook his head so fast his features blurred. "No. But a young girl is. I'm not related to her. A man did something to me. Felt as if he remote-controlled my body—well, whatever I have—and used me to possess this girl, making her walk straight into a group of kidnappers."

"Bastard," whispered Dorian. "We need to find this son of a bitch fast."

Kirsten's face flashed hot from anger, but not at this ghost. "Tell me as many details as you can."

"My name is Wilbert Yong. I died forty-one years ago and—"

"About the kidnapping," said Kirsten, nearly yelling.

Wilbert raked his hands through his hair. "Sorry. I'm all kinds of messed up right now. If they hurt that kid…"

"Please, try to stay calm and tell me the situation as best you can."

"Okay." Wilbert lowered his arms. "A man found me in the parking deck of my old office building. I've been stuck there since I died at work."

"Ouch," said Dorian.

Kirsten grimaced.

"So, he looked at me and the next thing I know, everything around me looks way different. Like forty years went by in an instant. The walls got all dirty and all the cars changed. I didn't want to, but I started walking off."

"Did he say anything?" Kirsten opened her armband terminal to create another Inquest file.

"Maybe. I've kinda been stuck re-living my death over and over, not really aware of the world around me too much. Umm. The next part's a bit blurry. Don't remember going from my office to this fancy residence tower, but there I am in the lobby. Somehow, I know to go up to the eighty-fourth floor, apartment 84-8, and possess this girl named Kena Carlin. I made her sneak past the security officer, leave the apartment, and go outside. Couple blocks from the building, I take her into an underground parking garage and over to a car waiting for her."

Grumbling, Kirsten looked up 'Kena Carlin' in the system, getting a few hundred hits. "How old is this kid? Do you remember her address?"

"Like fourteen or so, at a guess. Never had the address. I just knew where to go. Kinda like how I found you."

Kirsten limited the search to ages thirteen through sixteen. Three hits came up. "Manageable…" She opened the first record, displaying an ID photo. "Is this her?"

"No."

She swiped at the holo-panel, moving it to the next image. "Her?"

"Yes." Wilbert pointed. "That's her."

The slim-faced girl flashed a bubbly smile up from the holo-panel at her. Long, dark brown hair cascaded down over the shoulders of a private school jacket, the type of academy rich people sent their kids to where they still attended classes in person. Her light brown skin, features mixed of too many different ethnicities to count, landed her in the ninetieth percentile. It stood out for being a little strange. Wealthy or prominent people with kids at high risk of abduction often had prenatal gene tweaking done for a rarer 'look,' like freckled redheads, pale blondes, or went the other direction with extremely dark skin. Her friend Nicole's parents turned her into a pale redhead purely because they liked the aesthetic, not out of worry she'd be kidnapped.

Uniqueness stood out on missing child announcements.

Kena's parents letting her keep her natural looks made Kirsten think they probably loved her more—not forcing her to be someone else purely for convenience. The girl suffered from the same curse as Kirsten, appearing young for her age, and somewhat reminded her of an elf from the Monwyn franchise, except for not having pointed ears. At a glance, she'd have taken the girl for thirteen, though her ID record listed her as fifteen. She cross-checked the parents' files. The mother, Naomi, worked for a film studio as a producer of feature-length holovids, the father, Xander, was an executive, junior VP of engineering for NinTek Corporation.

"Do you know why you were sent to help abduct her?" asked Kirsten.

"They're trying to force her father to do something related to the business, threatening to kill her if he doesn't do what they want. I don't know exactly what they're asking for, but I can take you right to the office where they are keeping her. Not much time."

Kirsten nodded. "What are we dealing with here?"

"It's not a big operation, but they are dug in deep on a second-level sub-basement and will hurt her if they think the police have found them. I don't know how many employees of the other company are involved. Seemed like a fairly small group is aware of the plan."

"Another company?" asked Dorian. "Which one?"

"Sencor Electronics." Wilbert pointed northeast. "The people waiting for her in the car work for their security team. They injected something into the girl to knock her out and threw her in the trunk. Whatever controlled me stopped as soon as she went unconscious. Uhh, I totally freaked, but I followed them. They have her locked in a room by herself, bunch of armed security officers guarding the hallway."

Dorian squeezed his hands into fists. "This man is extremely fortunate I lack the substance necessary to perform summaries."

"So are you." Kirsten gave him a sad glance. "Not worth the black mark on your soul."

"Umm." Wilbert's body gave off a mild pulse of phantasmal light. "I think they're going to kill her anyway. The guy in the suit said something about punishing Xander for betraying them to work for another company."

Kirsten scowled. "This is not the ACC. Corporations here aren't supposed to behave like they freakin' *own* people."

"Don't mind her," whispered Dorian. "She's got a severe case of chronic idealism."

"I can help you get her out." Wilbert looked Kirsten up and down. "But I know they're going to kill the kid if they see cops. The room she's in is rigged with an incendiary device. Please believe me. I didn't want to do this. As soon as I saw where they put her, I started running around trying to find a way to get help. Another spirit told me about you."

"Get in." Kirsten hurried into the patrol craft and turned on the drive system.

Dorian faded into view in the passenger seat. A transparent Wilbert walked into the car, standing through it. He looked down at himself for a few seconds before attempting to sit in the rear seat. As soon as his body no longer pierced a solid object, he resumed his lifelike appearance.

"Never been in a car before?" asked Dorian. "As a spirit?"

"No. Never really went anywhere but the building where I died. Mostly stayed in the lab where it happened, but sometimes, I wandered."

Kirsten pulled the patrol craft into the air. "Comm, Officer Logan, Tactical."

A few seconds later, her friend's holographic head appeared in the middle of the console.

"Hey!" chirped Nicole. "It's too early for you to be off shift, so you must be calling about work."

"I need some backup, but we have to keep it low key. We're going to need civilian clothes… and a total disregard for normal procedures. It's time to cheat."

"Woo hoo!" Nicole clapped, grinning. "What's the mission?"

"Recovering a fifteen-year-old kidnap victim before her abductors kill her."

Nicole's smile fell flat in an instant. "Shit. I'm in. Tell me where to meet you."

"Just go to my PC."

"Will do. Be there ASAP." Nicole reached at the image and the holo-call dropped.

Kirsten levelled the patrol craft off to a standstill hover at 700 feet, rotating it in a continuous clockwise spin. "Okay, Wilbert. Point me where to go."

URBAN ASSAULT TRAINING

One block from the Sencor Electronics office tower, Kirsten dropped out of the hover lane and flew into the forty-ninth story parking level of an office building belonging to Innova Corporation.

The delivery bot containing the clothes she'd ordered had been chasing them for the past two minutes. It pulled up beside her as soon as she landed in a parking space. After collecting her purchases, she took off her boots, utility belt, and uniform top. She kept her uniform pants, since under a skirt, they didn't appear much different from black leggings. A loose-fitting top and baggy jacket allowed her to conceal the E-90. Alas, the forearm guard and terminal would give her away, so she'd have to rely totally on her NetMini. Kirsten piled the gear she couldn't bring with her on the back seat—then called Captain Eze.

While she explained the situation to him, another Division 0 patrol craft glided through the large, rectangular opening in the side of the building, crossed the parking area, and landed in the next space. The door swung up, revealing her friend, Nicole Logan, already in civilian clothes: half top, microskirt, and 'cute boots' as she called them. She, too, had a baggy jacket on, likely to conceal the E-86 she carried in an underarm holster. Kirsten settled for stuffing her weapon into an inside pocket.

"Nikki, I said civilian clothes, not go full catgirl."

Nicole laughed. "This isn't full catgirl."

"You know what I mean. Could you have worn a smaller skirt? This is a serious mission."

"Maybe she's trying to blind the bad guys?" asked Dorian, his voice emanating from the NetMini on Kirsten's belt.

"Ha. Ha." Nicole rolled her eyes. "I'm not *that* pale."

Kirsten and Dorian gave her a 'yeah you are' stare at the same time.

"Fine…" Nicole ran around to the trunk of her patrol craft and traded the micro-mini for baggy cargo pants, not caring she had both an audience and a lack of underwear. At least only Kirsten and two ghosts were around to see her.

Even if anyone had been there, people wouldn't bat an eyelash at her. Some Neko modders walked around completely naked and seldom got more than casual glances—perhaps because most people considered them nuts, but still, Kirsten blushed for her.

"All set." Nicole slammed the trunk. "Are these boots okay? Or should I avoid anything with heels?"

"You know my luck with heels." Kirsten showed off her flats. "But those things don't have big heels. I'm planning to cheat as much as possible. If we get into a hand-to-hand fight, we've already screwed up."

"Nice." Nicole nodded. "Eze cool with us going off the leash?"

"Yeah. As long as everything we do is directly related to recovering the girl. He's reaching out to Div 1 already. Our part of this is to get in there, locate and secure the kid, then dig in and keep her alive until backup shows up."

"How'd you score on the UAT course?"

"The what?" asked Kirsten.

Nicole whistled. "Oh, shit. You never ran the urban assault course?"

"I know what UAT means. Making a sarcastic comment about how it went for me."

"What did you score?"

"Didn't finish. Died a third of the way in. They didn't make me repeat it since 'all I do is talk to ghosts.'"

Nicole rolled her eyes. "Girl, you seriously need the training if you're gonna be doing crazy stuff like sneaking into corporations. This is like spy movie stuff."

"Spies don't have Suggestion and Mind Blast." Kirsten looked at Wilbert. "Nor ghosts helping them."

"True." Nicole looked around. "So where is it?"

"Another building. C'mon. Didn't want anyone there seeing a pair of police patrol craft going too close. If they get spooked, they're going to blow the girl up."

Dorian slapped Wilbert on the shoulder. "Did you disable the detonator in the firebomb?"

"I don't know how bombs work." Wilbert shrugged.

Kirsten and Dorian face-palmed at the same time.

"Wait." She pointed at him. "You possessed this kid but you don't know basic ghost stuff, like draining electricity from stuff or making electronics shut off?"

"I *did* kinda live in my own little world. Never possessed anyone before this. Didn't realize how easy it was."

Kirsten raised an eyebrow. "It's not supposed to be easy. Even non-psionic people have a good chance to resist a spiritual possession. If you think possessing people is easy, you either have a talent for it or you're not being truthful about having no experience at it."

"Maybe the control this guy used on him gave him hyper-focus?" asked Dorian.

Wilbert grimaced. "Well, perhaps I've been helping myself to some scientists so I could continue the work I'd been doing. Nothing dangerous or bad. Honest."

Dorian gestured in a 'let's get going' way. "Time is wasting."

"Yeah." Kirsten hurried toward the elevator. "We go down to street level, outside, and into the Sencor building. I'll make the security people at the desk issue us badges. Then we can walk in and go to wherever Kena is being held. Whatever we need to do short of killing people to get there, we do."

"What if they point weapons at us?" asked Nicole.

"Shoot them." Dorian smiled.

"What he said," muttered Kirsten. "Or TK disarm them."

"I can't hear Dorian." Nicole raspberried her.

Kirsten grumbled mentally. "If they point weapons at us, do whatever you normally do when criminals point weapons at you."

"Got it." Nicole grinned.

At the middle of the parking area, Kirsten approached a wall with five elevators and pushed the button to call one. "Obviously, we use self-defense. I meant we don't run in there guns blazing and kill everything."

"Right." Nicole put a hand to Kirsten's forehead. "Are you feeling okay? You know me better than that."

"Yeah." Kirsten stepped past the doors as soon as they opened. "Just making sure you understood I'm not telling you to kill everyone we see."

Nicole followed her into the elevator and poked her in the side. "I know *you* better than that."

Kirsten exhaled. "Thanks for helping me on this."

Dorian pushed the button for the ground floor.

"No problem. I love this stuff." Nicole grinned. "Besides, you're a lieutenant now and I'm just a TO. I kinda had to."

Kirsten raspberried her back. "I didn't give you an order. Call me a bad officer, but it feels weird to 'give orders' to my former roommate. I've known you since I was thirteen."

"Problems of being smart and talented." Nicole tapped her foot.

"Yeah, yeah…" Kirsten swallowed, too worried about Kena Carlin to find much of anything funny.

The elevator descended to the ground floor, letting them out at the innermost end of the lobby, opposite the doors out to street level. Giant backlit silver letters spelled the word Innova on the wall to the left beside a logo that might've been a cockroach crawling out of a pineapple… or merely an abstract design of shapes. Kirsten hurried across the lobby, disregarding two small silver orb bots floating over to say hello and offer their assistance to visitors.

Once out on the sidewalk, Wilbert took the lead. He moved in a series of blurry sprints, too fast for a living person to keep up with. Whenever he realized he'd left Kirsten and Nicole behind, he'd stop and wait for them to catch up.

Rather than go to the front entrance, Wilbert hooked a left into an alley beside the Sencor building, heading for a ramp leading down to a parking area below surface level. He kept going across a large, open room containing hundreds of ground cars to a bank of elevators along the wall.

Dorian made a contemplative face at the security camera.

"Wait here a bit, okay?" asked Wilbert. "I'm going to soften things up for you. The elevator goes to a small lobby and a security checkpoint."

"All right." Kirsten lowered her voice to an almost-whisper. "Suri, please send Captain Eze a message and tell him we're in the building."

The NetMini in her jacket pocket beeped twice.

Wilbert floated up into the ceiling. Dorian shrugged, then followed.

"So creepy," said Nicole.

"What?"

Someone used a ghost to kidnap some kid? Nicole shivered. *You know Command is going to want to keep that quiet. It'll freak people out.*

"Yeah." Kirsten sighed at the ceiling, then looked into her friend's dark blue eyes. *It's only one person who can do this. Once I find him and bring him in, no more ghosts working for corporations.*

Nicole nodded. *Shitty the corporations gotta involve a guy's daughter. One thing going after him, but the kids? Below the belt.*

"Again, yeah."

They stood there for a few minutes, waiting. Two women and a guy, all in suits, emerged from the mass of parked cars, heading toward the elevators.

"Like, seriously, can Dad take any longer to come let us in?" Nicole overacted an exasperated sigh. "Dunno why he wants me to be here at all. I'm too old for this stuff now. This tour crap is for thirteen-year-olds, like you."

Kirsten didn't have to work hard to pretend to be a teen. Nicole, at least, looked her age. Amazing what an extra two inches of height did for people's perceptions of age. She'd be twenty-three in another month. However, she could pull off seventeen or eighteen with the right attitude.

"You know he's busy," said Kirsten in a morose voice. "Too busy for us."

"Aww, don't be like that." Nicole hugged her.

The employees went into the elevator, paying little attention to them.

As soon as the doors shut, Nicole released the hug.

"Thirteen? Really?" deadpanned Kirsten.

"It's the innocence in your expression... and the epic shortness."

"Five nothing isn't epic shortness. It's ordinary shortness." Kirsten exhaled. "Sorry. I'd laugh but..."

"Kid in danger, I know. It's fine." Nicole eyed the wall. "Speaking of 'Dad' taking too long to come get us, do you want to try Plan B or keep waiting?"

"Another few minutes."

"Okay."

A holo-panel activated on the wall near the elevator a little over a minute later, displaying the face of a man in a dark grey security uniform. "Kirsten?"

"The heck?" asked Nicole.

"Wilbert?" Kirsten approached the screen.

"Yes." The security officer smiled. "Borrowing this man for the time being."

In most cases of possession-by-ghost she'd observed, the victim had a trancelike demeanor and slurred speech. Seeing this security guard acting natural convinced her Wilbert had far more experience at possession than he'd admitted to. A ghost wouldn't be able to make a person act so normal unless they'd had a ton of practice. If Wilbert possessed other scientists to continue his research, he would have needed to master the art of possession to be able to perform fine tasks, likely why the suspect she chased chose him for this job.

"Why?" asked Kirsten.

"As I said before, to make your job easier. I put the poor kid in this position, unwillingly, and I have to do as much as possible to fix it. I've taken care of the security control room. Possessed the manager. Any alerts come through this guy, so no one is going to warn the IRT you are here."

"IRT?" Kirsten raised an eyebrow.

"The issue resolution team. Basically, thugs willing to do whatever the corporation wants done. Most companies have a group they refer to as the IRT, even the more law-abiding ones… though those tend to be defense teams or act only in retaliation or rescue capacities."

Kirsten waved for him to get going. "I am aware of the concept, just not the acronym. All right. We're on the way in. You said she's on sublevel two?"

"Yes, but you can't get to it from the parking elevator. You'll need to go up to the ground level, get past the check in desk, and head down the main hallway to the central intersection. The blue elevator will access the basement levels. You'll need an access badge with high clearance to get to sub-two. Maintenance access works only for the first basement. I'll stay here at the control room and keep them in the dark as much as I can until you get to her."

"Okay."

Nicole frowned. "I better get the chance to break at least one nose."

She and Nicole stepped into the elevator when the door opened.

"I'm sure you'll get the chance. There are people guarding her."

Nicole cracked her knuckles.

The elevator went up one level, opening to a plain lobby area decorated mostly in unpainted plastisteel. Floating blue glowing letters spelled out the word 'Sencor' in front of a blue-on-black stylized circuit board wall behind a large security-slash-reception desk. Both entrances to the building's interior stood behind weapons scanners. Signs nearby advised all employees to check any firearms with the desk before entry, not an uncommon arrangement. Something like eighty-four percent of the adult population carried a gun.

Kirsten approached the security desk, targeting a late-twenties guy in a uniform similar to the man Wilbert possessed, sitting closest to the scanner on the right.

The man smiled. "Hi. You ladies must be new. Don't recognize you."

A random object on the left end of the desk fell to the floor, attracting the attention of the other three security people.

"First day." Kirsten leaned up on her toes and stretched closer to him, lowering her voice. "I forgot my ID badge. Please *give me an ID badge. Full access.*"

The momentary glow of white energy in her eyes reflected in his. He stared at her for a few seconds blank-faced, then got up and went over to a cabinet at the middle of the desk, from which he took out a blank badge. Once he returned to his station, he inserted the badge into a socket beside his terminal.

"Hmm. Odd. It's asking for a supervisor approval. One moment." The guard poked a button on his holo-panel. "Mr. Torres, need you to look at this."

"What is it?" replied a voice from the terminal—the man Wilbert possessed. "Oh, yes, she's clear. Proceed."

"Great. Thank you, sir." The guard nodded at the screen, pushed a few more buttons, and handed her the badge. "Here you are, miss."

"Thanks." Kirsten smiled politely while taking it, then headed around the desk to the door, scooting around the weapon scanner.

The guy jumped up and ran over. "Hey, you gotta go through the scanner."

Nicole glanced left. A woman security officer yelped as her chair slid out from under her, again attracting the attention of the other two.

"*We did,*" said Kirsten. "*You saw us go through it.*"

He blinked. "Oh. Sorry. Long day. Go ahead."

Kirsten hurried to the door, swiping the ID badge to open it.

"You are scary, you know that?" whispered Nicole.

"Yeah… I know. You don't have to remind me why Div 9 is as likely to deal with Suggestives as we are."

"Lucky for you, you're also an angel."

"I just play one in the holovids." Kirsten clutched her left arm tight to her side, cradling the weight of the E-90 in the jacket so it didn't flop around so obviously.

They passed a few small conference rooms and some bathrooms before reaching a square room with corridors leading out at the center of every wall, one leading back the way they'd come from. The intersection node contained several clusters of cushioned seats and small tables, holographic plants, random art objects, and of course, elevators. Most of the elevators had silver stripes on the wall around them, but two larger ones—cargo elevators—had blue lines framing them.

Seven people ranging from expensive suits to business casual sat on the assorted chairs, most absorbed in their NetMinis. Two security officers, a man and a woman, loitered in front of a vendomat, annoyingly right between the cargo elevators.

Attempting to act casual, Kirsten approached the elevator on the left.

The security officers' conversation stopped.

"You don't look like maintenance," said the male guard.

"Or even employees." The woman approached. "How'd you two get in here?"

Kirsten glanced up at her. "The front door, why?"

"Are you here to visit your mother or father?" The woman pointed at the other elevators on the opposite wall. "You want those. These go to the basement."

"I know." Kirsten stared at the woman. "You look like you need to *pee really bad.*"

At the flare of light in Kirsten's eyes, the male officer reached for a stunrod on his belt. Nicole focused on him. He struggled to pull the stunrod out of the ring it hung from, but his hand appeared fused to his belt. The woman gasped, squeezing her legs together for a second, then hurried off down the hall to the bathrooms.

Kirsten locked stares with the man. "*Calm down.*"

He stopped fighting Nicole's telekinetic force.

"*We have permission* to go downstairs," said Kirsten.

The man's eyes fluttered.

Kirsten peered at the other employees in the room. No one seemed to be paying much attention to them, everyone too fixated on their devices to notice security officers making odd faces or squirming like a kid in dire need of a bathroom break. She swiped her ID badge at the silver panel on the wall, opening the large elevator, then darted inside.

Nicole telekinetically swiped the stunrod from the guy, caught it out of the air, and followed.

Kirsten pushed the button marked S2. The door closed.

"Hey," said the voice of the possessed security manager from overhead. "Got a ping in here someone's going to sub-basement two. Must be some interesting stuff down there if they auto-notify security every time someone goes there. I silenced it. Dorian and I are on the way. There isn't much more I can do here but keep this guy out of our way."

"You're not going to hurt him are you?" Kirsten peered up at the brightly lit ceiling.

"Nah. No need. Binders and a toilet bowl work well enough."

Nicole laughed.

"Oh, by the way," said Wilbert. "You're about to run into the IRT. Those guys *will* probably shoot at you unless you're wearing maintenance uniforms. They might try to detain you, instead, since you don't look dangerous. Go straight from the first room, turn right at the first intersection, left at the second, go past the next one, then left again. If you see a fire-suppression bot in a charging cradle, you're in the right place."

The elevator doors opened.

Kirsten debated pulling the E-90 out but decided against it, hoping to capitalize on the 'not looking dangerous' thing. As much as it annoyed her to be mistaken for a teenager, if being mistaken for a fourteen-year-old helped her avoid hurting people, she'd embrace it.

She stepped out into a large room containing storage shelves holding various things like air filters, fuses, and mechanical parts she didn't recognize, likely replacement components for larger machines. Lockers and worktables lined the wall on the right, more storage cabinets to the left. Two corridors led away from the storage room, one going straight ahead from the elevator, the other to the left.

Kirsten crossed the room, heading for the corridor straight ahead.

A man in dark blue coveralls came wandering around the end of the shelf. He gasped, jumping back at the sight of her. When he sucked in a breath to yell, a metal component the size of a shoebox flew from the shelf beside him and bounced off his face. He staggered backward, grabbing his nose. The component floated in the air next to him as if waiting for the hand to get out of its way so it could bonk him again.

Kirsten gestured at Nicole to wait. The instant the man looked at her again, she said, "*Quiet.*"

He opened his mouth in a mime of shouting, not making a sound... then paused, seeming confused.

"Do you know what's going on down here?" asked Kirsten.

While the guy silently talked, she scanned his surface thoughts, finding no knowledge his employer arranged the kidnapping of a teenage girl, merely an ordinary maintenance worker with clearance to work down here in the secure lab area. She concentrated on his mind, attempting a deeper-than-usual Suggestion implant. Usually, she employed short, verbal commands. More complicated compulsions, she'd only done a few times in a test setting at the PAC. Instead of speaking the command, she concentrated on the notion he should forget seeing them and go take his lunch break. She held the thought at the tip of her brain, pressing it into his consciousness until she sensed it take hold.

Of course, in an hour or two, he'd totally realize he'd been compelled. By then, it wouldn't matter.

The man walked off to the elevator.

A tingle spread over her brain from Nicole's telepathy. *Wow, nice. It worked! You really go out of your way not to hurt people. I like that about you. Me? I'd have knocked him out.* She levitated the component back to the shelf.

Trying to be quiet. Kirsten started toward the hall, waving at her in a 'c'mon, follow me' gesture.

They rushed down a plain plastisteel corridor to the first intersection. Kirsten slid to a stop against the wall on the right side, peering around the corner at an empty hallway. She eyed the next intersection where she needed to turn left.

Once she felt reasonably safe no one was coming, she scooted around the corner and fast-walked. Three steps later, she paused at the sudden appearance of a woman in black body armor coming out of a doorway on the right side about thirty feet ahead. The corporate soldier appeared not to have noticed Kirsten and Nicole, as she smoothly cornered out of the door and strolled away from them, no hesitation.

Kirsten glanced at Nicole. *Cover the room. I'll get her.*

Nicole gave a thumbs-up.

Kirsten attempted to sneak up behind the armored woman.

Unfortunately, the clicking of Nicole's 'cute boots' on the plastisteel floor made the issue resolution woman pause to peer behind her—right at them.

"Drat," whispered Nicole. She reached both hands forward in a grabbing gesture.

Feeling stuck with no time to think of anything else, Kirsten fixated on the sense of the woman's consciousness and hammered it with a barrage of random, erratic sensory information. The Mind Blast knocked the woman senseless the same instant she flew forward, crashing to the floor as though she'd been tackled from behind. Hard body armor slid easily on bare plastisteel as Nicole dragged her up to them.

"Ngh," moaned the woman. "Baa… tru… larm."

"Ooh, you hit her over the head with the giant squeaky hammer, didn't you?" whispered Nicole.

Kirsten blinked at her, stunned anyone would refer to Mind Blast as a 'giant squeaky hammer.'

As practiced as any Division 1 patrol officer, Nicole disarmed the woman of a combat rifle, handgun, and two knives—both vibro-blades. Since the corporate soldier obligingly carried a small pack of plastic riot binders, Nicole hogtied her.

"How long is she going to be out of her head?"

Kirsten bit her lip. The quick spur-of-the-moment Mind Blast amounted to the mental equivalent of a rabbit punch. While it most likely wouldn't leave any lasting effects, the disorientation would only pacify the woman for about five minutes. "Not long. Three to ten minutes."

"Can you hit her again?"

"I could, but it could mess her up for a while if I hit her too hard."

"She kidnapped an innocent kid," deadpanned Nicole. "Does it really bother you if she has a headache for two weeks? Better than shooting her."

"Well, when you put it like that…" Kirsten shrugged.

Nicole made a silly face. "Better than *me* knocking her out. A hard enough hit to the head from Telekinesis will cause a concussion."

Another, slightly more forceful Mind Blast stopped the woman's babbling and left her drooling. Nicole and Kirsten grabbed her by the arms and dragged her into the room she came from. They entered a squad room style area with two cafeteria-style tables, six bunk beds, and a row of vendomats along the opposite wall. Two men and another woman in the same black body armor sat at one of the tables, playing some manner of holographic board game.

They all looked up at Kirsten and Nicole dragging their drooling, hog-tied associate in.

"So much for quiet," whispered Nicole. "I think we got noticed."

Kirsten stared at the man on the left. *"Hug the floor!"*

The other two gasped in fear.

While one man dove to the floor, the other two scrambled to collect combat rifles off the table in front of them and get up.

Both rifles leapt out of their hands, flew a couple feet, and hit the floor, sliding over to Nicole.

"Damn. I don't have a body cam on. Can't put them on my Wall of Derp."

"What the fuck?" the woman went for her handgun, staring at Kirsten in terror.

The remaining man sprouted a pair of twelve-inch metal blades from each hand, cybernetic claws concealed in his forearms. Nicole grunted. The woman drew the handgun, aiming at Kirsten.

"*Drop it!*" Kirsten's eyes flared white.

Like a horrible glitch in a video game, the man's legs blurred rapidly, but he didn't go anywhere.

The woman's fingers snapped open, releasing the handgun, which fell straight to the floor beside her.

"Problem!" said Nicole. "He's got speedware and vibro-claws."

At the mention of vibro-claws, all the muscles in Kirsten's back tensed in fear. The only thing she dreaded more than Evan getting hurt was losing limbs to extremely sharp blades. More technically correct, she irrationally dreaded the idea of cybernetic replacements, even though as an active-duty officer, Division 0 would have no problem covering the cost of tissue regeneration.

Still, vibro-claws tweaked her panic button.

Kirsten clenched her jaw to contain a scream part war cry part fear, and unloaded a Mind Blast on the augmented corporate soldier. The amount of energy she put into it felt as though her brain squeezed out one eye socket and went flying like a bullet, leaving her with a dull headache. He lapsed into a convulsing, twitching fit, held upright in midair by Nicole's telekinetic grip. His speedware went crazy, struggling to interpret the scrambled signals coming from his brain, making his arms and legs flail about too rapidly to see them. When he at last went still four seconds later, Nicole dropped him in a heap, scrunching her nose.

"I think he shit himself."

Kirsten cringed, feeling a touch guilty. "Probably did. Brain loses all control of everything with a slam that hard." She pulled her E-90 out and pointed it generally at the two remaining corporate soldiers. "Don't move."

The woman stared at her, thinking various things like 'oh, shit, a fucking psio. I'm dead.' Or 'I hate psio freaks.'

Kirsten frowned at her. *"Get down."*

Dorian and Wilbert sank into the room from the ceiling.

"Perfect timing." Kirsten wagged her E-90 at the man. "Mind killing their weapons' battery packs."

"On it." Dorian raised a hand.

Faint beeps came from all three corporate soldiers.

Nicole ran over and secured the woman in zip ties. Kirsten couldn't hogtie the man since his legs refused to bend up enough, so she merely secured his ankles together.

"How long's the aug gonna be out?" asked Nicole.

"Couple hours. I'm a little phobic of vibro-blades. Might have hit him slightly too hard."

Wilbert pointed at the wall. "There are two men in a small area in front of the last corridor. I'm a bit drained, but I can try to possess one of them."

"If you're feeling weak, don't worry about it." Kirsten walked out of the IGT's squad room. "Let me guess, those two guys ahead of us have the button to fry the room?"

"Yes. It's on the desk."

"Dead man switch?" asked Dorian.

"Dead teen girl switch more like." Wilbert looked down, guilt all over his face.

"No, I mean if it loses power, will it activate?"

Wilbert shrugged at Dorian. "I don't know."

"Nope," called Nicole. "This woman doesn't think so. And thank your ghost friend for messing up their communications. She's trying to warn the other two guys, but her headware isn't working."

"I shut off the comm channel," said Wilbert. "As soon as she figures it out, she'll call them on a personal line."

Kirsten ran back into the squad room, grabbed the woman by the hair, and forced her to make eye contact. *"Do nothing."*

The woman stared vacantly into nowhere.

"Okay. Let's go!" Kirsten dropped the woman's head—her cheek hit the metal floor with a *smack*—and ran out into the corridor.

She zoomed to the intersection and went left, continuing past doors marked only with numeric codes. When she reached a four-way intersection, she ignored it, continuing straight. Another sixty meters later, she slowed to a silent creep, approaching a leftward corner and leaning against the wall, E-90 held up in both hands. Nicole scooted up behind her.

Dorian walked around the corner. "Two guys up ahead playing video games on their 'Minis. I'd have no trouble just shooting them since they're ready to murder an innocent kid as soon as someone tells them to push a button, but I know you are squeamish about it. So... give me a moment to kill their weapons."

"Thanks," whispered Kirsten.

"What?" asked Nicole.

"Who's there?" called a man.

Nicole leapt past Kirsten, whirling around the corner, her E-86 raised. "Police, Division 0. Drop your weapons."

"Fuck!" yelled a guy.

A dark green laser beam flickered from Nicole's weapon. A male voice screamed in pain.

"What the f—?"

Nicole fired again. Another man screamed.

Kirsten leaned past the corner, aiming her E-90 down the corridor at a small, square security checkpoint where the hallway widened into a tiny room for a short span. One guy in black body armor rolled around on the floor, clutching his right thigh. Another man staggered, left hand clamped over a smoking hole in his right shoulder.

"It seems these two fine gentleman had a weapons malfunction." Dorian smiled.

Kirsten Mind Blasted them one after the next, knocking them senseless. The beginning of a headache swirled around the back of her brain.

"I really don't get it." Nicole jogged toward the men.

Kirsten followed. "Get what?"

"Why so many people are so afraid of mind blasters. You're like the soft and fuzzy version of combat psionics. Knock people out of commission without hurting them. I'd be way more afraid of a pyro than a mind blaster." Nicole got started putting zip ties on one guy.

Kirsten took a knee by the other man and secured his wrists behind his back. "It's because of people like Commander Ashford. If someone develops Mind Blast powerful enough, they can permanently wipe out a brain. Throws someone mentally back to infancy, every trace of who they were, gone."

"Okay, that's kinda scary."

"But it's rare. Very few people with Mind Blast can do it... but no one stops to think about it. They just hear the two bad words and think we'll erase them if they spill coffee on us or something. Also, Mind Blast doesn't care about body armor. Pyros still have to burn through it."

"Idiots." Nicole stood, looking around. "Okay, where's the kid? I don't see any doors here."

"Down there." Wilbert pointed at another hallway leading away from the small room.

Kirsten rushed into a corridor lined with red, green, and black pipes. Dozens of electrical cables hung from mounts on the ceiling. This didn't look like a place people generally went to unless they had to fix something smelly, wet, or full of high voltage. The passageway ran maybe forty meters to a dead end of metal cabinets loaded with buttons, meters, and valves.

"There's nothing here. No doors."

Wilbert strode past her. "Little bit down on the left. She's in a chamber. The door is partially hidden behind all the pipes."

He stopped a little less than halfway down and phased through the wall. Kirsten walked over to the spot, examining the plastisteel. It took her a moment, but she spotted a likely seam for a door easily mistaken for a simple gap between different metal plates.

"Electric motors in the walls." Dorian stuck his arm into the door.

"Should be able to open it bypassing the circuitry and giving the motor itself some power."

Wilbert's head stuck out of the wall. "Bomb's safe. I killed the battery."

A rectangular section of wall sank inward an inch, then slid to the left, revealing a doorway. The various pipes running the length of the corridor obscured the upper third of the opening. Kirsten ducked under them, peering into a tiny chamber. Kena Carlin sat on a cot tucked into the distant left corner, wearing a man's white T-shirt as a dress, her left arm stretched out to the side, dangling from a pair of metal binders, the other end locked around a vertical pipe against the wall. A small food reassembler sat on a shelf by the pipe. The opposite corner from the cot held a metal sink-toilet combo. An autoshower tube stood in the near corner on Kirsten's right.

The teen didn't appear hurt, though she mostly hid her face behind her knees, trembling visibly. The restraint allowed her just enough freedom of motion to reach the toilet and food reassembler, but not the autoshower or the door out of the room.

Overjoyed to find the girl unhurt, Kirsten scooted into the cramped chamber. "Kena?"

The girl pressed herself back into the wall. "Go away! Leave me alone!"

"My name is Kirsten. The woman behind me is Nicole. We're the police, Division 0. We're here to take you home."

Kena glanced at Nicole, then back to Kirsten. "You guys don't look like cops, and there's no way the police would even know where I am. Nice try."

"We needed to go undercover because we didn't want the people who took you to see us coming and hurt you." Kirsten examined the binders. Standard electronic ones, military grade, but not from the same manufacturer the NPF used. The girl had such a delicate wrist her captors had closed it all the way. She frowned at them and gave Dorian a 'would you please?' look.

He squinted. Tiny sparks crackled over the metal. A faint whirr came from the motor and the end around her wrist popped open; the binders fell off her, clattering against the pipe.

"Holy crap!" Kena yanked her arm back against her chest, rubbing the red mark the binders left. "How did you do that?"

"I'm surprised you aren't asking how we found you." Nicole ducked in under the pipes. "What kind of idiot designs a door half covered by water and sewer lines?"

Dorian smiled at her. "One who doesn't want anyone to think there's a room here."

"What he said." Kirsten gestured at him.

"Huh?" Nicole blinked. "Whatever. Wow. Tiny room. Why the hell does a corporation have a hidden prison cell in their sub-basement?"

"I believe it's more of a panic room intended for VIPs to hide in." Wilbert gestured at a button on the wall. "She could have easily opened the door if she wasn't chained to the pipe."

Kirsten repeated what the ghost said.

Nicole twisted to her right, peering at the shower and obvious red 'open' button. "Oh. Yeah. Okay. Panic room."

"Yeah, no kidding. I've pretty much been panicking the whole time I've been in here." Kena shifted her legs to one side and sat up. "You guys are seriously cops?"

Kirsten pulled out her NetMini, brought up her ID—which had a photo of her in uniform—and held it up so the girl could see it. "Yes. Are you hurt? Did they do anything to you?"

"My wrist is sore and I feel dizzy. I remember like sleepwalking or something outside. Men grabbed me. One guy stuck me in the neck and I woke up here."

The girl's surface thoughts didn't contain memories of anything worse than someone pressing a stimpak-like autoinjector into the side of her neck.

"Comm." Kirsten held her NetMini up. "Captain Eze."

Ten seconds later, he appeared on the holo-panel. His dark, bald head bore a sheen of nervous sweat.

"We found her. She's secure. Go ahead and kick down the doors," said Kirsten.

"Cry havoc and let loose the hounds of war," shouted Nicole. "Or at least Division 1."

Captain Eze leaned back in his chair and grinned broadly. "With pleasure. Are you all right?"

"Little bit of a headache, otherwise fine. We're in the second sub-basement level in what appears to be a panic room."

This kid is sitting on top of a firebomb, said Nicole telepathically. *She doesn't know. Distract her while I get it out of here. We can use this room as a defensive position in case the shit hits the fan.*

"Wonderful." Captain Eze's smile became even wider. "Stand by." He looked to his left. "Bianca, my people have secured the hostage. Give your team the green light."

A female voice in the background said, "Nice, Jonathan. Time to rock and roll."

Must be another captain if they're using first names.

Kirsten stood to block the girl's view of a large box sliding out from under the cot and going into the corridor seemingly by itself.

"What happened to me?" asked Kena. "I don't understand why I walked from my bedroom to the garage where these creeps kidnapped me. My body just did it."

Kirsten bit her lip. She'd feel horrible not being truthful with the kid but telling her a ghost possessed her might traumatize her for life, leaving her constantly afraid of a repeat attack. However, she felt far more comfortable being honest—gently. "What happened to you is a little outside events people expect from the ordinary world. It's an extremely rare situation, and also the reason we found you."

"You guys are like the psionic cops, right? Did someone have like a vision of me? Clairvoyant, right?"

The girl's lack of fear or derision around the word 'psionic' surprised Kirsten. She smiled. "Clairvoyant is what we call anyone who can see people or places far away, but it's not how we found you. There's someone out there doing bad things. He made a ghost take over your body and kidnap you."

Kena fidgeted. "I never saw a ghost, but I caught some EVPs in my apartment building."

"Wow." Dorian gestured at the teen. "Nice to run into someone who doesn't think you're crazy."

"I didn't know ghosts could take people over and control them." Kena relaxed somewhat, lowering her legs so her knees no longer blocked most of her face. "Did I make one angry?"

"No. The ghost who attacked you didn't want to do it. Someone forced him to. As soon as the control stopped, the spirit came to me and told me what happened so I could help you."

"Umm. Weird. Why did he find you?"

"She does all the ghost stuff." Nicole grinned. "Much easier for spirits to get help from people who can see and talk to them."

"I can explain everything once we get you out of here and safe, okay?" Kirsten glanced down at the E-90 in her lap. "We're going to sit here and protect you until Division 1 secures the building. This looks like a panic room, so it should be a good place to defend for now."

Kena tugged the T-shirt down, trying to make it cover more of her thighs. "Okay. Why did they steal my clothes?"

"To hide evidence. Didn't want any identifiable materials in the building. Or maybe they were worried you had trackers sewn into whatever you'd been wearing." Nicole looked away, her expression saying she likely thought the kidnappers wanted to hide evidence in the ashes when they set off the device in here.

"Oh." The girl shivered.

"Captain?" asked Kirsten. "The spirit mentioned a possible extortion or demand of the father. Can you please have someone inform him we've got her safe?"

"Of course. I will call him right away."

"What's the ETA on Div 1?"

Captain Eze glanced at another screen to his left. "They should be landing outside right now."

Kena leaned closer, looked at the captain's image on the screen, and seemed to shed the last of her doubt the police and found her. She grabbed Kirsten from behind. "They were gonna kill me, weren't they?"

A lump formed in Kirsten's throat, but she swallowed it,

positioning herself to shield the teen from bullets coming in the doorway. "I'm not going to let anyone hurt you. Stay behind me." She raised her E-90. "Anyone who tries to get in here is going to regret it."

"Damn right." Nicole took a knee in the door, pointing her E-86 down the hall. "Not bad, K. I still can't believe you never reattempted the UAT course."

Kirsten rolled her eyes. "They didn't think I'd ever need it. Remember, I'm supposed to walk into a completely safe scene and investigate what the ghost did."

"Not working out quite the way they expected it to," said Dorian, his expression grim.

"Wilbert?" asked Kirsten.

"Yeah. I'm still here." The ghost phased out from the wall, ending up inside the autoshower tube for a moment, fogging the plastic. He stepped away from it, fading from transparent to seemingly solid. "Was keeping an eye on the hallway."

"Do you know where the man is who forced you to attack Kena?"

"Not exactly. He found me at my office… but I can go look for him. Assuming he doesn't control me again."

Kirsten peered through the E-90's ring-dot sight at the door. "Please… just keep a good distance. Depending on how strong an astral he is, he'll be able to feel your presence if you get too close."

"Understood." Wilbert ran back into the wall.

A blaring alarm tone sounded out in the hall, followed by a man's voice.

"Attention: by authority of the National Police Force, the Sencor Electronics building is on lockdown. All occupants are to consider themselves detained at this time. Security personnel are hereby ordered to disarm themselves immediately and move at least fifty feet from any weapons. Noncompliance may result in lethal force."

"Here we go," whispered Nicole.

Kena shivered.

"Don't worry. The hard part's over." Kirsten squeezed the grip on her weapon. "We're just being extra careful."

RISK MANAGEMENT

Hours later, Kirsten sat at her desk in the squad room, filling out a form while slurping down a strawberry-chocolate latte.

Division 1 had basically detained everyone inside the Sencor building, processing them individually and releasing anyone who they had no reason to suspect knew about the abduction. Fortunately, Kirsten, Nicole, and Kena didn't need to sit there the whole time. As soon as armored patrol officers found them in the panic room, they escorted them outside.

The most difficult part had been trying to convince Kena's mother not to try suing the ghost, which turned out to be harder than convincing her parents ghosts existed at all. Dorian appearing briefly made getting past their skepticism relatively easy.

With the girl home safe, her parents gearing up to sue the hell out of Sencor, and the rash of random hauntings seemingly over, Kirsten set herself to the task of stopping the not-so-random hauntings. Unfortunately, Abernathy and Elan Mendoza had little success in Carlos Bennett's office beyond overhearing someone confirm 'the fixer' had been successful in arranging Mendoza's death. Elan's revenge would be petty, chilling every hot meal Bennett tried to eat for as long as it took him to get bored doing it.

She finished filling out the form to request video from the office building Wilbert Yong haunted, hoping to catch a glimpse of the rogue astral. It seemed almost an odd coincidence for him to also have Suggestion. Marley didn't, nor did Hannah—the teen Division 0 activated in East City to fill the same (or as same as possible) role as Kirsten in the west. Hannah couldn't lash, so her only recourse for nasty spirits was a bound sword.

Captain Eze's voice came out of her terminal. "Wren? Got a minute?"

Since she hadn't done anything even close to questionable lately, and his tone sounded concerned, the usual twisty feeling in her gut whenever he summoned her to his office didn't happen. "On my way."

She submitted the request, locked the terminal, and got up.

Not seeing the captain waiting for her in the doorway also indicated good news—or at least the absence of bad news. She walked in to find him seated at his desk, no particular emotion on his face.

"Yes, captain?"

He gestured at the chairs facing his desk. "Merely looking for an update. You have an astonishing number of open Inquests pending report completion."

"Oh. That." She exhaled into a slouch, then sat, staring into the carved eyes of mini African tribal masks standing in a row along the front edge of his desk. "I know they've been piling up, but it's been one after another after another. Trying to put the fires out first before I waste time in the office typing reports. Not saying reports are a waste of time, but I figured it would be better to find the reason so many spirits are going crazy first."

"Understandable. Kirsten, the kidnapping of Kena Carlin set off a shitstorm with the brass. I need a status update, something I can give them to explain the situation."

She squirmed, worried how Command would react to someone weaponizing ghosts. "We had two separate issues going on at the same time. Marley Santiago, the other astral I registered a few days ago, is the reason the random hauntings spiked by a thousand percent. She didn't realize she had psionic abilities. Her getting so emotionally invested in her music, plus being high on Placid Rain, affected the emotions of people and spirits around her. Somehow, her Telempathy integrated with her Astral Sense. It's not quite the same as me, since Lash is totally different from Mind Blast. In her case, she's using Telempathy on spirits, which doesn't work normally. Also, her radius of effect on spirits is noticeably larger than on live people depending on what kind of audio equipment she has set up. In her apartment, where the walls mostly contained the sound, she affected only people up to about four stories overhead. Spirits could hear her music for over a mile. If she played at a concert, she'd affect her entire living audience."

Captain Eze pursed his lips. "I did notice the influx of haunting calls had dropped off again, thankfully."

"Yes. Since she's now aware of her ability, she's able to contain it. I showed her how to Blockade her home studio. It should contain her power, at least so it doesn't affect spirits."

"How did she accidentally influence a ghost to possess and abduct this girl?" Captain Eze brought his hands together, steepling his fingers in front of his chest.

"She didn't. Marley had nothing to do with the Carlin case. We have a second problem." Kirsten hesitated. A few seconds of delay gave him a few seconds where he might not be tempted to lie to Command. "It's scary bad, sir."

He raised an eyebrow.

"I have reason to believe there is another astral sensitive out there who has figured out how to use Suggestion on spirits. I haven't really worked on my Suggestion enough to do much beyond short command phrases, but this guy is able to implant complicated... umm... almost programs. Wilbert Yong, the ghost who possessed Kena, sought me out as soon as he broke free of the command." She explained meeting him, his plea for help, and everything leading up to going into the Sencor building undercover. "The suspect ambushed Wilbert at the office he haunts. Lennox Beake, another ghost, told me a man mind-controlled him to attack a construction site with the intent of driving the workers off and forcing the company to abandon the project. This guy is basically an underworld fixer, sir. But instead of liaising between shady people with money and mercenaries willing to break the law, he's arranging for spirits to unwillingly do the job." She explained the ghostly spying at Lyris Corporation, which resulted in suspicious stock market trading—and a call from a Division 2 detective. "I wasn't sure if it would be wise to tell Detective Winfield exactly what happened."

"What is making you hesitate? Think he'll laugh about the idea of ghosts?" Captain Eze smiled.

"No, sir. Think about it. How could anyone possibly defend themselves against a spirit? They could go anywhere, watch anything. Eavesdrop on the highest levels of a corporate boardroom meeting or even the Senate."

Captain Eze exhaled. "This is potentially the scariest thing that's ever happened."

She blinked, then started to smirk, but stopped herself. "Hardly."

"I mean to the brass." He chuckled. "Someone capable of sending ghosts anywhere to do anything with total impunity?"

They stared at each other. She bit her lip, remembering how Theodore and *The Kind* put pressure on Senator Winchester at her request. Even a man as powerful and connected as him could do nothing whatsoever about ghosts. The look Eze gave her said he knew she could, in theory, ask ghosts to spy on anyone the same way as the suspect. But then again, she wouldn't have to. Anyone capable of Astral Projection could do simple spying themselves.

"It's not quite the same," whispered Kirsten, fighting off a twinge of guilt. "This guy can *force* ghosts to do whatever he wants. I can only ask. And ghosts are not the most helpful of beings. Most of them can't or don't want to go very far away from where they haunt. Even Wilbert, the ghost who possessed Kena? He literally *couldn't* leave the place where he died. The poor man had no perception of reality, being unable to see live people the way normals can't see ghosts. He re-lived the moment of his mortal death over and over like a residual haunting. He'd been possessing people in the lab where he died continuously, trying to keep working, unaware of how much time had passed since his death. This guy yanked him out of that and fired him off like a guided missile."

Captain Eze took a moment to process her words. "Off the record, because I know you would never do anything like this... but if you were inclined to use a spirit to obtain secret information for financial gain, how likely is it you could succeed?"

She gripped her knees. "Well, umm... speaking purely in a theoretical sense, I wouldn't have to. Just spying on people can be done via Astral Projection. No need to affect physical objects. However, if someone with Astral Sense couldn't project or didn't want to for some reason, they would have to find a spirit capable of going to the place they need, one who isn't bound to their remains or scene of death. Then, they'd have to somehow convince the spirit to help them out. Depending on the integrity of the ghost's mind, they may or may not be able to remember everything clearly or could always make stuff up. Nine out of ten ghosts would probably tell them to go away. The astral would almost *have* to find a spirit with an unfulfilled need, like 'go get this info for me and I'll kill the person who killed you' or a similar situation. If it even worked, the ghost would only help once. They couldn't keep asking the same ghost to do job after job." She paused to breathe. "I suppose it's maybe possible for someone to threaten the spirit's remaining family, or even save the life of their grandkid or something and earn long time gratitude they can use as leverage for favors. Doing stuff like hurting people can't be done by a projection since we're totally intangible. Assassination or scaring people away would require ghosts—but the same complications of finding one willing to help apply, plus finding one old and powerful enough to affect the physical world. Ugh. I feel sleazy even talking about this."

Captain Eze leaned forward, resting his arms on the desk. "Sounds like it's not terribly plausible."

"Not really. I told you about, umm, certain parties no longer being a threat to me or Division 0, thanks to the intervention of certain ghosts, but… totally different scenario."

"Of course. And, if you ask me, completely above board." His expression said, 'serves the bastard right.'

Kirsten picked at her uniform leg. "I have no idea yet where the suspect is located, but I'm working on it. Gotta stop this guy before astrals end up being declared a national security risk."

"That entirely depends on the impression we make on Command. Based on what you're telling me, this is something of a one-off situation. The complications involved in an astral doing anything like this when they lack the ability to forcibly *control* spirits makes it impractical."

"Yes. Even calling it 'impractical' is a bit soft. I'd say impossible, but it's not. Just really, really unlikely. It would totally be easier to hire living people."

"All right. Let me know if there's anything I can do to help."

She smiled. "I just submitted a request for video surveillance. You could approve it."

Captain Eze laughed. "Consider it done."

CULPABLE

K irsten's armband gave off an alarm tone simultaneously with Captain Eze's terminal.

After almost two weeks of near-constant 21-47 calls, the tone made her want to scream 'what now?' but she held back. She raised her arm, the holo-panel scrolling into view automatically.

"Lieutenant…" The image of a twentyish man in an Admin uniform appeared on the screen. "We have a high-priority situation at the Division 1 precinct office in Sector 2514. I'm not sure what code to use because it's a complete mess. Officers down. Electronics and tech going crazy. Reports of unexplainable paranormal events."

Kirsten jumped out of the chair, glanced briefly at Captain Eze who spoke to someone on his holo-panel, and decided this situation couldn't wait for him to finish, so she ran out the door. "Don't worry about codes… officers are down? What's going on?"

"It's difficult to get information since communications in or out of the precinct station are extremely distorted. Audio-only contacts report a heavily augmented individual rushed the front doors and opened fire. Officers have been unable to defend due to equipment failure."

Son of a bitch is attacking police now… She growled, sprinting harder down the hall to the elevator. Due to her arm moving rapidly from running, the call to Dispatch leapt to her earbud.

"Trying to get more information, but all I'm hearing is gunfire and screaming."

"Shit," yelled Kirsten, jumping into the elevator and mashing the button for the ground floor. "2514 isn't far from here. Like thirty miles. I'll be there in like a minute. Console, power up the patrol craft and open my door."

"Copy, lieutenant," said Dispatch. "Monitoring."

"Command confirmed," replied a placid female voice from her forearm guard.

Kirsten squeezed herself between the elevator doors as soon as they started to open and sprinted down the hall to the garage. Her patrol craft already gave off a cloud of cryonic mist and sparks, the driver-side door open.

She jumped in, yanked the door down, and accelerated so hard the enormous hovercar squeaked the tires. The emergency lights and audible warning signal activated seemingly on their own as Dorian appeared in the passenger seat.

"Caught me napping. What's going on this time?"

"Our guy sent a ghost to shoot up a Div 1 substation." Kirsten pulled a hard turn, leaning against the door, and lined the car up with the exit ramp.

Dorian looked over at her. "If this *is* our guy, I hope you reconsider your opinion of summaries."

She'd gotten the patrol craft up past eighty miles an hour already in the garage. When she hit the ramp up to street level, the car caught serious air. She switched to hover mode, the ion thrusters coming online with seconds to spare before the car nosed into the ground. The drivers of several land cars and a pedestrian or twelve probably cursed her out for being thrown by the ionic downblast. She narrowly avoided plowing into the wall of the high-rise across the street from the open courtyard behind the PAC, levelled off, and accelerated through a storm of advert bots and flashing holograms.

Due to the relatively short distance, it worked out being faster to drive at 300 MPH or so between high rises than waste time climbing high enough to do 600 in a straight line over them. She held altitude at forty feet, flying over the centerline of the street.

Nausea swirled around in her stomach. She couldn't tell if he said it in jest or seriously wanted her to execute someone. True, almost every other cop would gleefully put a bullet into the face of a cop killer, but she still had a problem with taking a life when not in immediate danger. If she had a half-second to react and *not* killing someone would mean she—or an innocent—died, she could do it. But pointing a gun at a pacified suspect and killing him like an executioner? The mere thought of it made her ill.

Would it be the same if I astrally bound the sword and let Dorian do it? She swallowed bile. *Yeah... and I don't want him to darken any more. The Harbingers finally seem okay with him.*

Rather than slalom city blocks, she flew straight east to Sector 2150, then pulled a ninety-degree left turn and headed north. Comm chatter on the local Div 1 channel contained lots of screaming and cursing. She couldn't follow the chaos too well but heard enough to know someone *still* shot up the station. Sounded as though the officers managed to establish a defensive position, but most yelled about their weapons being dead.

"Familiar trick," said Dorian. "What do you think we're walking into?"

"Dispatch said it's an aug. Probably possessed. It takes a lot of concentration to possess someone. There has to be another spirit helping out by draining power."

"Agreed."

The speed, and low altitude, of Kirsten's patrol craft sucked small ground vehicles into its wake, knocked pedestrians over, and sent advert bots spiraling into windows behind her. In any other situation, she'd feel awful for banging people around, but cops had been shot, possibly killed, and more could die for each second longer it took her to get there.

When the precinct building came into view, the lowest eighteen floors of a high-rise otherwise containing residential apartments, she extended the ground wheels and decelerated hard. The harness restraint punched her in the sternum, catching her as she rocked forward. Growling, she fought the control sticks, diving the patrol craft once her speed dropped below 150. Rubber screamed on the traction-coated plastisteel road surface. The patrol craft skidded to a halt halfway up on the sidewalk near the shot-to-pieces main entrance.

The rapid chattering of automatic fire thundered inside, azure muzzle flare flickering in the windows.

"Any closer and you'd have landed in the lobby!" yelled Dorian. "Gonna shut down his gun."

Kirsten drew her E-90 while jumping out of the patrol craft. She sprinted up to the precinct entrance, taking cover at the door and aiming into a standing wall of smoke. In between pulses of gunfire, two male voices muttered, "Kill all cops," simultaneously. The louder voice, gruff, overly deep and tinged in electronic crackling, sounded mortal. The other voice sounded more ordinary, but trancelike.

Dorian ran past her, unconcerned about being shot.

Seconds later, the machine-gunning ceased. Kirsten dashed forward into the smoke, heading across a waiting area of empty benches toward confused grunting and the repetitive slapping of a metal hand against a metal firearm. The smoke thinned at the far end, allowing her to see an interior security entrance beside a bulletproof glass window. The armored door lay on the floor, twisted up into an unrecognizable scroll of plastisteel.

Kirsten took cover behind the wall by the front desk, aiming through the breached door into the office beyond.

A large, mostly open room of green-and-white checkered tile contained more smoke, a handful of bodies in Division 1 armor or blue uniforms. Four confused ghosts—all in cloth Division 1 uniforms, bloody and riddled with bullet holes—stood over their remains, gawking in astonishment. Various holo-panels on the walls flickered as static, displayed errors, or kept turning off and on. Cleaning bots zipped back and forth in crazy, unpredictable ways.

The slapping drew her attention to a dark mass in the haze, the indistinct outline of a wide-shouldered human figure easily two feet taller than Dorian. Gaps and struts in his enormous arms revealed them to be entirely robotic.

Dorian, and another ghost—who appeared to be a gang punk—wrestled nearby.

Thirty or so cops tried to shoot at the aug over multiple portable barricades—collapsible plastisteel walls—at the opposite side of the room, but their weapons only emitted the faint clicking of electronic triggers connected to dead batteries.

Kirsten drew a bead on the aug's head just in case, then reached out psionically. She sensed both surface thoughts and a paranormal presence, confirming her suspicion the aug had been possessed.

"Console, interface, PA system."

Her armband beeped.

"Division 0 coming in the front door," said Kirsten, her voice booming from overhead speakers. "Don't light me up."

The aug, predictably, spun around to face her. He stepped closer, revealing a body covered in grafted plates of shiny dark grey plastisteel armor. The crude, older cyberarms with their exposed actuators and struts looked as though he'd stolen robotic limbs from a hovercar assembly plant. A bundle of steel-encased hoses dangled from the center of his back, connected to various points on his arms and legs. Baggy grey pants concealed his legs, though she suspected they had to be metal as well to hold up the weight of his inhumanly large, augmented torso and arms.

Red lens-eyes surrounded by black star tattoos brightened. Smoke peeled up from his lime green spiked hair. When a vibro-blade the size of a medieval broadsword sprang out of his left hand, it occurred to her all four armored Division 1 officers on the ground had vicious stab or slash wounds. His machinegun could penetrate patrol officer armor given a good enough angle, but not reliably.

"*Stop.*" Kirsten's eyes glowed white. "*Do not move.*"

"The fuck's a Zero doing here?" yelled someone behind the barrier.

"Who gives a shit why she's here?" shouted a woman. "She stopped the son of a bitch."

Dorian threw the ganger ghost to the floor and went to pounce on him, but the other spirit manifested a knife and stabbed him in the side. Groaning in annoyance, Dorian rammed his forearm into the ghost's face, knocking him flat on his back.

Another spirit exuded from the aug, his body stretching like molten cheese stuck to the immobile cyborg. He grunted, straining to move, but unable to.

Kirsten concentrated on the lash, extending the long, shimmering energy cord out from her hand. She rushed closer, swiping the glowing whip at the gang spirit, missing Dorian by less than a foot.

He flinched.

The ghostly punk howled in pain when the lash smacked him in the chest. He forgot all about Dorian and grabbed the 'wound'. Kirsten swung her arm up and around, the shimmering blue-white ribbon trailing gracefully after her hand. Flicking her arm, she sliced the energy strand at the towering augmented cyberganger. A faint *whud* accompanied a blast of pale glowing light radiating outward from the point the whip made contact.

Another ganger flew out of the aug, spun over twice, and landed flat on his chest by the portable barriers thirty feet away. None of the cops noticed him, primarily due to his being a ghost, but also because they mostly stared at Kirsten and the painfully bright energy ribbon coming from her hand.

"This is Lieutenant Wren from Division 0," said Kirsten in as commanding a tone as she could muster. "Everyone stand down. The aug is neutralized. Medics, now!"

"You call that neutralized?" Dorian gestured at the large vibro-blade.

"He won't be able to move for at least another three minutes. I have time to determine if those ghosts were compelled or malevolent," said Kirsten, forgetting she'd routed herself to the PA. "Console, PA off."

Most of the officers stood cautiously out from behind the barrier, still aiming handguns or rifles at the giant cyberganger.

"You…" Kirsten approached the ghost who stabbed Dorian, since he appeared less disoriented, and raised the lash. "I hope you have a good explanation for why you and your friend over there attacked a police station."

The gang ghost raised his hands. "No idea! This *pendejo* just kinda gave me the evil eye. Mean, ain't losin' too much sleep over some dead pigs, but I'm a little past this bullshit, now, ay?"

"I'm supposed to believe someone made you do this?" asked Kirsten, hoping the guy would give more information.

"Yeah, *chica*, 'cause it's true." He rolled back to his feet, glaring down at her.

A group of medtechs appeared clustered in a doorway behind the barriers.

Kirsten waved at them. "Get over here before there are more damn ghosts. I think everyone in armor is still alive. The aug is paralyzed."

The medics ran into the fray.

"The guy who you claim *made* you do this, what'd he look like?" asked Kirsten.

"Why'm I gonna tell you, bitch?"

She whacked the lash across the ghost's chest, slicing him momentarily in half before his essence reintegrated.

He shrieked, collapsed to the floor, and let out a wail loud enough for all the normals to hear.

Everyone—except the medtechs—froze, staring around while making 'WTF' faces. The medics disregarded a random disembodied scream, too focused on their work attending to the wounded officers.

"Because, I get the feeling you're the kind of spirit Harbingers would really be interested in. Another hit or two from this, and they'll drag you off where you don't want to be. The only reason I'm not already hammering you into the Abyss is because I already know about the guy who mind-controlled you. If you don't want me to arrange a date for you with tall, dark, and vaporous, tell me what this guy looked like."

Dorian raised both eyebrows.

"Uhh, little younger than him." The ghost pointed a middle finger at Dorian. "Black dude wit blond hair. Purple eyes."

"He should be easy enough to spot in a crowd," whispered Kirsten. "Big guy?"

"Nah. Average. Found me in my alley. No idea where he came from."

The spirit who'd been inside the aug grumbled a whole bunch of curse words and walked toward the wall.

Dorian started after him.

"No point. Both of these spirits were compelled." She looked at the ganger. "Where were you when you ran into this guy? Do you have any idea where he could be?"

"Probably under the city. He had the charge to him."

Kirsten narrowed her eyes. Thousands of spirits dwelled in The Beneath. The forgotten old city held darkness, sorrow, and pain as thick as a physical fog. Spiritual energy soaked into a living person who spent a significant amount of time down there as sure as bad smells saturated the clothes of people who worked at chemical plants. Spirits could feel it on a person. They referred to it as 'the charge.' Granted, someone who lived near a breach would also get it, but few normal people could tolerate the negative energy. Humans weren't wired for it. Even the least psionic person in the world would feel uneasy near a breach and come up with some excuse to go elsewhere.

"Did he get into a car or anything?" asked Kirsten.

The gang spirit offered a disinterested shrug. "Nah, walked."

"Where do you haunt?"

"The Sixty-Sevens." He puffed out his chest.

Kirsten tilted her head. "I'm not in a gang task force. Your crew or...?"

"Yeah. We're in Sector 4067. We call ourselves The Sixty Sevens. *Mi casa* is the alley behind The Penis Merchant."

Dorian blinked. "Well, there's a Navcon search that'll get you a meeting with HR."

The ganger laughed. "Nah, it ain't a brothel. Cyberware shop specializing in... augmentation."

"And they say there's no truth in advertising anymore." Dorian snickered.

Warmth spread over Kirsten's cheeks. "Alley near a cyberware store in Sector 4067."

"Yeah. You'll know you got the right place if you see a bunch of people hanging out with the number sixty-seven on them somewhere."

"Thanks. Worth checking out. Go on back home... and you might want to try rearranging your priorities. The Harbingers will eventually catch up to you."

He laughed. "You're a funny one. Talkin' shit about cops ain't gonna get them vaporous shitheads mad." After mockingly saluting her, he walked out through the wall.

Sighing, Kirsten approached the aug. *"Drop the gun."*

Metal fingers snapped open with a *click.* The squad machine gun clattered to the floor.

"Blade away."

He retracted the vibro-blade.

"You're... controlling me?"

"Yeah."

"Why? You could ask."

Kirsten bit her lip.

"Honestly, I have no idea why I'm here." The huge man sighed. "I don't expect you will believe me, but I think someone hacked my NIU and took my systems over. Spent the past hour wandering around like a damn remote-control android. You're psionic. Go ahead and read my mind."

Kirsten shrugged, and dove in with Telepathy.

He thought back to a few hours ago when he'd been wandering a black zone in search of anyone needing food or medical help, machine gun in one hand, backpack of supplies over the other shoulder. Despite the terrifying appearance of the being in front of her, the brain inside the nearly eight-foot-tall killing machine belonged to Dr. Hasan Kouri, a former cyber-surgeon specializing in neural implants. He'd been the victim of an attempted assassination for warning the authorities about some unethical practices his former employer—White Orchid Corporation—had been engaged in. Though he'd survived, his biological matter consisted of a brain, heart, one kidney, stomach, and a scrap of intestines stuffed into the only cyborg frame he could find on short notice.

In his memory, cold washed over him, his body disobeying his brain, walking off by itself from the Sector 18 black zone due south from here, heading to the nearest police station—or the first one he saw, which turned out to be here. His effort fighting the spirit for control of the body likely prevented several deaths by throwing off his aim ever so slightly.

"Oh..." Kirsten covered her mouth. "I'm sorry."

A dozen or so armored Division 1—and three Division 5 cyborg interdiction squad members—approached. The Div 5 officers pointed their ABR20 rifles, enormous shotgun-style weapons chambered in 20mm armor-piercing explosive rounds, at Dr. Kouri's head.

"Considering my appearance and augmentations, plus what happened here, I don't blame you." The doctor tried to look at the cops approaching behind him, but still couldn't move.

The medtechs rushed several wounded out of the room on hover gurneys.

Kirsten raised a hand at the Division 1 officers. "This man was... mind-controlled. Believe me, I'm every bit as furious as you are, but he's not the one responsible for this attack."

"Bullshit," said a muscular Division 1 cop. "I watched him do it."

"Officer Gonzalez," said Kirsten. "Did you not hear me say he was mind-controlled?"

The lone female Division 5 officer snapped her ABR20 up into firing position.

"*Don't shoot.*" Kirsten glared at the woman, the momentary glow in her eyes sapping some of the animosity radiating from the cops.

The Division 5 woman shuddered, trying to fight the command, and failing. "Bitch mind-controlled me."

"That 'bitch' is a lieutenant, Squad Officer Parson," said Dorian, his voice taking on a weird echoing quality. "You're an E4. Be glad she's not one of those officers who adores outranking people. Even second lieutenants are smart enough to fill out insubordination report forms."

"Uhh, who the hell said that?" asked the woman.

"I said, stand down." Kirsten tried her best impression of Captain Eze's body language when he tried to be forceful. "This man was mind-controlled."

"What in the nine towers of Fuckstantinople is going on out here?" shouted a gravelly voiced man, stomping over to them.

Kirsten opened her mouth to tell him to calm down but noticed captain's rank insignia on his nameplate and collar. She saluted him. "Captain Serrano, I'm trying to deescalate an extremely tense situation. The augmented man behind me was the victim of paranormal mind-control. Someone else had control of his body, using him like a puppet."

Squad Officer Parson grunted, again trying to fire, but couldn't overcome the suggestion not to shoot. Scowling, she lowered the giant rifle.

Captain Serrano set his fists on his hips and looked around at the carnage. "Some talking trash can kicks in my door, goes apeshit shooting up my people, and you're going to try and make excuses for him?"

"It's not an excuse, sir. A spirit possessed him, took over his body, and made him—"

"Spirits now?" Captain Serrano bellowed a manic laugh, more angry than amused. "Look, hon, I have no idea what the hell they're doing to you kids over at the PAC, but this is the real world. Someone shoots up my fucking precinct house, they're going out of here in a damn plastic baggie."

"Sir, if you'll—"

Captain Serrano gestured at the aug. "Why is this son of a bitch just standing there?"

"I commanded him not to move. He's a victim here, too. No different than if a hacker got into his NIU."

"Except, hackers exist. If you weren't a Zero, I'd have you sent for psych evaluation for talking nonsense." Captain Serrano glowered at the Division 5 officers. "What are you three just standin' around for? Aerate that sumbich."

A glowing aura of shimmery spectral flames surrounded Dorian's body as he faded transparent. "There's a time for summary executions, and cop-killers are definitely one of them. This man is not the one responsible."

One unarmored Division 1 officer fainted.

Everyone else, including Captain Serrano, stared at Dorian, their expressions ranging from 'whoa' to 'holy shit.'

A few seconds later, Dorian's vaporous aura ceased with an audible *whump*, leaving him once again looking solid to Kirsten. Visibly tired, he slouched.

The whole precinct fell silent, save for the occasional sparking buzz from shot-up terminals.

"This is related to an active Inquest. I'm already chasing the man responsible for this attack. It isn't Dr. Kouri." Kirsten looked over the stunned faces gawking at her. "I assure you, this man is a victim. I read his mind. If you shoot him, you'll be committing murder."

Captain Serrano pointed at her. "I don't like this. But I can't explain it. I expect to see a full report. Who's your immediate superior?"

"Captain Jonathan Eze."

Serrano frowned. "Look, lieutenant, you stopped this rampage and likely saved lives here. I don't mean to diminish what you did. But then you go an' take the side of the killer?"

"I'm not taking the side of the killer, sir. I'm taking the side of an innocent man the actual killer used as a proxy. UCF Criminal Code, section 0.18-00177, a person who is acting under the influence of a psionic against their own free will to commit crimes is not considered culpable for those crimes. Section 0.18-00178 defines legal culpability for crimes committed by a proxy under psionic duress as falling on the psionic responsible for controlling them. The actual cop-killer is still out there."

Dorian golf-clapped.

"Never heard of section zero-point-one-eight." Captain Serrano folded his arms.

"Sir, those sections were added roughly seventy years ago when Division 0 became official. Everything in the UCFCC starting with a 0 prefix is related to psionic crimes. You wouldn't really have much reason to learn it."

Captain Serrano huffed. "Well, *lieutenant,* what do you think we should do with this man who blew the piss outta my precinct?"

"Dr. Kouri is the gun in the hand of the suspect I'm pursuing. If this guy survives arrest when I find him, he's most likely going to end up on an asteroid mine. He'd probably *prefer* SO Parson atomizes his brain with her cannon."

Squad Officer Parson snarled.

"As far as Dr. Kouri is concerned, he is a victim. I need to check him for any residual psionic issues, latent trigger commands, or injuries. Once I'm done, as far as I'm concerned, he's free to go. If you want to give him a hard time after I finish, I can't stop you. But it's unnecessary."

"That monster's a damn doctor? Are you being sarcastic?" asked Officer Gonzalez.

"Not being sarcastic." Kirsten growled mentally at the time wasted tap dancing in front of a Division 1 captain when she should be out hunting the rogue astral. "He's a doctor who barely survived his former employer trying to assassinate him for exposing something illegal."

Serrano scowled.

"Pardon me, captain. Let me finish with him so I can go find the man responsible for this attack." Kirsten sidestepped to stand in front of Dr. Kouri. *There isn't anything dangerous remaining in your head. I said it to buy a little time and let them cool off.*

Dr. Kouri nodded.

Why the spiked green hair? Makes you look like a crazed cyberganger.

"Came with the body, but it helps me blend in out there. Easier not to get shot at when the locals think I'm one of them."

"Okay." Kirsten opened her armband terminal. "I'll try to be as quick as I can, but a mess like this is going to take a while."

"I understand." Dr. Kouri looked at the cops half surrounding him. "The actions you observed my mechanical body performing were not a product of my conscious mind. I remained trapped in a prison of my own cerebellum, forced to watch as your brethren fell. Perhaps it was a mistake of me to choose this body, but my options at the time were limited. I have not tried to access my finances and purchase a more appealing shell for fear my former employers will realize they failed to kill me and try again. It had not occurred to me such an event as being possessed by a spirit even approached the realm of possible."

The cops exchanged glances, evidently not the least bit prepared to hear an eight-foot hulking cyber-thug speak in such an educated tone.

Dorian stepped up beside Kirsten. "Spoke to the four victims. They all want you to talk to their families for them."

Kirsten bowed her head. As the adrenaline of the moment wore off, tears gathered at the corners of her eyes. Four officers dead. *I have to find this bastard fast.* "Of course."

28

ONCE MORE BELOW

Sector 4067 appeared unremarkable on the Navcon system but had quite a different story in the NPF database.

Though lacking in the blight of a grey or black zone, this particular five-mile-square slice of West City boasted a 400 percent increase in homicide rate compared to national average—which put it about on par with the northern third of East City. While letting the auto-drive run, Kirsten skimmed the stats. Most of the fatalities for the past few years in Sector 4067 involved known associates of street gangs. Namely, the Sixty Sevens, CR954 Crew, and the Sirens. The last one had a tag linking to a Division 0 record, so she clicked it.

The Sirens' leader, Natalia Kuznetsov, was a registered psionic as well as an emigre from the ACC. Despite being involved in a street gang, the woman claimed to use her abilities purely for self-defense. The ramifications of a telempath being the madam of a sketchy brothel didn't escape Kirsten. She'd declined to join Division 0 or even go in for help developing her powers. No surprise, an escapee from the Allied Corporate Council had a strong fear of the law.

I can't even imagine living somewhere they kill psionics on sight... having to hide who you are from everyone...

The majority of homicide incidents connected to The Sirens

involved low-level members, a startlingly high ratio of them being the killer rather than victim. With few exceptions, the incidents went into the system as justifiable self-defense. Kirsten had her suspicions. A little telempathic sympathy could go a long way in making a Division 1 cop take things a certain way. Considering the dead in all cases belonged to other gangs, the police wouldn't have put a ton of effort into investigation.

She hated the 'just a gang punk, they did our job for us' attitude prevalent in Division 1.

However, in a sector like this where street gangs reenacted the Wild West on a thrice-a-week schedule, if people had to die, better it be the reckless idiots rather than innocent bystanders—which still happened, naturally.

It seemed almost crazy how this sector hadn't descended into grey by now. She looked a little deeper for an explanation why people not involved with gangs would stick around such a violent location… and discovered the answer. The gangs fought over a highly lucrative trade in recreational chems. This single sector produced seventeen (rounded) percent of all chems used in West City. It also had a medical facility, Omni Community Care, providing services at no cost to anyone who could prove they lived inside Sector 4076. People from the adjacent sectors bordering 4076 enjoyed massive discounts. The UCF government required all medical facilities to provide care at no cost to minors under age eighteen, but this place waived fees on adults, too—provided they had a permanent address in the sector.

"Wow, check this out." Kirsten pointed. "No wonder people stay here."

Dorian leaned left to read the holo-panel floating over the console. "Bet it started off as the big gangs throwing money at the hospital to keep it open for their people, and it evolved from there. Keeping the sector out of the grey makes life easier on the chem producers. They probably don't really even notice the cost. *One* sector is responsible for seventeen percent of the entire chem profit in West City?" He whistled.

"Unreal," muttered Kirsten.

"People will put up with living in a warzone if it means medical insurance doesn't take everything they have—or sign their death warrant."

Kirsten tapped her fingers on the control sticks, debating turning around and going back to get a suit of PSI armor. Sector 4076 looked dangerous, but she didn't plan on being there too long. Also, the gangers mostly shot at each other. Civilian casualties happened primarily from stray bullets or the occasional crash when an advert bot strayed too close to a gunfight trying to sell ammo. Since Evan hadn't panic-called her yet, she figured she wouldn't have too much trouble.

A short while later, she dove out of the hover lane, descending to street level, landing on the road a little over a block from The Penis Merchant. Except for the name, nothing else about the cyberware shop stood out as inappropriate from the outside. Like most commercial properties in West City, it occupied the ground floor of a high rise, the outer walls a suggestive light brown skin color, as opposed to the shiny silver plastisteel-and-glass above the first level.

Pedestrians made their way along both sidewalks, a little over half of them appearing to be ordinary citizens, the rest fringers or off-gridders likely here to buy chems. She had an easy time recognizing the residents, as pretty much everyone wore body armor, even children. Being in a place where even five-year-olds ran around in tiny versions of combat infantry suits made her second guess not going back for her armor.

I should probably start keeping it in the trunk.

She parked on the side of the street and got out.

People going by on the near side stared at her. Most had helmets or face guards on, hiding their expressions, but she read worry, suspicion, or confusion in their eyes. A maybe seven-year-old girl in bright purple body armor bearing a faerie image on the chest waved at her while yelling, "Hiii!" in a cheerful voice.

Kirsten smiled back at her, returning the wave.

A boy about Evan's age in body armor covered in cartoon animals saluted her.

She saluted him back, forcing a smile past the somber sight of children not even in double-digit ages wearing armor. At least the little ones didn't carry handguns. Some adults wore armored vests, others full suits. Advert bots approached her in seconds, trying to sell body armor, medevac care plans—since she didn't have a registered address in this sector—and stimpaks.

Ignoring them, Kirsten crossed the street and headed for The Penis Merchant, specifically the alley next to it. In case anyone happened to be watching her, she avoided looking at the place.

Dorian noted her blush, but kept his mouth shut.

Perhaps someday, the idea of sexuality wouldn't remind her of the two worst moments in her life and she'd think only of Samuel Chang. At least Konstantin had been more or less a near miss; however, *almost* having sex with a man who'd mind-controlled her bothered her almost as much as the bastard who took advantage of her in the Beneath eleven years ago. Forcing those thoughts aside, Kirsten attempted to realign sexual thoughts entirely with Sam. Didn't work terribly well, but she tried. Maybe if she kept trying, it would eventually work.

The alley behind the racy cyberware shop had an unusually low amount of random garbage. Then again, this place hadn't become a grey zone, so the infrastructure didn't ignore it. An alcove behind the building held six large trash compactors as well as a handful of twentysomethings in mismatched, cheap clothing. They all wore the numeral 76 somewhere, on patches, glowing NanoLED tattoos, giant T-shirt logos, and so on.

One woman in her early twenties attempted to swim on the ground, behaving as if the plastisteel surface was water. Two guys and another young woman lay in a heap, staring straight up at the sky, making faces like they watched a comet plummeting out of the heavens right at them.

"Remember kids, don't do drugs," said Dorian.

Kirsten stared aghast at the gangers out of their minds. "Seriously."

"Old slogan. The government used to try to prevent drug use. Now they kind of encourage it. Keeps the fringers pacified."

"They do not *encourage* it."

"Not treating chems as illegal encourages it."

She frowned, unable to dispute his point. Only a few—really awful—chems got police attention. Lace, because it was so damn addictive and killed everyone who used it in six months or so. Phindara because it took away free will, acted as an aphrodisiac from hell, and had an association with human trafficking. Nightcandy sat on the borderline between something the police would ignore and prosecute, depending on the situation.

The Seventy-Sixers largely ignored Kirsten as she walked by. A guy with cobalt blue hair and a glowing cyan NanoLED raccoon-mask tattoo waved at her in a casual 'hey, what's up' manner. Not wanting to be rude—or provoke them—she waved back.

Hmm.

Kirsten stopped, considered a moment, then approached him.

Except for the swimmer and the comet-watchers, the rest of the group tensed up… though her small size and black uniform appeared to calm them enough not to run or go for weapons.

She peered up at the guy with the glowing raccoon mask. "Not here to mess with you guys. Looking for a psionic suspect. Have you seen a man in his late thirties, blond hair, dark skin, long black coat? Possibly had glowing purple eyes."

The more coherent gang members' surface thoughts varied from being impressed at her 'balls' for not wearing armor in this area to wondering why the police hired young teens. The blue-haired guy who waved at her thought her adorable and hoped she got out of here before anything hurt her. Two had seen the guy she described, though didn't consciously remember him or know where he lived.

"Maybe," said the blue-haired man. "Lot of people come by here looking for product. Hard to remember anyone who don't do crazy stuff."

"Okay. Thanks." She waved, then headed deeper into the alley.

"Didn't take much convincing." Dorian chuckled.

"I cheated."

"Ahh."

She glanced at him. "If we find this guy, be careful. Don't go charging in. He could affect you."

"And you can snap me out of it."

"I don't want to hit you with the lash." She squeezed her fist.

"No need to haul off and wallop me with it. Just a poke ought to do —if needed."

The Monwyn theme erupted from her NetMini, Evan's ringtone. While she would normally adore a chance to talk to him, receiving a sudden call from her mildly precognitive son in the middle of her duty shift while in a dangerous area scared her.

Kirsten grabbed the little device off her belt, swiping to answer. "Ev?"

His face appeared on the holo-panel, wide-eyed with fear. The boy seemed at the edge of crying, but within seconds of her answering, his emotions shifted to relief. Walter, Shawn, and another boy she didn't recognize peered over his shoulder. Scenery of an empty classroom behind them told her the boys worked on citizenship points.

"Mom! The hatch is gonna blow up!"

"Hatch?" Kirsten looked around but saw nothing 'hatch' like.

"The ones in the ground to go down. I saw you opening one and it exploded." He pressed a hand to his chest, trying to slow his breathing. "Scared me!"

The ghost said this guy had 'the charge.' He's gotta be in the Beneath. If Ev saw me opening a hatch, it means I'm going to end up going down there soon.

"I won't let a hatch blow me up." She wanted to hug the hologram, but it wouldn't do much good. "I'm sorry for scaring you."

"You didn't scare me. My brain scared me." Evan wiped tears. "You're gonna be okay now, pretty sure."

She bit her lip. "I'll be careful. Call right away if anything else happens, okay?"

"Yeah, totally." He nodded so hard his hair went everywhere, then made an earnest face at her like he really needed a hug.

"I'll find you as soon as I'm at the PAC."

He grinned. "Love you, Mom."

"I love you too, Ev."

It didn't fully hit her the boy saved her life until after she hung up. Kirsten stood there a moment, too choked up to see or think. Eventually, she barked a tearful laugh.

"I'm missing the humor here." Dorian rested a hand on her shoulder.

"Not funny. Just thinking it's backwards. I'm the mom. I should be saving his life, not the other way around."

"You already did, K. He's just returning the favor."

She sniffle-laughed and wiped her eyes. "Okay. There's an access hatch to the Beneath around here somewhere."

"Rigged with a bomb, no doubt. Probably this guy's booby-trap."

"My thoughts exactly. We're in the right place. Can you kill the bomb?"

"As long as it has an electronic detonator. If it's an old mechanical switch, I'd have to set it off." He smiled. "I've always been curious what it would be like to stand in the middle of an explosion."

"Hah. Sure you have." Kirsten accessed her armband terminal, pulling up a detail map of her immediate area. "And setting it off might alert him someone's coming. I'd rather be quiet."

"Better loud and alive."

"If you can't kill the bomb"—she located the nearest access hatch on the map, thirty-one meters from her present location—"I'll go in a different hatch and walk."

"We don't know what kind of defenses he has down there. Is this guy in the plate or all the way down on the ground?"

"Pretty sure he's on the ground or spirits wouldn't feel the charge on him."

Dorian held up a finger. "Valid point. And I can feel electromagnetic energy in sensors and cameras."

"It's like having an entire Division 9 team for a partner." Kirsten started walking toward the hatch.

"I don't kill anywhere near that many people," said Dorian in a fake English accent.

She sighed.

A few minutes later, she stopped at the mouth of another alley, slightly more trash-strewn but devoid of any people. The hatch, thirty feet away at the end, appeared innocent and normal. West City had innumerable similar hatches, intended to allow maintenance crews access to the guts of the plates. An elevated layer of plastisteel and technology twenty-five meters thick formed an even, contiguous surface upon which civilization rested. Workers often went into the plates, but few descended past them to the Beneath. At its lowest point, the natural ground lay seventy to eighty meters below the underside of the city plates, everything down there abandoned in the state it had been centuries ago.

Entering the Beneath felt like going through a post-apocalyptic time machine.

Dorian went down the alley and climbed into the shaft despite it being sealed. A minute or so later, the hatch emitted a hiss and a blast of pale white fog before rising upward on motorized struts.

An olive drab box stuck to the bottom, connected by a thin wire to the electronics inside the hatch.

Kirsten eyed the NetMini on her belt. When it didn't ring, she exhaled out her nose and cautiously approached the opening, giving Evan plenty of time to call her if he had to.

"Probably a code." Dorian poked his head up out of the hole in the ground. "Enter the wrong code to open it and boom. It's not going to detonate until someone replaces or recharges the battery unit."

"I don't know what I'd do without you." Kirsten crouched by the hole, braced her hands on the plastisteel alley surface, and stepped onto the ladder.

"Probably leave this stuff to Tactical teams." He chuckled, gliding down to the floor inside the plate.

Kirsten hit the button to close the hatch, then descended the ten-foot ladder to the first sublevel. "Tac would still be debating how to get past the bomb—if they even knew about it."

Faltering LED light bricks every twenty meters or so offered enough illumination for maintenance crews to see the walls. Alas, they weren't bright enough to conduct a proper investigation of the area. Kirsten started to concentrate on Darksight but decided against it. While the astral power would let her see the environment, it worked by peering into the Astral Realm. Disturbances wouldn't reflect in the shadow world until they'd been there for a significant time. A piece of dropped trash, for example, wouldn't become part of a place's astral shadow for months.

Oh, wait... idea.

She activated Darksight, shifting the narrow metal hallway from a string of lantern-like glowing spots in the dark to an overall even brightness tinged in sepia brown. She'd used the power so often, the wavering quality of the world's astral echo no longer made her feel as though she lived inside a disturbing dream.

Nothing appeared out of the ordinary. Using Darksight let her see the environment clear of darkness, exposing all the junk and garbage collected along the hallway. She switched on the utility light in her forearm guard. The intense—but small—spot of glow washed over the astral world wherever she pointed it, chasing some objects out of existence, making new ones appear, and changing others from sepia to full color.

Kirsten focused on anywhere the debris vanished or appeared.

If the physical light made something appear, it meant the object hadn't been there long enough to develop an astral copy. Anything the light erased from view existed only as an astral shadow, proving it had been moved recently. Objects shifting to full color under the physical light remained where they'd been for a long time. Sweeping the light back and forth soon revealed a trail in the garbage leading to the left. The disturbance had to be from the suspect going back and forth to the ladder.

"What are you doing?" asked Dorian. "I don't think I've ever seen you use the utility light before."

"Comparing reality to the shadow. Someone's been walking back and forth here often enough to make a trail."

"Genius."

She shook her head. "Hardly."

"You're smarter than you give yourself credit for."

A phantom weight settled on her chest. According to Dr. Loring, four years of Mother screaming at her constantly telling her she was stupid, evil, and worthless made it difficult for her to accept not being any of those things. Maybe thinking of comparing the difference between reality and the Astral Realm had been a little smarter than 'something any idiot would've thought of,' but it still sounded awkward to hear Dorian call her smart.

"Doctor Loring says the same thing."

He smiled. "You should listen to your psychologist."

Kirsten looked down, about to sigh, but froze at the sight of a bare footprint far too small to belong to a grown man. It only appeared in the electric light and looked rather like the footprints she'd likely tracked all over the place during the time she lived down here. Part dirt, part sticky mystery slime, the print appeared to be the size of a child's foot. She found prints pointing in both directions, proving the kid went back and forth. The small footprints appeared to target open spots, suggesting a careful attempt to avoid disturbing trash.

Either this kid has a flashlight or they can see in the dark.

It also meant the child couldn't be responsible for the trail she followed. The kid avoided junk, not plowed through it.

The Beneath had no shortage of children. Primitive settlements existed down below, and of course, whenever men and women lived together, babies happened. The living boy she met when she'd lived down here climbed back up into the plates to sleep and rarely came down. For whatever reason, he always went to the surface for food, never to the ground. He didn't want to be found by the natives. Maybe he thought every adult down below would be like the Discarded and possibly dangerous. One day when he went to the surface for food, he didn't come back. Most likely, he'd been picked up by the cops and given a better life. By now, he'd probably be in the military—the usual end point for non-psionic orphans taken in by the cops.

Seeing evidence of a kid being in the plate worried her, since they'd likely not be from a settlement.

Still, she followed the trail. Once she had this rogue astral in custody, she could take her time hunting for the kid. For all she knew, this child might have parents and a reasonably decent—for the Beneath—home. They could've come up here on an adventure. Obviously, they hadn't opened the hatch, or the bomb would've gone off.

The trail led her down the narrow maintenance passage. Wherever the floor became metal gridding instead of flat plates, she lost the child's footprint trail, but the disturbance in missing (or rearranged) trash continued. Relay boxes, electrical cabinets, and pipes went by on both sides, so filthy she didn't want to breathe near them.

Guess I'm no longer feral if the dirt disgusts me.

She became furious all over again at Mother for making her prefer this place to a proper apartment. What ten-year-old wouldn't prefer a filthy tunnel to constant beatings, burnings, and a locked closet?

The trail led around a corner to the right, through two doors, and finally to an opening in the wall containing a ladder down. She descended to sublevel two. A pair of prominent footprints at the bottom made her picture the kid playfully jumping off the ladder. The sight of the black marks practically made her feel the stickiness on her soles. Due to Mother's neglect, she'd spent most of her childhood barefoot, including the two years she'd been down here. Thanks to the mystery gunk, her feet used to adhere to everything they touched. Sometimes, she'd made 'shoes' out of plastic cartons by stepping on them so they stuck to her. The horrible-smelling black ooze collected in places within the plate, sometimes puddles, sometimes deep pools capable of swallowing an adult entirely. Tiny lakes of it also existed at ground level. She had no idea what the crap was, but it got *everywhere* down here. As a child, she thought it the 'city's blood.'

Not too long ago, a trip into the Beneath resulted in her going headfirst into a swimming pool of it. Her uniform had clung to her body as if glued. The sight of her wadded-up underwear sticking to the wall when she tossed them aside would haunt her for the rest of her life.

Waving the flashlight side to side like a sweeping scanner, Kirsten continued following the trail the suspect left in old cups, discarded meal cartons, boxes, old fuses, and so on. She scowled at packing cartons left behind by official maintenance crews. They hadn't even taken the broken parts away, leaving them on the floor in the hallway. It sorta made sense for off-gridders to throw trash everywhere, but the actual repair crews?

How damn lazy can a person be?

Eventually, the trail led her to a square chamber awash in a faint breeze blowing up from a hole in the middle of the room. The suspect no doubt used this as his entry point to go between the Beneath and the city above. Kirsten crept over to the hole and crouched, peering down through the opening in the eight-inch-thick underside of the city plate. The top and bottom surfaces of each plate represented a staggering amount of plastisteel, its components mostly harvested from asteroids. She wondered if humanity had effectively made the Earth heavier by bringing space minerals back here.

The opening overlooked a ladder going all the way to the natural ground down the side of a massive support column. Unlike some, this twenty-foot-diameter shaft didn't pierce the roof of a building. Those who built the elevated city centuries ago hadn't bothered clearing thoroughly, destroying only enough of an old-world structure to put up the support pylons. At least here, they got a break with a big parking lot.

Trash littered the ground at the bottom as well, but not enough for there to be a trail she could follow.

"Drat. No idea where to go down there." She leaned away from the opening to peer at Dorian. "Think he's got cameras on this ladder or is he not that paranoid?"

"Bombing the hatch is pretty paranoid. I'll go have a look."

"Okay." She glanced at the mound of trash against the wall. "I'll wait here. Maybe get lucky and he'll come to me."

"A stakeout. How exciting," deadpanned Dorian.

She chuckled. "Hopefully, I'm not here all damn day. Please find something."

Dorian saluted her and stepped off the edge, falling into the hole.

Wiseass.

She crawled into the mound of plastic trash, burying herself in a seated position under a scrap of old tarp so she could still peer out at the room. Both her flashlight and Darksight would give her away due to the bright glow, so she turned them off.

Ugh. Stinks down here. She didn't honestly expect the suspect to walk past her, at least not within the hour or two she'd be willing to sit there waiting. Sending a ghost to find a man capable of mind-controlling ghosts sounded like a stupid idea, but she trusted Dorian would keep his distance.

If he's not back in half an hour, I'm going down.

29

ERRAND GIRL

S itting in a mountain of discarded plastic trash brought back bad memories.

Not as bad as her memories of home before running away, but still unpleasant. Being at the constant edge of starvation and wearing only a scrap of cloth, tarp, or plastic bag hadn't been happy times. Of course, back then, she regarded it as pleasant freedom. Running around the Beneath like a feral creature far surpassed being with Mother. She had plenty of spirits to look after her and guide her to food or away from bad places. Hours every day to explore and play. Up until the man tricked her into trading her body for food at age twelve, being an orphan in the Beneath had something of a wistful romantic quality like one of those old stories of children on an abandoned island or living without adults in the aftermath of a world-ending war.

After the man who took advantage of her, she'd been willing to risk the cops picking her up and dragging her back to Mother to make sure he never saw her again. She'd gone to the surface for food, and couldn't bring herself to go back down, deciding to sleep in an alley. Kirsten sat in silence, remembering the past and trying to think only of the fun parts—the exploring, the thrill of finding food, having multiple sets of ghostly grandparents taking care of her.

Soon, her thoughts returned to the present, specifically Johanna Beck and her daughter Tamsen. The attack on them occurred quite far from Marley's apartment. She now knew for a fact some of the ghostly attacks had been deliberate as a result of mind-control. The ghost who tried to kill the Becks even looked like a heavy corporate assassin—the show up with a giant machine gun style of assassin, not the ninja type. However, he didn't stop trying to kill them the instant she lashed him. Dacre, Lennox, and Dr. Kouri all snapped back to their senses as soon as she hit them.

It's almost like the ghost tried to kill them of his own free will. But why? There's no reason. If this suspect did send the ghost to kill them, how long would he wait before realizing she'd obliterated his assassin and send another spirit?

Kirsten activated her armband terminal and placed a vid call to Johanna Beck.

The woman answered in a few rings. "Oh... umm, hello. Is something wrong?"

"I've got new information. Things are really starting to look like the spirit who attacked you and your daughter might have been sent on purpose. It's possible the person who did it will realize the ghost failed and send another one. I'm calling to make sure you let me know right away if anything even remotely weird happens."

"Umm... okay." Johanna looked down, guilt all over her face.

"Is there something you aren't telling me?"

Johanna shrugged. "Nothing too important."

"Is keeping this secret worth Tamsen's life?"

The woman shot her a glare, but her expression softened. "Maybe there's something. My wife, Arielle... but we'll manage."

Kirsten tried to sound as sympathetic as possible. "Is she doing something illegal? Messing with shady people? I'm only trying to keep you and your kid alive. My jurisdiction is only spirits and psionic matters."

After a long pause, Johanna exhaled. "Arielle's part of a small group of hackers not related to her job. They go after corporations for being shitty. Robin Hood type stuff. Yeah, it's against the law, but the stuff they do is on moral high ground. I don't know any details, but if someone found out who the real person is behind her online persona, there are probably a few companies out there who'd try to kill her."

"All right. Thank you for being honest. Nothing else has happened yet?"

"Not that I've noticed."

"If this guy becomes aware his ghost failed, he might send another one. You and your family should avoid hovercars or going anywhere with fast-moving bots or other things a ghost could use to kill you via making electrical power fail for now. I'll let you know when I get this guy but be careful."

"They've been after Arielle's online persona for a long time. Did they discover who she is in meatspace?" asked Johanna barely over a whisper.

"I can't answer that. Maybe they resorted to hiring this guy and a ghost since spirits can find information people can't. It's quite possible the living world still has no idea who she is."

Johanna slouched in relief. "All right. I'll tell Ari to be careful."

Kirsten nodded. "As soon as I know more, I will call you again."

"Thank you."

She hung up.

Grr. Why was the ghost there different? He didn't break out of the control. Had to be willing to do a contract killing. What did this guy have to offer him? He sure looked like an assassin. Maybe he did it for fun?

Soft pattering came from the hole.

Kirsten froze. It didn't sound like a grown man climbed the ladder, rather a child. The bastard could wait a few hours. She'd do for this kid what no one did for her, get them out of here and into a proper home.

Moments later, a girl of about nine climbed up into the room. She wore a tattered but fancy dress, torn and stained, one sleeve missing. The garment had once probably been shin length, but now ended in shreds halfway to her knees. She didn't appear dangerously thin despite seeming to have been down here for a long time. Silent, the child padded across the room to the door. In the dark, Kirsten couldn't make out much of the child's appearance beyond her having long, probably brown, hair.

The kid had no surface thoughts but gave off an astral presence. Before Kirsten wept at seeing a child ghost, her thinking mind caught up to her reactionary heart. The spirit sense coming from the kid didn't feel strong enough to be a ghost. Ghosts didn't leave footprints, nor did trash usually rustle out of their way.

Kid looks like she's been down here for years but she's not starving. No surface thoughts... is she a WellTech doll? The company manufactured artificial children as companions for lonely older people, couples who wanted a child without all the responsibilities, and so on. By law, the dolls couldn't be made with fully sentient AIs, otherwise the law would consider them 'people' and consequently, illegal to own. Except for cutting them open, a person had two ways to differentiate a WellTech doll from a real child. One, they had to answer yes if asked. Two, checking their physical anatomy. Like clothing store mannequins, off-the-line dolls had no genitals despite appearing otherwise indistinguishable from actual humans in every other way.

Of course, both methods could be compromised. Hackers could rewrite the AI to ignore the question—or illegally replace them with a sentient AI. Certain black market cyberdocs could modify the dolls into disgusting toys for pedophiles. The mere idea of it made Kirsten physically ill, but better those abominations preyed on a machine than real children.

Thinking of it reminded her of how the man had been waiting for her at the bottom of the ladder, staring right up her tarp dress as she climbed down. She hadn't understood what he did at the time, or why he'd been smiling at her.

She leaned to the side and threw up a little.

If that kid is a doll, there's a ghost possessing her. It. Ugh. Whatever.

The distant *pwoosh* and sucking noise of the surface hatch opening echoed out of the corridor.

Kirsten blinked. *The doll went to the surface?*

A few minutes later, the *thump* and hiss of the hatch sealing broke the silence. Soon, the soft sticky noise of the girl's bare feet peeling up off the plastisteel ground came from the hallway. Kirsten sat as still as she could make herself be. The same nine-year-old entered the chamber, carrying a white box almost big enough for her to curl up in, a Speedy-Nom logo on the side.

Dolls don't need to order a week's worth of food.

Kirsten tried unsuccessfully to peek into the girl's head with Telepathy again. Confident she looked at a doll and not a living girl, she got ready to move. The only reason a robotic child would get food is to bring it to her owner. An astral presence within the fake girl meant one thing—this doll had to belong to her suspect. At least, nothing else made sense. The ghosts who looked after her years ago never once ordered her food from above. For a ghost to possess a doll and use it to pick up a delivery implied the spirit interacted with someone capable of placing the order. People who lived in the Beneath would sooner try to eat a NetMini than use it to order food.

It had to be him.

Ten seconds after the doll disappeared down the ladder, Kirsten climbed out of her hiding place, trying not to make too much noise. Fair bet, the ghost 'piloting' the doll would assume her a sleeping off-gridder. Her suspect likely operated under the belief no one in the world would ever be able to detect him using ghosts as weapons. The rarity of astrals plus the general disbelief among the public in spirits would no doubt give him a total sense of being untouchable. Hiding down here kept him away from Division 0—or so he thought. While it stopped him from being casually discovered and approached, it wouldn't protect him from her.

She peered over the edge, watching the faux child descend to the ground, step off the ladder, and walk away across the old parking lot in a creepily adult manner, devoid of playfulness or hesitation. The instant the doll had her back turned, Kirsten lowered herself through the hole and made her way to the ground.

Two ruined cars sat in an area large enough for a thousand. To the left, the remnants of a huge grocery store gradually collapsed in on itself. Considering the age of everything down here, most of it appeared in remarkably good shape. The modern, elevated city protected structures in the Beneath from the ravages of wind and weather, turning it into the world's largest indoor museum of the past. Open areas near the city's western edge by the ocean as well as north and south ends suffered the most decay, long ago having decomposed into fields of rubble. A giant wall blocked off the eastern border of the city from the Badlands, leaving much of the old construction intact.

Or as intact as almost three centuries of total neglect could leave a place.

Kirsten reactivated Darksight so she could see, then followed the ersatz child out of the parking lot to a six-lane paved road, going past various old shopping centers and stores. The sight of such massive— but short—buildings baffled Kirsten. Nothing over two stories tall in sight. Granted, before the Corporate War, the entire nation hadn't crammed itself into the coastal areas. In a time before the Badlands existed, people could spread out. It didn't matter if one hardware store took up almost as much space as a city block and only had one story.

The girl walked past all the stores, following the old highway out of the commercial district to a field of rubble and dirt where a long-ago explosion had levelled most of the buildings. Undeterred, the android child carried the package across a dirt field, heading toward an interstate overpass a little more than a hundred meters from the highway she'd been following.

Electric lights shone within a walled area beneath the overpass. It looked as though someone—hopefully her suspect—had established something of a stronghold here. She didn't see anyone moving around, nor any obvious defenses. A good, tough wall would be more than adequate to hold off the usual sort of dangers lurking in the Beneath. Automated sentry turrets or bots would be overkill.

Light would attract interest, especially Discarded, known for stealing anything they could carry from electronics to scrap metal to junk. She figured the guy had to have *some* defenses beyond a wall.

Briefly, she considered going for backup, but few cops—even within Division 0—would be willing to come down here. Most believed the wild stories about mutants and horrible monsters down here. Much of it came from ghosts not wanting to be disturbed mixing into the folklore of the Badlands. Some people spoke about a demonic entity ruling over the desolation out there. Few claimed to take the idea seriously, but no one really had a good explanation for why no serious attempt to retake the center of the continent had ever happened or why the exploratory attempts all failed disastrously.

Down here, her suspect wouldn't have any reason to hesitate before killing a cop. If she went in, she'd have to be prepared to handle it all herself. This, of course, meant shooting him if need be. The man had, after all, been responsible for the death of four police officers, Elan Mendoza, two construction workers, plus anyone else he'd attacked she didn't know about. A rogue astral sending ghosts out to kill people could have been going on for years undetected.

She wouldn't go in there intending to kill him, but if he forced her to, so be it.

Kirsten beaconed for Dorian as the fake child disappeared into a doorway in the barrier below the overpass.

I really shouldn't be completely reckless and do this alone.

A COUPLE OF FRIENDS

Dorian appeared on the road to her left, running at the speed of a fast-forwarded holovid.

She breathed a sigh of relief, overjoyed to see he hadn't stumbled into the guy and ended up under control. When he came to a stop beside her, she drew the E-90. "Think I found him."

"Impressed. Seems I went the wrong way."

"Not totally confident. Going off a hunch here."

"Why this place?"

Kirsten gestured the E-90 toward the overpass. "WellTech doll went by, possessed by a ghost—I think. She picked up a box of food from a delivery bot at street level. Followed her back here. Ghosts don't eat, and the locals down here don't know about delivery bots. Half of them think they're stuck on a giant spaceship after the Earth exploded."

Dorian chuckled. "Reasonable theory worth checking out."

"It's a stupid story. We're not on a spaceship."

"I meant your hunch the guy is here." He gestured at the 'fortress.'

"Yeah. I know. Teasing you. Here we go."

Kirsten trusted the darkness to hide her approach, keeping her gaze down so her glowing white eyes didn't appear too obvious to someone far away. She stepped off the road into the dirt field, navigating chunks of concrete, metal scraps, and smashed appliances. Subconsciously, she gravitated toward large dense objects, the ones useful as cover if someone started shooting at her. Her heart raced in anticipation. At any second, she expected to have the Monwyn theme song shatter the relative quiet. If Evan called, she'd dive for cover before trying to answer.

"Suri," whispered Kirsten. "Ring silent, send it to the earbud."

"Okay," chirped a voice in her ear. "But you know I have no signal down here."

She swallowed saliva. Evan *couldn't* call her now. Her stomach in knots, she forced herself to continue, trusting he'd have warned her going down here would be deadly when he called last time. He'd only worried about the hatch exploding. A rat or something small and furry darted out of the debris on her right. She dove away from it, hitting the ground behind a crushed car.

"Are you okay?" Dorian blinked at her. "Last I checked, rats haven't figured out how to use firearms."

"On edge."

"I noticed."

"We're offline down here. Ev can't call me."

"You did fine before you had him to warn you. Trust your instincts. You shouldn't get complacent and think you're going to be untouchable as long as he doesn't have a panic attack."

"I know. I know." Grumbling, she got back up and continued.

When she'd made it a little past halfway across the field, a strong paranormal presence welled up in front of her. She risked looking up, exposing her glowing eyes to anyone who might be watching her from the little fortress beneath the overpass.

Six ghosts stared at her. Three men in heavy tan coveralls, likely killed by accidents during the construction of the city overhead, two men wearing prewar hoodies and jeans, and a skinny man sporting two black metal cyberarms and a partially exploded head stood in a line in front of her as if to block her way forward.

"Leave him alone," said a muscular construction worker wearing a blue syn-wool hat.

The taller of the men in hoodies waved her off. "Look, we don't want no trouble wit' you. We all know who ya is. Anyone else, we'd give a good damn reason to stay away."

"We do?" asked the exploded-head guy. When he looked to his right at the others, he revealed the hollowness of his skull, as though a bomb inside his brain blew everything out the back left side. More than likely, he'd been killed by extreme voltage on the uplink cable… black ICE. "Who is this?"

Kirsten winced.

"Just a lost little girl who doesn't belong here," replied Blue Hat.

"She's the one who dwells between worlds." A short, stocky construction worker leaned back as if afraid of her.

Kirsten walked right up to them. "I'm not halfway dead. What I am is here to stop a man who is abusing his abilities to make slaves out of spirits."

"We have an arrangement with him," said Exploded Head. "And part of the arrangement includes keeping people out he don't wanna see. Which is everyone who ain't dead."

She gawked at him. "This man is controlling spirits against their will, using them to kill, kidnap, steal…"

"Yeah, so?" asked Hoodie Two. "Ain't no skin off our ass. He does shit for us if we need."

"Wait, you six are willingly assisting this man?" asked Dorian. "Not under control?"

"Shit, yo." Hoodie One laughed. "Do we look controlled? Holmes takes care of our peeps up top, those of us what have peeps up top."

"You're worried about baby chickens?" Kirsten blinked.

The construction workers and Exploded Head laughed.

"Marcus, no one uses the term 'peeps' anymore," said Blue Hat.

"Unless they're talking about marshmallows." Dorian smiled. "There's no reason this has to become unpleasant. Please stand aside."

Both ghosts wearing hoodies gestured at him while chuckling.

"Get a load of this guy," whispered Hoodie Two. "He ain't even fifty yet. Talkin' shit like he'd do something about it."

Kirsten fidgeted. The men in hoodies had to be close to 400 years old as spirits, having lived here prior to the Corporate War. The construction workers could be anywhere from 300 to 200 years old. Exploded Head seemed to be the youngest based on his cybernetic arms; their appearance didn't look out of date.

Still, she didn't like the idea of getting violent with five ghosts as old as Theodore at the same time. While they'd be marginally less of a threat to her than fighting five living men at once, a five-on-one fight never went well for the one—unless they happened to be a Division 9 doll operative fighting normal people.

These spirits are awfully casual about this guy enslaving other spirits and committing crimes. Good chance they're not terribly nice people.

"What is this guy doing for you that you're standing here protecting a man who could mind-control you if he wanted?"

"Revenge," said Exploded Head, grinning. "Killing the bastards responsible for boiling my brain, and as many other idiots in the company as he can."

"Making life difficult for General Fab," said Blue Hat. "Fuckin' company blamed *me* for falling to my death. Didn't pay out on the policy."

"Tossin' credits at my peep—mean family up top. Takin' care of anyone givin' 'em problems," said Hoodie Two.

"You're like over 400 years old." Kirsten stared at him in disbelief. "You have family up top?"

The guy grinned. "*Distant* family, but they still blood. Gotta do right by 'em."

So much for offering to help instead. No way am I going to kill people or steal for these spirits. She tapped her foot. Talking her way past them wouldn't work. Fighting didn't seem like a wonderful idea. Even if a good shot with the lash scared one off, this place had thousands of random sharp objects they could drag her over to and hang her on. She didn't relish the idea of spending the rest of eternity dangling as a corpse from a length of exposed rebar.

I wonder... don't want to destroy them, but these guys seem kinda sinister.

Kirsten stared into space, trying to beckon Harbingers. For some reason, they couldn't or didn't attack old spirits until they'd been weakened somehow. But... as her old friend Ritchie proved, ghosts with dark enough souls had an irrational fear of Harbingers. Even if they couldn't lay a single shadowy claw on them, their mere presence would create panic.

If you can hear me somehow, I could use a little help here. This man is going to keep killing and hurting people if I can't get to him. Any chance a couple of you could show up and maybe scare these spirits out of my way?

"C'mon, kid. You got outta here once already." Blue Hat pointed up. "Go back where ya belong."

"I can't do that." Kirsten locked stares with him and put her E-90 away. "This man killed four cops, and a bunch of other people."

"Hah!" Exploded-Head laughed. "Only four? Shame."

Kirsten summoned the lash. "I'm going to ask you nicely one more time. Get out of my way."

AS USUAL, A COMPLETE MESS

The six ghosts leaned back in response to the energy whip.

Dorian once compared it to being worse than the way a living person felt having a laser sword waved in their face. Not only did it give off a painful amount of heat to ghosts, even the newest spirit registered a sense of dread the instant they saw it, knowing full well it could annihilate them.

"Aww, man." The stocky construction worker grumbled. "Look, kid. We really don't want to hurt you. All of us know ya from your last time down here. Well, all except for Soft Boiled over there."

Exploded Head gave him the finger.

"I'm here to protect spirits, not harm you." She tried to step forward, but Blue Hat got in her way. "You're helping a man who hurts ghosts as much as the living."

"So?" asked Exploded Head. "Hey, why you guys getting all soft on this kid? She's a cop."

"Cadet?" asked Hoodie Two. "What are you, girl, fifteen?"

"Nah, she's gotta be in her twenties by now." Blue Hat rubbed his chin. "Less my sense of time is crappin' out."

A sense of foreboding welled up behind her.

Kirsten smiled. *Thank you.*

"You guys are pussies." Exploded Head lunged forward, thrusting his hand into her chest, grabbing her heart.

Kirsten snapped the lash upward while jumping back—three icy points scratched at her heart as his hand slid out of her. The energy whip caught him in the groin, slicing upward all the way to the top of his head. For an instant, two severed halves of spirit gawked at her in stunned silence. She staggered away from him, grabbing the cold spot on her chest. Both halves of Exploded Head crashed together as he let off a wail of pain.

The other spirits seemed conflicted, close to jumping on her, but hesitating.

Pain in Kirsten's chest resolved, seeming more a product of her fear the ghost might've tampered with her heart rhythm than actual tampering. Snarling, she snapped the lash at him again, nailing him in the back as he tried futilely to jump aside. Howling, Exploded Head fell to all fours, writhing in agony.

"Whoa," said Dorian.

"I didn't hit him *that* hard."

"Not what I meant." He pointed behind himself.

Kirsten looked back.

A mass of Harbingers flowed across the open field toward her like a crashing ocean wave of infinite darkness. She counted at least a dozen pairs of sparkling silver eyes. The instant she processed the sight, she knew they had a particular interest in Exploded Head. Kirsten spun back to face the ghosts, concentrating on the dead hacker's essence. He didn't feel too weakened yet.

"Aww shit, girl," said Hoodie One. "What the fuck you do that for?"

Before she could offer up an answer, the spirits ran away from the approaching wall of Harbingers. Exploded Head scrambled upright into a run. Kirsten sprinted after him, taking advantage of her long reach via a wide horizontal swipe. The lash scored across his shoulders, swatting him sideways into a roll.

His essence changed, drained past a teeter point by the third hit. One more would obliterate him.

Kirsten stopped chasing him and lowered her arm.

The Harbingers drifted past her, an icy wind whipping at her hair. Though their presence still brought on a powerful sense of dread, she respected them. Roughly half chased Exploded Head into the ruins, the rest peeling off one by one after the others.

Dorian shivered like someone dumped cold water over him. "Well, I'm awake. You have to expect our guy sensed this."

"Yeah." Kirsten released the lash and pulled the E-90 again. "No point being subtle now."

She ran the rest of the way across the field to the door the WellTech doll entered. Somewhere off to the right, Exploded Head shrieked, begging and pleading the Harbingers not to take him. Kirsten didn't have to see to picture him being swarmed and dragged down.

Predictably, her police override code didn't work on the door—but a shot from the E-90 did. She melted the locking bar and shoved the door inward, gun up, aiming at a more or less open space between four ancient concrete pillars holding up the overpass. Glowing blue fiberoptic cables ran from several computers on a table to the left, going up along the pylon to the overpass, likely connected to the GlobeNet somewhere inside the plate.

The child doll sat in a chair straight ahead beside a coffee table loaded with junk, her expression bored. A much larger table holding electronic parts, disassembled bots, and tools stood on Kirsten's right along the front wall. Beyond it, a portable autoshower tube, reassembler, and fridge. Three power cables ran along the overpass support behind the fridge, no doubt spliced into the city's electrical grid up in the plate.

Kirsten scanned the walled-in area, not noticing anyone else there —until she reached out telepathically in search of sentient minds. One directly above her. She peered up at the underside of a filthy metal platform spanning the doorway, reminiscent of battlements in an ancient fort.

"Shit," muttered a man.

She dashed forward and spun, aiming her E-90 up at a guy in a trench coat. Fluffy blond dreadlocks surrounded a dark face with glowing white eyes—Astral Sight. His surface thoughts went from panic at the tremendous feeling of doom coming from the field outside to shock at seeing another person in his fortress to anger at the other person being a Division 0 cop. He considered going for one of the handguns on his belt.

"I wouldn't do that," said Kirsten. "My preference is to bring you in alive even if you did kill at least seven people, four of whom were Division 1 officers. But don't think for a second I won't click this trigger if you reach for a weapon."

The man stared over Kirsten's head.

Her E-90 went dark.

"Sorry," said a little girl voice. "Trev made me."

Trev yanked a handgun off his belt. Kirsten leapt forward, taking cover under the platform he stood on.

"Got it." Dorian smiled. "His gun's as dead as his sense of feng shui."

"Help me," said Trev. "Kill the cop."

Dorian shivered. He glared murderously at Kirsten for an instant, then grabbed his head in both hands, growling.

Kirsten reloaded, stuffing a new e-mag in the E-90, then firing straight up into the metal plate. Small globs of molten steel fell from the tiny hole.

"Fuck!" shouted Trev, leaping off, the bottom of his trench coat on fire.

She swiveled to aim at him. He landed in a somersault, springing back to his feet. "Shoot the bitch."

The child doll picked a large handgun up out of the junk on the coffee table next to her chair.

Kirsten darted to the side, putting Trev between her and the doll, aiming at his face. *"Tell her to stop."* Light from her eyes flashed briefly over him.

"Gah!" Trev also grabbed his head in both hands, trying to fight her suggestive command. "Dammit. Shit. No!"

The doll stepped around him and fired, her little arm flying upward from the recoil of the giant handgun. Fortunately, the spirit's aim sucked. Kirsten hit the deck a second after a bullet struck the metal platform over the doorway with a *clank*. Dorian continued growling and squirming, he and Trev both momentarily unable to do anything other than fight against forces attempting to control them. Despite it being a machine, Kirsten couldn't quite bring herself to shoot the child doll. She dashed for cover behind a thick concrete pylon on the left, running to put it between her and the armed android. Another shot rang out as she ran, but the bullet didn't hit anything close enough to tell where it went. Kirsten stopped at the end of the overpass support, transferred the E-90 to her left hand, and called the lash.

She found herself in a narrow space between the bridge support and the wall of scrap Trev—or some prior denizen of the Beneath—built to enclose the area. Shelves held various boxes of old technology, most of it covered in dust. The space made her an easy target, so she hurried forward to the other side, pausing at the end.

The soft scuff of small feet drew closer to the corner in front of her, the doll fearlessly coming after her like a miniature combat android. Kirsten kicked a plastic bottle out past the concrete wall.

Bang!

The bottle exploded into a twist of shredded plastic surrounded in a puff of dirt.

Hoping to take advantage of recoil fouling the false child's aim, Kirsten rushed out from cover. The doll stood only a few feet away, teetering back, both arms over her head, the hand cannon practically flying out of her grasp. Kirsten swiped the lash at the doll in a hasty, weak attack. The energy whip struck a squishy-solid mass as it passed through the little body, which ought to have been insubstantial to it. The strike launched a blurry, spectral mass of light away from the doll, sending it zooming off almost to the wall surrounding the fortress before it coalesced into the shape of a young woman in a miniskirt and puffy jacket bearing the logo of the Jade Scorpionz gang.

"Oh, no," said a little girl voice from the doll. "I'm not allowed to touch weapons." She tossed the handgun aside like a hot potato.

"Please don't be angry with me. I don't know where it came from. I'm sorry."

The ghostly woman gawked at Kirsten. "Freakin' ouch! And thanks!" She ran through the wall.

"Get back here," yelled Trev.

"Eat a dick!" shouted the woman from outside.

Kirsten whirled to face him. He almost stood straight up, twitching like an android having a logic circuit breakdown. "I don't think she likes the controlling type. *Get on the ground.*"

"Grr." Trev squatted. He started to shift to all fours but froze with only his left hand touching dirt. Growling, he forced himself upright. "How are you doing that to me? I'm not a ghost."

"How do you do it to spirits?" She pointed the E-90 at him. "Trev, whatever your last name is, you're under arrest by authority of Division 0. On the ground, now."

"Go away!" he yelled, a tiny flicker of purple light coloring the white Astral Seeing glow in his eyes.

She barely noticed a tickle at her psyche. Even if she didn't have Suggestion, his attempt to use it on her would have failed.

"Shoot him in the damn knee." Dorian growled, still struggling to fight off the command. "Put him on the damn ground."

"Not a bad idea," said Kirsten, completely bluffing. "Three… two…"

Her E-90 went dark again.

She sighed, glaring to her left at a ghostly Discarded pointing at her. Tattered rags and grey fabric covered every inch of him, including his face except for eye holes. "Ooh, damn that really is annoying."

Trev roared, charging in to grab her. She weaved to the side, avoiding him while stuffing the dead E-90 back in its holster. He crashed into the junk-covered coffee table, kicking it over on his way into the wall. Growling, he shoved himself back, spinning into a roundhouse kick. Kirsten ducked, then launched herself at him, trying a jiu jitsu takedown. She seized his shoulder and arm, sweeping his leg while crashing all her weight into him. He tried to catch her, but stumbled due to her trapping his leg, and fell over backward, Kirsten on top of him.

The Discarded ghost blurred over, trying to grab her. Spectral hands pulled at her chest, freezing cold, but having no solidity to get a grip. The shock of sudden, extreme cold paralyzed her for a second, allowing Trev to throw her to the side. She rolled over twice before coming to a halt on her back. Trev pulled a knife off his belt and leapt at her. Kirsten swung her right leg up, deflecting his pounce via kicking him in the groin. He flew past her, landing in a heap on the ground.

Still on her back, Kirsten called the lash and smacked the Discarded ghost across the face and chest. He emitted a screech like an electrocuted hog before disappearing entirely—most likely jumping back to his remains.

"I said kill her dammit!" yelled Trev.

Dorian snarled, shaking from his battle against compulsion. "K. Shoot him. Please, just shoot him in the face."

Kirsten scrambled upright, as did Trev.

"*Stop!*" yelled Kirsten, her eyes flaring white.

"Yeaaargh!" bellowed Trev, stagger-leaping at her.

She blocked his punch, smoothly flowing into a counterattack kick at his face. He caught her ankle and held it. *Grr.* Furious, she locked stares and Mind Blasted him. Drooling, Trev let go of her leg, stumbling off to the side in a drunken sway, holding his head. She jumped on his back, trying to tackle him, but lacked the body mass to take him down. He wobbled back and forth around the fortress wearing her like a backpack, bouncing off two tables before wrenching himself around in a hard spin, flinging her off. She flew onto the bed, landing on her chest. He drew another knife, grasping it in an icepick grip and hammering it down at her back.

Kirsten shoved herself aside, rolling out from under the attack; the blade plunged to the cross-guard in the old-world cloth mattress.

"Can I dance, too?" asked the WellTech doll. "Looks like you're having fun! I love dancing."

"Adorable," muttered Dorian. He'd stopped visibly fighting,

standing rigidly. His expression shifted from serial killer to normal to serial killer.

Kirsten scrambled off the side of the mattress into a side kick, ramming her boot into Trev's chest. He stumbled back, losing his grip on the knife, which remained impaled in the mattress. *He's stronger than me, but I don't think he's got any training.*

Trev recovered his balance.

She narrowed her eyes, concentrating on Mind Blast. Her eyes vibrated in their sockets under the barrage of chaotic sensory information streaming into his brain.

His eyes crossed. Trev screamed, "Border router overrun pickles and rabbits" while lunging at her, swinging his arm around in a wild, unexpected haymaker.

Concentration slowed her reflexes too much to avoid the attack. His knuckles mashed into the side of her face, throwing her back onto the bed. Spots danced in her vision. The hit to the head elevated the dull Mind Blast headache into a nauseous nuclear bomb between her ears. Kirsten rolled on her side, vomiting onto the mattress in front of her.

Whimpering, Trev grabbed his face and sank to his knees, repeating the words "Cake ribbons" over and over.

"What on Earth did you do to him?" asked Dorian, red-faced.

Ugh... I hate Mind Blast. The paradox irritated her. Developing the power would get her used to it and lessen the annoying side effects, but also result in it becoming more powerful, rate higher, and consequently, scare everyone in Division 0 into treating her like Commander Ashford. Admittedly, he took Mind Blast well past simply being able to bonk people over the head and not get a headache. She didn't need to develop it anywhere near as much as him.

Kirsten spat bile, coughed, then crawled the rest of the way across the mattress, grasping the edge in preparation to stand. Trev grabbed her by the hair, dragging her upright. She screamed at the pain, focusing it into another Mind Blast.

"Data syncing." Trev fell over backward like a plank, his fingers raking through her hair, dragging her hair clip out. "Poodle server. Fiberoptic neuro chicken."

"Ow, son of a…" Kirsten sank into a crouch, cradling the back of her head.

Dorian ran up to her. "You're bleeding from the nose. Bind the stunrod so I can tune this guy up."

"Memory pudding," muttered Trev.

"Uhh, seriously… what the hell did you do to him?" Dorian glanced at the twitching man.

"Mind Blast. Nothing unusual." She rubbed her face. "Ow. I've never zapped a psionic with it before. Maybe he's partially resisting it. No idea why he's babbling nonsense."

Dorian held his hand out. "Stunrod please."

"Are you free of control or just asking me for the stunrod so you can use it on me?"

"Oh." Dorian lowered his hand. "Free, but if you give me the rod, he's going to try taking me over again. Better not do it. Just shoot the son of a bitch."

Trev sprang upright again, screaming, "Mind fuck pickles" over and over while rapidly punching at her.

Kirsten dodged and blocked most of his uncoordinated onslaught, but even blocking sent her stumbling a few steps each time due to her size. The instant his barrage slowed enough to give her an opening, she stomped on his knee and rammed her forearm guard into his face, exploding his nose into a spray of blood. He grabbed her throat in both hands; she punted him in the groin. When that didn't make him stop trying to strangle choke her, she thrust her arms up between his and went for his eyes.

Roaring, Trev threw her aside like a ragdoll.

"Ooh, throw and catch me!" called the WellTech doll. "I want to play, too."

Kirsten landed on the table of tools and disassembled bots—the exact opposite of a comfortable mattress. She cried out in pain, momentarily stunned from crashing onto a bed of sharp. Trev staggered around in a drunken stupor, staring fearfully at her for a few seconds before pointing at Dorian.

"Make sure she doesn't follow me!" Trev stagger-sprinted for the only exit. He missed, crashing into the doorjamb, clinging to stay on his feet.

Kirsten groaned and started to sit up, but Dorian jumped on her and pushed her down. A cluster of sharp points jabbed into her back.

"Ow!" yelled Kirsten.

"Do it." Dorian shuddered, rasping, "Do it... can't resist."

Trev slipped out the doorway and ran.

Kirsten extended the lash. Rather than fling it like a whip, she mentally commanded the energy cord to stab Dorian in the leg like a striking snake.

"Shit!" He yelled and jumped around as if he'd been shot in the foot. "Damn, that stings."

"I'm sorry!" She sat up, reaching for him.

"Don't be. Broke the compulsion. Way harder to resist a command to be irritating. He couldn't make me hurt you. Hope it pissed him off."

Kirsten slid off the table to her feet, rubbing sore spots where metal pieces jabbed her. She smiled at him but couldn't afford to get too sentimental at the moment. Being able to resist the compulsion to kill her proved he loved her at least like a kid sister, or a real partner.

"Aww. Did he have to go home? Are we done playing?" asked the WellTech doll.

"Yeah," muttered Kirsten. "We are definitely done playing."

32

SANDCASTLES

Kirsten ran out the door in the fortress wall, stuffing her last e-mag into the E-90.

She still didn't want to kill Trev, but the medics could replace a knee easily enough. Taking one of his legs out bothered her less than another Mind Blast, which could cause permanent damage. She'd already tenderized his brain quite thoroughly. Besides, the more she used it, the more the ability would develop. People in Division 0 already acted afraid of her for having a fairly low rating in Mind Blast. If she ranked higher in it, she worried they'd start avoiding her like they did Commander Ashford. The man could silence the PAC cafeteria merely by entering it.

Trev neared the edge of the dirt field by the time she emerged from the fortress. Though a class 4 laser weapon laughed at a mere hundred-meter range, the iron sights of a handgun didn't fill her with confidence. She'd be lucky enough to hit him at all, much less surgically take out a leg. Fortunately, he still stumbled along in an ungainly, lopsided gait as a result of repeated Mind Blasts. He'd likely be suffering loss of motor control for a few hours at least.

Kirsten powered past the soreness and dizziness, forcing herself into a run, weaving around debris. Trev went left at the highway, loping along a little faster than a highly motivated jogger. She gained on him easily, until he glanced back and noticed her step onto the highway. Shouting curses, he found the clarity of mind to straighten out his run. His larger size and longer stride made up for his disorientation. She took a stimpak out of her belt case and injected it in her thigh, mostly for the energy boost.

A second wind hit her a few seconds later, along with tingles in her nose from nanobots repairing blood vessels. The stimpak hit her like a triple shot of high-grade espresso. On the wings of synthetic adrenaline, she started catching up to him again.

I have nine more stims. He'll eventually collapse. Don't have to shoot him. I have a stunrod.

She eased off to conserve energy, matching his speed rather than trying to run him down. An endurance marathon worked to her advantage, being lighter and smaller. Settling in about sixty feet behind him, she paced him down the highway, waiting for him to run out of breath.

A thunderous, screeching moan of stressed metal rolled overhead.

For an instant, it sounded as though the entirety of West City was about to collapse on top of her.

She gazed upward, her eyes drawn to a large object falling from the underside of the city plates sixty or so meters above, directly in front of her. Kirsten stopped short, staring aghast at an enormous machine component plummeting toward the highway.

"Trev!" shouted Kirsten. "Look out! Stop!"

He ignored her, continuing to run for two more seconds before the dumpster-sized box slammed into the road on top of him. The *whump* of metal striking the ground echoed over itself four times into the distance. She caught sight of a massive blood splatter an instant before a huge cloud of dust obscured the impact point.

Kirsten cringed, looking away. "Gah!"

"Ooh. He's going to need way more stimpaks than you're carrying," said Dorian.

"Shit!" yelled Kirsten. "What the hell was that?"

"Looks like a power transformer. Maybe a capacitor unit."

She gave Dorian side eye. "No, I mean where did it come from? How the hell did it fall perfectly aimed to hit him."

The sense of a weak spirit manifested in the dust cloud. She cringed at the confirmation Trev died, as if a thirty-foot wide blood spatter didn't already tell her.

Dorian pointed upward.

She followed his finger to a hole in the underside of the city plate—and locked eyes with Dacre peering down at her. As soon as he realized she'd spotted him, he backed out of sight.

Kirsten sighed.

"Don't have to worry about feeling guilty." Dorian smiled at her. "After all, the man *did* say he would be hunting the one who controlled him."

"He's dead." Kirsten shook her head. "I didn't want to kill him."

"You didn't kill him. The dead have their own rules. The laws of mortals are as impermanent as cobwebs."

Kirsten opened her mouth to make a sarcastic remark about his poetic dismissal of her concerns of someone being splatter killed right in front of her but froze at a sudden upwelling of dread in the air.

Three Harbingers emerged from the ground nearby, flying as streaks of billowing shadow after Trev's disoriented spirit. She winced as they pounced, sinking their vaporous claws into his ethereal form. In seconds, Trev's screaming ghost sank beneath the dirt under a mass of darkness.

"Seems they decided to hang around and wait." Dorian folded his arms. "Wonder if they knew he was going to die."

She exhaled out her nose. "Probably."

"He deserved it and you didn't do it." Dorian patted her shoulder. "And, you know for sure he deserved it. They wouldn't have gone after him otherwise."

"I wasn't trying to kill him." She sank into a squat, cradling her head in both hands. Exhausted, heart racing, head throbbing, body shaking from excess adrenaline, she lacked the mental fortitude to do anything other than take a breather.

Dorian pointed upward. "You didn't. Something like this would have happened to him, eventually. If not Dacre, another. Trev left a long trail of angry spirits."

"True."

"Unless you're carrying a sponge, it's going to be difficult to bring his remains back to process."

She gagged, pulling her NetMini from its belt clip. "I at least need to document the scene."

33

NEW RECORD

The blare of an alarm clock slapped Kirsten out of a dreamless sleep.

Groaning, she rolled on her side to reach the infernal device and silence it. A few breaths later, she dragged herself out of bed. Only the hopeful relief things ought to be quiet for a while gave her the strength to keep moving. The warm autoshower almost turned her sore muscles to jelly. She daydreamed about Sam massaging her as the water jets worked their magic. Her idle fantasy morphed into an embarrassing idea of asking him to do it for real. Of course, she'd have to make some arrangements for Evan to spend the night at Nila's first.

After the hot air cycle ended, she dragged herself out of the tube, elbow bumped the white box on the wall so it spat out a plastic-wrapped pair of clean panties, and staggered into her bedroom. Once dressed, she went to the kitchen. Since she didn't see Evan in his room or the hall bathroom, she approached the tall cabinet beside the fridge and opened it.

Evan stood inside it, naked, eyes closed, left arm up over his head, rubbing his hand up and down his side as if scrubbing himself in the shower.

She tapped him on the shoulder. "Morning, sweetie. You're in the closet. Not the shower."

"Oops. I stayed up too late." He backed out and yawned.

Kirsten kissed him on top of the head. "I know. I was with you."

"Oh yeah." He laughed dazedly.

The precognitive vision of Kirsten blowing up at the hatch had freaked him out. Kirsten spent most of last night sitting with him on the sofa while they watched Monwyn episode reruns. The day would come when he got too old to like it when she 'got squeezy,' but for now, she'd adore every second of it.

While he plodded off to the hall bathroom to take a real shower, she whipped up a breakfast of egg burritos. They both ran a little late, but these, they could eat on the way to the PAC. Soon, Evan returned to the kitchen, dressed and ready for school. She handed him his breakfast, took hers, and hurried out of the apartment to the elevator.

KIRSTEN GRINNED LIKE AN IDIOT AS SHE WALKED DOWN THE CORRIDOR toward the squad room.

It may not have ended the way she hoped, but Trev would no longer pose a threat to anyone. Captain Eze would be thrilled to report up the chain of command, especially when she told him an additional reason a situation like this wouldn't work out long term. Eventually, pissed off ghosts would have their revenge. The threat of another psionic able to force ghosts to act against their will, despite being quite unlikely, would inevitably backfire on the person. Perhaps Trev's reasons for living in the Beneath came from fear of his former spirit victims rather than the police. Up top, ghosts had thousands of ways to kill someone from a distance if they wanted to, mostly thanks to advert bots or delivery bots whizzing around everywhere. Some of them had the size and mass to kill a person in a crash.

The lab rats would, undoubtedly, be annoyed at not being able to study Trev's brain to research how he'd managed to mind-control ghosts. She had a sarcastic 'well, grab a sponge and follow me' ready for them if they demanded she recover the body. They did, however, have a few computers he'd been using. The devices no doubt contained at least some records of the various contract jobs people or companies hired him for. While no court in the UCF would prosecute a corporation or individual for 'hiring a ghostly mercenary,' they might ignore the details and treat it the same way as any shady entity paying off a fixer to arrange violence or criminal activities. Division 1 sent a bomb squad to deal with the trapped hatch at least. One thing Kirsten didn't have to do herself.

Johanna Beck would be relieved no more undead mercenaries would threaten her family. Whether or not living ones might be a threat, Kirsten couldn't say—and had no jurisdiction over. True to her soft-hearted nature, Kirsten brought the WellTech doll up out of the Beneath. She couldn't leave it there since it acted too much like an abandoned child. Nicole thought her cute and took her home.

Also, with Marley happily adjusted to life knowing she had psionic talents, there wouldn't be a constant surge of hauntings. Kirsten crossed her fingers she'd have at least a few days of relative peace and quiet.

The woman who always seemed nervous, sad, or exhausted walking around the Division 0 wing wearing a massive smile drew strange looks from everyone—except Nicole who merely beamed back at her, excessive happy being her normal.

Kirsten eased herself into her chair, adoring the idea she'd be able to spend the whole day here in the office.

"Coffee?" asked Nicole.

"Absolutely," said Kirsten.

"Yes," replied Morelli.

"Peach green tea here." Kurosawa raised a hand.

Montez also waved at her. "Triple espresso and a caramel latte."

Nicole bounced out of her chair. "What'cha want, K?"

"Can't decide between mocha or the strawberry one. You pick."

"Okay."

Kirsten unlocked her terminal. A screen popped up showing three pages of Inquests, all flashing yellow warning icons at her for having reports overdue.

"Aaaaaaugh! Noooo!" Kirsten threw her head back, wailing like she'd found a dear friend dead.

Everyone stared at her.

"They nagging you about range certification again?" asked Kurosawa.

"Ooh, sounds like someone's been naughty." Nicole laughed. "That's the scream of a whole bunch of reports needing attention."

Kirsten groaned.

"Thirty?"

Kirsten groaned again.

"More?" Nicole blinked.

Kirsten groaned louder. "Forty-three."

"Wow, I think you set a record. I'm gonna get you *both* flavors. You're going to need two coffees today." Nicole wagged her eyebrows and hurried off to meet the delivery bot at the garage.

Groaning again, Kirsten folded her arms on the desk and beat her forehead into them a few times.

"Look at it this way," said Dorian from his desk behind her. "No one's getting hurt and you have a nice quiet few days here in the squad room."

She lifted her face off her arms. "Here's hoping." She exhaled hard, glowering at the flashing yellow dots. Forty-three Inquests, each with a thirteen-page report form attached. "Going to start with Trev's first... Captain Eze will need it to talk to the brass."

The Monwyn theme played from her NetMini.

Dorian whistled. "I sincerely hope filling out those reports isn't a threat to your life."

Nervous, Kirsten plucked the device off her belt and answered. "Hey, kiddo."

His face appeared on the screen, beaming. "Mom! Mom! Guess what!?"

Whew. He doesn't look freaked out. Guess reports don't kill. "Umm, the school decided to ban homework?"

He laughed. "Naw, I wish. I'm done with cit points! They forgave the last 150 for bein' good and gettin' a bunch of hundreds on tests."

"Awesome!" Kirsten smiled. "I think this calls for a few hours at the big Monwyn VR Saturday."

"Yay!" Evan cheered. "Okay, Mom. I gotta go. In class. Just had to tell you. Bye!"

He hung up.

"That boy's happy enough to take the pain out of having to do forty-three reports."

"Yeah." Kirsten put the NetMini back into its holder, cracked her knuckles, and poked the screen, bringing up the Inquest for Trev. "Maybe if I find the true name of the report, I can kill it."

"Reports aren't elder demons," said Dorian past a chuckle.

"No, but they were made by one." Kirsten narrowed her eyes. "Time for battle."

---

fin

ACKNOWLEDGMENTS

Thank you for reading *The Shadow Fixer!*

Kirsten's adventures will continue in book 7.

Additional thanks to Lee Hargrove for editing and Alexandria Thompson for the cover and interior artwork!

ABOUT THE AUTHOR

Originally from South Amboy NJ, Matthew has been creating science fiction and fantasy worlds for most of his reasoning life. Since 1996, he has developed the "Divergent Fates" world, in which *Division Zero, Virtual Immortality, The Awakened Series, The Harmony Paradox, and the Daughter of Mars series* take place. Along with being an editor at Curiosity Quills press, he has worked in IT and technical support.

Matthew is an avid gamer, a recovered WoW addict, Gamemaster for two custom RPG systems, and a fan of anime, British humour, and intellectual science fiction that questions the nature of reality, life, and what happens after it.

He is also fond of cats.

Visit me online at:
    Facebook: https://www.facebook.com/MatthewSCoxAuthor
    Amazon: https://www.amazon.com/author/mscox
    Pinterest: https://www.pinterest.com/matthewcox10420/
    Goodreads: https://www.goodreads.com/author/show/7712730.Matthew_S_Cox
    Email: mcox2112@gmail.com

OTHER BOOKS BY MATTHEW S. COX

Divergent Fates Universe Novels

Division Zero series

- Division Zero
- Lex De Mortuis
- Thrall
- Guardian
- Harbinger
- The Shadow Fixer

The Awakened series

- Prophet of the Badlands
- Archon's Queen
- Grey Ronin
- Daughter of Ash
- Zero Rogue
- Angel Descended

Daughter of Mars series

- The Hand of Raziel
- Araphel
- Ghost Black

Virtual Immortality series

- Virtual Immortality
- The Harmony Paradox

Prophet of the Badlands Series

- Prophet's Journey

Divergent Fates Anthology

(Fiction Novels - Adult)

The Roadhouse Chronicles Series

- One More Run
- The Redeemed
- Dead Man's Number

Faded Skies series

- Heir Ascendant
- Ascendant Unrest
- Ascendant Revolution

Temporal Armistice Series

- Nascent Shadow
- The Shadow Collector
- The Gate to Oblivion
- The Queen of Discord

Vampire Innocent series

- A Nighttime of Forever
- A Beginner's Guide to Fangs
- The Artist of Ruin
- The Last Family Road Trip
- The Phantom Oracle
- How Not to Summon Demons
- Ordinary Problems of a College Vampire

- A Vampire's Guide to Surviving Holidays
- An Introduction to Paranormal Diplomacy

Standalones

- Wayfarer: AV494
- Axillon99
- Chiaroscuro: The Mouse and the Candle
- The Spirits of Six Minstrel Run
- Sophie's Light
- The Far Side of Promise anthology
- Operation: Chimera (with Tony Healey)
- The Dysfunctional Conspiracy (with Christopher Veltmann)
- Of Myth and Shadow
- The Girl Who Found the Sun

Winter Solstice series (with J.R. Rain)

- Convergence
- Containment
- Catalyst

Alexis Silver series (with J.R. Rain)

- Silver Light
- Deep Silver
- Silver Quarrel

Samantha Moon Origins series (with J.R. Rain)

- New Moon Rising
- Moon Mourning

Vampire For Hire series (with J.R. Rain)

- Moon Master
- Dead Moon
- Lost Moon

Maddy Wimsey series (with J.R. Rain)

- The Devil's Eye
- The Drifting Gloom
- Dark Mercy

Samantha Moon Case Files series (with J.R. Rain)

- Blood Moon

Immortal Operative series (with J.R. Rain)

- Broken Ice

Four Elements series (with J.R. Rain)

- The Elementalist
- The Black Rose
- The Wakefield Curse

Young Adult Novels

The Eldritch Heart Series

- The Eldritch Heart
- The Cursed Crown

Evergreen Series

- Evergreen

- The World That Remains
- The Lucky Ones
- Nuclear Summer

- Caller 107
- The Summer the World Ended
- Nine Candles of Deepest Black
- The Forest Beyond the Earth
- Out of Sight

Middle Grade Novels

The Adventures of Ubergirl series

- My Dad is a Mad Scientist
- Aliens Ate My Homework
- The End of all Halloweens

Tales of Widowswood series

- Emma and the Banderwigh
- Emma and the Silk Thieves
- Emma and the Silverbell Faeries
- Emma and the Elixir of Madness
- Emma and the Weeping Spirit

Standalones

- Citadel: The Concordant Sequence
- The Cursed Codex
- The Menagerie of Jenkins Bailey

www.ingramcontent.com/pod-product-compliance
Lightning Source LLC
Chambersburg PA
CBHW020506260626
47156CB00006B/1884